CALLING FRANK O'HARE

HAZEL WARD

Hope St Press

1

SO MANY POSSIBILITIES

Frank opened the French windows that led from his studio to the back garden and was nearly knocked over by two big dogs, excited to get out for their first romp of the day. Turf flew this way and that as they tore up the patchy lawn and crashed through daffodils that were already past their best. Good job he wasn't precious about these things. A third, much smaller dog trotted between his legs and took a more sedate amble around the garden's perimeter, keeping a dignified distance from her altogether larger and more boisterous offspring.

Frank turned his attention to the studio, bathed in morning sunlight and perfect for painting. It had been a breakfast room once and still was when his lovely Netta stayed over, but most of the time he painted in it. Living alone had its plus points, mainly being able to choose how you lived. And for the next two weeks, Frank was choosing to live as a full-time artist, rather than someone who fitted it in around his other job. It was officially the first day of the Easter holidays. Until his college re-opened, there would be no guiding non-plussed sixth formers around the intricacies of Shakespeare, Austen et al. There would only be painting, and that filled Frank with a pleasing, if somewhat smug sense of contentment. It was a feeling he rarely felt in his day job, so he allowed himself a brief wallow in it.

Wallow over, he set out his paints and checked his brushes. All clean and ready to go. Just one stretch before he got going because, according to Netta, it was good to stretch and keep yourself loose. Particularly when you had a minor back problem, as he did. Not that he was in bad shape for sixty-one. A tiny bit overweight maybe, but nothing life threatening, and he still had a good head of hair. It was better than most men of his age, although it wasn't what it used to be. The old back did give him a bit of jip now and then, but he couldn't complain. In fact there was very little to complain about in his life. He got on just great with his daughter, Robyn. She had moved to Edinburgh, which was a long way from Birmingham but not prohibitively so. The woman he loved lived next door, handy but not in your face, and they had a good thing going, as the song said. There was an exhibition in the autumn to look forward to, and he was about to start on a new canvas in readiness for it. All in all, Frank was happy. And comfortable. He was happy and comfortable. Not a bad place to be.

Satisfied with his stretch and his life, he selected the first tube of paint. It was a new one, as yet unopened. Frank loved a brand new tube of paint. There was so much potential in them, so many possibilities. He unscrewed the top and broke the seal. Time to get started.

Then the phone rang.

He checked the caller ID. It was his sister. Frank tutted and screwed the top back onto the paint. He was going to have to take this, whether he wanted to or not.

'Frank, it's Siobhan, your sister.'

'I know who you are, Siobhan. What's up? Is it the parents?'

'Now why would you ask me that?'

'You don't usually call.'

'I could say the same for you, Francis. They're grand. There's nothing wrong with them.'

'What is it then?'

'Who is it, you mean.'

'Ah.' There was no need to say more. He knew what was coming next.

'It's Martin.' Of course it was. Wasn't it always Martin? 'He's gone missing. Well, not completely missing. There's been sightings.' She stopped, her last word left dangling over a cliff edge waiting to be rescued.

Frank let a few more seconds pass but since no further words were forthcoming, he embarked on the rescue mission. 'Sightings?'

'Scotland.'

'Scotland's a big country, Siobhan. Any particular part?'

'Glasgow. Cousin Finn bumped into him. He was half-cut.'

'Finn, or Martin?'

'Martin I think, but it could have been either. Or both. Anyway that's where we think he is. Would you go and get him?'

Frank looked longingly at the tube of paint he'd abandoned moments earlier. 'I'm sure he'll be fine.'

Perhaps he'd said it too quietly or perhaps his sister wasn't listening. Either way, she carried on as if he hadn't spoken. 'You know what Martin's like. He needs minding sometimes.'

'Only sometimes? Did Finn get his address?'

'Of course not. Finn's almost as useless as Martin.'

'What are the odds of me finding him without an address? Besides, I can't go. I have responsibilities.'

'Responsibilities? And what would they be now?'

As usual, Siobhan said it in a way that implied he was a complete numpty. He could tell she was waiting for an answer to pour scorn on and he knew before he opened his mouth, he was about to give her one. 'Dogs. I have dogs to look after.'

'Dogs?' An incredulous laugh told Frank exactly what she thought of his responsibilities. 'And they're more important than your brother, are they?'

Yes they were, but he knew better than to say so. It would cause an awful fuss. 'I'm home alone, in charge of three dogs.'

'Three dogs? Well aren't you the big man, so? I'll tell Ma. She'll be over the moon.'

'It's just—'

Too late. She left Frank hanging in mid-air, wondering what he would have said if he'd had the chance to finish. It's just that Netta's away. It's just that I'm about to start work on something that means a lot to me. It's just that I really don't want to see my brother if I can help it. All of those statements were true, but he probably wouldn't have admitted that last one to anyone, especially Siobhan.

He stared at the phone, wondering if he should call her back and explain further. No point. She'd only ridicule him. Best to get on and pretend nothing had happened. He shifted his gaze to the blank canvas. Suddenly it didn't seem so appealing.

2

THE PAST IS NEVER FAR AWAY

Even though his heart wasn't in it, Frank picked up his brush and began sketching an outline. What was it about his sister that always managed to wind him up? They hardly spoke these days but whenever they did, he was always left feeling both idiotic and angry. Did that make him an angry idiot? Almost certainly, from Siobhan's point of view. His thoughts strayed to Cousin Finn. So he was in Glasgow now. No wonder Martin had turned up there. Those two were always hanging onto each other's coat tails, and neither of them had an ounce of sense between them.

The dogs came in from the garden. His own dog, Fred, lay at Frank's feet, as he always did when Frank was painting. Fred's sister, Betty, flopped down in front of the French windows, leaving no option but to step over her if you wanted to go outside. Their mother, Maud, pottered into the kitchen.

Frank put down his brush. He needed a coffee. 'Will we have a biscuit, dogs?'

Betty and Fred shot up and followed him into the

kitchen. Maud was waiting by the cupboard where the biscuits were kept. Frank gave each one a pat and a biscuit, took a couple for himself, made a good strong cup of coffee, and went back to the easel.

He compared the photo he was working from with the strokes he'd already made on the canvas, satisfied he'd caught the outline correctly. It put him back in the right frame of mind and soon he was lost to everything but the paint. Not because that was the way he worked, he wasn't one of those sort of wankers, but because he refused to let any thoughts of his bossy sister and his imbecilic brother ruin his day.

Frank's second call of the day came as he was finishing up. Netta's name flashed up on the screen. She was in Brighton, visiting her friend, Claire.

'How's it going? I hope the dogs are behaving.'

'All good. We've settled into a nice cosy domesticity. Maud's keeping us all in check.'

Her laugh tinkled down the line like fairy dust, spreading warmth and love as it passed through his ear and went straight to his heart. God, how he loved that laugh.

'You're not getting too lonely then?' she said.

He glanced at the half-finished painting he'd spent the day creating. He'd managed to get a fair bit done in the end. 'Just about coping. I'm keeping myself busy.'

'Good. Only I might stay an extra day, if you can manage a bit longer. Doogie's come down to see Merrie, and it's been ages…'

Damn. He'd booked a table for tomorrow night. Just the two of them, all nice and romantic in a cosy little place in

Harborne. 'No problem. You stay. It'll be good for you to catch up. We're all fine here.'

'Okay, thanks. No other news?'

'No. All very quiet.'

'Not too bored?'

'Never.'

'Good. I have to go. We're out on the razz tonight. I'll try to ring you later.'

Frank was on his second lap of the park with Fred and Betty. Maud had elected to stay at home. She knew her own mind, that one. His stomach rumbled. It was too late to cook now. He'd stop off for fish and chips on the way home. He should have taken the healthy option and made dinner before the walk, but it was too much effort when it was just him. Although that never stopped him before he met Netta. He was a dab hand at meals for one back then, and he'd fully intended to cook for himself tonight. It was just that he'd been put off.

It was the lying, for one thing. Okay, so it wasn't a big lie but still, he didn't know why he'd said there was no news when clearly there was. His fool of a brother had upped and left his wife. Presumably. Siobhan didn't say he'd left the wife behind, but the clue was in the word "missing". And if Cousin Finn was to be relied upon, which was something of an imagination leap, Martin was on this side of the water. A bit too close to home for Frank's liking, and even closer to Robyn's home. Luckily, Robyn had just gone on holiday.

Then there was the old boyfriend, Doogie, to be thinking about. Old boyfriend to both Netta and Claire, mind you, albeit not at the same time. Jesus, the man had even impregnated them both. Sadly, Netta had lost her baby, but Claire's daughter, Merrie, was twenty now. Amazingly, the three of them were still really tight. He couldn't understand how Doogie had pulled that one off.

Frank had yet to work out how he felt about Doogie. He was almost certain he wasn't jealous, but if he had to pinpoint his feelings, it would probably boil down to curious but uneasy. There was some part of him that wanted to know more about the man that everybody seemed to love, come what may, but uneasiness always held him back. A Pandora's box kind of uneasiness. Consequently, he'd resisted meeting the guy. Perhaps when they did finally meet, they'd get along just grand and all this unease would disappear. Then again, perhaps he was just kidding himself.

Fred dropped a stick at his feet. It was a big solid thing, a broken branch from an oak tree. Its shape reminded Frank of a rifle. He picked it up and tossed it, sending the dogs bounding after it. A scene popped into his head from eons ago. Him, Martin, Finn, and Billy Mac with their stick rifles. Baby paras shooting down the soldiers. Naturally, the soldiers were imaginary. Pretending to be the enemy was against the rules.

The sound of yapping and shouting broke his absorption. Some way off, the dogs were trying to make friends with a little fluffy thing, one of those breeds with a big head and very little going on in the legs. Its owner, a young woman, picked it up and tucked it under her arm. It didn't stop it barking. A second woman was flapping her arms at Fred and Betty who seemed to be trying to make up their minds whether this was some kind of game that didn't involve the throwing of sticks.

Frank attempted a sprint in their direction, conceding

that it probably looked more like a slow jog to an onlooker. Eventually he reached his destination, flushed and out of breath. 'Sorry. They're quite harmless. It's their size puts people off.'

The woman with the dog under her arm shot him a look. Then she smiled. 'It's Mr O'Hare, isn't it? You taught me A-level English.' Frank couldn't catch her name over the little dog's noise but she did look vaguely familiar. 'I don't suppose you remember me, it was fifteen years ago.'

'Of course I do. I never forget the good pupils,' he said, searching his memory banks for a name.

'Well I certainly wouldn't forget you. You were my favourite teacher. Are you still at the college?'

'Yes, still there.'

'God, that's dedication that is. I'd better take this noisy madam away. So nice to see you again.'

'You too.' Fifteen years? Jesus.

Fred batted Frank's leg with the rifle stick. Old pupils and childhood games. The past is never far away. Frank clipped the dogs' leads onto their collars and followed the two young women along the path, keeping a distance suitable enough to rule him out as a stalker.

'Ooh you were my favourite teacher,' said his former pupil's friend in a namby-pamby voice, obviously not realising it was carrying now the barking had stopped.

'Well he was. All the girls fancied him. He was actually quite hot,' said the ex-pupil.

Quite hot eh? He had no idea. Foolish, vain and entirely inappropriate as it was, he couldn't help being a tiny bit impressed with himself.

'Not that you'd know it now,' she said.

And with that, Frank's bubble felt a little pin prick and

burst. So that was him then. The man who used to be quite hot. Not even fully hot. Not then, and certainly not now.

He veered off the path before the last vestiges of his pride were shattered to smithereens. 'C'mon dogs. Fish and Chips. And drink. I need a drink.'

3

MA AND THE MOTHER OF ALL HANGOVERS.

Day two of the Easter holidays had not begun well. Frank had woken that morning with the mother of all hangovers and a feeling that something catastrophic was on its way. To say he felt crap was quite the undersell. A long shower and strong coffee had barely revived him. He really shouldn't have drunk that much last night.

As he watched the dogs doing their morning tour of the garden he heard a ping coming from the living room. It took some locating but eventually he found his phone behind the cushions on the sofa. Netta had messaged him:

'Looks like I had a missed call from you last night. Did you mean to phone me? Sorry, it was really late when we got back. Too late to call.'

Frank closed his eyes and put his sore head in his hands. Had he phoned her last night? He racked his brains and then wished he hadn't when he recalled a drunken attempt to convey his love for her. Please God, don't let him have left a message. He checked the length of the call, about two minutes. Probably not long enough to say anything stupid. He muttered a thank you to the air and tapped out a reply:

'Sorry, must have pocket dialled you.'

'Okay, no problem. I'll ring you later. Love you x.'

He eased himself back against the soft cushions, grateful to have got away with it. Then he noticed he'd had a message from Siobhan in the early hours of the morning:

'Are you on the pop? Get yourself off to bed and stop messaging me, you dickhead!'

Oh. A quick scroll through the messages he'd sent to his big sister during his spell of inebriation confirmed that he'd had a drunken rant which, in a nutshell, stated that Martin was a moronic arsehole, Finn wasn't much better, and Frank would definitely not be going anywhere near either of them. He made a mental note not to drink alone again and went into the studio.

He pulled up a tall stool in front of yesterday's half-done painting. It was an old bar stool, salvaged from a minor refurb at the Hope and Anchor, a pub he frequented far too often. Mostly on account of it belonging to his friend, Adrian. He was painting a landscape, the inspiration coming from a photo Netta had taken a few years back. It was a beautiful sunset on the western shores of Scotland. She'd wanted to take him there and show him the colours. He'd have loved to go and experience that clarity and those colours himself, but there was a problem. One that he wouldn't admit to Netta because he was a cool guy who took things in his stride; Doogie lived there. So Frank made do with a photo and his imagination.

He mixed up the first colour he'd be working with, adding bits of yellow and brown to get a perfect egg-yolk gold. His head was still throbbing and he felt mildly sick, but it was okay. He'd be fine once he got into the painting.

He laid down the paint in long, thick strokes and thought about his night of lonesome debauchery. He should have gone to the Hope and Anchor and had a few beers, traded a few insults with Adrian, maybe had a game of darts. But no. Instead, he'd sulked on his sofa waiting for Netta to call, with only three dogs and his old records for company. He'd started with Van Morrison, for old time's sake, he was a Belfast boy all after all. The Undertones came after that, followed by a rather sorry musical journey through Frank's past. It was probably the Undertones that had set him off messaging Siobhan.

Frank worked on. Next came fire red, slicing through the deep azure lines at the bottom of the canvas. Bit by bit, he built them up, until they met the golden yellow and merged into a delicious blood red orange. He could almost taste it, that moment, that place. He'd go up there one day and see that sunset himself. For sure. One day.

His headache was lifting now. As he'd guessed, working had helped. He was going to be all right. Netta would be home tomorrow and they'd have some time together before the rest of her family returned from their trips. His brother would turn up in Belfast, all apologetic, and everyone would just shake their heads and say: 'That Martin. What is he like?' Everything would be back to normal and he'd be comfortable again. That was all he wanted.

The shrill ring of his phone startled him. He hoped it was Netta. A glance at the screen told him it wasn't. 'Feck.' He could just ignore it. No, she'd only keep calling. Frank put down his brush. 'Siobhan.'

'Frank.'

'Here we are again.'

'We are. He's at Cousin Finn's.' At least she didn't mention last night's messages. That was something to be grateful for.

'I take it you mean Martin? So everything's in hand then. Finn's taking care of him. Nothing to worry about.'

A hysterical giggle flew down the line and almost shattered his eardrums. 'In hand. Are you mad? In what universe would Finn taking care of Martin mean everything was in hand? Hang on. Ma wants a word.'

Frank put his hand over his eyes. His headache was back. Not Ma as well.

'Hello Francis. Is that yourself?'

'It is, Ma. How are yer?'

'How do you think I am? I'm sick with worry.'

'Ma, he's nearly sixty. He can look after himself.'

'Oh Francis. If only I had your faith. Now listen, son. Could you not do me, your mother, this one favour and get your brother home before he goes completely off the rails?'

'It's not that simple, Ma. Netta's away. I'm looking after her dogs and mine. And I have a lot of work on.'

'Netta. I take it that's his new life-partner?' shouted Siobhan in the background.

'Actually, we've been together a few years, so she's not that new,' said Frank, defensively.

'That's nice,' said Ma. 'I'm glad you've someone else at last. After all that Ellen business. When is she back?'

'Not sure. Tomorrow maybe.' He winced at his falseness and wondered whether Ma could tell he was lying.

'Oh good. I'll hand you back over to Siobhan and she'll give you Finn's number. You can go and get your brother when Venetta gets home. God willing, he won't have killed himself by then.'

'Netta, Ma. Her name's Netta.'

'Netta. Foreign, is she?'

'She's English.'

'That's what I said. Maybe I'll be fortunate enough to meet her before I die.'

Frank sighed. There was that feeling again. Something catastrophic was on its way.

4

A CUP HALF EMPTY

'All sorted, Siobhan. Francis will be going up to Scotland tomorrow,' said Ma, obviously not realising that the phone was turned up so loud, Siobhan would have been able to ascertain that fact if she'd been halfway up the road instead of a few feet away. 'Give him Finn's details. I'll put the kettle on.'

Siobhan took the phone and put it to her ear in time to hear a deep sigh at the other end. It made her smile. Maybe a touch too wickedly but she took her fun where she could get it these days. 'So that's you away to Glasgow, is it?' she said, stifling a snigger.

'Looks like it.' There was a tightness to Frank's voice that made her smile again. 'I don't suppose there's any chance she'll be talked round?'

'None whatsoever. She's put the kettle on now. That's it done and dusted as far as Ma's concerned. You're under orders, Francis.'

Another sigh. 'Right. I'll book a plane ticket. I had plans, yer know. Lots of plans.'

'Didn't we all.' If he was expecting sympathy, he was

talking to the wrong person. 'How long has it been since you last saw Finn?'

'A while. We kind of lost touch.'

Lost touch was a neat and tidy way to describe it. If you were Frank anyway. As far as Siobhan remembered it wasn't quite that neat and tidy. 'Well you might notice a few differences in him since then.'

'I don't doubt it. I'll prepare myself for the worst.'

She allowed herself another little smile. 'You do that. I'll send you his address and phone number. Go there and get Martin home. We'll take it from there. Got it?'

Yet another sigh. 'Yes.'

'And stop sending me drunken messages in the middle of the night. I'm not interested in your pathetic musings on your childhood, our brother, Cousin Finn, or your awful taste in music. Call me when you've got your hands on Martin. Preferably around his neck. Goodbye.'

Ma came in with the tea. 'It's semi-skimmed. I'm trying to reduce your father's cholesterol.'

'I prefer skimmed myself,' said Siobhan.

'I know you do but that's a step too far, in my opinion. You'll have to make do.'

Siobhan took a cup off her and had a sip of tea. It was too thick and creamy for her taste but she would make do, as instructed. Sure, wasn't that always the way?

Ma sat down. By the look on her face, you'd have thought the chair was a bed of nails. Siobhan knew that look. Ma was building up to saying something. She sipped on her tea and waited.

It was a short wait. Ma was nothing if not consistent. 'Are you sure you can't go, love? I really don't think Francis is up to it.'

'I can't get any time off this week. It's our busiest period. You know I would if I could.'

Ma stared into her eyes. It was like she was looking deep into Siobhan's soul, searching for all the lies she'd ever told.

'I practically got down on my bended knees and begged them.' She was overcompensating now. She knew it but she couldn't stop herself. 'Honestly, Mammy. Frank will be there tomorrow and Martin will be back in no time.'

Ma sniffed. 'We'll see. I wish I had your confidence.' It was one of those sideways statements, like when someone pays you a backhanded compliment and you instantly know they don't mean it. It was a good job she hadn't let on about Frank's messages. The man was clearly deranged.

'What was it you called that Venetta woman?' At least Ma had moved on from Frank's lack of capability.

'It's Netta, Ma. I said she was his new life partner. It's just another way of saying the person he's settled down with.'

'Are they living together?'

'As far as I know, she lives next door.'

'So she's just his neighbour then?'

'No, they're a couple. They just don't live together.' It sounded like a very sensible arrangement to Siobhan. She couldn't imagine anything more irritating than living with Frank. Well, yes she could actually. Living with Martin would be even worse. She really didn't know how Bronagh stood it. Dermot had been bad enough but at least in the last few years before the divorce he'd had the decency to spend most of his spare time at the pub.

'You know an awful lot about Frank's living arrangements. I didn't realise you talked that often,' said Ma.

'We don't. I talk to Robyn more than I talk to Frank.'

'I talk to Robyn as well. She hardly ever mentions this

neighbour who's supposed to be her father's new life partner.' Ma bobbed her head about and did air quotes when
she said life partner.

'I expect she has more interesting things to talk to you
about.' Siobhan unlocked her phone and opened up her
photos. 'Do you want to see the new dress I'm having made.
It's for a big work event. I designed it myself.'

Ma stood up and whipped Siobhan's mug away. 'You
spend far too much money on clothes.'

Siobhan was about to protest that her cup was only half
empty but she decided not to bother.

5

FRANK, THE STRANGER

Netta had been blethering on about the wonderful time she'd been having with her old pals for ages before it occurred to her that Frank wasn't listening. He was making the occasional noise every now and then, so she knew he was still on the line, but it wasn't what you'd call interaction. This was unusual for Frank. He was normally attentive, and very involved in their conversations, but not today. 'Frank, is everything all right?'

'Why do you ask?' He sounded as if she'd just accused him of something. The heinous crime of not being all right, presumably. This was very much not Frank. He was usually so laid back.

'You seem a bit, I don't know, not quite yourself. *Is* everything all right?' She did her best to make it sound like an empathetic enquiry rather than a blunt accusation.

There was a moment's silence, his soft breathing the only evidence that he was still there, then: 'Yes. Except... I was going to wait until you got home but since you ask, it's my brother. It's nothing really, but it seems he's left his wife.'

'Oh that's a shame. These things happen, I suppose.' It

was an inadequate response but the news had rather taken Netta by surprise, mainly because she didn't know Frank had a brother. She knew that his parents were still alive, and that he had a sister, but she couldn't recall any mention of a brother.

'Yeah, well, these things have a habit of happening to Martin, that's for sure.'

'Martin. That's your brother? Are you close?' Clearly not, seeing as the name Martin had never passed his lips in her company before, but she asked the question anyway. Mainly because she was intrigued.

Frank made a noise that was difficult to put a label on. Not so much a laugh as a mangled exclamation. 'Not really. Anyway, it seems he's walked out and come across the water. He's staying at Cousin Finn's in Glasgow.'

'Cousin Finn?' Another new name.

'Yes. Sorry. There was already an Uncle Finn when Finn came along, so he's always been known as Cousin Finn. Although Uncle Finn's dead now, so I suppose we could just call him Finn but, you know…'

'The name stuck.'

'Exactly. Anyway, the thing is, I might have to go up there and see to things.'

'See to things?'

'Pack him off back to Belfast so the family can deal with him. I'm under orders. I've had phone calls.'

She couldn't tell if he was joking, so she decided to not to laugh at the idea of Frank having phone calls that carried orders. 'I'll be leaving here first thing in the morning. I'll be home by lunchtime. You can tell me all about it then if you want to. Unless you'd rather talk about it now.'

'No, I don't want to waste any more time than I have to on this. Tell me what you've been up to.'

'Let me see. Where to start…' and she began all over again. She'd been right, he hadn't been listening to her at all. Frank really wasn't himself. Mind you, she'd guessed that when she heard the message he'd left last night. It wasn't like him to profess his undying love in the style of a pub singer. And then there was something about his late wife, Ellen. He'd been so drunk she couldn't make out what it was, other than Frank assuring someone that she wasn't Ellen. Who that someone was, Netta had no idea, but given he'd apparently spent the night in, it could only be the dogs or himself. And since Frank was pretending to have called her by accident, it wasn't the right time to ask.

Netta turned into her road. She'd set off early enough that morning but the drive from Brighton had taken longer than expected, thanks to roadworks and a lorry blowout. So it was with some relief that she finally pulled up outside her house. Frank and the dogs came out to meet her, the dogs being infinitely more excited about her return than he was. But while he wasn't exactly bouncing around in celebration, it was obvious Frank was happy to see her. He hugged her so tight you'd be forgiven for thinking she'd been away for months and not just a week.

She thought about his strange message as she kissed him. 'Missed me?'

'So much,' he said, his arms still enveloping her. He smelt as if he'd just stepped out of the shower.

She ran her hand against his smooth face. 'You've shaved.'

He grinned. 'Special occasion.' This was her Frank, not the one she'd spoken to yesterday. The man she knew and loved was back.

She landed another kiss on his lips. 'Let's not waste it then, shall we? Come on you. We've got some catching up to do.'

She took him into her house, the dogs following behind like a mini dog parade. Only when they got upstairs did the parade come to a halt. Frank closed the bedroom door to shut them out. 'Sorry dogs, you're gonna have to wait this one out.'

A few hours later, they were in the lounge. Outside, the skies had turned grey and wet but inside, they were cosied up on the old leather sofa. Netta stretched her foot out to stroke Frank's leg with her toe. 'What's the news on Martin?'

'I'm going up there tomorrow. Sorry. It would have been good to have a few days to ourselves.'

'It would, but it doesn't matter. We'll have other times. I didn't know you had a cousin in Glasgow.' She was building up to asking about his brother in incremental steps. Cousin first, brother next.

'Neither did I. I mean I knew Finn was my cousin. I just didn't realise he'd moved. My own fault. I don't keep in touch with the family nearly enough.'

'I don't think I knew you had a brother either.'

'Didn't you? I'm sure I must have said. Yes, I must have. I have mentioned Martin to you before, haven't I?'

'I think I'd have remembered.'

'Hmm, maybe you're right. He's not someone I think about very often. Apart from being brothers, we don't have a lot in common. Not these days anyway. To be honest, he's hard work.' He stared at the fireplace and sighed. 'We should make the most of the few hours we have left. Do you fancy going out for a meal tonight?'

He made it sound as if they were on the verge of extinction. Netta squeezed his hand. 'Good idea. Better not get too drunk though. You don't want to be travelling with a hangover.' Or leaving any more rambling messages, she added in her head.

'So, Doogie turned up then? I take it you weren't expecting him?'

'It was all a bit last minute. You know Doogie. You didn't mind me staying for the extra day, did you?'

'Of course not.' Frank flashed her a smile that didn't quite reach his eyes. That stranger was back again.

6

THE MAN WHO WAS AGEING
BACKWARDS

The plan was to get to Glasgow, locate and dispatch Martin, and return home as quickly as possible. Ordinarily, he'd have stopped off to see Robyn and made a trip of it, but she was away in Thailand. Basically then, there was no joy to be had in this visit. It was simply a matter of completing an unpleasant task and getting the hell back home in one piece. Frank could do this. He could absolutely do it. He'd told himself this numerous times on the flight, and was still repeating it in his head as he walked out of arrivals and searched for Cousin Finn.

If Finn hadn't called out, Frank would have walked past him. The last time he'd seen his cousin, Finn had been lying face down in a pizza, sleeping off a forty-eight hour drinking binge. That was at Martin's wedding, thirteen years ago. Binge drinking and food pillows were pretty much par for the course with Finn back then. Frank did the age calculations. Finn must be fifty-nine now. Given his history, he'd been expecting him to have aged badly. In fact, he was amazed Finn was still alive. And yet the man that stood before him now looked younger than when Frank had last seen him. Surely that wasn't possible?

This new Finn's eyes sparkled. His hair shone, his skin glowed, his firm muscles flexed as he pulled Frank into an uncomfortably tight bear hug. 'Frankie Boy. It's great to see ya.'

Released from Finn's grip, Frank gave his cousin the once over to confirm he wasn't imagining things. 'What happened to you?'

'What? Oh this?' Finn gestured to his lean, athletic body. 'I just cleaned myself up.'

'You look great.'

'Thanks, man. You look … good yourself.'

Frank, the man who used to be quite hot, remembered his ex-pupil's words. 'No I don't, I look like shite, but thanks for trying. Is Martin not with you?'

'He's not here.'

'Okay, so he's at yours?'

Finn shook his head. 'He's not.'

'So where is he then? Oh no, don't tell me he's given you the slip? For the love of God, Finn, don't tell me that.'

'He has so. He was gone when I got back from work yesterday. On the positive side, I know where he's gone. I hope I do anyway, because if it's not him that's nicked the camper van then I really should report it.'

Frank folded himself into Finn's Mini. 'So let me get this straight. You got home yesterday and found both Martin and your campervan gone, and he hasn't called or anything?'

'He has not. Although he did leave the note.'

'The note? What did it say?'

'Sorry. I just need some space.'

'That was it?'

'It was. There was no mention of the van, but I assumed it was too much of a coincidence that they'd both be gone at the exact same time. So I tried calling him and I heard his phone ringing in the spare room.'

'He's left his phone behind? On purpose, do you think?'

'I think so, yes. Probably got himself a new one, so we couldn't contact him. Unless he's decided…'

'Unless he's decided what? To top himself?'

'I was going to say, unless he's decided to go off grid. I've been talking to him about how it helped me sort myself out. I thought it might give him something positive to think about. I didn't think it would give him ideas, like. If he'd only said, I'd have been happy to take him on a trip. He didn't have to steal the fucking thing. I love that van.' Finn pulled up onto the drive of a small, modern terraced house. 'Here we are. This is home.'

If he'd been asked to describe the house of a single, fifty-nine-year-old man with a one-time serious addiction to partying, Frank was pretty sure Finn's house would come close. Except maybe for the Buddha statues. He'd been in four rooms so far and there was one in every room, including the bathroom. Other than that, there were no ornaments, paintings or pictures of any kind. Just modern, comfortable furniture and a lot of electronic equipment. If Frank's house hadn't been decorated by Ellen, and moulded by Robyn, it would probably come close to this. Although he'd definitely have paintings on the wall, and not one single Buddha.

He came out of the bathroom and found Finn in the kitchen. 'Coffee?'

Frank noted the super-sleek top of the range coffee maker. Yeah, he'd probably have one of those too. 'That'd be grand.'

They sat at the kitchen table on chairs that looked like they were fresh from the showroom.

'So what do we do now?' said Frank.

'We go get it back.'

'It?'

'The van. Martin too, of course. I've made the arrangements at work. We'll head off in the Mini tomorrow.'

'Where are we going?'

'On a road trip. Cheer up, Frank. It'll be like the old days, you, me and Martin. When we catch up with the sneaky bastard anyways.'

Frank sighed. In the old days they were kids, not old men. Well, he was old. Martin was less than two years younger than him but he was probably no better. And God only knows what kind of pact with the devil Finn had made, because he was probably the only one of them that seemed to be ageing backwards. So no, it was not going to be like the old days. Anyway, how could it be, when they were missing a key player in their little gang? Not Martin, obviously. That useless shite was only ever a liability.

'There's just one thing we need to work out quickly,' said Finn.

'What's that?'

'We need to work out what we're going to say to your Ma and Siobhan. They'll be calling us soon.'

From nowhere a tune floated through the air towards them. For a second Frank thought that maybe Finn's Alexa had misinterpreted their conversation and thought they'd requested the kind of music you might hear while having a soothing back massage. Then he looked down and saw that it was actually Finn's phone ringing.

Finn glanced at the phone and then at Frank, his expression a cross between resignation and panic. 'Oh.'

GOLDEN BOY DISAPPOINTS

Siobhan could not believe her ears. Martin, the shifty fecker, had absconded yet again. 'So you've lost him.' She made sure to put extra emphasis on the word "you've" because Ma had a face of fury on her, and Siobhan did not want to be on the receiving end of it.

'Only temporarily,' said Cousin Finn.

'Temporarily doesn't make it okay, Finn. No matter how hard you try to gloss it up, you were supposed to hold onto him and instead you've lost him.'

'Yes you could say that, Siobhan. I prefer to take a more optimistic view.'

Oh for Christ's sake, Finn was back on to that karma shit again. She had to put a stop to it right now. 'Finn, there is no optimistic view to be taken here.'

Ma interrupted her flow: 'What's optimism got to do with it? Is that Finn talking nonsense again?'

Siobhan took the phone away from her ear. 'Yes it is, Ma. He said he prefers to take a more optimistic view.'

Ma muttered something under her breath which may

very well have been a swear word. Meanwhile Finn was doing his best to squirm out of trouble by roping in the other eejit. 'Hang on Siobhan, I'll put you on speakerphone, then you can talk to the both of us.'

Speakerphone was it? She'd give them speakerphone. 'You do that, Finn. I'll put mine on as well, so Ma can join the conversation.'

'Oh okay. Hello there Auntie Clodagh. How are yer?' Ha! Finn didn't sound so optimistic now.

Ma bent over the phone. 'Don't you come here with your hellos and your how are yers, Finn Moran. You were given a job to do and you failed, although why I'm surprised about that I have no idea. Is Francis there with you?'

'I'm here, Ma,' said Frank.

'And you're no better. If you'd gone when we asked you to, this would have all been done and dusted by now and you'd have been back with those dogs you're so fond of. And don't be telling me no one else could have looked after them for a few days, you've plenty of friends. I'm not the idiot you take me for, Francis. I've spoken to your father about this and we are very disappointed in you. Very disappointed. You are both very disappointing.'

'Is Da there with you?' said Frank.

'No he is not, and don't try to change the subject,' hissed Ma.

Siobhan had to work hard to conceal a smirk, it wouldn't have gone down well. Still, at least she was off the hook. 'What are you going to do now?' she said to the phone.

'We're going to follow his trail. I promise you, we will track him down.' Finn was back again with that annoyingly positive optimism. Frank was notable in his silence. Licking his wounds probably. Nobody likes to be called disappointing by Ma. Not even the golden boy.

'Has Martin's wife heard from him at all?' The golden boy had found something to say. Maybe his ears were burning, except that was when someone was talking about you, wasn't it?

'Her name's Bronagh, in case you forgot.'

'Yes, I do know, Siobhan.'

'No she hasn't. He's not answering his phone either.'

'Well he's left his phone behind, so that'll be why,' said Frank.

Why would he do that? Surely he wasn't...? No, not Martin. Bronagh would have told her if she thought he'd been in that frame of mind. Wouldn't she? Siobhan glanced at Ma but saw no outward signs of panic. She herself was feeling unsettled. She'd had enough of this call. 'Just find him and get him home so we can sort this mess out.'

'And if anything happens to Martin, I will never speak to either of you again,' added Ma. That seemed a little melodramatic and highly unlikely, but Ma was Ma, she liked to end an angry conversation with a flourish.

'Why do you think Martin left his phone behind?' said Ma after they'd hung up.

Siobhan shrugged and tried to look convincing. 'I don't know.'

'Yes you do. I told you not to leave it to those two. You should have gone after him.'

'What am I, a bounty hunter?' She forced out a laugh when really, she wanted to scream. Why was she always expected to sort out everyone else's mess? 'I'll put the kettle on. I've some nice cake.'

Ma gave her a withering look. 'I'm not a child, Siobhan. Do not treat me as one.'

'Sorry Ma.' Siobhan groaned inwardly. It seemed she was still on the hook. Fecking Martin. Fecking Frank and Finn. Fecking, fecking men.

8

ALL THE BEST GANGS HAVE NICKNAMES

Frank woke up in a strange bed feeling anxious. When he remembered he was in Finn's spare room, the feeling of strangeness went but the anxiety persisted. His hastily made plan to get his brother back into the bosom of his family had been scuppered. So too had the one to get back home to Netta and his paintings. He was stuck up here for the foreseeable, or at least until they found Martin. Not to mention Finn's campervan.

The call from Ma and Siobhan had clarified the situation on two specific points. Firstly, if he'd got off his arse quicker instead of procrastinating with all that rubbish about dogs, Martin would have been home by now for them to talk some sense into. Secondly, if he and Finn didn't get off their arses right now and haul Martin back before he did anything stupid, they would never be spoken to again. Finn and Frank had briefly held each other's eye at that declaration. Finn looked as if it wouldn't be such a bad thing, and Frank probably did too, if he was honest with himself. Maybe if it was Siobhan, rather than Ma that had said it, they'd have entertained the idea a bit longer. But it was Ma and so it was only a fleeting thought and then it was gone. They both knew they had an obligation. Martin had disappeared on their watch. It was their job to retrieve him.

Frank got up, took a shower and went downstairs. Finn was in the living room on a yoga mat. He lowered himself from downward dog into a plank, and stayed there as if he was just having a wee rest. Frank watched him, mesmerised by his taut, rippling biceps. When they were kids, Finn was always the skinny little runt they couldn't get rid of. When they were older, he was the booze monster they were always apologising for and still couldn't get rid of. Both of those people seemed a long way off from the Finn of today.

'Nearly done. Help yourself to breakfast,' said Finn, without even one bead of sweat on his forehead.

There was granola, yoghurt and fruit on the kitchen worktop. Frank made probably the healthiest breakfast he'd ever eaten and countered it with a cup of coffee. Back in the living room, Finn had transitioned into a meditative pose, so Frank headed the other way into the tiny paved garden where he found another Buddha, a few pot plants, a table and two chairs.

When he finished eating, he rang Netta. They'd spoken last night but her parents were there so he'd kept it brief.

She answered straight away. 'Morning. I was just having breakfast.'

'Me too. Granola, yoghurt and fruit.'

'Isn't that a bit healthy for you?'

'Yes. Cousin Finn appears to have been taken over by some health cult. He's doing a spot of yoga as we speak. It's all quite surreal. If I had my way I'd be running for the airport before you could say hot buttered toast, but I have to stay up here. We're going on a road trip. Martin's made off with Finn's campervan and we're about to follow his trail. In a Mini, no less.'

'All sounds very exciting. How long will it take?'

Exciting wasn't the word on Frank's lips at that moment. Annoying more like, and that was putting it mildly. 'Not sure. Not too long I hope. Finn's confident he can find him.'

'Where are you going?'

'North. The Highlands. Finn's got it all in hand. I'm just following his lead.' The irony of that made him laugh.

'What's so funny?' said Netta.

'Nothing. It's just that Finn was always the loser who followed us around. We were always having to get him out of trouble. It's crazy and more than a little scary to think he's the one I'm relying on now.'

There was a cough behind him. It was Finn. Despite his yoga and meditation, he wasn't looking very zen.

Finn had filled every vacant space in the Mini except for the two front seats. He'd done it without uttering any more than a few words, and those words had been: 'I'll try not to get you killed,' although he'd sounded very much like getting Frank killed was currently high on his priority list. Possibly even higher on the list than getting his campervan back.

Frank didn't answer. He was too busy being piqued by the fact that Finn had left no room for his small suitcase. He pulled the passenger seat forward and the contents in the back shifted enough to allow him to shove his case in. Before everything toppled, he rolled the front seat back and jumped in, only then realising it was now so far forward his chin was almost resting on his knees. All attempts to push it back were met with resistance and Frank realised the contents had shifted because they'd fallen into the space behind the seat.

'Do you want me to take everything out and repack?' said Finn, looking more than a bit pleased with himself.

'No. I'll manage.'

Finn switched on the engine. 'Okay then. Let's go'

They stopped and started, weaved and wound through the busy Glasgow streets, until they reached the motorway, passing places Frank had heard of but never visited. Within an hour they'd reached Loch Lomond. It took a while to get to the other end but Frank was so lost in the beauty of it that he didn't care. The gloriously clear day helped, but the images, the light bouncing off the water, and such colours. The blues – cerulean, ultramarine, midnight. The greens – sap, viridian, phthalo. His head was full of compositions.

'Quite a sight, eh?' said Finn.

'Indeed.'

'There's more to come. This is just the beginning.'

They carried on until they stopped to stretch their legs in Glencoe, its snow-capped café au lait and moss green mountains dwarfing the Mini. Frank imagined all the great artists that would have travelled here in the past to capture it and the awe they must have felt on their first sighting.

'I love this place. The power of it, it's just breathtaking,' said Finn.

If one of his colleagues from college had said that, Frank wouldn't have batted an eyelid but this was Finn, although not the Finn he used to know. 'I'm sorry I called you a loser.'

Finn rolled a stone around under his foot. 'You were only telling the truth. But that was a long time ago, Frank. I'm a changed man now. I guess I was just hoping that wasn't how you still saw me.'

'Finn, I haven't seen you for years. Give me a chance to get used to the new you.'

Finn nodded. 'I was sorry to hear about Ellen. I would have come to the funeral but I didn't think you'd want me there.'

'It was in France. No one came. There was just me and Robyn, some French people, and the man she'd left me for.'

'Oh. I thought she came back to you.'

'She did. And then she left again.'

'Okay. Well I'm still sorry she died. I liked her.'

Frank glared at Finn. He might be a cleaner version of himself but he still didn't know when to keep his mouth shut. 'I know you did. Let's get back on the road.'

'Keep an eye out for a yellow campervan with renegade written large on its side. Or an orange one with rebel without a clause on the back. Not such big writing. They've both posted sightings in our WhatsApp group,' said Finn.

'Rebel without a cause?'

'No, clause. He's a retired solicitor.'

'I see. It's a joke only solicitors would find funny.'

Finn smiled. 'Yeah. He's a good guy though. The other guy's a scientist of some kind. It's a diverse community.'

'And what do you do these days?' Back when Frank saw more of him, Finn was always in and out of jobs. More out than in, it had to be said.

'I have my own business. Personal training, yoga, wellness.'

Well that explained a lot. 'Wasn't it difficult to drop this trip on your clients?'

'A bit, but I don't do so much teaching these days. I have a team I can fall back on. There's Rebel.'

Up ahead of them a bright orange campervan was parked on a dirt patch at the side of the road. As they turned into it, Frank spotted rebel without a clause written under the back window. A little man in a loose fitting T-shirt and baggy chinos appeared from the other side of the van. This, presumably, was Rebel.

Finn jumped out to greet Rebel. Frank got out too, more to stretch than anything. He was still travelling with his knees close to his ears and was beginning to feel it. He caught a whiff of something meaty cooking and his stomach rumbled.

Rebel nodded in his direction. 'I've got the barbie on. Can I interest you guys in a steak?' It wasn't the Scottish accent Frank had been expecting but very much English home counties.

Frank was so hungry his mouth was watering by the time Rebel served them up juicy pink steaks with barbecued peppers and thick crusty bread, washed down with a beer.

Rebel tore at a piece of bread and mopped up the meat juices on his plate. 'Picked up some supplies earlier from Fort William. Stayed there last night, which is where I saw your man. I recognised your van, Finn. He said you'd lent it to him.'

'He borrowed it,' said Finn.

'Yes, I see the difference. I did think there was something unreliable about him. I was going to message you but then I saw your post.' Rebel turned to Frank. 'Apologies, I know you're all related.'

Finn shook his head. 'Don't worry about it. You called it right. Martin is definitely unreliable. Did he say where he was going?'

'All the way up north. He mentioned Durness. I wrote down the best overnight stop off points for him. I photographed it before I gave it to him. Let me send it on to you.'

Finn stood up and shook Rebel's hand. 'We'd better get on. Thanks, man. I appreciate it.'

'Not at all. I'm going up that way myself so we may bump into each other. Good to meet you, Frank.' Rebel shot his hand towards Frank.

Frank shook it, half-expecting some kind of secret signal, as if he'd been initiated into some private organisation, but it was just a normal handshake. Firm but friendly. 'Good to meet you, Rebel.'

'Actually, it's Duncan. Rebel is just a joke name someone in our group gave me because I'm the least rebellious person you could meet.'

Frank pointed to the phrase on the back of the campervan. 'You don't mind it though?'

'Not at all. Something to live up to. Besides, all the best gangs have nicknames for each other, don't they?'

Frank eased himself back into the Mini. He turned to wave to Rebel but he'd already gone back to his chair and was opening another can of beer. He'd have liked to have stayed there with him, shooting the breeze, or just taking in the scenery rather than driving north to look for his idiot brother and a stolen campervan.

'What did you think of Rebel?' said Finn.

'I liked him. So what's your nickname then?'

Finn winked and shook his head. 'That would be telling.'

'You're part of the club though?' Rebel had called them a gang, but Frank had stopped short at that. It didn't seem right somehow.

Finn's face broke into an embarrassed grin. 'Yep.'

Frank looked out of the window at the vast mountains and his mind drifted back to four young eejits who once thought they were the only gang worth being in.

9

TEENAGE KICKS – 1978

Ma stood in front of the kitchen door, refusing to let him pass. 'Francis O'Hare, if I find out you're up to no good, I will personally make sure your father deals with you.'

'I've done nothing.' Frank held out his palms and did his best to look innocent of all charges, even though he wasn't sure what the charges were. Probably because Ma didn't know either. She just had this uncanny way of recognising when he was about to commit an offence.

'That may be so, but you've no good in mind. I can tell. You're looking awful shifty. Tell me where you're going, or you'll be going nowhere.'

'Only to Billy's. His ma's away. I'm just keeping him company.'

Frank's ma squinted at him. She didn't believe him, but Frank knew he was on safe ground because she wouldn't ask more details about Billy Mac's family arrangements. They were too loose for her liking, too close to potential indecency, and she, as a decent woman would not be drawn into discussion on them. 'Well you make sure you keep away from trouble.'

'I thought I'd stay at Billy's tonight.' He threw it in, casual like, in the hope he might get away with it.

Ma folded her arms. 'You will not. You've school in the morning and you're in the middle of your exams. You're lucky I let you out at all. I want you home by nine. And you can take Martin with you.'

Frank threw his arms in the air. 'You've got to be joking?' How come he was always lumbered with that clown? Billy would do his nut.

There was a loud cough from the living room and Da said: 'Take Martin, or you'll be going nowhere.'

Martin was in the kitchen before Frank could protest any further, although he knew protestations were a waste of breath. His brother had that butter wouldn't melt look on his face that Frank could never pull off. 'Can Finn come?'

'Good idea. Less chance of you getting into trouble if you've two youngers to look after.' Ma stepped away from the door to let them through. 'Nine o'clock, Francis. Do you hear?'

Frank gritted his teeth. 'Yes.'

'And if Billy's on his own, he can stay here tonight.'

'Youse two are not coming, so get that right out of your heads.' Frank stormed up Billy Mac's street, mad as hell. Martin, the sneaky bastard, had done it again. Every time he tried to do something on his own, Martin sneaked his way in. And if that wasn't bad enough, now he had an extra liability. Wee Cousin Finn. 'You are definitely not coming,' he said again, in case they hadn't heard him the first time.

Finn ran at his side. 'Where are we not coming to, Frank?'

Frank walked even faster. 'It doesn't matter because you're not coming.'

'We're going to the Battle of the Bands,' shouted Martin, full of himself because ever since he'd found out Frank's little secret, he'd been trying to get in on it.

Frank stopped and swivelled round. 'Will you shut your big mouth? Do you want us to get killed? 'Cos if Ma finds out, we are dead.'

'You will be. Not us. Because we're not going. Apparently. I suppose I could go back right now and tell her. Then you won't be going either and she'll still kill you.'

Frank didn't bother answering. He knew that no matter who went and who didn't, he'd be in for it. If Martin told on him, he'd get walloped for trying to go, and for thinking it was okay to take Martin and Finn with him, even though he didn't think it was okay to take them with him. If he let them come and by some miracle they got in, he'd get walloped for missing the nine o'clock curfew and leading Finn and Martin astray. Whatever happened, he couldn't win but at least if he got to see a concert, a real live concert, it would be worth it.

They reached Billy's street and dodged the kids playing games. One of them was Billy's wee brother. He fired an imaginary shot at them with his stick gun. Martin pretended to catch it in the guts and stumbled along the pavement.

Frank rolled his eyes. They were way too old for those kind of games now, they had other interests. At least, Frank and Billy did. The only interest Finn and Martin had was following Frank around like he was some kind of fucking messiah.

The fellas hanging around on the corner gave them the once over as they passed. Frank nodded at a couple of them he knew from school. He was used to being watched when he visited Billy, so it was no big deal. It was the mixed marriage thing that made Billy's family so interesting. Two religions in one household, not that either of his parents ever went to church. Since Billy's Protestant da had walked out on them, his ma had made a special effort to stick to her own side. You'd have thought that would have made her less interesting, but not so. Maybe it was the kind of people she chose to stick to. Billy didn't help matters either. He was the only boy in their Catholic school with a Protestant name, and the only one to openly state that all religion was a pile of shite. It gave him an edge and was a recipe for distrust. Having Billy for a friend was the only edgy thing about Frank.

Billy opened his front door and gave Martin and Finn a cursory glance. 'What the fuck have you brought them for?'

'The parents made me. Martin'll tell if we don't let them come.'

Billy looked up at Martin. He was sixteen, the same age as Frank, but he was smaller than Martin and only a bit taller than Finn. 'You wouldn't do that, would yer Marty?'

Martin folded his arms and stuck out his chin. 'I would so.'

'Jeez, you're a bag of shite. You know that, don't yer?' Billy pulled the door further open. 'You'd better come in. We're going to have to do something about Finn. He's never gonna get in.'

Inside the house, Frank changed into the ripped jeans and T-shirt he'd stashed there. For Martin and Finn, they tore into two of Billy's T-shirts and scrawled *'Anarchy'* and *'Bollocks'* across them, then added some safety pins. Then they mixed up sugar and water and pasted their hair to make it stick up like Johnny Rotten and Sid Vicious.

'Sure, don't we look like proper punks.' Finn was bouncing off the ceiling with excitement.

Billy checked himself in his ma's dressing table mirror. 'We are proper punks. Well, me and Frank are. Youse two are just hangers on. Aren't they Frank?'

Frank gave Martin a shove. 'Too right.'

Martin looked a bit hurt but it was his own fault, he deserved everything he got.

The concert was at the university, nearly an hour's walk away. They added a bit more time in case they got held up at the checkpoints. You never knew. As they walked, they talked tactics and kept their eyes out for trouble. It was pointless trying not to draw attention to themselves. Belfast was a city full of big ties and flares. How could they not get noticed?

When they got closer to the university hall they started to see other lads dressed like them. Girls too. Frank recognised one girl from Good Vibrations, the record shop where he'd heard about the Battle of the Bands. He wasn't sure but he thought she might be one of the enemy. She caught him looking at her and stuck out her tongue and laughed. He grinned and looked away, embarrassed by his burning cheeks.

'Who's she?' said Martin.

Frank shrugged. 'Dunno. Just someone I see around.'

'She's awful pretty.'

'You can't call a punk girl pretty. That's a real insult.' He tutted to emphasise just how stupid Martin was. Secretly though, he agreed. She was awful pretty.

When they got to the hall, they circled around Finn. Frank and Martin lifted him by the elbows to make him look taller. When one of the bouncers on the door noticed Finn rising up, it occurred to Frank that he would have been less conspicuous if they'd left him to walk.

'How old are you?' said the bouncer.

'Eighteen.' Finn put on a gruff voice which was actually pretty impressive.

'Oh yeah? I suppose if I asked your date of birth you'd have one ready to go?'

'Yeah,' said Finn.

The guy shook his head and laughed. 'On your way, big man. But if I catch you at the bar, you're out.'

Walking into the hall was like they'd crossed the pearly gates and gone to heaven. Punk heaven to be precise. Their parents would probably think it was hell. Frank, Martin and Finn's parents that is. Billy's ma probably wouldn't have noticed either way, and his da didn't count anymore.

Billy's eyes opened wide. 'Who'd have thought there were so many of us. Makes you feel special.'

The other three nodded, too awestruck to answer. Up on the stage, the record shop owner made an announcement they couldn't hear properly over the noise. Four lads came on and took their places. The drummer's sticks crashed into the opening bars and the room vibrated with thundering guitars and hundreds of people bouncing up and down.

'I can't see,' shouted Finn.

Billy was already pogoing. He grabbed Finn's arm. 'Do this.'

They all started leaping and crashing around, knocking into the other punks. Everyone was doing it. No one seemed to care which side you were on. They were too busy having a good time.

Somebody leapt onto Finn's shoulders and sent him tumbling down. Frank pulled him up before he got crushed. 'You okay?'

Finn's eyes were wild. 'I'm fucking fantastic, Frankie Boy.'

Frank laughed. Only Billy called him Frankie Boy. But it was okay, he'd let it ride for tonight. Finn was just a kid trying to be one of them.

In the break between bands, Frank and Billy pooled their money together. They only had enough to buy two pints so they'd have to share. Being taller than the others, Frank looked the oldest so he went to get them. He waited to be served, memorising in his head what he had to ask for. He didn't want it to be obvious it was his first time. The girl he'd seen earlier was at the other end of the bar with a group of lads he knew for sure went to a Protestant school. That was it then. She was almost certainly the enemy, so she wouldn't be interested in him.

'Yeah?' said the barman.

Frank gulped and told himself staying cool was the key to success. 'Two pints of lager.'

'Which lager?'

Which? Bollocks, he hadn't thought of that. Frank's eyes shot across the taps in a panic. 'Er, Harp.'

The barman gave him the beady eye, but he still poured out two pints and took his money.

Puffed up and triumphant, Frank took the drinks back to the others. When he reached them, he found Martin and Finn had their own pints. 'Where'd you get them from?'

'They were left on the bar. Will we get some more?' said Finn.

Frank stopped him before he headed back. 'Fuck no. You'll get us killed. I mean, really killed. Proper dead.'

Martin supped on his stolen beer. 'Suit yourself.'

Billy took his drink from Frank. 'No one's gonna kill them and at least we all get our own pints.'

Frank shook his head. Sometimes Billy was worse than the other two, and they were bad enough.

The record shop fella came back on stage and announced a band from Derry. Everyone was bouncing up and down to their first song, except for one person. Frank stood, open-mouthed. It was the most perfect song he'd ever heard in his life. Too perfect to do anything other than stop and listen, and take it in. He was grinning, that much he was aware of. He was probably the only one in the room not moving, but Frank couldn't care less. Nor did he care about stolen drinks, or getting his head kicked in by some angry fellas looking for their pints. Nothing mattered now that he'd heard 'Teenage Kicks.' Nothing.

The band seemed to be on the stage for just minutes and then they were gone.

Billy's eyes were popping out of his head. 'What were they called again?'

Frank stared at the stage. 'The Undertones.'

'Are they really one of us?'

'They must be. They said they were from Derry.'

Billy grabbed hold of him. 'We have to get that record.'

On the way home, they were stopped twice by the soldiers and narrowly missed getting locked up, thanks to Finn who'd managed to get drunk on hardly more than a sniff of lager. By the time they got to Billy Mac's, it was getting on for midnight.

'Ma said you can stay at ours if you want to,' said Frank.

Billy snorted. 'You must be joking. I don't wanna be

around when your ma blows a gasket. Anyway, I have to help get the wee ones to school in the morning.'

Shit. Frank had forgotten about the curfew. The parents would be going up the wall with worry by now. Ma probably had the search parties out as soon as the clock ticked past nine. And the ould man wouldn't be much better. Frank was going to be in so much trouble when they got home, but it didn't matter anymore. He walked the rest of the way with 'Teenage Kicks' running through his head. So what if he was going to get battered. He'd just had the best night of his life.

10

FB AND YODA GET COSY

They'd been on the road for several hours since they'd left Rebel. Frank had lost track of time so it was difficult to tell exactly how long. On top of that, he had no idea where they were. He could ask Finn but the answer would mean nothing to him. All he knew was that it must be time for them to stop for the night. He checked. It was eight-thirty, although it was so bright you'd never guess it. His back ached and he had cramp in his legs. In the morning, he'd be sure to readjust that seat but for tonight, he just wanted to stretch out on a comfortable bed. 'Will we be stopping soon?' he said.

Finn looked startled, as if he'd forgotten Frank was there. 'There's a place just up the road here with facilities. We'll stay there tonight, as we've no facilities of our own.'

'So long as it's got a comfortable bed, a shower and a toilet.'

'Well it has toilets. One out of three ain't bad.' Finn turned off the main road, up a side road towards what looked like nothing more than a toilet block.

Frank looked at him, aghast. 'You're kidding me?'

Finn pulled up next to a motorhome and cut the engine. 'Nope. We're pitching up here tonight.'

'Pitching? In a–'

'Tent. Yes. Come on, Frankie Boy. Where's your sense of adventure.'

Frank eased himself out of the car and made for the toilet. Once inside, he glanced at himself in the mirror and noticed he was bent over. Road trip day one and he was nothing short of a wreck. Wait till he told Netta. Of course, he couldn't tell her because he'd lost his phone signal ages ago. And now he was going to sleep in a tent. A fecking tent! And in the morning he probably wouldn't be able to walk. This was all Martin's fault. It was always Martin's fault.

Finn was busy setting up the tent when Frank came out of the toilet block. Someone was helping him, a big guy maybe in his late thirties or early forties, his long hair pulled up in a bun. The motorhome that they'd parked next to was gone and in the space that would have been next to it, there was a yellow campervan.

Finn looked up as Frank got closer. 'Ren, this is my cousin Frank.'

'All right, Frank?' Renegade stood up to his full height and dwarfed Finn. He even made Frank feel small.

'You must be Renegade,' said Frank in response.

'I am, mate. Right, let's get this baby up so's we can get on with a few bevvies.'

They had the tent up in no time. Frank was relieved to see it wasn't one of those little two-man things that only a small child could lie down in. That said, it was still pretty cosy. Not the comfy, put your feet up kind of cosy either.

'I've got a chilli on if anyone fancies it. Come over when you're ready, Yodes,' said Renegade.

Frank waited for Renegade to go. 'Yodes? Don't tell me your nickname's Yoda?'

Finn threw two sleeping bags into the tent and zipped it up. 'Yeah. Like I said, I'm a different man these days.'

'That bit I can believe, but Yoda?'

'It's just a joke, okay. Like Rebel's not really a rebel, and Renegade's not a renegade. Except for that time when he blew the whistle on his old company for bad practices, but that doesn't really count because it was for the public good.'

Frank held his hands up in defeat. 'Okay, okay, I get it. I'm sorry for taking the piss.'

Renegade made a mean chilli, particularly when you considered he'd done it in a little van with two gas rings and no space to speak of. Frank was a messy cook. He needed surfaces and lots of room. He couldn't imagine himself whipping up a meal in what was basically a tin can on wheels. But he had to admit, there was a simplicity in it that he could see the appeal of, especially when you could eat the meal in surroundings like these.

Renegade was obviously from the Midlands. Just hearing his accent made Frank homesick. Partly because there was a nice comfy bed there, but mostly because he missed being with Netta. He knew that was a bit needy of him since he'd only seen her yesterday morning. Was that really only thirty-six hours ago?

'The show's about to start.' Renegade pointed to a stretch of water down the hill. Four red deer appeared on the other side of it and started grazing. Another two were drinking the water. Just ahead of them, keeping a watchful eye was a magnificent stag.

'Wow,' was all Frank could manage.

Renegade poked at some coals he'd loaded into a fire-box. 'Yep. They come down from the mountains most nights. I stop off here just to see them. Never get tired of it.'

They sat around the fire, eating chilli, drinking beer and following the deer's progress around the lochan. Before their eyes, the sky changed to the colours of a furnace, casting its fiery reflection on the water and Frank's only thought of home was that he wished he'd brought his paints with him.

Frank had been on a high for the rest of the night and it was only now, as he wrestled with his sleeping bag and lay on the cold, hard ground that he was beginning to come down. Between him and the ground was a rubber mat, and it may as well have not been there for all the good it was. His back ached, every bone in his body ached, and he felt ancient. Renegade had offered him a camp bed but he'd refused, because he already felt like an old man next to him and the new, clean Super-Finn. Now he was wishing he hadn't been such a twat and accepted the offer.

'Are you awake, Frank?' Finn's voice sounded eerie, like it was stranded in the dark without an owner.

'Yes.' He could have added that he was so uncomfort-able, he was likely to be awake all night, but he restrained himself.

'I know we're on a mission and all, but it's good to see you again, FB.'

FB. He hadn't heard that in a long time. Frank smiled in spite of himself. 'Do you know what I was thinking about on the drive up? That time we went to see the Battle of the Bands. Do you remember it?'

'How could I forget? What a night. I got drunk for the

first time that night. Me and Martin stole so many drinks. The Undertones have a lot to answer for.'

'Listen Yoda, the Undertones are beyond reproach. Don't you be blaming them for your bad habits.'

Finn didn't answer. Frank assumed he'd dropped off but then, out of nowhere, he said: 'Wasn't that the night you met Eve?'

11

THE GIRL FROM THE WRONG SIDE – 1978.

When they'd got home after the Battle of the Bands, Finn's ma wept tears of joy. She'd been convinced he'd be dead, 'or worse.' Frank couldn't imagine anything worse than being dead, but expressing that opinion would have been the final nail in his coffin, so he kept quiet and hoped for the same response from his own mother. As soon as he saw her, that hope crumbled. Ma was in such a rage she was practically foaming at the mouth. Da walloped Frank in every room of the house, with Ma bringing up the rear, screaming 'Hit him harder, the worry he's put us through.'

Nobody had thought to do the same to Martin. Apparently, it was considered enough of a deterrent to watch his big brother being battered. Martin wept like an eejit, even though no one laid a finger on him. Although to be fair, when questioned, he didn't let on where they'd been. Da had been round to Billy Mac's so they knew they weren't there, but Martin said they'd been in the park. He was a dab hand at the lying. But Martin, being Martin and never knowing when to call it a day, added bells and whistles. He told them they'd taken the drink Billy's ould fella had left behind and drank so much they lost track of time. The result was another battering for Frank and more tears from Martin, even though everybody knew that couldn't have been true because Billy's ma would have downed the lot before Mr Mac had quit Belfast.

Before they'd left Billy's, they'd changed their clothes back, and washed the sugar out of their hair so no one would be any the wiser. Five days later, they were still congratulating themselves on the parents believing Martin's story when Siobhan let it be known they'd been seen by her friend's brother at the university. In a forbidden zone, no less. Before Frank knew it, he was getting another walloping, and even Martin got slapped for lying.

Frank was still feeling battered, bruised and resentful. It was a Saturday afternoon and he was stuck in the house, helping his dad decorate the living room. It had been nearly three weeks since that night and he was still under house arrest. Not Martin though. He was off the hook and was out with Finn and Billy. Ma was out doing Ma things with her sisters, and Siobhan was out doing Siobhan things with her friends. It wasn't fair.

Da threw a rag at him. 'Stop moping and wipe down the table like I showed you.'

Frank wiped away the sticky wallpaper paste that had left a rectangular outline along the table. 'I'm just saying, it's not fair that I'm the only one.'

'You were supposed to be minding your wee brother and cousin, and you got them drunk. And could have got them killed. Fairness doesn't come into it.'

'Martin's only a bit younger and—'

'Francis, I do not want to hear any more of your nonsense. You did wrong, now take your punishment like a man. And fetch that roll of wallpaper.'

. . .

Martin was looking awful smug when he got back for tea. It was only when they went to bed that Frank found out why. 'We went to that record shop, Good Vibrations.'

'You're not supposed to leave the area.' Part of Frank wished Martin would have been seen there like they'd been seen at the concert. Maybe then he'd get what was coming to him for once, because no one could blame Frank this time. But then Martin was just the kind of jammy bastard that would find a way to turn it round and get the finger pointed in his direction, just like he always did.

'So don't say anything. Otherwise, I can't be your go-between.'

'My what?'

'That girl was there. The one from the concert. She was asking about you.'

Frank shot up. 'What did you say?'

'I said you were busy. Better to play it cool,' he said, like he knew anything about playing it cool, but at least he hadn't let on that Frank wasn't allowed out. That would have made him look like an absolute kid. 'She asked your name.'

'What did you say?'

'FB. Her name's Eve, in case you're interested.'

He had to wait another two weeks before he was set free. Two whole weeks. It should have been a week, a month's house arrest in all, but he'd made the mistake of asking when he could go out again. Apparently, that meant he'd shown no remorse, so Ma extended it for another week.

Frank insisted he was the most remorseful fella in Belfast, but she stood firm and two weeks it was.

It was Saturday. His first day of freedom and he knew exactly where he was going to spend it. For the last two weeks the boys had been coming back with news from their secret visits to Good Vibrations. At school, all they talked about was who was there, what they were wearing, and what the latest records were. Billy had found out that there was a pub called the Harp Bar where punk bands played. He brought flyers in to show who was on. He'd even been there. It was easy for him. He didn't have parents who ruled him with an iron fist. He didn't even have parents half the time.

According to Martin, Eve was usually in the shop when they went, and she always asked about Frank. Frank was going to make sure he was there today, even if he had to wait all day to see her.

They got changed at Billy's again. His ma was back from her travels but she wasn't at home. Billy said she'd got herself a fancy man, the sort it was best not to look in the eye. No one wanted to be in that house when she and her man returned, so they got ready and got out pronto.

As usual, they walked into town, steering clear of places they were likely to be seen in and reported back on. Anyone that looked like they might know Siobhan was avoided like the plague, being as she took great delight in dobbing them in for entering any of the parents' designated no-go zones. Great Victoria Street was definitely a no-go zone but it held the place that was their mecca and their sanctuary, so they went anyway.

Eve wasn't in the shop when they arrived, but Frank had plenty to occupy him while he waited. He had five lost weeks of new releases to sort through.

She sneaked up on him while he was looking through the singles: 'So what does FB stand for?'

He swung round and nearly smacked her in the face with the record. He was about to tell her but then she might think it was stupid, or that he had something to hide, which of course he did. His actual name would have immediately marked him out as being on the wrong side. But maybe she knew that already.

She looked straight into his eyes. 'Aren't you gonna tell me?'

'Frankie Boy.' His throat had gone dry and it came out like his voice hadn't broken yet.

'So your name's Frank?'

He coughed and tried to sound like a man rather than a pipsqueak. 'Yep.' He wasn't lying exactly. Frank was his preferred name. It was nice and neutral. A no man's land of a name.

She nodded slowly. He shoved his hands in his pockets to stop himself fidgeting and waited for her to make up her mind. He was about to accept defeat and go back to the records when she flashed a smile at him. 'Do you wanna take me for a drink?'

12

FRANCIS DRIVES A HARD BARGAIN – 1978

Ma and Da sat on the other side of the kitchen table. Ma looked like she'd received bad news, but then she had that kind of face. You could tell her the paras had laid down their arms and were best mates with the enemy and she'd still have a face on her like the world was about to end. They'd been up to a meeting at the school. It was about him. That much Frank knew. He didn't think he'd done anything wrong but that didn't mean he wasn't in trouble. He'd been summoned to the table. That in itself was worrying.

'Well, son. It seems you've been hiding your light under a bushel. It seems you're brighter than you act.' Da's eyebrows were nearly reaching his hairline.

'Your teacher says you're very intelligent!' Ma made it sound like this had come as a complete shock.

Frank couldn't think of anything else to say except: 'Oh.' It wasn't news to him that he was clever, but it obviously was to them.

'Very talented,' she went on. 'Especially good at the

English and the art.' Ma looked at Da, her eyes popping. 'Imagine.'

Da gave her a look that suggested his imagination was struggling with the concept. 'Anyway, son, you've to stay on at school and do your A-levels. Then we'll think about the university.'

The idea of university had been mentioned to Frank at school but he'd assumed it would be out of the question. Anyway, he wasn't sure he wanted to go. Him and Billy had plans. Well, Billy had plans and he was expecting Frank to go along with them. Unfortunately, his parents also had plans. It was one thing telling Billy he couldn't meet his expectations. Telling his parents was a much more terrifying experience. He dug deep and found some inner courage: 'Don't I get a say in it? It is my life we're talking about.'

'No,' said Ma.

Da held up his hand. 'Hang on now, Clodagh. He has a point. What do you want to do, Francis?'

Frank was stunned into silence. He'd never been asked such a question before. University sounded like it might be cool. Hadn't Eve told him she was going there as well? And Billy's plans might not work out. He'd have to let Billy down but he could make out he'd been forced into it.

Da was watching him, his face blank. He wasn't giving anything away. Ma was twitching, impatient for an answer. Frank knew he might never be asked again. He should make the most of it and try to wheedle some concessions out of them. 'It's not that I mind staying on, Da. Especially if it's what you both want. It's just that I won't have any money.'

Ma's arms folded. 'You could get a Saturday job.'

Da's hand went up again. 'We could give you a bit of spending money.'

'Okay. But if I was working like Siobhan, I'd have more freedom. I'd be allowed to go out later.'

Ma winced. 'You'll have your homework to do.'

'Exactly. I mean, I wouldn't have that if I was working. Although, if I was allowed a bit more freedom I could still have that and do homework.'

Da looked him in the eye. 'So what you're saying is, you'll be fine staying on if you can have a bit of spending money and we loosen the reins a bit. And if we do that, you'll work hard at school, do your homework, and make the most of the brains God's given you. Is that the sum of it, Francis?'

Frank gulped. This suddenly felt like serious grown-up stuff. 'Yes.'

'And you won't let us down?'

'No Da, I won't.'

'Good man. That's settled it then. We've a deal. You drive a hard bargain, Francis.' Da stood up and patted him on the shoulder as he walked past. 'Looks like those teachers were right about you not being stupid.'

Even Ma smiled at that. Frank decided to make the most of her good mood. 'Is it okay for me to stay out till ten tonight then, now that we've got a deal?'

Ma got up and put the kettle on. 'Don't push your luck, Francis. School is still compulsory for you until the end of term.'

Ah well, it was worth a try. 'I'm away to Billy's.'

Ma looked out of the kitchen window. 'You might think we're hard on you, but we're just trying to keep you safe. This could be your chance to get on in the world, get away from all of this. Don't mess it up.'

.   .   .

Billy was not impressed by Frank's news. He'd lined them up to work as roadies for a band he'd seen at the Harp. That was his big plan. The pay was peanuts but Billy didn't care. It was better than a factory job. Or no job at all. But Frank knew it wasn't promised. It was one of those maybe jobs that Billy often talked about. Ma would have said it was a pipe dream, like when Siobhan said she wanted to be a fashion designer. That came to nothing and Frank guessed it would be the same with the roadie job. Besides, now that he'd settled on it, Frank actually wanted to stay on at school and go to university. He wanted something different. For once, he was in agreement with Ma. This could be his chance. Still, he couldn't leave Billy high and dry. 'You could stay on too. You're better than me at some subjects.'

'Why the hell would I want to do that? I hate school.'

'Because we'd carry on seeing each other every day. Nothing has to change.'

Billy laughed. 'You're such a kid sometimes, FB. Anyways, in case you haven't noticed, things have already changed.' He was having another dig about Eve. It was one of his favourite topics. When it first started, Frank bit back and Billy would tell him to stop being so touchy, he was only joking. It wasn't much of a joke in Frank's eyes. As far as he was aware, your best friend was supposed to be on your side. Martin and Finn got on great with Eve. A bit too well sometimes, you couldn't get rid of them. Billy was the only one who had a problem with her, although he wouldn't admit it. Instead, he said snide things about her and complained that she hung around too much.

The reality was, Eve was his girlfriend but he only ever saw her on Saturdays in and around the record shop, unless they had enough to buy a drink at the Harp Bar, or they went to a concert. They were the only places they felt safe going to. That didn't stop him thinking about her the rest of the time though. All week he'd store up things to say to her. Funny things preferably, because she thought he was funny. In a clever way, she'd once added. After that he aimed for funny and clever. When he wasn't doing that, he was scouring Billy's music mags for interesting facts about their favourite bands that he could share with her. Maybe Billy was right. Maybe things were already changed, and maybe Billy couldn't handle it. In which case, he had some nerve saying Frank was a kid.

Eve was a lot more positive about him staying on at school. Frank had earned some extra cash helping his dad decorate a neighbour's bedroom, so they went to the Harp. She grabbed his hand under the table. 'So we'll both be students then? Get us.'

'That would be weird, us both going to the same university, wouldn't it? In a nice way though.'

'Weird and unlikely. I'm not staying here. As soon as I can, I'm away over the water.'

'Over the water?'

She giggled, the way she did when he made a funny joke. 'Close your mouth, Frankie Boy. It's not that shocking.'

Maybe not for her, but it was for Frank. 'Why do you want to go over there?'

She stopped laughing. 'Because it's not here. Have you been there?'

He shook his head.

'Then you wouldn't understand. I've been plenty of times. We have family over there. I'm not saying it's anything special, but at least you can ride a bus with a reasonable assumption you're not going to get blown up or shot. And you don't have soldiers on every corner looking for any excuse to touch you up. And you can be friends with whoever you want. You can even sleep with the enemy, if you want to.' She winked at him and her smile was back.

She had a point, but even though she'd said it as fact, Frank still couldn't get his head around it. So he brought it back to reality. His reality anyway. 'What about your parents, are they okay with it?'

'Mum is. We haven't told Dad yet. He's old-fashioned. He still thinks I'm going to settle down with a nice fella and have kids before I'm twenty.' She shook her head. 'Not this girl. I'm going to be a journalist.' She kissed him. 'Come with me, Frankie. We could run away together.'

'Are youse two gonna buy another drink or are you gonna sit there all day nursing your empty glasses?'

Frank didn't realise the barman was talking to them until Eve asked him if he had any more money. He hadn't.

'Me neither. Let's go back to the shop then. It costs nothing to hang around there.'

It was raining when they left the pub. They ran for the shop, splashing through puddles. As they passed a bombed-out building, Frank grabbed her arm and pulled her in to what was once an entryway. She stood on her tiptoes and kissed him on the mouth, pushing her tongue around his teeth. It was like an electric shock to him. He pulled her closer and kissed her again. 'Did you mean it?'

'Mean what?'

'That we could run away together.'

Eve opened her mouth, but the sight of a soldier standing a few feet away clamped it shut. They put their hands up over their heads and walked back out onto the street.

Frank blinked the rain away from his eyes. 'Sorry, we were just-'

'So I saw.' The soldier's eyes darted around the street. 'Go on then. Fuck off before I change my mind.'

The others were reading a fanzine in the shop when they got there. Billy showed it to Frank. 'We could do one of these. They'll let us sell them here.'

Frank looked it over. It was good and probably not that hard to do, but it was all handwritten. That took time. 'What about the roadie job though, Billy?'

'They took someone else on. Guess I'll be going back to school after all.'

Frank couldn't stop a smile from forming on his lips. They were staying together for a bit longer. Things were working out just grand. 'Good. Hey, Eve could help with the writing. She wants to be a journalist.'

Billy's eyes flitted over to Eve for a second then returned to Frank. 'Okay. If she wants to.'

Eve snatched the fanzine from him and scanned the pages. 'Yeah, all right. I'll have to call myself by another name though. My dad would go crazy if he found out.'

'You should make it real punky, like Poly Styrene,' said Martin.

Eve laughed. 'Yeah! That's your job this week, Martin. Think of a name for me.'

Martin blushed. 'Anything for you, Evie.'

Frank waited for Eve to look the other way before eyeballing him. Martin's face was all innocence, as usual, but Frank wasn't fooled. That sneaky fecker was up to something, and it had better not have anything to do with Eve.

13

JOHN LENNON'S AUNTIE

Frank had been awake for twenty minutes. He'd woken up alone. Finn had probably gone to climb a mountain or something equally fit and healthy. He, on the other hand was struggling to move. Not because he didn't want to, but because he was physically unable to. His back was gone. But full bladders paid no heed to broken backs and he was a man with a bladder that lacked the retention capacity of youth. He had to get up before he embarrassed himself.

Unzipping the sleeping bag didn't pose a problem. Rolling onto his side, no matter how carefully he did it, sent a pain shooting up his left buttock. He pressed on through it and forced himself onto all fours, then manoeuvred round to face the front of the tent. He managed to open it, relatively pain free, and crawled outside. Renegade's van was still there but the man himself was nowhere to be seen. Neither was Finn, although it was fair to say Frank's area of vision was somewhat restricted, what with him being on his hands and knees. What was in sight was the toilet block. He considered crawling over there, but he'd have to get up some time. Bit by bit, he brought his hands closer to his legs, and eased himself up, first into a kneeling position, then onto his feet. Somehow he managed to stand, put one foot in front of the other, and get to the toilet.

When he came out, he was still alone. He walked slowly around the parking area until he felt muscle and bone loosen a little. Then he did another lap and took in the colours this Scottish morning had gifted him. Last night's fiery sky had given way to thick gunmetal cloud and a mist hung over the water. It could have been a Turner painting.

He heard the sound of something moving behind him and gingerly turned his whole body towards it. Just a few yards away, at the foot of a winding path leading up the mountain, a stag was watching him. Frank held his breath, not sure what to do. Did stags charge like bulls? He was a city man and had no idea.

They remained like this for some time, neither seeming to want to turn away from each other, until the sight of Finn and Renegade further along the path broke both their concentration. The stag dipped its head, then turned and climbed up the mountain. Frank saw then that the rest of the herd were up there behind the vegetation and once again, the stag had been keeping guard.

'He's a fine looking fella,' said Finn. 'That's more than I can say for you though, FB. You look like shit.'

'It's the back. It plays up sometimes.' Since he wasn't sure he'd be able to get back in that Mini, there was no point in trying to hide it.

'Well why didn't you have Ren's camp bed, you stupid fecker? Where does it hurt?'

'Just here. No, don't touch it. Finn, I said don't. What are you... Oh!' Frank had no idea what the hell Finn had done but whatever it was, it worked. The pain had gone.

Finn shrugged. 'My pleasure. C'mon let's get some breakfast.'

They were back on the road again straight after breakfast. The car had been repacked to give Frank more legroom. Finn said they'd make more stops so he could stretch but they'd still make Balnakeil before nightfall. 'I think that's where Martin is.'

'Oh right. That's good then.' Frank was only half-listening. He was thinking about that stag protecting his family, and for some reason it made him think of Eve's dad.

'What made you ask about the Battle of the Bands last night?' said Finn.

'I don't know. I've been thinking about it. Only since coming up here, mind. I haven't thought about it in years.'

'I think about that time a lot. I used to believe they were great years. The best.'

'Used to?'

'Aye. Then I realised they were the worst of my life. Don't get me wrong, I loved being with you and the boys but I drank myself stupid. I tried anything going. It was a way of coping with all that fucked-up-ness. I know that now. You did the right thing getting out. The others blamed you for breaking the gang up, but I never did.'

'They blamed me? I never knew that.'

Finn nodded. 'They blamed Eve too, but I didn't see it that way.'

'It wasn't her fault.' Frank checked his phone, suddenly desperate for a message from Netta. Still no signal. That's what he got for hanging onto such an old knacker. The first thing he was going to do when he got home was purchase a fancy new one with a signal you could pick up from Mars.

.   .   .

They'd reached the coast. Finn found the last spot in a small car park sandwiched in between a graveyard and the beach. 'I'll ask around, see if anyone's seen the van. You should take a look in the graveyard. John Lennon's auntie's buried in there.'

'Really? Are you messing with me, Finn Boy?'

'I am not. Take a look. The walk'll do your back good.'

A memory resurfaced of him carrying Finn home because he'd passed out. Another came. Him and Martin stopping Finn from throwing himself off a balcony because he was stoned and was convinced he could fly. Now Finn was fixing his back and telling him to take walks for the sake of his health. What had the world come to? Still, John Lennon's auntie? That was worth a look. Just to see if it was true.

He walked up and down reading the gravestones, then realised he didn't actually know the name of John Lennon's auntie, so unless it was obvious, he had no way of finding her. But it was a nice, solitary place to heal your body and be alone with your thoughts. He remembered what Finn had said that morning about Billy and Martin blaming him for going away. He'd always had a sneaking suspicion. But then he'd had suspicions about many things. Perhaps some of them were true and perhaps they weren't. He'd probably never find out. But blaming him for breaking up their gang, that wasn't fair.

Suddenly his phone pinged. He pulled it out of his pocket with all the excitement of a kid who'd just been given a bike for Christmas. He'd had several messages and at least six missed calls from Siobhan. More importantly, there were a couple of messages from Netta. Nothing earth shattering, just asking if he was okay. She'd left him a voicemail message too. He tapped out the number, cursing his fat fingers for pressing the wrong ones. He got through and heard her voice, her sweet, lovely voice: 'Hi Frank. Just saying hello. I hope you're looking after yourself. No real news here. The dogs are fine. The kids are fine. Speak to you soon. Have you found Martin yet?'

He checked the time. He might just catch her before she left work.

'Well hello. I guess I can stop worrying that you're stuck up a mountain somewhere now,' she said.

'I'm at the seaside actually, in a graveyard.'

'Oh. You go to all the best places. Are you okay?'

'I had a bit of back trouble this morning but Finn put me right. I'm still coming to terms with his drift from debauchery to sainthood but other than that, I'm doing all right. Sorry I haven't been in touch. This phone is useless. It can't seem to cope with all this Highland scenery.'

'That's okay. I had the same problem when I visited Doogie and my phone's a lot newer than yours. Have you found your brother?'

'Almost. We're hot on his trail.'

'Where are you?'

'Right at the top. A place called Balnakeil.'

'Not sure where that is but I think it might be quite a way from Doogie.'

Doogie again. She'd mentioned him twice and they'd only been talking for a few minutes. He changed the subject: 'It's wonderful up here, Net. The colours.'

'I knew you'd like it. We should go up together sometime. You can paint and I'll stand behind you and say how wonderful it is.'

'I'd like that.'

'Hang on, I'm losing you. Are you there? Fra…'

Gone. She was gone. Frank looked at his phone in disbelief. 'Fucking piece of shit.' There was so much he had left
to say. He wanted to tell her about the stag and the mist on
the water. He wanted to tell her he was missing her. He just
wanted to talk to her.

Desperate, he ran around the graveyard trying for a
signal. Nothing. It was useless. He looked up to the sky,
cursing the god he didn't believe in. And then he saw him,
standing by the church ruins. The big gormless eejit was
grinning from ear to ear. Martin, sneaky fecker, O'Hare.

14

THE ABSENCE OF BROTHERLY LOVE

Martin opened his arms out as if he was waiting for Frank to run into them, a big, stupid grin still plastered across his big, stupid face. Frank took deliberately slow steps towards the ruins, all the while refusing to look at him. He didn't deserve a look. And if he thought Frank was going to let him throw his arms around him, he'd better think again. There'd be none of that brotherly love stuff here. That ran out a long time ago. If it ever existed in the first place.

'Frankie Boy!' Martin took a step towards him, looking ready for a full-on bear hug.

Frank swerved in the nick of time. 'Does Finn know you're here?'

'Aye. He's waiting on the beach for us. Sure, you're looking great Frank.'

No he was not looking great. He was looking like a dog's arse, and if Martin wasn't such a bullshitter, he'd have said it. 'C'mon. Let's find Finn.'

Frank left the graveyard, none the wiser on John Lennon's auntie. Martin danced around him and jabbered on like a daft fool: 'This is some place, huh? Beats city life, what? Did yer see the deer, did yer?'

They got down to the beach, a stretch of long white sand that was deserted except for a couple of walkers and Finn, sitting watching the turquoise waters crashing into foaming white waves. Martin dropped down next to Finn. Frank eased himself carefully onto his backside. Finn kept his eyes on the sea and stayed silent. He didn't appear to be angry. In fact he seemed completely devoid of emotion. It was like looking at a blank canvas that some other artist was about to fill in. He let out a single long breath and blinked, then he was with them. 'You found each other then. Good.'

Martin leaned back on his elbows. 'Aye, we did. So how are yer, Frank?'

How was he? The cheek of him. The fecking cheek of him. Frank had been trying to keep a lid on it but that was the limit. 'How do you think I am? I've got Ma and Siobhan calling me non-stop, insisting I come after you. I've lost valuable work time, and my back is probably fucked. But hey, it's not all about me. How've you been Martin?'

'Me? Oh I'm grand.' Martin smirked. It was pure wickedness, and it took Frank right back to their childhood.

'Of course you are. Why wouldn't you be? Never mind that you've left your wife and kids, taken advantage of Finn, and had everyone in the family worried about you. And don't even trouble yourself that you've got me up here on a wild goose chase. You're grand. That's all that matters.'

'Sorry. Sorry I nicked your van, Finn. But I had to do something drastic to get us back together again.'

Finn sighed. 'Could you not just have called and suggested a holiday, or emailed a proposed itinerary?'

Martin shook his head. 'You wouldn't have come. Frank won't even answer my calls.'

Finn screwed his face up. 'Sure, that's not true. It's not true, is it Frank?'

Frank looked out to the sea and kept his mouth shut.

'Tell me it's not true, FB,' said Finn.

Martin filled in the gap that had been left open for Frank: 'He's not returned my calls for years.'

Frank scooped up some sand and let it run through his fingers. It left a silver residue on his hands. Finn and Martin were staring at him, no doubt waiting for an answer. 'You make it sound like you've been calling every week. It's only been a few times, and I was busy.'

'I've called you at least twenty times in the last three months. You must be a very busy man.'

'Why?' said Frank.

'Well if you'd picked up the phone, you'd already know wouldn't you? I was calling because I needed to talk to you. And I wanted to see you.'

'Now why would you want to see me? It's not like we've ever been close.'

Martin stood up. 'Never mind.'

'Well, we're here now,' said Finn.

'And we're sending you back home,' cut in Frank.

Martin was staying in a field belonging to a crofter who was amenable to them pitching the tent up. Finn's campervan turned out to be pretty high spec. It had what Da would call, all the mod cons, as well as its own small bathroom. Small being the operative word here. It was a squeeze for big men like Frank and Martin to get in. Aside from that, there were no other amenities. Frank would have dearly loved a shower. There was one of sorts in the bathroom but after a thorough inspection, Finn announced that they were low on water and a shower was out of the question. There was some good news, however. Finn insisted Frank have the bed, on account of his dodgy back, and the crofter sold them some lamb steaks. Frank was not going to argue about the bed, and he tried not to look at the poor wee lambs in the next field.

Surprisingly, Martin had stocked up well on food and drink. It was almost as if he was expecting them, which of course he was. As he'd already said, he'd hijacked the campervan for the sole purpose of getting the old gang back together again. Except for Billy Mac. Perhaps Martin had a plan to get him over here. Surely even Martin wasn't that stupid?

Finn was clearly happy to be back in his van. He soon had a barbecue set up and was whipping up what looked like a very decent meal. Like his home, the van felt very much like a man's space. Frank wondered if there was anyone in his life. He'd always had girlfriends. They didn't last long but there were plenty of them.

Martin handed Frank a beer. Frank waited for an accompanying smart arse remark but none came. He just settled himself down in the chair next to him. In the end, it was Frank who spoke: 'We have your phone in the car. Just thought I'd let you know in case you want to call home.'

Martin didn't answer. If he was trying to niggle Frank, he was succeeding. 'Have you called home since you left?'

Martin took a mouthful of beer. 'Nope.'

'Do you not think Bronagh deserves to know where you are?'

'You think she wants to know?'

'She's your wife, man.'

Martin laughed. 'That counts for nothing. You of all people should know that.'

'That's not the same. You can't just walk out on her and say nothing.'

'I didn't. Bronagh threw me out.'

Frank frowned. 'Siobhan didn't say. Ma didn't–'

'Well that doesn't make it any less true. My wife is sick of the sight of me and she doesn't care if I'm alive or dead. So don't you be telling me to go home to the family. Fuck the family.'

'Oh Martin, what have you done this time?' Finn said what Frank was thinking.

'I honestly don't know. If I'd been unfaithful to her, I could understand it. But I haven't. I'm not a gambler. I don't do drugs.' Martin nodded towards Finn. 'Not since you left anyways. Sure, I like a drink, but no more than the next man. She just told me she'd had enough. Then she threw me out of the house. I mean physically pushed me out the door!'

Frank rolled his eyes. 'Ah come on. You're exaggerating. Bronagh's a wee woman and you're twice her size.'

'That's what made it all the more shocking.' Martin shook his can to make sure it was empty then screwed it up in his fist.

'She is a feisty woman,' said Finn, as if it all made sense.

It made no sense to Frank. He wasn't buying it. 'You must have done something. From what I remember she was a very reasonable woman. Feisty, but reasonable.'

'She is. And I'm sure you're right, Frank. I must have done something wrong, but I haven't a clue what.'

'Have you tried asking her?'

'I did, when I went back to pick up my clothes from the front garden. She just said to work it out for myself.'

'Is that why you came over here? To work it out,' said Finn. It made Frank think of Netta's mum when she was in what Netta called her counselling mode. Perhaps counselling was another string to Saint Finn's bow. Unless perhaps, he'd been counselled himself. That was always a possibility.

'I suppose so.' Finn's suggestion seemed to come as a welcome surprise to Martin. If you were suspicious you might say it was a handy excuse to latch onto. Frank was definitely suspicious. He wasn't sure if he was one hundred per cent signed up to this idea of Bronagh throwing Martin out for no reason.

'Dinner's ready.' Finn loaded the food onto plates and passed them round. 'Let's get this down, have another beer, and work out what's to be done.'

15

OH FRANK

Netta let herself into Frank's house. He'd cut out midway through the call earlier, so she hadn't had time to ask him if she should come over. She decided to come anyway, mainly to check the food he'd left behind. It was all very well leaving stuff when you were expecting to be back in a couple of days, but if he ended up staying for the whole of the Easter break, some of it wouldn't last.

A quick scan of the fridge and cupboards produced a small assortment of fresh stuff that she'd need to use up before they went bad ways. The bin would also need emptying before it started to smell.

She checked his studio and found the wastepaper basket nearly full with chocolate bar wrappers and crisp bags. 'Tsk tsk Mr O'Hare. Up to all sorts of naughtiness when I'm not here to keep an eye on you.' The thought made her smile. Never mind the food going bad ways, Frank was doing a decent job of sliding into it himself.

His unfinished painting caught her eye. As with all of Frank's paintings, the colours arrested you, they drew you in, just like the photo he was taking inspiration from. She recognised it as one she'd taken when she'd visited Doogie in the Scottish Highlands. Frank had printed it out. His response had been quite muted when she'd sent it to him and even more muted when she'd suggested they went up there together. He'd said something about not feeling confident enough to meet Doogie. Before then, Netta had never seen him as anything other than a man comfortable in his own skin. It seemed there were some things that even Frank wasn't immune to. Or rather, some people. All the same, the photo must have triggered something if he was trying to capture it on canvas. The snap didn't really do it justice. Seeing it in real life was a much more sensual experience, and Frank could be finding that out himself right now.

The evidence of Frank's food indulgences were emptied into the kitchen bin. Netta filled a jug with water and fed the wilting basil plant on the window sill, then moved onto the lounge where a few cacti lived.

Most of the time, the lounge was kept reasonably tidy so it was a surprise to find records spread across the floor. She noticed there was a single still on the stereo turntable, 'Teenage Kicks' by the Undertones. Netta put it on and sang along as she checked out the other records. Some of the covers were pretty battered. He'd obviously had them for years. They were probably bought in Belfast when Frank was a kid. She didn't know all of the names. Perhaps some of the bands never made it out of Belfast. She slipped one of the unknowns on and realised it was the background noise in the message Frank had left when she was in Brighton. Like the first one, the song was over in a few minutes and she had to look around for another. She'd forgotten how attentive you had to be with singles. It was quite tiresome now that she thought about it. No wonder albums took off.

She flicked through the albums and picked out one called *The Undertones*. As the vinyl slid out of its cover, one of those old handwritten fanzines came out with it. She'd bought some herself back in the eighties. This one was written in 1978 and was called *Can*. Next to the name was a drawing of a half-open tin can on its side with worms spilling out of it. Worms with Mohicans and safety pins, no less. It was, by all accounts, the first edition and was priced at 20p.

Netta put the album on and sat on the floor for a read. It was just like the ones she used to buy, mostly pictures of punk bands of the day, some gig and record reviews, and one full length article, *'Battle of the Bands: Was I in Punk Heaven?'* by someone called Ana Manic. She wondered how long it had taken to come up with that name. The other names listed on reviews were far less on trend for the time – FB and Billy Mac. Ana Manic sounded much more interesting.

Her phone rang just as 'Jimmy Jimmy' began. It was Robyn, Frank's daughter. 'Hi Netta. Sorry to bother you. It's just that I can't get hold of Dad and I promised I'd let him know we got to Thailand safely. I've messaged and called but he's not picking anything up, so now I'm worried. Is everything all right?'

'Oh yes, no need to worry. He's had to go up to Scotland. His brother's there.'

'What's Uncle Martin doing in Scotland?'

'I think that's what your dad's trying to find out. Martin left Belfast without telling anyone apparently, but then he turned up in Glasgow at Cousin Finn's.' Netta still couldn't say the name Cousin Finn without wanting to laugh. She hoped that wasn't evident down the line. 'They're up in the Highlands now, trying to track Martin down.'

'Oh yeah, I heard Finn had moved to Glasgow.'

'Oh. I don't think your dad knew.'

'No, I didn't mention it to him. Is dad okay with all of it?'

'I'm not sure. I think he's finding it a challenge.'

'That makes sense. He kind of went off them, don't know why. Has he still got that crappy old phone?'

'Afraid so. That'll be why you can't get hold of him. But I did manage to speak to him earlier. He's alive and well, although not particularly happy.'

Robyn laughed. 'He'll be all right once he gets used to the idea of seeing Finn and Martin again. Can you tell him I'm okay and having a great time, and I'll call him when I get back?'

'Will do. Bye. And enjoy your holiday. Give my love to–' Too late. Robyn had gone. Netta had been too slow, distracted by something tucked away in the gap between the stereo cabinet and the sideboard. A closer look told her it was actually two things, one empty wine bottle and one that was almost empty. The not quite empty one was just cheap plonk Frank normally used for cooking.

Netta sat back on the floor and chewed on her lip. 'Oh Frank. What on Earth is going on with you?'

16

THE NEW ROAD TRIP

'I'm not saying youse fellas are wrong, but it has to be The Clash, October 1978.' Martin was waving his plastic glass in the air, as if he was about to raise a toast to The Clash. They were arguing which was the best gig ever. Frank and Finn had said Battle of the Bands, no question, but Martin disagreed.

Frank poured them all another whisky. They'd run out of beers pretty quickly, but Martin had bought a couple of bottles of whisky somewhere on his journey to the top of the country. 'So you are saying we're wrong then.'

Martin thought for a minute. 'I suppose so, now you put it like that. C'mon now, FB. Surely you remember that buzz.'

Frank smiled. 'I do. The Clash were special, I agree with you there. But Battle of the Bands. The Undertones. That was our first. The first is always the most memorable.'

Martin tittered. 'Sure, you never forget your first.'

Frank rolled his eyes. 'You're like a big kid, you know that?' As soon as he said it, he thought of Billy Mac telling him he was such a kid sometimes. He considered asking about him, then stopped himself. What would he do with the information if he got it? Probably beat himself up with it. It wasn't worth the effort.

'Will you shut up and look at that sky,' said Finn. 'Forget the past. Focus on the here and now.'

Easy for him to say. Most of his past was best confined to life's waste disposal unit. But certain things, certain moments were worth remembering. For Frank anyway. Martin caught his eye for just a beat and then they both looked up to the black viscous sky encrusted with endless sparkling diamonds. Frank heard a gasp. At first he'd thought it was Martin, but then he realised it had come from him.

'All this must really stand out to you, with your artist's eye,' said Martin, quietly.

'It stands out, but I can't say whether it's more or less than you,' said Frank.

'We're all unique,' said Finn.

'Fuck off, Yoda. Next, you'll be telling us you believe the children are our future.' Maybe it was the whisky he'd just swallowed, or maybe it was because the other two laughed at his joke. Whatever it was, Frank felt all warm inside.

'It's great to be back together again,' said Martin. 'The old gang on tour, eh?'

'We're missing–'

'Let's do this one road trip back down the coast.' Martin cut Finn off before he had a chance to finish the sentence.

'We're supposed to be getting you back home,' said Frank.

'One week. That's all I ask. I'll go back after then. You can spare me a week, can't you Frankie?'

The answer was no, he couldn't spare a week. He had paintings to do, coursework to prepare for the new term, and a woman to see. One he cared for very much. All the same, there was something about this country that made you hanker after losing yourself in it. Then again, did he really want to spend a week with Finn and Martin? And how was he going to manage with the few clothes he'd brought with him in his overnight bag?

'I'm up for it.' Finn was looking at him. The years fell away and all Frank could think of was the wee boy who would do anything to be one of their gang.

Frank sighed. 'Okay. But only if we square it with the demon sister and mother. And only if there are showers involved, and somewhere I can wash my clothes.'

When Frank had woken up, his first thought was his back, but he'd had no sense of pain coming from that area. Whereas his head had been a different matter altogether, and his tongue appeared to have acquired a fur coat overnight. What's more, he was still in yesterday's clothes. It had been a long time since he'd gone to bed without getting undressed, but this is what he'd come to. This mad trail was taking him back to his youth, and not in a good way.

Now he was driving the Mini behind the campervan. Finn was driving the van, adamant that he was not going to let Martin back behind the wheel, and Martin was in its passenger seat. That suited Frank. He welcomed the solitude. He was happy in his own company. Not a hermit exactly, but there were definitely times he liked to retreat into himself. Just him, a canvas and his trusty young dog at his feet. He sometimes thought Fred was the ideal companion, although he didn't tell Netta that.

Seeing Martin again hadn't been as bad as he thought it would be. Perhaps the distance of time had been good for them. Perhaps it wouldn't be too awful to spend a week with him and Finn in this place. He could do worse things.

There was another deer up on a ridge ahead of them. It reminded him of the stag from yesterday, the way it looked straight at him, taking the measure of him. That must have been why he'd thought of Eve's dad. Although it could have easily been Ellen's father too. He'd only seen Eve's dad once. That had been enough.

They'd been going together for a year before Eve told him her dad was a cop. He didn't blame her. The RUC weren't exactly flavour of the month and loose talk cost lives, on both sides. But one day she just came out with it. Maybe it had taken that long to build herself up to it. More likely, it had taken that long for her to trust him. They were officially on opposite sides, after all. She made him promise not to say anything. Not that he was going to. His family weren't like that. They kept themselves very much under the radar and tried not to get involved. She'd only told him, she said, because she wanted him to understand why they needed to keep everything low key. They couldn't draw attention to themselves. Her daddy wouldn't like it. She never said what it was exactly that her daddy wouldn't like – them going together, or his profile being raised – and Frank didn't ask. In hindsight, he wished he had.

They reached a pretty village called Ullapool. Frank followed the van into a campsite on the shores of the loch. This was the place they were staying for the night, if they had room. He waited in the car while Finn went in to enquire. When he came out and did the thumbs up, Frank nearly wept with joy. It didn't matter that he'd be sleeping in the campervan again tonight, he'd be clean and he'd be able to wash his clothes. He might even get a signal on his shite phone. Right now, this was a good as civilisation got.

The campsite delivered as promised. They'd showered and shaved and done a laundry wash and dry. Finn had also emptied out and topped up all that was needed to keep them going for several days. So in the space of a few hours they were clean and presentable, and ready to venture out. Except that first they had to make some calls.

Frank had already tried Netta's phone but it had gone to voicemail. After another unsuccessful attempt, he left a message to tell her the plan and said he'd try her again in the evening. He took a picture of the loch and sent it to her: '*We're in Ullapool and we have Martin.*' He added a smiley face to make it look more cheery.

When he got back to the van, Finn and Martin were debating who they should call with their news, Siobhan or Ma. In the end, they decided Ma was the lesser of two evils. They also decided it should be Frank who called. Frank tried to back out of it but they were adamant, it would be better coming from him.

'Use my phone, not that ould brick of yours.' Finn pressed dial and handed it over.

To Frank's relief, it was Da that answered the phone.

'Hello, Da. It's Frank. I'm calling with some good news. We've got Martin.' It was only after he'd said it that Frank realised he sounded like an SAS man reporting back on a special mission.

'Hello, son. That's grand. Your ma will be happy. She's away to the shops right now. Will I tell her you'll call back?'

The other two shook their heads. They could hear every word on account of Da being a bit deaf these days and thinking it necessary to shout down the phone.

'Ach, the signal's bad here, we might not be able to. I

just thought you'd want to know we've got him and he's safe. And we're going on a trip, the three of us.'

'A trip? What kind of a trip?'

'Just along the coast for a wee while, Da. No more than a week. We'll put him on the plane home after that.'

'Good man. Your ma said we could rely on you, Francis.'

That was a statement Frank never expected to hear. 'Well it was Finn really, Da.'

'Finn? Aye. Quite the transformation there, what? I hope he's holding up okay. Poor wee fella. Would you put Martin on, son?'

Martin took the phone and walked away to the loch. By the look on his face, Da wasn't giving him too hard a time.

'Da said he hoped you were holding up,' said Frank.

'Ach, Uncle Gerry's always looked out for me,' said Finn.

'What did he mean?'

Finn glanced up at him. 'You're not the only one who's lost someone, Frank.'

Martin's return put paid to finding out who Finn had lost. Frank would have to wait for another opportunity to ask his cousin who was now staring at the loch with an expression Frank couldn't make out.

In contrast, his brother was looking mighty pleased with himself. 'All sorted. Da's going to square it with Ma.'

'And Siobhan?' said Frank.

'Ah to hell with Siobhan. Bossy ould cow. There's a woman who's had too much time on her hands since her divorce. She's probably the one who put Bronagh up to it. They've been thick as thieves since she became newly single.' Martin did the air quotes thing when he said newly single.

Finn smiled. 'You could do with being more in touch with your feminine side, Marty.'

'Or even just being more in touch with the real world,' added Frank.

He and Finn laughed at their little joke. It wasn't that funny but it cut the tension. All the same, Frank had this inexplicable feeling that he was somehow to blame for Finn's loss, which was ridiculous. How could he be when he hadn't seen Finn for years? That didn't shake the feeling though. Because if it wasn't Finn's loss he was responsible for, it had to be something else.

17

SIOBHAN GETS A BAD ACHE

Siobhan was about to get her roots done when her phone rang.

Shayne stopped stirring a pot of brownish black gunk and raised one eyebrow at her reflection in the mirror. 'Do you want to get that?'

'No, I'll leave it.'

'Are you sure now? We both know what you're like.'

'Yes, I'm sure. Or maybe I should. Do you think I should, Shayne?'

He put the pot down. 'Are you really asking me whether you should answer your phone? For feck's sake, Siobhan.'

'All right, I'll answer it.' But it was too late, the ringing had stopped. 'It's Ma. I'll call her back later.'

Shayne did the one eyebrow raise again. 'She won't have left a message?'

'This is Ma we're talking about.'

'Fair point. You don't want to call her back then?'

'Shayne, just slap that shit on my head and stop probing, will yer?' Siobhan threw him a no nonsense look. One of the plus points of having a hairdresser who was also one of your oldest friends was that you didn't have to do the small talk. But sometimes it had its drawbacks. Right now it would have been nice to talk about what she had planned for the rest of the day or where she was going on holiday this year, even if the answers were nothing and nowhere.

Shayne's lips pinched together as he picked up the pot again. 'I wasn't probing. I just know it'll be playing on your mind and you won't be able to relax. Look at you, you're all tensed up.'

She eased her shoulders away from her ears which was harder than it should be, thanks to the knots in between her shoulder blades. 'I'm sorry I shouted. I'm just so, yer know.'

'You need a relaxing massage. Glenda upstairs is quiet today. Will I ask one of the girls to pop up and book you in?'

She wasn't too sure about that. The last time she'd had a relaxing massage from Glenda, it was a week before she could walk straight again. 'I don't think I have the time.'

'You've just said you have the day off.'

'Yeah but… Okay then. But tell her, just a gentle massage.'

Siobhan inched her aching body into the car. Never. Ever. Again. Fecking Glenda didn't know the meaning of the word gentle. And God only knows where she got her so-called qualifications from. One of those joke places off of the internet probably. People like her should be banned from laying their hands on another living body.

Ma rang for the fourth time in the last two hours. She considered ignoring it, just as she'd done the others, but decided it might actually be something important.

'Where have you been? Have you not seen my calls?' Ma started before Siobhan had even said hello.

'I couldn't come to the phone. What is it?'

'They've gone on a road trip, whatever that's supposed to mean.'

'A what? Never mind, I'm on my way.'

Da opened the door to her. That should have raised alarm bells in itself. Ma was usually like one of those troll gatekeepers when it came to the front door. Now Siobhan had knots in her stomach to go with her aching back. 'What's going on?'

Ma was in the hall in an instant. 'They phoned while I was at the shops. A road trip. That's what Martin called it, wasn't it Gerry?'

'It was.' Da put his arm around Ma. 'Come on now, Clodagh, it's not that bad. It's only a week. Martin gave me his word that he'd come home and sort things out with Bronagh after that.'

'Daddy, you do know Martin's word is worth diddly-squat?' said Siobhan.

'Let's give him a chance to prove us wrong. Anyways, it'll do them good to spend some time together. Give them a chance to clear the air.' Da smiled. It was the kind of smile that had been enough to make everything all right when she was a girl. But she was a mature woman now and a patronising fatherly smile didn't quite cut it.

Ma looked pained. Like she wanted to believe him but something was stopping her. Not that she would admit it, because that would mean she'd have to contradict him which was something she never did. Not in public anyway.

'Well I'm away upstairs,' he said.

'Will you be wanting a cup of tea, Gerry?' said Ma, still looking like she had a bad case of trapped wind.

'That'd be grand, love. And have we any of those chocolate biscuits left?'

'We have,' she almost sobbed. 'I'll bring you a couple up. Away you go.'

Da went off to paint his wee pictures. As a younger man, he'd been a master at the decorating. When Siobhan and Dermot got married, they'd bought a shithole of an old house because it was all they could afford. By the time Da had given it his magic touch, it was like a show home. The first time she saw it, Siobhan cried. The love he'd poured into that house just broke her heart. Da didn't do kisses and hugs. He showed he cared in other ways.

She'd worked out long ago that the decorating had been his escape. It kept him going through the Troubles and every other disaster that had come their way. When the decorating got too much for him, he'd scaled down. Nowadays, he hid himself away in Siobhan's old room and got lost in his watercolours. Although he had less to escape from, as far as she knew.

A future scene flashed before her. Da, not long buried and her having to go through all those paintings of his, deciding which to let go of. And of course it would be her. It was always her. She felt an ache that had nothing to do with Glenda. Her parents weren't getting any younger, but then none of them were. She was too old to be running around after her brothers. It was about time she had a life that didn't involve cleaning up other people's messes.

'What's wrong with you? You look like the Hunchback of Notre Dame,' said Ma.

'I had a massage from Glenda.'

Ma did a sharp intake of breath.

Siobhan put her hand up. 'I know, I know. Shayne

suggested it and I'd already upset him once so I couldn't refuse.'

Ma tutted. 'You know your trouble? You don't know how to say no.'

Siobhan dropped her bags on the kitchen worktop, took a ready meal lasagne out of one of them and stuck it in the oven.

Before she'd finished putting the rest of her shopping away, Ma was on the phone again. 'I'm awful worried, Siobhan. Do you think they'll be all right? Martin's not the big man he pretends to be. And Frank's not been right in years. Not since Ellen. Then there's poor wee Finn. He's never had any luck.'

It was on the tip of Siobhan's tongue to ask what about me? What have I had? But she stopped herself. The words would only have fallen on stony ground. Ma would have said she had a good job, three great kids, and if she'd worked harder at it, she could still have a husband. That was all very well but she hated her job, her kids were long gone into the world, and maybe if Ma looked at how hard Dermot had worked at their marriage, she'd see exactly why Siobhan no longer had a husband.

'It's only Scotland. It's hardly an expedition to the Antarctic, and they're grown men, Ma. They'll be fine. I'll try calling them again.'

It took half an hour to talk Ma down, by which time the lasagne was more than a bit crispy around the edges. Siobhan stuck it on a tray, poured herself a large glass of wine and went into the living room to catch up on the soaps.

· · ·

'Don't fall for it, love. He'll just impregnate you and go off to the pub while you're up to your neck in shitty nappies.' She was shouting at the TV again. She'd been doing this a lot lately. She'd have to stop watching all this rubbish romantic shite. It wasn't doing her any good. She poured the dregs from the wine bottle into the glass. Getting drunk on her own was another thing that needed to stop.

She turned the sound down and tried Frank again. No answer. A call to Finn was just as fruitless. Siobhan knew it would be. She knew they were avoiding her, otherwise why phone the parents and not her? Road trip, her arse. Well, if they wouldn't speak to her, she'd let them know exactly what she thought of their pathetic little trip. She tapped out a message and sent it to both of them. She'd have sent it to Martin too if she knew the selfish fecker's new number.

18

THE HARDSHIP OF LOSS

Frank let Siobhan's call ring out. A minute after it stopped, Finn's phone started up.

'Don't answer it,' said Martin. 'She'll only be having a rant.'

Finn's hand hovered over his phone. 'That's not very fair though, is it? She's got a lot on her plate.'

'Well on your head be it. That's all I'm saying,' said Martin. 'We've had a nice day, but if you want to spoil it, go ahead.'

It *had* been a nice day, even though they'd only been to the shops and stocked up on provisions and, in Frank's case, extra clothing. For dinner, they were treating themselves to fish and chips by the harbour.

'You know she's a HR manager now?' said Martin. 'Siobhan, a HR manager. Can you imagine anyone less suited to the job?'

'Ah come on now, Marty. That's enough.' Finn's hand continued to hover until the ringing stopped, then he went back to eating his fish and chips.

'Let's find a pub after this to christen our road trip,' said Martin.

'Okay, so long as we don't go as mad as last night,' said Frank.

Finn's phone pinged. A few seconds later, Frank's did the same. Finn read his message and winced. 'She's not happy.'

Frank opened his up:

'A road trip for fuck's sake. What are you, the fecking Blues Brothers?'

Siobhan was indeed not happy.

Martin read it over his shoulder. 'That's actually quite funny. Hey, we should get some dark glasses. D'ya think we could find somewhere that sold trilbies around here? We could do a selfie and send it to her.'

Frank pictured his sister's face as she opened up such a photo. 'Absolutely not.'

'First round's mine.' Martin was already on his way to the bar, so they didn't argue.

They left Martin to make himself at home chatting to the locals at the bar and found a table. He'd always had an easy way with him that people warmed to. It was the only thing Frank envied about him.

Finn was studying the drinks menu. It seemed as good a time as any to ask him about his loss. 'What you said earlier about losing someone. Do you want to tell me about it?'

Finn put down the menu. 'There's not a lot to say. I met the woman I wanted to spend the rest of my life with, and then she died.'

'Jesus, Finn. I had no idea. I'm so sorry.'

Finn shrugged. 'I wasn't the only one to lose someone then. She was one in a cast of thousands.'

'Covid?'

'Yeah. She was a nurse. This is her. Her name is, was, Orna.' He passed his phone over to Frank. 'Scroll through as many as you like. It's mostly her on there.'

Frank looked at one picture after another of a middle-aged woman smiling into the camera. She wasn't classically beautiful but there was an obvious warmth and vibrancy about her. There were some of Finn and Orna together. It was Finn as Frank had never seen him. He seemed to be glowing. 'She looks lovely, mate. I wish I could have known her.' It was an insincere thing to say. Frank knew it and by the look of Finn's expression, so did he.

'Yeah well, you could have, Frank. But it was your loss.'

'Will you look at the faces on yer. We're supposed to be enjoying ourselves.' Martin put three pints on the table.

'We were talking about Orna,' said Finn.

Martin sat down next to Finn and put his arm around him. 'Ah fuck, I'm sorry fella. Me and my big mouth. Let me take a look at those photos again. You can see the loveliness of her shining through, can't you Frank?'

'You can,' said Frank, keen to leave the talking to Martin.

'She was one of the nicest women you could meet. And funny too, yer know? She'd have you laughing, great big belly laughs. She must have been a great nurse.'

Finn cleared his throat. 'She was.'

Martin squeezed Finn into him. 'I know you only had a few years with her and you're still hurting like hell, but one day you'll look back on your time together and realise you were lucky to have known that kind of love, Finn. Lucky.'

'I was. I'm just away outside for a…' And with that Finn got up and walked away.

Frank felt bad all over again. He shouldn't have asked. He should have let it lie. 'Shall we go after him?'

'Nah. Let him alone. He'll be back when he's swallowed enough sorrow.'

'That was a beautiful thing you said to him. I didn't–'

'Think I had it in me? I'm not always the complete shitebag you think I am, FB. And she was a lovely woman.'

'I was going to say, I didn't know. Why did no one tell me?'

Martin's head jerked back. 'What would you have done if we had? Would it have made any difference?'

'Of course it would. I'd have called him, or mailed him.'

'Would yer? Would yer really though, Frank?'

Frank didn't answer: Finn was on his way back and anyway, Martin was probably right.

Before turning in he found a quiet spot to ring Netta. She answered straight away which gave him some hope that she was missing him as much as he was missing her.

'I got your messages,' she said. 'Your trip sounds like fun.'

'I'm not so sure you'd call it fun. I'm just hoping it's not awful. I've already upset Finn, and Martin's ... well, he's just Martin.'

'I'm beginning to think you don't like them.'

Not like them? It hadn't occurred to Frank that he might not like his brother and cousin. They were his family. He might not much like being with them, he might even try to avoid contact with them but actually not liking them, that was a different thing. 'It's kinda complicated. It goes way back. There's a lot of history and it's not all good.'

'Do you want to tell me?'

'Maybe when I get back. Talk to me about home. Are the kids back from their travels now? Is your dad still going to his allotment? Are the dogs behaving themselves?'

Netta's laugh was like a sweet kiss. He ached for her, ached to be lying next to her, listening to his old soul records, all nice and comfortable. 'You've only been away for a few days. You make it sound like it's been months.'

'Indulge me.'

'Will's decided he's not coming home for Easter. Liza returned for a day, then took off again. I won't see her now until she comes back for the start of term. Yes, Dad is still going to his allotment and yes, the dogs are fine. The big news is Robyn called because she couldn't get hold of you. I filled her in and she said to let you know she's having a great time and she'll speak to you when she gets back. She seemed a bit surprised that you were with Martin and Finn.'

'She's not the only one.'

'Is it going okay? Are you okay, Frank?'

'I'm absolutely fine. It's just a bit disconcerting. Like stepping back into the past.'

'And that's a bad thing, is it?'

'I don't know yet.'

'It doesn't have to be all about the past. Or the future even. It can just be about the moment. This week could be an adventure for you. Something new.'

'Aye, I suppose.' It had been a long time since Frank had an adventure. It wasn't something he was good at. But anything was better than it being all about the past. Only problem with that was the past hadn't got the memo. The bloody thing refused to go away.

19

EMBRACING THE DANGER – 1980

Frank and Billy walked into the Harp Bar together, each looking for different things. Billy was looking for a good time. Frank was looking for Eve. It used to be that being with Eve was Frank's idea of a good time but lately, things had been going downhill.

It had started with the fanzine that never was, unless you counted ten copies of the first edition. Like most of Billy's ideas, *Can* didn't get very far. Frank, Billy and Eve had all written pieces for that first edition and Frank had done the artwork as well. He'd even helped Eve to write the article about the Battle of the Bands being punk heaven. Then Billy decided splitting the tasks would make it more like a professional production. Billy and Eve would do the words and Frank the art. Martin and Finn's jobs would be the sales. It all sounded great, except nothing ever got done.

Sure, they'd talk about content. They were good at coming up with ideas but they never turned them into something readable, in spite of how much they discussed them. Frank had stopped counting the number of times Billy and Eve, Martin and Eve, or Billy and Martin had said they'd made a start on something. Because by now, Martin had decided he was going to be a content consultant, even though he couldn't spell to save his arse. It seemed to Frank, it was just an excuse for them to go to the Harp while he was at home either studying, or drawing something for their next big idea. And what Martin was up to was another concern. He'd been getting nice and cosy with Eve ever since he came up with that name for her. So when Billy had hinted that Martin was using those meet ups to make a play for her, it was enough for Frank to throw in the towel. He didn't tell them it was because he was trying to keep his girl-friend and devious bastard of a brother apart. He just said he'd had enough. Eve had been in a sulk about it ever since. Not just with him but with Billy as well. According to Billy, she blamed him for Frank's decision, even though she didn't know that Billy had tipped him off about Martin.

The next thing to rock the boat was their choice of university. For months, all Eve would talk about was how she was going to get away from Belfast and study in England. She talked about it so much that Frank got swept up in the idea of it and began to think of it as their great adventure. Soon, all he could think of was the two of them together in the same university, doing what the hell they liked.

Surprisingly, his parents were all for him leaving the country. This was his big chance they said. Although they might not have been so keen if they'd known about Eve. So Frank sent off for the prospectuses and filled in all the forms with one parent or another watching over his shoulder, making sure he'd made no mistakes. Eve applied for the same places. Or so he thought. Last week, she'd let slip that instead of Manchester, she'd applied for Queen's as a fall-back. Just to keep her daddy quiet. This time it was Frank's turn to be pissed off.

Billy nudged him. 'Her Highness is over there. I'll get the drinks in but I won't stop. You know she hates me.'

'She does not. You just wind her up sometimes.'

Eve was sitting with the crowd she usually hung around with. She patted the seat next to her. 'Where's Marty, is he not with you?'

Frank stiffened. Marty now, was it? Billy was right about those two. 'He's doing his homework. Why do you need to see him?'

'I don't need to see him, I just like to see him. He's a real joker. He makes me laugh.' She caught sight of Billy on his way over. 'What d'you bring him for?'

Billy may or may not have heard her but he didn't need to, he got the gist by the dirty look she threw at him. 'Don't worry I'm away. Here, love. Peace offering. Across the divide.'

Eve's lip curled at the sight of the drink he'd put on the table. 'What's that?'

'Babycham. I thought you could do with sweetening up.'

'You're fucking hilarious, Billy Mac.' She turned to Frank. 'And what the hell are you smiling at?'

Frank put his arm around her. 'Ah come on now, Eve. I thought you liked a joke.'

She pushed him away. 'Fuck off. And take your wanker pal with you.'

Frank and Billy stumbled out of the Harp, onto Hill Street. Eve had come round in the end. She'd even had a laugh with Billy. She'd even put her hand down Frank's pants and squeezed his dick when she kissed him goodnight. Maybe things weren't as bad as he thought.

Billy lit up a cigarette. Smoking was his new thing. He

took a drag and blew a smoke plume out of his nostrils. Like a tiny white cloud, it hung in the cold February air before fading into the night. 'Have youse two done it yet?'

'Have we fuck. There's nowhere to go, is there? When we get over the water, we are gonna shag until we can't shag no more.' He put on a Yank accent when he said it. He thought it would make him sound manly, like Van Morrison but as soon as he said it, he realised it made him sound like one right eejit.

Billy laughed all the same. 'I'd let you go to mine but my ma's man would be straight on the blower to his contacts. You and her Highness are gonna have to wait.'

'I think Eve's warming to you, Billy.'

'My easy charm must be wearing her down. She'll be granting me a dance at your wedding, the way things are going.'

'Who says we're getting married?'

Billy stopped walking. 'Oh, you radical you! All this talk of over the water's gone to your head.'

'Not so loud, people might hear.'

'You know, FB, you've got no sense of adventure. Embrace the danger for a change. C'mon. I've got something to show you.'

All the way home, Billy wouldn't say what it was. He just kept saying he didn't want to spoil the surprise. But when they got to a bombed out shop near their neighbourhood, he put his fingers to his lips and signalled for Frank to follow him.

Frank had a bad feeling in the pit of his stomach, but he still followed Billy round to the back of what was left of the shop. The only thing still standing in the yard behind the ruins was a brick shed, although calling it standing was an exaggeration. The door was padlocked but the lock it held together was hanging off, making it easy for Billy to open it.

'Billy, I don't think–'

'Shh.' Billy went inside and pulled back an old sack curtain from the window. The shed filled with moonlight.

Frank stood in the doorway. He relaxed when he saw that the inside was just a messier version of his da's shed. He couldn't understand why Billy had brought him here, unless he was suggesting that it might be somewhere to bring Eve. But this was a Catholic area, so that would be crazy.

Billy grabbed some empty petrol cans from the floor and tossed them into a corner. Underneath was some rotting cardboard, and underneath that, part of an old door. He lifted it up and handed it to Frank. 'Do something with this.'

There was a sound in the near distance. A movement maybe, Frank couldn't be sure. Something cold crept over him. It wasn't an entirely new experience so he knew what it was. It was fear. He grabbed Billy's arm. 'We need to go.'

'Aye, in a minute. Nearly there.' Billy pulled his arm away and lifted up some tarpaulin. And then Frank felt sick. Beneath the tarpaulin were two boxes. There was no need to open them. They both knew they were guns.

'Shit,' was all Frank could say.

Suddenly, there was another sound, louder and closer than before. Frank's heart leapt into his mouth. 'What was that?'

Billy dropped the tarpaulin. 'Run!'

He pushed Frank back round the side of the shop, just as a beam of torchlight found them. They ran for their lives, instinctively taking the opposite direction to home, and didn't stop until they were far away from where either of them lived.

Frank's eyes searched the shadows and dark entries but

saw no one. There was a film of sweat on his forehead. He wiped it away with his sleeve. 'Did they see us?'

'Who knows.'

'How did you know about them?'

'My ma's man. I heard him talking.' Billy's face lit up. 'Don't tell me you didn't get a buzz from that.'

'You're fucking mental, Billy.' Frank looked around again. Still no sign of anyone. They might just have gotten away with it. He laughed, out of relief and because Billy was right. It was the most frightening thing he'd ever done in his entire life. It was also the most thrilling.

20

LOOSE TALK COSTS LIVES – 1980

Ma walked in with her shopping bags just as Frank came downstairs. She scanned him from top to bottom. 'You look ridiculous. Where are you going?' He'd been wearing his punk clothes openly for a while now and she still hadn't got used to it.

'Billy's.' He wasn't lying exactly. He was going to Billy's first. Then they were away to Good Vibes. Eve would be there. They'd been getting on great since that night in February when Billy showed him the guns. It was probably coincidence but Frank was convinced it had something to do with it. Nothing had happened to them afterwards. Months had passed and the Balaclavas still hadn't come knocking. They'd gotten away with it, and because of that, Frank had become bolder. Instead of hiding his punk gear at Billy's, he brought it home. The first time he'd walked into the living room with it on, jaws dropped. It gave him a kick to see the shock on Ma's face. Da only glanced up from his paper but Frank was sure he detected a little smile. Spurred on by that success, he'd begun to stand up for himself more with the parents, and also with Eve. It seemed to have a positive effect. He didn't get battered for being cheeky and more importantly, Eve was all over him. She promised when they went over the water, they'd have sex all the time. They'd even agreed which university they'd choose if they got places. Birmingham.

Ma put her shopping down on the table and folded her arms. 'You've made all that effort, in your get-up there just for Billy, have you? You be careful, sonny. You don't want to be getting some girl in trouble.'

Siobhan came in to help Ma unpack the bags. 'Dressed like that? I don't think you've any worries there, Mammy.'

They both had a laugh at that one. Frank ignored them. What did they know?

'Mother of God, there's another one of them.' Ma wiped her eyes but it was wasted, seeing as her and Siobhan fell about laughing all over again.

Martin came in wearing his new bondage trousers. It hadn't taken him long to follow Frank's lead. He did a twirl for Siobhan and Ma, setting them off again. It didn't bother Martin. He was all for the attention. 'Are you away to Billy's? I'll come with yer.'

'Have fun, Sid and Nancy,' said Siobhan, at which point, Ma was so hysterical she had to sit down.

They left the women splitting their sides and knocked on Finn's door. It was still morning and he already looked half-cut. He put his arm around Martin. 'How are yer, Marty?'

Martin pushed him away. 'You stink like an alchie. Where'd you get that from?'

'It's me ma's medicinal brandy. Just a couple of mouthfuls.'

'You better pray she doesn't get a cold or you'll get battered,' said Frank.

'I added some water. She won't notice.'

'You need to reel yourself in, before it becomes a habit.' Frank couldn't believe he was saying this, but someone had to point out that Finn was getting a bit too mad for the drink. As usual, it was left it to him.

'He's not that bad.' Martin watched Finn nearly fall off the kerb into the road. 'Okay, maybe he is that bad. Finn, you need to ease off.'

Finn nodded. 'Okay. I'll have to stop anyways. If I add any more water, there'll be no brandy left. Are we going to Billy's?'

Martin took his arm. 'No. I couldn't say indoors, Frank. I saw Billy this morning when I went to get Da's paper. He said he had to go somewhere first, so he'll meet us there.'

When they reached Musgrave Park, Martin said they should take a different route. 'I heard there was some trouble on Lisburn Road. We should go up Malone Road.'

'Fair enough.' The last thing Frank wanted was trouble. Next week was his final exams and he couldn't afford to get picked up and miss them.

They took a right and headed towards Malone Road. It meant they went by the university which Frank liked because it filled him with anticipation for his and Eve's new life of freedom that was almost within touching distance now.

Just before they got to the university, they passed the edge of the Botanic Gardens. On dry days, people sunbathed on the grass. Today was grey and drizzly and the grounds had a deserted look about them.

'Is that Billy and Eve over there?' said Finn who'd been sobered up by the long walk.

They saw Billy and Eve talking on a corner, over on

University Road. Billy had his hand on her arm. Finn called out to them but they didn't hear.

'C'mon.' Frank took a few steps closer. But that was as far as he got. Martin pulled him back. Frank saw then that two cars had pulled up next to Billy and Eve. Three men in balaclavas jumped out of the first one, shoved Billy into it, and drove off. Another man got out of the second car. He said something to Eve. She shook her head and backed away, but he grabbed hold of her.

Frank was seized with urgency. He shot off before Martin could stop him again.

He was just feet away when Eve saw him. The man saw him too. 'What, is this another one?'

'No. He's no one.' Eve opened the passenger door. 'Can we go home now, Daddy?'

So this was her dad, the big RUC man.

'Get in the car, Eve.' He walked up to Frank until he was no more than a couple of feet away. Frank could smell the familiar scent of Old Spice. Da had some that he wore on special occasions.

Eve's dad fixed his eyes on Frank. They were dark grey. Opaque, like sheet metal. Frank knew the worst thing he could do right now was to show weakness, but he still had to fight against his instinctive urge to turn away.

'This is your lucky day, son,' said the big RUC man. With his unflinching stare set on Frank, he walked backwards to his car.

A cold shiver ran through Frank, just like the one he'd felt the night Billy had shown him the guns. He watched Eve's dad drive her away, not noticing Martin and Finn were next to him.

'Who was that?' said Finn.

'Eve's ould fella,' said Frank.

'Is he one of their paras?' said Martin.

'No. He's a cop.'

'Cops don't hang around with the Balaclavas in broad daylight. Billy could be dead already. What'll we do?' Martin clenched his jaw. If he was trying to be strong, his eyes gave him away. He wasn't equipped to deal with this. None of them were.

Finn began to shake.

Frank put his arm around him. 'We should go home.'

Ma and Da listened to their story without cutting in. On any other day they'd have been furious with them for going into a no-go zone but there was no time for that. 'Someone needs to tell Billy's mother. I'll go round there now,' said Da.

'What about Billy?' Finn hadn't stopped crying since they got back.

'I'll speak to that fella she's taken up with. He might have some idea if it's our side, but there'd have to be a reason if it was. If this girl's father's involved, I don't understand why he would go for Billy if it's you who's been carrying on with her, Francis. Is there any other reason you can think of?'

'No. Except…' Frank didn't dare say it.

Da frowned. 'Except what?'

Frank told them about the guns. And that's when Ma slapped him straight across the face.

The six o'clock news came on. Da was still out. He'd been gone for hours. Normally he watched the news religiously and then they had their tea, but not today. Today it was Ma watching the news and no food was anywhere near being cooked. 'Francis, get in here now,' she shouted.

Frank had been sitting on the stairs, waiting for the front door to open, waiting for Da to come in and say everything was all right. He went into the living room. Ma was on her feet, pointing to the TV. 'Is that it? The guns. Is that the place?'

The news was showing the old bombed out shop. The reporter was saying a cache of guns had been found. Frank couldn't speak. His head was full of Billy and all the things those men were doing to him now, if he wasn't already past punishment. But he didn't need to say anything. Ma had read his face. She put her hand to her throat. 'Holy Mother...'

The phone rang. Siobhan ran into the hall to pick it up. 'It's Da.'

Ma pushed past Frank and took the phone from her. They all stood around watching, hoping. 'Oh thank God. Are you coming home now, Gerry? Are you hungry? I'll get us a fish and chip supper. No, I'll go. I can't risk letting the kids out. Okay, love. If you're sure. Just be careful.'

She put the phone down and sniffed into her hankie, then straightened out her skirt. 'Billy's been found. He's in a bad way but he's alive. They've had to take him to the hospital. Your da's on the way home. He'll bring some fish and chips back with him. I'll not be cooking tonight. And we'll none of us be going out. Francis, go and spread some bread and butter. Siobhan, put the kettle on.'

Siobhan slammed the kettle down, lit the gas and threw Frank a dirty look. 'I was supposed to be meeting a fella tonight. Now he's gonna think I've stood him up. This is all your fault, you big eejit. I can't wait until you leave.'

· · ·

The first time Frank saw Billy in the hospital he wanted to howl. Billy's face was so swollen you couldn't see his eyes. Both his legs were in plaster and so was one of his arms. Billy's ma said he was lucky to be alive. If it hadn't been for her fella and Da then he probably wouldn't be. No one said anything about the guns, or Eve.

Frank's own ma wouldn't let him or Martin out of her sight. Along with Finn, they had to suffer the indignity of being walked to and from school. Although what she would have done if the Balaclavas did come for them was anyone's guess. Apart from school and visiting Billy under escort, they were kept under lock and key. There was no going back to Good Vibes, or the Harp and no chance of seeing Eve. Frank could only hope they'd meet up in Birmingham.

It was difficult to talk to Billy about what happened. He was in a room on his own so it should have been easy, but someone was always there to chaperone them. It was as if they couldn't even be trusted to speak to each other.

The day after Frank's exam results came through, Da took him to the hospital to see Billy. Billy's ma was in there with him. She spent a lot of time there, considering she was never that bothered before the beating.

Billy's face was back to normal, except for a few broken teeth but he was a long way off being his usual self. It wasn't a good time to tell him Frank's news but it had to be done. 'Looks like I'll be going to Birmingham. I got the grades I need.'

Billy said nothing. His ould lady got up. 'Is your da out in the waiting room, Frank? I'll go and say hello.'

Billy waited until she'd left the room. 'You're definitely going then?'

'Aye. I'm sorry. I don't wanna leave you like this.'

'No. You go. Don't let me stand in your way, Frankie Boy.'

The way he said it narked Frank. It wasn't like it was his fault Billy was in such a mess. 'Where were they from, those men? Were they our side or theirs?'

Billy zipped his mouth with his good hand. 'Loose talk costs lives.'

Frank tutted. It was a bit late to be worried about loose talk. 'What were you doing there with Eve anyway?'

'Saving your skin.'

The door opened and a nurse came in. 'Visiting time's over.'

Frank nodded. 'I'll see ya, Billy.'

Billy looked at the open door. 'Yeah.'

21

DARK TIMES AND BAD SMELLS

The next morning, while they were having breakfast, Finn announced he was keen to get on the road. 'I want to get us set up early so's we can go on a hike before the weather turns.'

There were two elements to Finn's summary that raised alarm bells. The first was the mention of a hike. The second was the casual way he'd dropped in the possibility of the weather turning. Martin's eyebrows lifted. He must have been thinking the same thing.

Finn caught him in the act. 'When I say hike, I mean walk. Don't you be worrying that I'm taking you on a long trek. I don't think I could handle two cardiac arrests. One maybe.'

Martin put down his coffee. 'I'm quite affronted by that accusation, Finn Meister. I'll have you know I can walk the hind legs off a donkey.'

Finn Meister. Frank had forgotten their name for Finn's alter ego. 'I think you'll find it's talk the hind legs off a donkey. You can certainly do that, brother. Not sure about the walking element though.'

Martin grinned. 'Okay then, a nice wee walk it is.'

They'd been driving for a couple of hours when the campervan turned off the main road. Frank followed it up a mountain track, and then along what seemed to be not much more than a dirt path, until they came to a halt on a space of flattened earth.

Finn jumped out of the van and opened up the Mini's boot. 'This is us. Come on and help me pitch the tent, Marty. Frank, can you make sandwiches to take with us?'

Frank looked at Martin and they both smiled. The Finn Meister was taking charge. It was a never seen before phenomenon.

With their lunch and drinks packed up into a backpack, they set off, Finn at the front with the bag and a compass around his neck. To Frank's relief, they were going along the side of the mountain and not up it. At least that's what he thought. It wasn't long before he noticed an uphill gradient had sneaked into their wee walk and it was getting decidedly rockier. Up ahead, Finn was skipping along the terrain like a mountain goat. Martin, although heavier on his feet, also seemed to be managing quite easily. He was the only one stumbling along.

They carried on and on, up and along, up and along, until – hallelujah – Finn said they should stop for lunch. Frank staggered up to the other two and flopped down onto the ground.

Finn handed him a bottle of water. 'Are you okay, FB? Have I pushed you too far?'

'By the looks of him, it was too far as soon as we left the van,' said Martin.

Frank got his breath back. 'Feck off. You both have proper walking shoes on. All I have are my trainers.'

Martin nodded. 'Oh that'll be it then, for sure. Nothing to do with the fact that you're completely unfit.'

'I am not completely unfit. I walk every day. I'm just…'

'Old?' said Martin.

Finn thrust a pack of sandwiches at Martin. 'Enough now lads. Let's have a nice civilised lunch and admire the scenery. Then we'll walk a bit further, only if everyone's up to it.'

They sat in silence eating their food, Frank quietly fuming. He was not old. He was … what? Comfortable sprang to mind, just like it had done when he was at home preparing for two weeks of painting and relaxation. Comfortable wasn't such a bad thing. He was happy being comfortable. Although he probably did need to work on his fitness when he got home. Two things to do on his return. One. Buy a new phone. Two. Embark on a fitness programme.

'If you can manage it, Frank, there's a great view further round that way.' Finn said it in the way you might cajole a small child into eating their greens. Frank was insulted all over again.

'Of course I can manage it.' He caught a flash of something from Martin. A look that said, ease off the wee fella, and he added humiliation to his current list of emotions. 'I'd love to see the view. I'll be fine.'

It was noticeable that Finn had slowed the pace down. Although Frank was glad of it, he was also more than a little indignant. Not so indignant that he wanted them to speed up though. Anger, humility, gladness and indignance. That was some range of emotions for a man who liked to keep things on an even keel. This trip was getting to him, just as he knew it would. Again, he thought about that day in 1980 when everything changed. The way Eve's dad had looked at him, like he would have gunned him down without a thought. Frank had had nightmares about that look for years after. Not now though. In fact he hadn't thought about it since Robyn, was born. If you didn't count this week, that is.

The thing he hadn't really thought about in any great detail was Eve's reaction. 'He's no one.' Sure, he'd heard her speak the words in those bad dreams, but they hadn't been the focus of his fears. If he ever considered them, it was just to be thankful that she'd saved him. And when she didn't turn up in Birmingham at the start of the first term, he'd just assumed her daddy had stopped her from coming to him. But what if she hadn't said it just to save him? What if the other possibility was the real reason she didn't turn up. What if she had really thought he was no one?

Frank had been so lost in his thoughts that he hadn't realised they'd slowed down to a stop. Martin and Finn were gazing at a loch surrounded on nearly all sides by multi-coloured mountains. Thick green trees at their base gave way to patches of yellow-green and rust, themselves giving way to slate grey topped with dazzling white snow.

'That is fucking amazing,' said Martin.

'It is,' said Frank.

'It was one of Orna's favourite places.' Finn stared straight ahead.

Frank knew that look. Finn was in a faraway place. A happier place. He put his arm around his cousin. 'Thanks for sharing it with us.'

Finn pointed to a dark cloud sitting over the peak of the

furthest mountain. 'That's coming our way. We should go back.'

They managed to cook up some dinner under the van's awning before the rain started, and it was another hour or so before it began to trouble them enough to pack everything away. Finn produced some cards and they played gin rummy inside the van while hailstones thundered against the roof and sides. When they got bored with that, the newly replenished beer stocks came out and they argued their way through their all-time top-fifty singles. That brought them back to Belfast and Frank's thoughts returned again to that day. 'I've been thinking about that time Billy got picked up by the Balaclavas.'

'Dark times, so they were,' said Finn.

'What in God's name made you want to think about that?' said Martin.

'I dunno. It must be seeing you two again.'

Martin rolled his eyes. 'I knew it'd be our fault.'

Frank ignored him. 'Something's just occurred to me. If we'd gone our usual route to the shop, we wouldn't have seen them on that corner.'

Finn frowned. 'I suppose so. It was lucky we did then, because Billy might not have gotten away with a beating if your da hadn't been on the case.'

'I guess so.'

Martin yawned. 'Sounds like the rain's stopped and I'm ready for bed. Are you coming sweet cheeks?'

Finn pulled back the side door. 'Aye. Let's go before it starts again.'

.   .   .

Frank was in the middle of getting undressed when the side door opened again and Martin's face appeared around it. 'Are you decent, dear? The tent's too damp. We're sleeping in here.'

Frank quickly pulled his pants on. 'What, all three of us?'

'Sorry, no choice. I'll take the top bunk. You two can share the bed.' Finn stepped in and raised the van's roof. Sure enough there was another bed up there.

Frank sighed. Then he remembered Billy Mac telling him to embrace the danger for a change. It might not be Billy's idea of danger but Billy wasn't about to sleep with Martin Thunder Arse, was he? 'Just don't snore into my ear. And don't get too close.'

Martin scratched his backside. 'Frank, we're two big fellas, sharing a bed in a campervan. Of course I'm gonna get too close.'

'Well at least turn the other way.'

Frank lay in the dark, his brother's back up against his and began to doze. A long whiny noise like a balloon being deflated made him start, and then a very bad smell invaded his nostrils. 'Martin, have you just farted on me?'

'I couldn't help it, it sneaked out.'

Finn groaned. 'Oh that's atrocious. I can smell it from here. It's hit the ceiling and rebounded on me. You're one dirty bastard, Martin Thunder Arse.'

Martin chuckled. 'Sorry guys. This is nice though, isn't it?'

'Not from where we're lying,' said Frank.

'Reminds me of when we used to visit you in your student digs. Do you remember that?'

Frank covered his nose and smiled. 'Aye, and you were one smelly bastard then as well.'

22

DA DELIVERS FREEDOM – 1980

Da steered the car into the boat's lower deck. Frank had never been on a ferry before. He'd never been anywhere outside of Ireland. But that was about to change. Today he was on the way to his new life, and he couldn't wait.

The summer had been endless, but not in a good way. He'd been stuck at home for most of it because of the guns and Balaclava debacle, and when he was allowed out, it was only with a chaperone. Sometimes the parents chaperoned him, which was bad enough, but other times it had been Siobhan and that was worse. She'd spent the whole time telling him what a fecking eejit he was. "Too many brains and not enough common sense" was a favourite saying of hers, along with "there are a million things I could be doing right now, if I wasn't stuck babysitting you". So to say Frank was ready for freedom was an understatement.

He was also dying to be with Eve again. He hadn't seen or heard of her since the day the Balaclavas took Billy. He hadn't seen a lot of Billy either. Billy was out of hospital now but the parents had added his house to the list of no-go zones, and Siobhan made sure he stuck to the rules. His sister was a pain in the arse and she was definitely the one he was going to miss least. Apparently, that was fine by her because, as she'd made clear on many occasions, she couldn't wait to see the back of him either.

With the car safely parked, Frank and Da went up to the top deck and watched Belfast get smaller and smaller as they sailed away. When they hit open water, Da pointed out and named the sea birds while they ate the sandwiches Ma had made for the journey. She'd shed a tear that morning when Frank said goodbye, then reminded him not to mess up. That was Ma in a nutshell.

They docked at Liverpool and drove on to Birmingham to stay with Cousin Eamon who'd moved there before Frank was born. The area Eamon lived in was full of terraced houses, some with tiny front gardens and others with doors that opened straight onto the street. You could stand at one end of his road and see a line of the exact same little houses stretching from one end to the other. It was a lot like Billy's road, without the soldiers.

After their tea, Eamon took them out for a pint. It was strange to be going to a pub with Da. Like he'd become a grown-up overnight. Frank sat listening to Eamon and Da chatting about home and thought about how Finn would never get to have a drink with his ould fella. Maybe Da would take Finn out some day just like this. Although it was entirely possible that Finn could already drink Da under the table.

Frank hadn't expected to sleep that night with so many new things to look forward to, but he ended up managing it quite easily. His last thought before dozing off was that when he got to the university tomorrow, Eve would be waiting for him.

· · ·

The next morning they went to the university and found Frank's halls of residence in Edgbaston. Then they explored the campus in a state of wonder.

'Sure, it's a fine place, son. Your mother will be very pleased when I tell her,' said Da.

They were sitting on the green in the middle of the campus watching students relaxing on the grass or wandering around with their parents. Frank was keeping an eye out for Eve but so far there'd been no sign. Probably just as well. He didn't want to run into her ould man.

'Do you think you'll be happy here, Francis?' It was a funny question to ask. The parents had never enquired about his happiness before.

'Aye, I think so.' He said it with more conviction than he felt. He was excited but it was a bit scary and he was already missing home, and Billy. He was even missing those two stupid eejits, Martin and Finn. Most of all he was missing Eve. But then, he'd been missing her since that day in June. Last night he'd been absolutely certain she'd be here. Now, he wasn't so sure.

'It's a place to build a life, without all that nonsense. Just look at Eamon.' Da was talking as if Frank was never going home again which was absolutely not the plan, as far as Frank knew anyway.

'Right. I'm away. Come on and walk me to the car, son.'

When they reached the car, Da put his hand on Frank's shoulder. 'Promise me you'll stay out of trouble, Francis.'

'I will, Da. I promise.'

'Good man. And try to keep a low profile until you've got the lie of the land. People have long memories. They're still hurting after all that pub bombing business.'

'Okay, Da.'

'And phone your mother every week, otherwise I'll get it in the neck.'

'Okay, Da.'

'Well, I'm away then. Definitely going. Look after yourself, Francis. You're doing the right thing.'

Frank waved goodbye with a heavy heart and a great lump in his throat. Da was staying another night at Eamon's before going home first thing. They wouldn't see each other again until Christmas. He was on his own now and he wasn't sure what to do with this new freedom he'd been so looking forward to. He'd been liberated from the tyranny of parental control and he could do whatever he wanted. He should feel happy, but all he felt was lost and alone. He remembered the three things Da had told him to do. Stay out of trouble, keep a low profile, and phone Ma every week. In the absence of anything else, those were the rules he would live by while he was over here.

With nothing else to do, he trekked back to the halls of residence to unpack his things. He passed a couple of games of football on the grassy areas in the student village. Some people had sorted themselves into groups and were drinking and hanging out. Frank walked on and found his building, then his room.

Ma had sent him with a box of groceries and they'd bought some fresh food that morning, so he took them into the kitchen and looked for some space in the fridge. Someone came in as he was putting his milk in there. 'You need to put your name on it, mate.'

'Huh?' Frank turned to see a tall, bulky, fair-haired guy wearing an Undertones T-Shirt.

'Your name. If you don't put your name on it, someone'll have it. Although it's no guarantee it won't be nicked if you do name it.'

'Oh right. I'll get a pen.'

'You can use mine when I'm finished. Found out the hard way, didn't I? Two yoghurts gone, just like that. Where you from?'

'Ireland.' Frank was thinking about rule number two, keep a low profile. He couldn't hide his accent but he didn't need to be handing out specifics.

'Anywhere near Derry? Or is it Londonderry? I'm never sure which.'

'Depends which side you're on. The Undertones call it Derry. I'm from Belfast. It's about seventy miles from Derry.' There he'd said it, but he was banking on this fella being like the punks back home. He pointed at the guy's T-Shirt. 'I've seen them in Belfast though.'

The guy whistled. 'Jammy bastard. Were they good?'

'Aye. The best I've seen.'

'I'm Adrian. Adrian Wilson.'

'Frank O'Hare.'

Adrian tossed him the pen. 'Here you go, mate.'

Frank emptied his groceries out onto the table and began to write his name on each item. Adrian was taking his groceries out of a cupboard to do the same. There was a sound of footsteps clop, clopping along the corridor. Whoever it was, seemed to be coming towards them.

'Have you seen a girl wearing a top hat and tails?'

Frank looked up, the pen still in his hand. Standing on the other side of the kitchen was the most incredible looking girl he'd ever seen in his entire life. She had long red hair that hung in waves around her and a face that could have been painted by Rossetti. She was tall. No, she was statuesque. And she had the kind of cut-glass accent Frank had only heard on TV. Usually someone from the English upper class talking about the Irish problem.

'Er, no,' he said.

'You're sure?'

'I think we'd have noticed,' said Adrian.

She frowned at them. 'Yes, I expect so. Damn.' Then she turned away and clop, clopped back down the hall.

Adrian raised his eyebrows at Frank. 'Well that was surreal. Fancy a pint?'

23

THE LADY OF SHALOTT – 1981

For the first time in his life, Frank had friends who weren't Irish. He even had friends who weren't British. That was how different his life had become. He'd thought it would be easy to stick to the three golden rules – stay out of trouble, keep a low profile and phone Ma every week – but he'd reckoned without Adrian's influence. By November he was already missing phone calls home, much to Ma's displeasure. By Christmas, no one in their right mind would call his profile low. Frank had become a regular on the party scene. In fact he was a regular on every scene that involved music and drinking. Everyone knew him and nobody cared where he came from, what church he went to, or even if he went to church at all. It was a revelation to Frank, an epiphany that hit him like a lightning bolt. He was really and properly free. All of a sudden, he was unstoppable in the pursuit of unmitigated hedonism.

It was March now, and the only one of his rules he hadn't yet broken was the first one, although Adrian believed it was only a matter of time before trouble came looking, the way Frank was carrying on with girls. It wasn't

Frank's fault really. It was just that these girls were mad for the accent. They couldn't get enough of it. He'd held out at first, hoping Eve would turn up. Every time he called home, he asked Martin if he'd seen her but the answer was always no. Billy might have seen her. He had his ear to the ground on these things, but he couldn't ask Billy because he didn't have a phone in his house, and Billy never wrote. So he gave up on Eve, and then came his second epiphany. Sex was fucking ace! And in this country, birth control was easy. Girls were on the pill, and if they weren't, a boy could buy johnnies without being subjected to the Spanish Inquisition. Frank could not believe his luck. As Adrian had a habit of reminding him, he went from virgin to a complete slag of the male variety, in the space of a few short months. So what? Frank was having too much fun to care.

This weekend he was giving Billy, Martin and Cousin Finn a taste of his new life. It was their first ever trip across the water and they were struggling to take in the everyday things that Frank had gotten used to.

'It's kinda weird without the soldiers and the checkpoints. It feels like something's missing. Like it shouldn't feel strange, but it does,' said Martin.

'You get used to it.' Frank was trying to put them at ease but one look at Billy told him he'd come across like he was showing off.

'Will you catch yourself on? You've only been here five minutes and you're acting like you've lived here all your fucking life. Just because the cops don't have guns, doesn't mean they won't kick your head in. Same goes for the rest of the Brits.'

Billy's words cut him down and he felt ashamed. Ashamed that he'd been crowing, rubbing their noses in it, showing off his newfound freedom. 'Sure, it's not perfect.

You still get shifty looks from the locals when they hear you talk, but I'm just saying, it's a wee bit easier once you get used to it. That's all, Billy.'

'Is that so?' Billy scanned Frank's room as he let them in, like he was on reconnaissance. Like he was expecting to find a stash of petrol bombs under the bed. It wasn't like Billy at all.

'Are we going drinking? I'm gasping.' Finn dropped his bag on the floor. He was working for a builder friend of Da's now. It had put some muscle on him, and he'd grown a few inches since leaving school so although he wasn't eighteen yet, he could pass for it.

'There's a party later on, but we can start at the Hope and Anchor. It's a bit scuzzy but the beer's cheap, and Adrian will be there.' Frank said it all casual like, as if they knew Adrian. They didn't. He'd mentioned his name to Martin and Finn a couple of times over the Christmas break, but he'd held back with Billy.

Billy stopped his room check to give Frank the evils. 'Who the fuck is Adrian?'

'He's a mate. A good guy. He likes the Undertones.'

'Oh well that's all right then. Is he some kind of fruit? Must be with a name like that.'

'No he's not, and leave off, Billy. What the hell's wrong with you?'

Billy took a sudden step back, as if Frank had just hit him, then he laughed. 'Just kiddin, Frankie Boy. C'mon let's go. Sure, I'm desperate for the craic.'

Frank glanced at Finn and Martin. They didn't look like they thought he was kidding either, but no one said anything.

. . .

The pub was full, as it always was on a Friday night. Frank spotted Adrian and the rest of his drinking mates squeezed together in the middle of the room. He held his breath while his Belfast gang eyed his Birmingham gang. It was the way you did things back home but it was out of place here.

It was Martin who eased the tension: 'Frank says you like the Undertones, Adrian.'

Adrian's face broke into a big grin. 'Mate, I fucking love 'em.'

It got everyone talking about music and for once in the whole entirety of his life, Frank was grateful to have a brother who could talk to anyone about anything.

After a couple of drinks, they moved on to a pub that was less crowded. Some girls Frank and Adrian knew came over to join them. Straight away, Finn and Martin were chatting them up. Martin was having more success than Finn.

Adrian nodded in Martin's direction. 'Runs in the family then, does it? Shame it was him got all the looks.'

'Up yours, mate,' said Frank. He hadn't noticed before but Adrian was right, Martin was good looking. Good looks and charm. Bastard.

'Isn't that the Lady of Shalott over there?'

Frank looked over to a table on the far side of the pub. It was her, the flame-haired beauty from his first day. He and Adrian often talked about her. They'd even given her that nickname, but they hadn't seen her since that day in the kitchen. 'Aye. Methinks the lady hath returned.'

'Methinks she hath.'

It was their private joke, this way of talking, whenever they mentioned her. They were being daft, but that was the fun of it. This was another of Frank's epiphanies since coming here. It was okay to be daft and say silly things, and it was even better when you had a friend who knew that. Billy was staring at them. More reconnaissance. It felt like being back home, always being watched. A not yet forgotten uneasiness crept over Frank.

They'd been at the party for a few hours when Frank saw her again, floating through the crowd like a vision. With her height and those flame-red locks she stood out among the ordinary people. He nudged Adrian. 'She's here. Twice in one night.'

'It's a sign. Go for it, mate.'

'You don't mind?'

Adrian snorted. 'She's way out of my league, Frank. You might stand a chance with your Irish charm and your good looks.'

'I thought you said I was ugly?'

'Only when you stand next to Martin. Get over there before he gets to her.'

Frank didn't need telling twice, especially as he could see Martin had noticed her. He went for her without really thinking what he was going to say. She was alone and had her back to him. Then she turned and looked him in the eye, as if she'd known he was there all along. He said the only thing that sprang to mind: 'Did you find her?'

Her lips parted. A little crease appeared on her perfect brow. 'What?'

'Did you find your friend with the top hat and tails? You were looking for her in our kitchen.'

'Oh yes. That was ages ago. Fancy remembering that.'

'It's not a question I'm asked every day. Especially when I'm being asked by a beautiful woman.' God almighty, did he just say that?

She did a little smirk and gazed straight into his eyes. 'I suppose not.'

Frank was sure his knees were buckling. How could he come back from that look? But before he had a chance to, some guy had his arm around her. 'Sorry pal, she's taken.' He had a cockney accent. Not what Frank was expecting. He'd thought she'd be with someone as posh as her.

He remembered golden rule number one, stay out of trouble. 'No problem. We were just talking.'

She winked at him. 'Catching up on old times.'

The cockney dragged her away and Frank went back to the others.

'Boyfriend?' said Adrian.

'Yeah. I think she likes me though.'

'Still a chance then. The Belfast lads have gone outside. Finn passed out. He likes a drink, doesn't he?'

Finn was back in the land of the living when Frank found them, although he was raging drunk. 'I love this place, FB. I'm gonna move over here. I've decided.'

'I think your mammy will have something to say about that,' said Martin. 'Who was that girl you were talking to, Frank? Is she a student?'

'Aye. I don't know her really. We've just bumped into each other once or twice.'

'Feck off. You fancy her,' snorted Martin.

Frank shrugged, trying to play it cool. 'Who wouldn't?' Of course he fancied her, but he didn't want Martin to know how much he fancied her. Because if he knew, he'd be bound to make a play for her, just to prove he could.

'I'll tell Eve you've forgotten about her then, will I?' said Billy.

Frank twisted round to face Billy. 'Have you seen Eve?'

'Aye, a few times.'

'She stayed in Belfast then?'

'Yeah. She's at Queens.'

'Does she ask about me?'

'Now and then.' Billy glanced over at Martin as he said it.

Martin's eyes dropped to the ground. Frank put two and two together and turned on him. 'You said you hadn't seen Eve.'

Martin shoved his hands in his pockets. 'I haven't. Well, only a couple of times.'

The lying wee shite. Frank pushed him. 'Are you going out with her?'

Martin steadied himself. 'Fuck no.'

Billy laughed. 'You really think Eve would go out with a loser like him? You're soft in the head, FB.'

Frank gave Martin the narrow eye treatment. Billy was right, he was being soft. Martin might be good looking but he didn't have a lot going on up top. Eve would never go with someone like him. 'Next time either of you see her, give her my address and ask her to write to me.'

Billy put his arm on Martin's shoulder. 'Sure. If there is a next time.'

24

PRIDE COMES BEFORE A FALL

They had just about survived the night, what with the torrential rain and Martin's rampant wind. That was Frank's view anyway. Finn was a lot less perturbed by the weather, although he did concede that the smell had nearly suffocated him at times, and that Martin was indeed a slob of the first order. 'It's no wonder Bronagh threw you out, if you were doing that sort of business every night,' he said, over breakfast.

Martin slugged back his coffee and wiped his mouth with the back of his hand. 'That's not why she threw me out.'

'I thought you didn't know why she threw you out,' said Frank.

'I didn't when we last talked about it, but I might have a clue now. I messaged her to tell her we were going on a road trip, in case she was interested.'

'And was she?'

'No. She told me to feck off and don't contact her again until I saw the error of my ways. Obviously, I asked if she couldn't give me a hint on the errors. To help me along, like.

She said if I paid her more attention, then I wouldn't need to ask the question. So, from that I've deduced I haven't been paying her enough attention.'

Finn topped up their coffees. 'Are you sure there's not more to it, Marty?'

Frank blew on his steaming mug. 'Finn's right. You've never paid Bronagh much attention. If that's all it is, I'm amazed she didn't throw you out years ago.'

'And how would you know, brother dear? When was the last time you saw me and Bronagh together? When did you last grace our humble shores?' said Martin.

'That's got nothing to do with it.' Frank didn't need to see Martin in action to know how things would play out with him and Bronagh. There was a reason why she was his third wife.

'It has everything to do with it. You don't know shit about us and our lives.' Martin jabbed his finger in Frank's direction. 'You cut us off as soon as you could, just like Billy said you would.'

'It's time you and Billy grew up.' Frank stood up and walked away before he said something that couldn't be unsaid.

He ignored Finn's pleas to come back and went in the direction they'd gone in yesterday. He'd been an idiot to agree to this trip. As soon as he cooled off, he'd drive the Mini back to Finn's house. There was no need for him to carry on, Finn could see to it that Martin got home. In fact Martin could get himself home. It was about time he took some responsibility for his actions.

He came to a point where the trail split into two tracks. Yesterday, they'd taken the one that led them uphill. This time he stayed on the flatter one, knowing it would be better for putting some distance between him and the van. He walked at a pace that made him breathless and he was starting to tire, but he was too full of indignation to stop. He knew he had nothing to be indignant about. Martin had spoken the truth, he had cut them off. But he'd had good reason to, hadn't he?

There were more deer up ahead. No stag this time. He probably wasn't far away though. The deer kept their eyes on him as he negotiated his way along the narrowing track.

His thoughts strayed back to that first time the boys came to stay with him in Birmingham. Billy had spent the whole of that weekend picking holes in Frank's new life. Birmingham was as crap as Belfast. His new friends were all middle-class wankers. The girls weren't as pretty as the ones back home, and they were slags too. It was embarrassing. Even Martin and Finn were embarrassed by the stuff he was coming out with. Frank hadn't relaxed until they were back on the train to Liverpool. All the same, he'd made Billy promise to pass that message on to Eve because he didn't trust Martin to do it. The next time he saw Billy, he said he'd done it, but no letter ever came. Not that it really mattered to Frank by then. He was over Eve the minute he saw Ellen, but it was the principle of the thing. He'd been more angry that Martin had been sniffing around her. He shook his head at his younger self and the callousness of youth.

He looked over to the deer again. To his surprise they were enveloped in fog and barely visible. It was time to swallow his pride and turn back before it got too thick to see. He turned and retraced his steps but the fog was descending quicker than he could walk. Frank sped up, his arms pumping. He could hardly see the trail now and the fog was getting thicker. He began to run. Suddenly his left foot connected with something slippery and slid forward.

His right foot went the same way and before he could stop himself, he came crashing down with a mighty thump.

He lay there for a few minutes, certain that he could see stars circling over his head like they do in cartoons. When the stars landed on his face, he realised it was just the heads of dead heather that had been disturbed by his fall. He pulled himself up to a sitting position and immediately realised that this time, his back was well and truly fucked. He reached into his rear pocket gingerly and took out his phone. Naturally there was no signal and to add insult to injury, the screen was cracked.

Frank rested his head on his knees. He really wanted to scream right now. Instead he closed his eyes and pictured Ellen noticing him for the first time at that party. She was so perfect. To look at anyway. He never did find out any more about the friend with the top hat and tails. When he got to know her better, he found she had a whole collection of oddball friends, so the need to know more about that particular one wasn't important. Besides, he'd only asked because he was too dumbstruck to think of anything else to say.

25

THE LADY RETURNS – 1981

It had been two months since the boys had visited. Martin kept asking when they could come again but Frank put them off. He was still angry with him about Eve, but the real reason was that he didn't want to risk Billy showing him up like the last time.

Adrian knocked on his door. 'Ready?'

Someone was having a birthday party at Snobs, a club in town, and everyone was invited. He had it on good authority that the Lady of Shalott was going to be there. He hadn't seen her since that party in March, but he'd found out her name was Ellen Montague. Frank took a last look at himself in the mirror. He was dressing to impress.

Adrian leaned on the door frame. 'Come on you tart, you look gorgeous.'

They positioned themselves on a walkway above the main dance floor in Snobs, along with a crowd of other fellas. Every now and then someone would shove or elbow them to get past, but they held their place because it was the best spot for watching the dance floor. They were both checking for somebody in particular. Adrian was looking for a girl on his course that he fancied his chances with, and Frank was looking for Ellen Montague.

'A Message to You Rudy' came on. Unable to resist it, they left their vantage point and went down to dance. So did half the guys on the walkway, causing the population on the floor to swell, along with the ratio of boys to girls. More 2-Tone records followed. They had everyone bouncing off each other. It made him think of the concerts he'd been to in Belfast. He thought of Eve sticking her tongue out at him and tried to imagine what it would have been like if she'd been here with him tonight. But she'd chosen Belfast over him so like it or not, she was history.

The music changed to something boring and main-stream. Adrian grabbed his sleeve. 'Let's go to the other room, see what's playing.'

The other room was playing older music. Tamla Motown. Frank recognised it from stuff his ma and da sometimes listened to.

When 'Baby Love' came on he saw her moving onto the floor, the vision that was Ellen Montague. She was with other girls. The cockney she'd been with before was nowhere to be seen. This was his chance. He turned to Adrian, but Ade was already on his way towards the girl he was after. Well then, he might as well do the same.

There were less people in this room so Ellen Montague clocked him before he got to her. She raised her eyebrows at him and watched him getting closer. Her long, slender arms opened and she wrapped them around him. He started to say one of the lines he'd been rehearsing all day, but she silenced him with a kiss. They danced, too slow for the record, but she didn't seem to care. Next came 'My Guy'. It was one of Ma's favourites. It seemed wrong somehow to be snogging to one of his mother's records, especially with a steaming hard-on, but Ma would never know.

Ellen Montague slid her hand between their bodies and held it against his dick. He felt he should apologise for the state of it but her eyes met his, and the colour of them – grey with flecks of gold – took his words away.

She leaned into his ear: 'We should do something about that.' Then she took his hand and led him off the floor and out of the club.

She pulled him into one of the taxis lined up outside. 'Let's go to yours.'

'I don't have enough money to pay for a taxi.'

She laughed. 'I do.'

All the way there, she kept rubbing his crotch. It was only the driver watching in the rear-view mirror that stopped Frank from exploding. When they got to his room he hardly had time to get his clothes off before she was on top of him. She hadn't even bothered taking off her skirt. Frank held on for as long as he could, which wasn't long.

Afterwards, they lay on his bed, him, half-naked, her, fully clothed except for her panties.

'Sorry it was so quick,' he said.

She shrugged. 'I'm amazed you managed to hold on for that long. I'm obviously not as sexy as I thought I was.'

He'd never met anyone so self-assured and confident. 'You're awful sure of yourself.'

'I am. Comes with the upbringing I'm afraid, Irishman.'

Frank laughed. 'You don't even know my name.'

She reached for her bag and produced a ready-rolled joint. 'Don't I? Do you know mine?'

'I do. Ellen Montague.'

She lit up her smoke. 'You've been doing your homework. Well so have I, Frank O'Hare. And guess what, you have a reputation. You're the boy who can't keep his dick in his trousers.' She blew smoke into his face and the smell of weed filled his nostrils.

'Is that why you jumped on me?'

'Thought I'd give you a road test before I decided.'

'Decided what?'

She smiled and handed him the joint.

Frank took a draw. 'What happened to the cockney you were with at that party?'

'Long gone, darling. Far too stupid and boring. Possessive too. The three worst crimes, in my opinion. Never, ever try to possess me, Frank. I hate being shackled.'

'I promise I'll never try to possess you. Till death us do part.' He made the sign of the cross over his heart.

She took the joint, had a long draw and then kissed him, transferring the smoke and taste into his mouth. 'Don't worry about the speed. We'll take it slower next time.'

'There's going to be a next time?'

'Oh yes. You're mine now, Frank O'Hare. I've decided.'

26

FRANK, THE CONDEMNED MAN – 1981

Ellen Montague was crazy. Crazy and completely unpredictable. One minute she couldn't get enough of Frank and the next she'd take off for days without telling him. Sometimes she could party like no other. Even Finn wouldn't have kept up with her. Other times, she'd drag Frank off to some relative's cottage in the countryside for long walks where they'd talk about the futility of life. Well, she'd talk. Frank would just make the right noises in the appropriate places.

It was the kind of craziness that Frank found irresistible. It would be easy to say it was because she was so very different to anyone he'd ever known, but there was more to it than that. At first he'd been attracted by her beauty. If he was honest, he'd always be drawn to that, but he was not so shallow that he couldn't distinguish between physical attraction and a deeper feeling. Even if he couldn't put a name to that feeling. Ellen was exotic. She was strange. She was an adventure. She was an expedition into the unknown. Other girls didn't come close to her and although she didn't seem to care if he was seeing anyone else, he had no interest in it. It could only end badly for him but Frank was falling for her.

It was obvious he was punching above his weight and she'd soon drop him, just like she'd done with the cockney. He kept reminding himself it was only ever going to be one of those encounters you remember with fondness when you're old and grey. Eventually, she'd settle down with a public school twat who played polo and every now and then, he'd recall the time he caught the attention of a high class girl who had a weakness for lower class boys. Or, as Adrian put it, a bit of rough. Frank was Ellen's bit of rough. He found that ridiculously thrilling.

It was the summer break that helped to get her out of his system a little, and put things into perspective. Frank and Adrian had spent the holiday bumming around Europe. It had given him the time and space to think about his future. Too much of his first year had been taken up with Ellen, and his end of year ratings had suffered because of it. He'd have to work harder for the next two years if he wanted to get a good job and stay in England. That was his plan now. He'd tasted too much freedom to go back home.

When the break was over, he'd been surprised to find that while he'd cooled off, Ellen had gone the other way. No more taking off. She was stuck to him like glue. It was kind of flattering, but he needed to knuckle down so he had to lay down some rules. She said he was boring but she stuck around.

Then her grandmother died, and she was in pieces. Frank was good with death. He'd seen enough of it to know how to behave. If there was one thing he'd learned from Ma, it was how to take care of the grieving. He held Ellen for hours while she cried herself out. He washed her clothes, washed her, cooked for her and made sure she ate.

On the day of the funeral, Adrian borrowed his dad's car and they drove Ellen to Surrey. She looked stunning in black, and Frank was ashamed of the stirrings in his groin. On the way to her grandmother's village, they drove along leafy lanes with cosy cottages and houses that looked like they were dripping with money. When they reached it, Ellen asked them to stop up the road from the church. 'I'll walk it from here. I'll have to go home afterwards for a few days, so don't wait.' She kissed Adrian on the cheek. 'Thank you. You're the kindest friend.'

Frank got out of the car with her. 'Are you sure you'll be all right?'

She threw her arms around him. 'I think I may be in love with you.'

He watched her striding off. There was a strange jitteriness in his chest. Did she just say she loved him? He got back in the car and caught Adrian wiping his eyes. 'What's the matter?'

'Well you know, it's sad isn't it?'

Yes it was, and yet Frank was the happiest he'd ever been.

So they were a proper couple now. Ellen had a flat she shared with two other girls, but she preferred to be in the house Frank and Adrian shared with their mates. She said it was because her flatmates were prim about sex. Ellen was not prim about sex. She loved it any which way, but most of all she liked to climb on top of Frank and ride him like he was one of her daddy's stallions. She'd only said her father kept horses, but the more Frank found out about Brigadier Hugh Montague, the more he assumed they'd be stallions. Maybe it was because he was big in the show jumping world. That was his hobby, making horses leap over poles and do silly walks, something called dressage, apparently. His job was killing people. Or at least it had been until he retired from the army. He worked the land now. That was what she called it. Somehow, Frank didn't think that meant he ploughed the fields and scattered, or milked the cows. His other assumption about the Brigadier was that he had people to do that sort of thing for him. They were loose assumptions based entirely on what Ellen had told him, but university was breaking up for Christmas and Frank was about to find out if his assumptions were correct. He was going to meet the parents.

The first shock for Frank was that someone met them at the station who was not a family member or friend. They were staff, or Ray, as he was officially called. To Frank's relief, Ray called Ellen by her first name. If he'd called her Miss, he wasn't sure his working class sensibilities would be able to stand it.

Ray was maybe in his forties. He wasn't a big man but he was muscular. He had short, neat hair. His clothes were casual but pressed. Everything about him screamed off-duty soldier. When Ellen introduced them, he nodded, his face blank. Frank did the same. They both knew how to play the game, even though they both also knew Ray had already noted every single detail about Frank as soon as he'd stepped off the train.

They got into the back of a Land Rover that was as clean and tidy as its driver. It cruised through Weybridge and out into the countryside.

Ellen wound the window down, the wind blowing her hair in Frank's face as the car picked up speed. 'Who's at home?'

'Everyone. Gavin got back yesterday,' said Ray.

'That's my darling brother,' she informed Frank. 'You'll meet them all straight away.'

'Looking forward to it,' he lied. 'Do you think they'll like me?'

She looked at him as if he was mad. 'God no. They'll hate you.'

Ray's eyes wrinkled as he glanced at them through the rear-view mirror.

If the news that he was about to be despised wasn't enough to make him crap himself, then the sight of the Montagues' farm was. It was nothing like any farm Frank had ever seen, not that he'd seen many. It was a massive mansion that was nearly as big as his old school. The entrance hall was probably the same size as his parents' house. Its walls were covered in portraits that dated back a century or two. The middle of it was dominated by an ornately carved staircase that shone so much there was light bouncing off it. This was no backwater retreat. It was practically a country seat.

Mrs Montague was waiting for them in the sitting room. She didn't embrace Ellen. She didn't even look pleased to see her. As soon as Frank spoke, her face dropped. 'You're from Northern Ireland.'

It wasn't a question, but Frank felt he should answer: 'That's correct.'

She sighed. 'Tea?'

Taking tea with Mrs Montague was a feat in itself. Before then, Frank had no idea that the task of drinking a cup of tea and eating tiny cakes could be so hellish. When they eventually escaped, Ellen showed him to his room where he found that another member of staff had not only taken up his bag, but had also unpacked it. Jesus Christ. Even Ma wouldn't have the brass to go through his private things. He hoped it was the last straw, but he had a horrible feeling there was worse to come.

Ellen pulled him onto the bed. 'Poor baby. We're disgustingly rich, aren't we? Try to let it wash over you. Maybe this will help.' She unzipped his flies and within minutes, all that mattered was that she was on top of him, riding him like one of her daddy's stallions.

They avoided the family until dinner which was being taken in the relatively smaller breakfast room as there were only four of them because Gavin, the brother, had gone out. Mr and Mrs Montague were waiting for them in the sitting room.

First sight of Mr Montague made Frank think of Eve's dad. He had that same proprietorial look about him. Maybe that was why Ellen got so het up about being possessed.

In the vain hope of making a good impression, Frank stuck out his hand. 'How do you do, sir.'

Mr Montague ignored the hand. 'Your lot killed my nephew.'

Frank looked to Ellen whose face was completely blank.

'Shall we go in to dinner?' said Mrs Montague, oblivious to the fact that her husband had just accused her daughter's boyfriend of being a murderer.

Frank gulped. He was a condemned man on the way to his last supper.

Dinner was of course, fucking awful. Not the food, that was the best he'd ever tasted. It was the company that made it so bad. Mrs Montague seemed to have decided it was best to pretend Frank didn't exist, so all her attention was on her daughter and the food, both of which she picked holes in relentlessly. Her husband, on the other hand, spent the entire dinner explaining to Frank all that was wrong with Ireland, with particular emphasis on the north.

Frank listened out of politeness, and because he was afraid the Brigadier might aim a hunting rifle at him if he dared to contradict.

The end of dinner was signalled by the Montagues standing up. The Brigadier threw down his napkin. 'Ellen. A word.'

For the first time that evening, Mrs Montague looked at Frank and added: 'In private.'

Frank left through some doors that led to a terrace and followed its steps down to the endless rolling lawn. It was dark but the clear sky was full of stars. The full moon illuminated a lake in the near distance that was surrounded by rushes and ancient trees. He carried on walking towards it. The crisp air burned his throat and nostrils but he sucked it in, glad to be away from the stifling atmosphere inside. He thought he heard an owl hooting. It was idyllic, and he had no idea what he was doing here. He should have gone home for Christmas and made his parents happy. He shouldn't have let Ellen trick him into coming here. Because she had tricked him. There was no doubt about it.

'You must be Frank.' A voice came from somewhere in the depths of a huge oak tree and made him jump. A guy who could have been Ellen's twin emerged from underneath its dark branches.

'Gavin?'

The guy took a bow. 'I am he. I take it the folks have been giving you a hard time?'

Frank liked him already. 'Correct. I appear to be on the wrong side. Although I don't believe they know which side I'm on.'

'It doesn't matter which one you're on. Both are wrong as far as they're concerned. That's why Ellen brought you here. You're her ideal man, my friend. I'd be amazed if she didn't propose to you before the end of the year.' He laughed. 'Get out while you can.'

The distant sound of a door closing made Frank look back at the house. Ellen was striding towards them.

When she reached them, she slipped her arm into Frank's. 'We're leaving in the morning.'

'That bad?' said Gavin.

She rolled her eyes. 'Don't ask. We're going to the flat. Frank, you don't mind do you?'

'Not at all.' In fact, Frank couldn't have been happier about it. 'Where is the flat?'

'London.'

The next morning Ray drove them to the station. Ellen went to the ticket office while Ray got the bags out. He held them out for Frank but didn't let go immediately. 'You're out of your depth with that one, son. You know that, don't you?'

'Go fuck yourself, Ray.' For a student of English, it wasn't his most eloquent moment but Frank had had enough of being told how shit he was. He seized the bags and walked, before he broke golden rule number one.

Her parents' flat was in Knightsbridge, and even that was bigger than his Belfast home. Frank wondered what Billy would make of it. Not that he was about to find out, because he was never going to tell him.

They spent the next two weeks living on takeaways and junk food, and making a dent in the Brigadier's extensive wine stocks. And when they tore themselves away from their bed, they visited museums and saw more art than Frank could ever imagine. Ellen could talk endlessly about almost any painting they saw and Frank drank it in, full of admiration. Her degree was in art history. It was her passion. Even though he'd taken the sensible option with an English degree, art was Frank's passion too. It might have been the only thing they had in common.

The night before they were due to return to Birmingham, she told him her grandmother had left her money to be held in trust until she was twenty-one. 'I can do what I want then. No more living by Daddy's rules. We could get married.'

Frank was speechless. It wasn't that he didn't love Ellen. Obviously, he did. It was just a shock. And the fact that Gavin had predicted it was even more of a shock.

She sat up and frowned. 'Wouldn't you like to have a rich wife?'

He found his voice at last: 'Not particularly. I'd rather just have a wife who loved me.'

Her brow wrinkled as she studied him. 'You're quite honourable aren't you? I think you may be the most decent person I know. Let's get some more wine.'

They went into the wine cellar which was actually a room behind the kitchen. Ellen picked out two dusty bottles from the shelves. 'Would you take these into the kitchen?'

Frank opened a bottle and set it down on the kitchen worktop. The sound of an almighty crash sent him running back into the cellar. Lying on the floor in front of Ellen was the shelf unit they'd just selected from. The floor was already staining red from the wine spilling out of the forty or so broken bottles scattered across it. 'What happened?' he said.

She smiled at him as if nothing was wrong. 'Just sending a message.'

27

RARE FLASHES OF INSIGHT

Just sending a message. Frank should have seen the writing on the wall there and then. Instead of concentrating on Gavin's prediction about the marriage proposal, he should have paid more heed to his other warning and got out while he could. But that moment of reckless vandalism had only made him love Ellen more. She was fighting his corner, telling her parents not to shit on her man. Or so he thought at the time. As with everything related to Ellen, the reality was more complicated than that. But at that moment, he'd adored her. He'd even helped her smash more bottles. It had felt good too. Vengeful and liberating. In those early days, being with Ellen was very liberating. If he ignored the money.

Oh the perils of having a rich wife. It never sat well with Frank. His parents weren't poor. They weren't well off either, but his dad had had a good job and he made money on the side with his decorating. None of that had prepared Frank for the kind of wealth and status of the Montagues. Not that it was thrown in his face. Old money like theirs didn't do that sort of thing. With old money, everything was implied. It was all about taste and connections. Both of which were alien to Frank. In spite of that, the money didn't get in the way, because he and Ellen compromised. She kept her wealth mostly to herself, and Frank mostly pretended it wasn't there.

If it ever did threaten to come between them, Frank remembered something Adrian had said to him after that Christmas in 1981. 'The money's not her, mate.' Simple but effective. That was Ade's speciality. That, and loyalty. Frank had lied when he told Finn no one else had gone to Ellen's funeral. Adrian had been with them. Adrian, who despite his deadpan piss-taking persona, came to say goodbye to one of his oldest and dearest friends, and cried like a baby as he did so.

Now, Frank edged himself up a little to test his back and concluded it was still fucked, although possibly not quite as much as it had been when he first collapsed into an unsightly heap, however many hours ago that was. Was it hours ago? He wasn't entirely sure. It certainly seemed like it, but time was an altogether different beast when you were wrapped in a damp fog, halfway up a mountain. In some ways it drifted along slowly and in others, it whizzed through decades, which was unfortunate because he didn't want to be back there in the past. The present was his comfort zone.

He wondered what Netta was doing now and if he'd ever see her again. Perhaps he'd die on this mountain, stuck between the woman he loved now, and the woman he loved then. Ellen would have found that hilarious, and then she would have told him what a sad old man he'd become. 'Well fuck you, Ellen. You're dead and I'm still here. How's that worked out for the both of us?'

Naturally, Ellen didn't answer, but in the distance he could hear someone calling his name. 'Over here. I'm over here,' he yelled.

'Keep shouting, so's I can find you.' It was Martin, and he was getting nearer.

'Here. I'm here. You're close.'

'I'm coming, Frank. I'm… What are you doing down there?' Martin appeared through the fog. First the top of him, like a disembodied head, then his entire self. His brother was here. His stupid, ridiculous, wonderful brother.

'I slipped. My back's gone.'

'Well aren't you the eejit? The fog's beginning to lift. We'll try and move you then.' Martin sat down next to him. 'Don't you be worrying, FB. We'll get you back. Even if I have to carry you.'

'I am an eejit, you're right. I shouldn't have stormed off like that. I'm sorry.'

One side of Martin's mouth slid into a half-grin 'Fucking hell, you apologising. That's a first.'

'Yeah well, don't let it go to your head. It won't happen again.'

'I'm sorry too. I shouldn't have gone off at you like that. I'm a bit touchy when it comes to Bronagh. We've had our moments but I really love her, you know. I will try to make it up with her. I just need some space to clear my head. Just give me this week, will you, Frank?'

'Okay.'

'So what do you think of the new Finn?'

Frank blew air out of his lips. 'He's a changed man. Was that his lady's doing?'

'Orna? I don't think so, but he's definitely upped the ante since she died. In my opinion he's gone a bit over the top with it now. Have you seen all those Buddhas in his house? That's fucking creepy.'

'He's grieving. Better meditation than drinking his liver to shit.'

Martin shrugged. 'I guess so. You'd know more about how that works. I hear you've a new woman in your life now. What's she like?'

'She's nice.'

'Nice? Is that the best you can do? Jesus, bro, where's the passion?'

'Hey, I can do passion. I'm a very passionate person.'

'Sure you are. I think the fog's lifted now. Let's make a move. Renegade and Rebel arrived after you left. It was like an oddball convention before we went out to look for you.'

He helped Frank stand and they limped along the pathway, stopping only to pick up some markers that he'd set down at different points, like a modern day equivalent of Hansel and Gretel's trail.

They managed to struggle back to the van. Rebel was the only one there. The others were still out searching. Frank was annoyed with himself for causing such a fuss, and also because he was now being eased down into a chair like some ancient ould fecker who was on his last legs, whereas Martin appeared to have turned into a latter-day Davy Crockett. He set off to retrieve the other two, leaving Rebel to tend to Frank's wounded ego.

'You look like a man who enjoys a good coffee, Frank. I have a very rich Colombian roast, if you're interested.'

Frank pushed his ego aside. 'You're correct in your assumption and right now, that Colombian roast sounds like heaven. Thank you.' He watched Rebel expertly make the coffee on his stove top. 'You've got everything you need in there.'

'I want for nothing, except the occasional bit of company.'

'How long have you been doing this?'

'About eight years, except for the dreaded Covid period. I spend the winter either at home or in sunnier climes. It's a good life.'

'Sounds it.'

'Not for you though?'

'I'm not sure I'm cut out for it. I'm comfortable where I am.' He'd said that word comfortable again. It was true, he was comfortable with his lot, but right now it didn't sound quite so palatable. 'I'm in a relationship, and I have my work.'

'I see. What do you do?'

'I'm an artist. I also teach English to college students, part time.' He surprised himself with his answer. Normally, he told people he was a teacher who did art as a sideline.

'Wonderful. I appreciate art immensely, but I'm a terrible artist. And teaching? Such a worthy profession.'

'I don't know about worthy. It's something I fell into. I met a woman recently who told me I'd taught her over fifteen years ago. Fifteen years. It makes you think.' The fact that the woman no longer thought he was "quite hot" was also making him think, but his preference was not to share those thoughts.

'It does. How's the coffee?'

Frank took a sip. 'Pretty damn good. You don't miss your old life?'

'Not one bit. Like you, the law was something I fell into. I quite enjoyed it for a long time, but then I got to a point when I realised I'd grown to detest it. It took a while for me to get there, mind you. It sort of creeps up on you. Ah, the wanderers have returned.'

. . .

Finn had Frank's back righted in no time.

'Where the hell did you learn to do that?' asked Frank.

Finn tapped his nose. 'That would be telling.'

'Our Yoda's a man of much knowledge and many talents,' said Renegade.

Finn's neck went a shade darker. 'Ah come on now guys, stop bigging me up. These two know I'm just a waster at heart. Frank's the intellectual around here, and Martin's got more talent in his little finger than I could ever have.'

'That's rubbish. I got lucky and made a few quid in property, and just because Frank's been to university doesn't make him any better than you. And you're no waster. Isn't that right, Frank?' Martin's eyebrows twitched upwards as he turned to Frank.

'Sure. Who wasn't a bit wild when we were younger? But look at you now, Finn. You've done so much, despite a terrible loss, and your life has so much meaning.' Frank was going to add against all indications to the contrary, but that would have spoiled the moment. Besides, Finn was welling up and it was triggering a rare flash of insight. Could it be that Finn had always thought himself inferior? Frank couldn't help thinking the answer was probably yes. With that came the possibility that the reason for Finn's excessive lifestyle might have been down to his need to impress their little gang. And whether he wanted to or not, Frank was forced to face the fact that he had indeed thought Finn was inferior. And because of that, he had to bear some of the responsibility for Finn's years of debauchery.

Renegade broke his train of thought. 'Here's a proposal for you. It's too late to set off for another camp now, so why don't we pool our resources and have ourselves a party?'

'Top idea. What d'you say, FB?' said Finn.

Frank smiled. 'I can't think of anything else I'd rather do.'

28

A LITTLE LIE AND A LOT OF GUILT

The first thing they did when they woke the next morning was get out of the van. The three of them had spent the night in there again and to say the atmosphere was a bit ripe was an understatement. The smell of light sweat and stale beer hung about their bodies and, once again, there had been farting. Not just Martin this time. Frank distinctly recalled a farting competition which Martin naturally won hands down. Or should that be arse down? Either way it was a good craic, something he never thought he'd say about a decidedly puerile activity that he hadn't indulged in for an exceptionally long time.

Rebel was up and looking very perky considering how much they'd had to drink last night. 'Beautiful morning.'

Frank looked up at the ice-blue sky framing the distant snow-capped mountains. It was indeed beautiful and not for the first time did he wish he'd brought his paints with him. In their absence he took photos on his sorry looking phone. 'To remind me when I get back home. I'd like to paint them,' he explained.

'No explanation needed. Now then, we have enough

food left to rustle up a rather unhealthy breakfast. What say we do that?'

Ren's side door slid open. 'I'm good with that. Fort William's close enough for a stock up.'

Rebel clapped his hands together. 'Let's get started then. Care to assist, Frank?'

'I would.' There had been a change in Frank. Nothing seismic. Nothing he could put his finger on, but it was just possible that he might be starting to enjoy this trip. Last night they'd sat around the fire talking until the early hours. Rebel, Ren and Finn had entertained them with their travel stories. Frank had taken his turn cooking on Rebel's luxury camping stove and made a one pot concoction that had received plaudits all round. When the skies cleared, they marvelled at the incalculable number of stars, and he was amazed at the contentment that was filling the soul he didn't even know was empty. This morning he felt good. Better than good. He felt alive.

'Where was that place you mentioned last night, Ren?' said Martin. 'The one with the beautiful beaches on the west coast.'

'The Ardnamurchan Peninsula. There's a good, quiet little campsite to the north of Sanna Bay. It's got the basic amenities, but that's it. The owner's a farmer. Nice lady. You can buy fresh produce from her. This time of year, you should be able to get in on spec.'

'I've been there before. It's a fine spot and it'll be grand for cleaning up,' said Finn.

Martin's face lit up. 'Sounds great. Will we go there next, lads?'

'Sure, why not,' said Frank before he realised that might be the place where Doogie lived.

·   ·   ·

After breakfast, they packed up and got ready to set off. They were going to Fort William first, for fresh supplies. Ren was going that way too before heading east. Rebel was aiming for the north.

'You don't fancy coming with us?' Frank was reluctant to see the back of them both, but it was Rebel that he knew he'd feel the loss of most.

'I've had my people fix for now. I need a few days of solitude.' Rebel shook Frank's hand. 'Goodbye, Frank. With any luck we'll bump into each other again. If not, I hope you find what you're looking for.'

'I'm not looking for anything, now that I've found Martin.'

'Ah. My mistake. Enjoy the rest of your trip.'

Frank got in the car, more puzzled than anything. He'd sensed a kindred spirit in Rebel, but he had no idea where he was going with that statement about finding what he was looking for. Still, he was a nice guy. He'd have to tell Adrian about him. Ade would find the whole trip very funny. It'd keep him going with piss-taking material for months. Now that he thought about it, he'd like to bring him up here one day. It had been a long time since they'd done anything together. Ade would probably enjoy it. Eventually. Maybe the four of them could do another trip. Him, Adrian, Finn and Martin. Although it could just as easily be five of them if Billy came too. But then, Billy wasn't likely to do that, was he?

He bought some watercolours and a pad in Fort William. Then he called Netta and told her about the adventures he'd been on since their last call, only missing out a few embarrassing details, like his fall and the farting contest.

What happens on the mountain, stays on the mountain and all that. 'We're in Fort William now. I'm strangely unnerved by its hustle and bustle, and it's not even that big.'

'That must be how Doogie feels when he comes away from his place.'

'What did you say it was called?'

'Oh, it's a funny long name. It's on the very western tip. I'd have to look it up. I can send it to you later.'

'No, don't worry. I don't suppose we'll be anywhere near it. I think we're heading back up north. Or possibly east. We haven't fully decided yet.'

'Pity. You'd like it there.'

'Well, you never know. I wouldn't rule it out,' said Frank, the guilt already stinging him for his little lie.

'Sounds like you're getting into the spirit.'

'I am. I've decided to embrace the danger.' He thought of Billy again, laughing at his idea of danger.

'Well, it's good to get out of your comfort zone sometimes.'

'You think I need to get out of my comfort zone?'

'Not just you. We all do, don't we? Otherwise life becomes a bit … you know, same old, same old?'

'Does it?'

Netta laughed. 'Frank, this is not a conversation to be having over the phone. Let's keep it for another time.'

'You're right. I'll let you go. I'd better call my sister before we head off. I love you, Netta Wilde.'

'I love you too, Frank O'Hare.'

But did she though? After all, hadn't she as good as said he was a boring git? Oh Jesus, he really needed to stop being so fecking insecure. He was a grown man, and Netta was not Ellen.

29

THE IMBECILE AND THE EXOCET MISSILE

Siobhan had all but given up on Frank, so it was a bit of a shock when his call came through. She leapt on it before he changed his mind and rang off. 'About time. I've been trying to get hold of you for days.'

'Hello to you too, Siobhan,' he said, sarcastic as ever. 'I liked your message.'

'Which one? The one about you taking the coward's way out and leaving the update about your little trip with Da, or the one about you being useless?'

'The one about the Blues Brothers. We all thought it was very witty.'

'Was that a hint of sarcasm there, Francis?'

'No. It was funny and very clever.'

Okay so that definitely was sarcasm. Siobhan closed her office door. 'Where the feck are you?'

'We're in Fort William. My phone's really crap. I've had a lot of trouble with the signal. Your messages only just came through.'

Just came through? She didn't believe that for a minute. 'Funny that you have to wait for my messages to pick up the phone. You couldn't just think of giving me a call to set my mind at rest?'

'You're right. Sorry. But you've no need to worry. Martin's fine. He's in good spirits.'

'I don't give a flying feck about Martin. It's Ma I care about. She gets herself into such a state with the worry.'

'Oh. I didn't know.' Frank sounded surprised, like he genuinely didn't know.

'Of course you didn't. How could you? How could any of you when you're never around to deal with the fallout from your little escapades?' Siobhan sighed. Sometimes it was like trying to get through to a simpleton when she spoke to Frank. For a clever man, he could be awful stupid. 'I'll tell her you're okay.'

'Thanks. By the way, Martin didn't leave Bronagh. She threw him out.'

Well, this was news. Whether it was accurate news was yet to be established. 'Did he tell you that?'

'Yes. Have you spoken to Bronagh?'

'Of course I've spoken to Bronagh. I'm everybody's fecking shoulder to cry on.'

'And she didn't tell you that?'

'No. I'll speak to her again. But it's not beyond that arse-hole to lie.'

'Bronagh?'

She tutted. 'No. Martin. Jesus, you're as bad as him. I'll call you back. Keep checking in with me. Don't cut me out, Frank. And don't let Martin out of your sight until you're sure he's on the plane home.'

'Okay. Are you all right, Siobhan? You sound a bit stressed.'

A bit stressed? A BIT STRESSED? He didn't know the half of it. 'A bit stressed doesn't even touch the sides, Frank.'

'Is there anything I can do?'

Imbecile. The man was actually an imbecile. 'Yes there's something you can do. You can get that slippery fecker back home, pronto.'

'Right you are then. I'll leave you to it.'

Siobhan stared at her phone in disbelief and not for the first time wished she was an only child.

Darcy, her PA, opened the door. 'Coffee?'

Siobhan adjusted her expression to serene but businesslike. She couldn't have the team seeing her with her demented face on, although that was getting increasingly difficult to hide lately. 'Yes please. How long before my next meeting?'

'Half an hour.'

Just enough time to try Bronagh. She waited until Darcy closed the door and got straight on the phone.

'How are yer, Bronagh?'

'I'm holding up. Have you any more news on the road trip?'

'They're in Fort William, wherever that is. Frank's just called me. He said it was you that threw Martin out. Is that right?'

'It is.'

Darcy brought in the coffee. Siobhan mouthed a thank you and waited for her to leave. 'Why didn't you tell me that in the first place?'

'I thought you'd be cross.'

'Why would I be cross with you? You're my best friend.'

'I know. I'm sorry, love. I'm just not thinking straight.'

Siobhan pinched the top of her nose. She'd known Bronagh for years. If she hadn't introduced her to Martin in the first place, none of this would be happening right now. Although calling it an introduction probably wouldn't have held water under the Trade Descriptions Act. A more accurate depiction was that Martin happened to be drinking in the same pub she and Bronagh had chosen for a night out. One look at the gorgeousness of Bronagh and he'd zoomed in on them like an Exocet missile seeking its target. All the same, Siobhan felt responsible for this mess. If only because she'd been slow in spotting Martin on that fateful night and didn't get Bronagh out of the pub before he'd had a chance to come at her, all guns blazing with the charms and the sparkling smile. She sighed. 'It's okay. Do you want to tell me why?'

'Not now. Can you come over later?'

She smiled at the prospect of an evening with Bronagh, even if it was listening to her pouring her heart out. At least it was better than sitting in your jammies and screaming at the TV. 'You bet. I'll bring a bottle.'

'Bring two. It's a long story.'

30

FRANK ASKS THE QUESTION

The place they were heading to was only about sixty miles away, but the journey involved a short ferry ride and mostly single track road that took them through scenery Frank could only describe as breathtaking. When Netta had told him about her journey to Doogie's cottage, he'd mentally sketched out the colours and the immenseness of the mountains, the sprawl of the lochs, and the vast expanse of the skies. Now that he was here, he could see he'd underestimated all of those things. Yes, it was breathtaking. No doubt about it.

By the time they reached the farm where they were staying, Frank had a strong feeling that it could be the place where Doogie lived. When he met the farmer, any remaining doubts were erased. Netta had mentioned the name before so when she introduced herself as Grace Buchanan, it was pretty cut and dry. Netta had also told him that Grace and Doogie were in a relationship. Five minutes in her company and Frank could see why. Grace Buchanan was like a horsier version of Netta, with a Scottish accent.

They got showered and changed, washed their clothes in

the rudimentary washing facilities and then walked down to the nearby beach before they lost the day. The light was already fading into mauves and purples that would soon be blue-black. Even at this time of day, the sand was a silvery white. Before Robyn was born, he and Ellen had holidayed in the Caribbean and the Far East. Paid for by Ellen, naturally. One of his compromises. They saw some of the most stunning beaches in the world. He'd never expected to see anything like them in the north-west of Scotland.

'I'm going to paint this tomorrow.'

He said it more to himself than anything. In fact, he hadn't realised he'd said it out loud until Finn replied: 'Okay. But tonight let's just make a fire and eat here. Grace said it's okay, if we make sure we put it out when we're done.'

They ate their food and looked out to the horizon without speaking. Words weren't necessary. When Martin eventually broke their silence it was almost in a whisper: 'Imagine living here.'

'Sure, you'd be bored after a month,' said Finn. 'You're too fond of the bright lights, Marty.'

Martin let out a long, contented sigh. 'Maybe. I'd be willing to give it a try though.'

Frank was thinking about Doogie, a city boy and party animal through and through, from what Netta had told him. How had he ended up in this remote place? He'd been looking out for him ever since he'd got here. Although he wasn't sure he'd recognise him if their paths did cross, since he'd only seen him once in a photo from back in the late eighties. He was hoping Doogie had aged badly.

He didn't want to kill the mood but he needed to talk about the call he'd had with Siobhan. 'I spoke to Siobhan earlier. Bronagh didn't tell her she'd thrown you out.'

'You think I'm lying?' Martin's expression was half astounded, half amused. When they'd been younger, it had been his go-to face when he was trying to bluff his way out of something. Frank hated it back then. He still hated it now.

'I didn't say that.'

Martin turned back to the horizon. 'Yep, I'd be willing to give this place a try.'

Frank was up early the next morning. He had the van to himself again and while it was nice to have the space, he kind of missed the other two. He bought some fresh eggs from the farm's honesty box and made them scrambled eggs and toast for breakfast.

'You're really getting into this,' said Finn.

'I am. I wouldn't mind doing this trip again some time.'

Finn and Martin's jaws did a collective drop. Martin was the first to recover from the shock: 'We could make it an annual trip.'

'Yeah, maybe. As long as Finn was with us to save us from disaster,' said Frank.

Martin nodded in agreement. 'Finn's the man.'

'Finn is the man.'

'Aw, you guys.' Finn put on a phoney American accent, but if they'd been in a room, he'd have been bouncing off the ceiling right now.

Martin starting singing 'I'm Waiting for the Man' with a very poor impersonation of Lou Reed.

'You know that song's about drugs, right?' said Frank.

'Yeah but you know … it seemed appropriate.'

Frank shook his head. 'As my daughter would say, it is so not appropriate. Not anymore.'

'How is wee Robyn? I heard she was in Edinburgh now,' said Finn.

'She's not so wee now. But yes, she lives there with her boyfriend. A nice fella from home.'

'Belfast?' said Martin.

Frank frowned. Belfast had never been Robyn's home. It had stopped being his home over forty years ago. 'Birmingham. I could give her your address Finn. I'm sure she'd like to look you up.'

Finn's eyes went glossy. For a minute, it looked like he was going to cry. 'I'd like that. Does she still look like Ellen?'

'Even more so.'

Martin scooped up the empty breakfast plates and threw them into the washing-up bowl. 'Her boyfriend's a lucky man then. Ellen was a beautiful woman.'

Finn caught Frank's eye. He looked like he was waiting for Frank to say or do something, but Frank wasn't ready for that conversation. He steered the subject back to the trip. 'I could drag Adrian along, if we did this again next year.'

'Adrian? Are you still in touch with that ould reprobate?' Martin laughed and Ellen was forgotten.

'I see him most weeks. What about you? Do you still see Billy Mac?' There, he'd done it. He'd asked the question that had been on his lips for days.

Martin stopped laughing. 'Not in a long time.'

'What about Eve?'

'Occasionally.'

Finn stood up. 'Right, let's get on. Frank, me and Marty are gonna go on another hike today to give you some time alone with your painting. Unless you'd rather come with us?'

'Thanks, but I'm good with the painting.'

. . .

They walked down to and along the beach together, until Frank found a good spot. He unfolded his chair next to a big boulder that would be perfect for resting his paints and water on. The dunes behind him would be good for sheltering from the wind that was blowing the sand about. There was no one else around. Martin and Finn were two distant figures now, heading further away.

Frank opened his pad and picked up a brush. So Martin still saw Eve occasionally? Interesting.

31

A STATE OF CONFLICT AND GUILT – 1982

'It's competition time.' Finn let out a loud rip. 'Beat that.'

'Ach, there's no substance to it. I'll beat you every time. You're completely useless. You can't even fart properly.' Martin let one out just to prove it. 'C'mon Frankie Boy, your turn.'

Frank tried to force one out. 'I can't. I've none left in me. You win again, Martin Thunder Arse.'

Martin started singing his favourite farting contest song, 'So You Win Again'. Errol Brown would not have been happy if he'd known his blockbuster was being used to such disgusting ends, but Frank and the boys weren't going to tell him.

Martin and Finn were here, on account of Martin getting into a spot of trouble back home. Da had managed to sweet talk them into a job at a cash and carry but Martin had messed it up by being caught red-handed with stolen goods literally down his trousers. It was decided Finn must be in on it too so they both got the boot. That was bad enough but the real trouble started because with no work they had nothing else to do but hang around the streets.

That didn't just put them on the soldiers' watch list, it also got them approached by what Ma always referred to as the wrong sort. So a month ago, they were packed off to Birmingham until Da could find them gainful employment back home.

They were supposed to be staying at Cousin Eamon's but Martin screwed that one up too by trying to get off with Cousin Eamon's youngest daughter at her seventeenth birthday party. Add to that, Finn drinking the house dry and getting himself spaced out on Eamon's wife's Valium, and Cousin Eamon had had enough. So they'd been dumped onto Frank with a promise that once they got back home, their ears would be well and truly boxed all the way from Belfast to Derry. Although why Derry was chosen as the final destination for the boxing of ears was unclear. All Frank knew was that he was under the strictest orders to keep them out of trouble until they all went home next week. It was a trip he couldn't get out of. Partly because no one trusted that pair to get home in one piece, but mainly because Siobhan was getting married. It was also the Easter break so he was going to be stuck there for the holidays.

Martin and Finn had been with Frank for almost a week, sleeping on his bedroom floor. It had been a good craic, but there was every chance that might change, because Billy was coming tomorrow and Frank couldn't be sure which way things would go. That's if he actually got here. Frank had a lecture to go to, and he was having to rely on the eejits to meet Billy at the station.

He turned over in his bed. It felt wrong sleeping in it on his own, but one of the downsides of having house guests was Ellen not being able to stay over. She was okay about it. She thought Martin and Finn were hilarious and naturally, they loved her. That was another downside, he had to keep

a good eye on Martin because from where Frank was standing, Martin was a bit too in love with her. And Frank still
wasn't one hundred per cent on whether Martin was seeing
Eve, or even if he'd made a play for her, back when she was
supposed to be his girlfriend. Basically, he didn't trust his
brother one bit, especially when it came to girlfriends. Past
and present.

Another fart ripped through the air, followed by a snigger. Frank pulled the blanket up over his nose. 'Contest's
over now, Finn. Go to sleep.'

When Frank got back from his lecture the next afternoon,
he was relieved to see the eejits had made it back safely with
Billy in tow. He was less relieved when he saw Billy with his
dirty boots up on the kitchen table. Frank had never seen
him do anything like that before, not even in his own house
when his ma was on one of her jaunts. The other thing was,
he was clearly rat-arsed. 'Here he is. Francis O'Hare,
scholar and gentleman.'

'How are yer, Billy?'

'Oh I'm grand. Martin said you've got yourself a posh
Brit girlfriend. When am I gonna meet her?'

'Later.'

'Can't wait. So where can you get a drink in this
shithole?'

When Ellen walked into the pub, every man's eyes turned
on her. Frank had grown used to it now and it didn't usually
bother him, but he hadn't expected Billy to do the same.
Billy followed her every movement until she reached their

table. His mouth hung open when she bent over Frank and kissed him.

Frank wanted to tell him to clamp it shut and stop drooling, but Billy was in a funny mood. There was every chance he'd kick off. So he said: 'Ellen, this is Billy.'

Billy waved his pint at her. 'Hiya doll. Frank didn't tell me you were such a looker.'

Ellen looked as if she'd just had the misfortune to walk in on one of their farting contests. 'Well if it's any compensation, he didn't tell me you were such a charmer either.'

Adrian raised his glass at her. 'Touché. Point to Lottie.'

Billy shot a sneer at Adrian. 'Who the fuck's Lottie? I thought your name was Ellen. Have you got two women, Frankie Boy?'

'It's a nickname, because he and Frank used to call me The Lady of Shalott. They think I look like the women in the painting. Do you know the painting? Perhaps you've heard the poem? Thought not.' Ellen grabbed Frank's arm. 'Let's go to the bar.'

'I'm sorry about Billy,' he said, as soon as they were far enough away.

'Oh forget him, I've got some news. I've been approached by a modelling agency. They want me to go to London next week. So I'll have plenty to occupy me while you're away.'

'That's great. I didn't know it was something you wanted to do.'

'I've never really thought about it, but seeing as I don't have anything else to do because you refuse to take me with you…'

'It's not safe for you to go.' They'd been through this so many times. If she came back to his streets and the Balaclavas got wind that she was an English brigadier's daughter, she'd be lucky to survive the first week. That was the truth of it. It was also a perfect excuse, because there was another truth Frank was keeping to himself. He was ashamed. Ashamed of the place he called home and the people who made that home. But he was also ashamed of her and everything she and her family stood for. He was in a state of constant conflict and guilt.

'Okay fine. I'll go to London instead. It will annoy the hell out of my parents.'

'Hmm?' Frank hadn't been listening. He'd been watching Billy having a go at Adrian. It occurred to him that the one person who brought out that conflict and guilt more than anyone else was Billy Mac.

32

A TELLING OMISSION – 1982

They were on the Liverpool to Belfast ferry. Considering he was going home, Frank was in a good mood. The weekend had gone better than expected. Once he'd settled down, Billy was less of an arsehole and when it was just the four of them, it was almost like it used to be. Another plus point was that Ellen thought he was an obnoxious fuckwit which pleased Frank no end. He'd seen Billy's look when Ellen walked into the pub, so it was good to know his lustful thoughts weren't reciprocated. Not that Billy would ever try to steal Ellen from him. That was more Martin's style. Billy had principles when it came to doing the dirty on a mate, and they were still mates.

Another reason for his good mood was that Ellen was so excited about this modelling thing she'd stopped moaning about not being able to come with him. She was always banging on about the restrictions her parents placed on her, but Frank sensed she was used to getting her own way. She'd been a pain about it for weeks. At one point, she had the kind of tantrum you'd expect from a toddler and he didn't see her for days after. But when she did return, it was as if nothing had happened. She was all kisses and cuddles again. This kind of behaviour was alien to Frank. In his house it would have gotten them a clip round the ear. Even Siobhan. There was no discrimination from Ma and Da in that regard. They were equally strict with all three of them. Well, sort of. Him and Siobhan didn't agree on much but there was one thing they were united on, Ma sometimes let things slide with Martin that neither of them would have gotten away with.

Da met them from the ferry. He patted Frank on the back. 'Your ma'll be pleased to see you, son. Do you want a lift, Billy?'

Billy threw his bag over his shoulder. 'Nah, you're okay. I'll make my own way. I'm not living near you anymore.'

Da would have known that, but he didn't say. Everybody knew everybody's business here, and Da always seemed to know more than most. Not that he ever let on. You had to watch his expression when someone told him what they thought was news. If you looked closely, you could tell his surprise was put on and that he'd probably known about it before it even happened. 'Right you are, Billy. We'll get off then.' He pointed to Martin and Finn with what they always used to call the finger of death. 'I'll deal with youse two when we get home.'

Martin winced. He was bigger than Da now, but that didn't make it any less scary. Finn gulped. His own da was long dead – one of the unfortunate innocents who happened to be in the wrong place at the wrong time – so Frank's da had become Finn's proxy da. Finn always gave the impression he was happy with the arrangement, but maybe not today.

Frank sat in the front while the other two quivered in the back. Martin was in trouble and for once, Frank couldn't be blamed. It was wrong to be pleased about it, but he couldn't help himself.

Ma was too busy raging to express her delight at Frank's return. She was in no mood to let Martin's indiscretions slide this time. As soon as the front door closed, Da had Martin by the scruff of his neck and was battering the hell out of him. Finn's ma was slapping him around the head with a rolled up newspaper, screaming about him being a waste of space. Determined not to be outdone, Ma added they were both a waste of space. Frank watched the theatrics with a warm glow. Maybe being home wasn't so bad after all.

'Frank's got a posh Brit girlfriend,' yelped Martin, on receipt of a spectacularly hard whack.

The battering stopped. The screeching stopped. Ma and Finn's ma turned to face Frank, their mouths wide open. Martin was triumphant. The bastard had saved his own skin by throwing Frank under a bus.

Ma folded her arms. 'Is this true, Francis?'

Frank cleared his throat. 'Aye.'

'How long have you been seeing her?'

'About a year.'

'A year, and this is the first we hear of it. This is how we hear of it. From your brother, who only spilled the beans because he thought it would get him out of trouble.' Her head swivelled round to Martin like an owl. 'Which it has not, by the way.'

'It's complicated.' He'd have liked to have left it there but Ma was having none of it. The look of fury on her made that quite clear. 'Her dad's a brigadier.'

Ma clasped her throat. 'A bri…'

'She's awful nice though.' Finn got another slap around the head for his trouble.

Ma dropped down on the nearest chair. 'This can't get out, d'you hear me? This must not get out.'

The front door opened and Siobhan came in. She took one look at Ma. 'What's happened?'

When Frank came down in the morning, Da was reading the paper in his armchair. He'd taken the week off work to ferry Siobhan and Ma about in the build up to the wedding, and to stop Ma exploding with the nerves of it all. On top of that he was decorating Siobhan's new home. Dermot, Siobhan's fiancé was rubbish at that sort of thing apparently.

Da looked up from his paper. 'Do you fancy giving me a hand finishing off at Siobhan's?'

'Sure. I've nothing else planned.'

'Good man, we'll get the place shipshape in no time.'

Frank stepped into the little hall of Siobhan and Dermot's new house. The smell of fresh paint and paper hit him straight away. Unlike some people, he loved that smell. It spoke to him of hours spent with Da, just the two of them, making something new out of something old.

Da pushed the living room door to fully open. 'We've only this room to finish papering. Get a brew on and I'll get started.'

They worked for a few hours and stopped to eat the sandwiches they'd brought with them. Frank made more tea and they sat in the kitchen, the only room with any furniture.

'Are you fond of this girl of yours, Francis? Is she a keeper?' said Da.

'Aye, I am. I think she is. Her parents don't like me though.'

'Did he serve over here, this brigadier?'

Frank nodded. Best not to dwell on Brigadier Montague's thoughts on Ireland.

'You'll not be bringing her over here anytime soon then. We'll have to come over to you if we're to meet her.' Da chewed on his sandwich, cheese and enough onion to blow your mouth off. Just the way he liked it. 'So you're over the other one then?'

'Yes. I haven't seen her since Billy got taken. I heard she stayed over here.'

Da nodded and took another bite on his sandwich. No feigned surprise this time but Da knew where Eve was now. Frank was certain of it. He definitely knew.

They finished up in the late afternoon. Da had done a great job on getting the house ready for the newly-weds. They packed up the tools and took a last look around. It was a nice house, with enough room for Dermot, Siobhan and a couple of kids.

Da closed the front door. 'Well, we've done all we can to get them off to a good start. The rest is up to them.' It was another thing that didn't get discussed, but Martin had told him he'd overheard the parents talking about Dermot. In their opinion, Siobhan was making a mistake.

Frank got into the car. 'Da, how come you never went into decorating full-time?'

'If I did that, what would I do for a hobby?' Da switched on the engine and the radio started up. They listened to it until the news came on and he switched over to Van Morrison on the cassette player. Da had a rule about the news. He had two designated news slots in his day. Six o'clock and ten o'clock. The rest of the day he kept news free.

When they got in, Siobhan and Ma were at the kitchen table, surrounded by papers. Ma glanced up at them 'We're just going over the final guest list and seating plan. Are you all done now?'

'Aye, all finished. It's like a little palace in there now, so it is.' Da dropped Siobhan's house keys on the table. 'There you are, love. All yours.'

Siobhan hugged him. 'Daddy you're a lifesaver. That's the best wedding present ever.'

'That and your brand new bed,' Martin called out from the living room.

'Shut up, Martin,' shouted Ma, Da and Siobhan. He was still very much in the doghouse.

Frank picked up the guest list. 'Let's take a look.'

'We're keeping it small and low key. Just family and close friends.' Siobhan was on the defensive. She didn't need to be. Frank got it. Small and low key was the same as keep a low profile, stay under the radar, stay out of trouble.

There was however one glaring omission that Frank didn't get. 'Billy Mac's not on the list.'

Siobhan snatched the paper away. 'He's your friend, not mine. Anyway, he's too high profile.'

'What do you mean?'

'You know why. His girlfriend.' She looked at Da, then back at Frank. 'Has nobody told you? Oh, for... He's living with your ex.'

'Eve.' Martin was in the doorway now. 'He's living with Eve.'

Frank pushed him out of the way and went through the

front door. Martin followed him out onto the street. 'Frank, wait.'

He grabbed Martin's shirt. 'You knew and you didn't tell me. You let me think it was you.'

'I wanted to. I just–'

'Wanted to make me look like a wanker.'

Martin shook his head.

Frank let go of him. 'Just give me the address, then fuck off out of my face.'

The house was on a street where only certain people lived, those that were living in sin, and those that had committed the even greater sin of marrying someone from the other side. Billy, being the product of a mixed marriage himself, had lived on a similar street to this before his ould man left. He was used to being an outsider, so it held no fear for him. It would be a new thing for Eve though.

She answered the door to him. Her hair was longer and the black eye make-up she always wore had been replaced by bright blue. She had tight jeans on and a big red jumper that hung off one shoulder. She looked so delicate. He'd gotten used to Ellen who was like an Amazonian compared to this tiny creature.

'Billy's not here,' she said.

Frank was irritated that she hadn't started with hello, or an apology for not keeping her promise about university. An apology for hooking up with Billy would have been nice too, but that was obviously too much to expect. 'How are yer, Eve?' He was going to take the moral high ground, even if she wasn't.

'I'm great. You?'

'Sure, I'm great too.'

'Moving on, I hear.'

'You too, it seems.'

She shrugged. 'Well, you know how it is.'

No, he didn't, but he didn't care anymore. He had Ellen and she was more than enough for him. He was only here because he wanted Billy to know he knew. He wanted to look Billy in the face and tell him he was a sneaky fucker of the highest order.

33

FACE TO FACE WITH A FRIENDLY FOE

Frank was in full flow now. Watercolour wasn't his favourite medium. He preferred the thickness and density of oils, or the speed of acrylic. But needs must, and he was pleased with the results. They were only sketches anyway. When he got home, he'd paint them in big bold canvases. The bigger the better.

He checked the time. Somehow he'd lost a couple of hours. Normally he'd blame it on the painting, but not this time. This time it was the past he'd got lost in. He was doing that a lot lately.

He never did hang around and wait for Billy to come home that day. He didn't ask Eve why she hadn't come to Birmingham, and she didn't offer an explanation. But after that, Billy stopped coming over with Martin and Finn. It was a relief. He could stop pretending that he didn't prefer Adrian's company, and he could stop pretending that he was ever going to move back to Belfast.

Ellen had still been away when he'd got back after that visit, but he didn't know that until he'd called at hers and her flatmates told him. These were the days before mobile phones made everything visible. He'd tried her parents' London flat from a phone box three or four times, but no one had picked up. So he'd waited. Two weeks later, she'd turned up on his doorstep, looking tanned and even more beautiful. She'd been on a photo shoot in Tunisia for a magazine, and she was still high on it. By then, she'd decided modelling would be her future. She carried on doing her degree but it took second place behind modelling. Everything took second place behind modelling, including him. But that was okay with him because the absence of all the Ellen and Billy distractions, had allowed Frank to carve out a life for himself in Birmingham. And anyway, he'd always expected her to tire of him. Even now, he never really understood what she saw in him.

That time was the start of him taking painting seriously, thanks to a girlfriend of Adrian's who got him interested in an art club. Next came a debating society. Finally, against all that he'd been taught about not sticking his head above the parapet, he became active in the students' union. He even broke golden rule number one and got arrested for protesting. He got off with a caution. Strangely, that reignited Ellen's passion for him. Although in hindsight, not so strange at all. Ellen did love a rebel. It was boring gits she couldn't stand.

A piece of driftwood landed on Frank's foot and pulled him out of his brooding. Sitting over it was a long, lean dog with a wiry coat. A lurcher, if he wasn't mistaken. The dog whined, picked up the wood and dropped it back on Frank's foot again.

'I suppose, you want me to throw this?'

The dog whined again.

Frank stood up and tossed the wood towards the sea. The dog went hurtling after it at a speed only greyhounds could match. He was back in less than a minute. Frank threw it again, a bit further this time. He wondered how Fred was getting on and whether he was missing him. Did dogs miss their owners? From the corner of his eye, he caught sight of a runner. A tall, slim black man was coming his way. Shit.

Still running, Doogie Chambers whistled and the dog came to his side. God, they looked good together, this long, lean man and his long, lean dog. The bastard had aged well. Doogie was the same age as Netta, so he was about five years younger than Frank, but Frank felt much, much older.

'Sorry mate, Spike gets a bit over-friendly sometimes.' Doogie was barely out of breath.

Frank patted the dog's head. 'No problem. He's a fine looking fella.'

'Yeah. Good company too.' Netta had said Doogie was originally from Nottingham and he still had the accent.

'I suppose it gets a bit quiet here.'

'We manage. You staying at the farm?'

'Yeah.'

Doogie nodded. 'Grace said she'd had some new visitors. I'll leave you to your painting. I'm just up the road a bit if you need anything. Come on, Spike.'

'That's good of you. Cheers.' Dammit. He was a nice guy. Frank was hoping he'd be a shit, like Netta's ex-husband.

He sat back down, deflated and no longer in the mood for painting, but then he noticed the sky had changed colour again and with it, the sea too. He had to get this down. He wasn't normally one for the outdoor painting, but then again he wasn't normally one for stalking his partner's former lovers. So there you go. Things change.

The woman he'd met in the park popped into his head.

The one who thought he'd once been slightly better than average looking. He'd taught her fifteen years ago. Christ. And this was the thing. That was only halfway through a thirty year stint. Dedication, she'd had called it. Frank wasn't sure what he'd call it, but it wasn't dedication. He remembered how he'd reversed his roles when he told Rebel what he did. Artist first, then teacher. Maybe there was something in that. Then again, he'd been juggling the two for a while now. Perhaps it was time to let one of them go. But what if he hated the choice he made? He recalled Da's answer when he'd asked why he didn't become a full-time decorator. 'What would I do for a hobby?' Was that why he'd stuck with teaching? Because it certainly wasn't for the love of it. Like Rebel, he'd enjoyed it at first, then it became convenient, then it became something to get out of the house for. Then it became, what? Something else he was too comfortable to change.

'There you are.' Martin appeared from the dunes behind him. 'I like your paintings there.'

'They're only sketches. I'll do them properly when I get home. I've an exhibition coming up in the autumn they'd fit into.'

Martin looked surprised. 'An exhibition? I had no idea you were that good.'

Frank shrugged. 'I do all right. Funny thing, I've been thinking about Da. Did he ever get you to help him with his decorating?'

'Nah. That was your thing, the two of you. He never asked me. Not even after you left. Ironic really, seeing as you don't have a practical bone in your body and I'm the one's made the money from doing up properties.'

'I'm insulted that you think I'm impractical, Martin, but

I take your point. What did you do with Da then? What was your thing?'

'Nothing. We didn't have a thing. It was always about you with Da.'

'That's not true. I never saw it that way anyway.'

'That's the trouble with you, Frankie Boy. You only see the things you want to see. The rest is just background.'

34

ADRIAN JOINS THE DOTS

There was a man at Frank's front door. Netta probably wouldn't have noticed if she hadn't decided to put the bins out. It had been an inadvisable decision because it was raining much harder than she'd realised and now she was getting wet. She couldn't see the man properly. The rain was in her eyes for one thing and, for another, he was wearing a waterproof coat with the hood pulled down. All she could tell was that he was a big man.

The man turned and saw her. 'You must be really desperate to get those bins out.'

Netta wiped the rain from her eyes. 'I didn't notice how bad it was until… Adrian, is that you under there?'

He raised his hood slightly. 'Yeah. Do you know where he is?'

She gestured towards her house. 'You'd better come in.'

The dogs started barking as soon as he stepped inside. He shook off his wet coat and hung it in the hall. 'All right you lot, I'm harmless.'

Fred began to whine. Adrian bent down and patted him. 'Hello, mate. What you doing here then? Where's Frank?'

'I'll just get these wet things off, then I'll make us a warm drink,' said Netta.

Adrian went off in the direction of the kitchen. 'Righto, I'll put the kettle on.'

When she got back downstairs, she found he'd made tea. It was a bit disconcerting because she normally only ever saw him in the Hope and Anchor, Frank's favourite pub.

'You've got it nice in here,' he said. 'You haven't changed it much but you've freshened it up a bit. It's good.'

'You've been in here before then?'

'Yeah, but not since you moved in, obviously. Anyway. Frank? Has something happened? It's just that he didn't turn up for a darts match, or our usual monthly get-together. I tried calling him and there was no answer, so I thought I'd come over.'

'He had to go up to Scotland for a family emergency.'

'Shit. Is Robyn okay?'

'She's fine. It's his brother.'

'Martin?'

'You know Martin?'

'I do. I know them all.'

'All?'

'Martin, Finn, Billy Mac.'

Billy Mac. Where had she heard that name before?

Adrian's brow furrowed. 'Haven't seen the lads in a while though. Must be … ooh, 2007? Around that time anyway.'

2007? Just how long had Frank known Adrian? She knew they were friends and Frank had been going to Adrian's pub for a long time, but neither of them had ever said how far back they went. 'I didn't realise you'd been friends that long.'

Adrian laughed. 'That long? Net, we've been mates

since university. Met on the first day. Has he never told you?
I'll have him about that when I see him.'

'Oh he probably did and I just forgot. So you would
have known Ellen then?'

'Yeah. She was a good friend. She was bonkers but, you
know.' He looked down at his mug of tea. 'Anyway, what's
this family emergency? What's Martin been up to this time?'

Adrian had stayed for an hour during which time he'd told
Netta more about him and Frank in their university years.
She couldn't believe Frank hadn't told her they'd known
each other that long. The other thing he hadn't mentioned
was that Adrian and Ellen had been great friends. Again,
why not? Surely he didn't think it would trouble her. It
wouldn't have, but she was troubled now because she
thought she knew everything she needed to know about
Frank O'Hare, when she clearly didn't. What's more, she
was beginning to wonder how much Frank thought he knew
about her, if he really thought she'd be jealous of his oldest
friend and his dead wife. Because that was the only reason
she could think of for his silence on the matter.

She let herself into Frank's house. Adrian had also given
her a few more details on Martin and Finn and the other
person who, so far, hadn't appeared on the scene. Billy Mac.
Apparently he'd been Frank's best friend in Belfast and a bit
of a wanker, in Adrian's opinion. That was when Netta
remembered why the name was familiar. It had been on the
fanzine she'd found in the record sleeve the last time she was
in here. She pulled it back out of the sleeve and took it
home to read properly.

When she got in, she tapped out a message to Frank,
read it, deleted it, and tapped out another. By the fourth

attempt, she was reasonably happy that she'd written something that didn't make her sound annoyed, hurt, or accusing:

'*Hi. Just to let you know, Adrian came round. I filled him in on your trip. He mentioned he'd known you since uni. I didn't realise. How lovely to have been such great mates for so long. All's well here. Fred's okay xx*'

Message sent, she stretched out on the sofa, surrounded by dogs and began to read *Can.*

She read it from cover to cover, twice, and concluded the article by Ana Manic was by far the best. Whoever she was, she had a way with words that really brought the experience to life. Frank had once told Netta he'd seen the Undertones in Belfast. Perhaps he'd been at the Battle of the Bands too. Perhaps he'd been there with Ana Manic, or Billy Mac. Or both.

So now she knew who Billy Mac was. The dots were beginning to join up. But the other two were still a mystery. Netta had a feeling FB might be Frank, although she didn't know what the B stood for. But who was Ana Manic? She'd only know that if she asked Frank, and she wasn't sure she wanted to admit she'd been snooping around in his personal things.

She flicked on the TV and wasted a few minutes channel surfing, quickly coming to the conclusion that there was nothing worth watching. She was bored. Late at night kind of bored, when you were too tired to do anything productive but not tired enough to sleep. She should have been snuggling up to Frank right now, or maybe doing the Sunday night quiz with him at the Hope and Anchor, not moping about and feeling sorry for herself. And certainly not worrying that Frank might not be the person she thought he was. In her heart, she knew he wasn't the secretive sort. If he'd neglected to tell her things, it was probably because he'd either forgotten or it wasn't important. Unless. Unless it was something he preferred not to remember. No. Not Frank. Not solid, dependable Frank. She was being silly.

Netta hauled herself off the sofa and let the dogs out for a final toilet trip before locking up for the night. Maud curled up in her usual armchair and the two younger dogs sprawled across the floor, their long legs criss-crossing each other.

'Just staying down here then, are you? Nobody wants to join me upstairs?'

Maud ignored her. At least Betty and Fred had the good grace to look guilty.

'Right. Just me then. All on my own in that big bed.'

They weren't moving. Netta gave up and switched off the light. Even the dogs didn't want her company.

An hour later she was still tossing and turning, unable to get Frank out of her mind. She knew the only thing that might settle her was to speak to him. It wasn't quite midnight. Late, but worth a try.

It went straight to voicemail. She put on her cheeriest voice and tried not to sound too desperate. 'Only me. I was just lying in bed thinking of you. I suppose you'll be on road trip day five when you pick this up. Or maybe day six. You really must get a better phone. Anyway, sleep tight, my love. I miss you.'

She lay back down and closed her eyes, but her head was too full of names that a week ago, she'd never heard of. And she couldn't stop wondering why.

35

THAT'S WHERE SOFTNESS GETS YOU

After yet another unsuccessful attempt to get hold of Frank, Siobhan tapped out a message to let him know she'd talked to Bronagh about their wayward brother. Although talked was putting it mildly. Yes, there had been some talking, along with some crying and a hell of a lot of drinking. It was a good job Martin was in another country, because if he wasn't, he'd be screaming for Ma to come and protect him, absolute shite that he was. And no doubt Ma would come to his rescue. She was always soft on him. Maybe one day, Siobhan would tell her that. Maybe one day she'd say: 'Look where all that softness got him. Look where it's got us, running around after him like he was still a helpless kid.' But no. She wouldn't say any such thing. Ma already knew she was guilty of turning the odd blind eye when it came to Martin. Why else would she have them all making such an effort to save his marriage? The woman was covering her tracks.

Bronagh was the other reason too, of course. Ma knew, as much as any of them, that it was Bronagh who kept Martin grounded. But that was only the half of it. The

parents were always going on about how Martin had done
so well with his business, but that was all down to Bronagh.
If it wasn't for her, Da would still be looking for favours
from old friends to give Martin another job to screw up.
Bronagh had saved Martin, and she'd also saved them all a
lot of stress. No wonder Martin had run for the hills when
she dumped him. No wonder Ma was half mad with worry.
That's where softness gets you, Ma. In the end, it bites back.

She stretched out on the sofa and rubbed her sick stomach. She felt ill. More than ill. Wrecked was what she was.
Absolutely wrecked. There was a time when she and
Bronagh could down a few bottles of wine, dance the night
away and still get up early next morning to take the kids to
football, ballet practice or whatever the fuck it was they had
on. Happy days. Happy, happy days. She'd kill for those
days again.

It was late. She should go to bed, but she had papers to
read for work and no appetite to read them.

Her phone went. She snatched it up quick in case it was
Frank. It wasn't. It was a name and number she hadn't seen
in a few years. What could he want?

'Hello, is that Siobhan?'

'Adrian? It's been a while.' She tried to remember the
last time they'd spoken. Probably five or six years ago. After
Ellen died, they'd had quite a few secret calls about Frank.

'Yeah. I kept your number from when you used to ring
me before. In case of emergencies. I hope you don't mind.'

'Not at all. Is there an emergency?'

'I don't know really. I feel a bit daft calling, all panicky
like, but it's Frank. Did you know he's gone to see Martin
and Finn?'

Adrian in a panic? She couldn't imagine it. He was so
laid back, he was practically horizontal. 'In Scotland, yes.

We sent him there. Martin's run off. Frank's gone to get him back.'

'So I heard. So Frank's okay with it, is he?'

'Not exactly okay, but needs must.'

'It's just that I only found out about it today from Netta. I thought he might have let me know he was going.'

'Netta? You know Netta? How well?'

'Well enough.'

'What's she like?'

'Great.'

Great? What kind of an answer was that? Typical man. 'Great can mean anything, Adrian.'

'Okay. She's lovely.'

'Lovely as in not like Ellen?'

'Nothing like Ellen.' She could tell he was smiling. Adrian had the kind of voice that reflected exactly what was going on with his mouth. 'Netta's just what he needed. She's brought him out of himself. You'd like her. You'd get on well.'

'Would we now? I think I'll be the judge of that.'

He laughed. 'Same old Siobhan. You should relax and let go a bit, you know. The world won't end tomorrow if you do.'

And he was the same old Adrian. Siobhan felt herself soften. 'Less of the old, Mister. And don't be so bloody cheeky. I'm relaxed as fuck.'

'Yeah, I bet. So he's all right then, Frank? I don't have to do an emergency dash up north with a defibrillator and a therapist?'

'I think you're good there, but it's nice that you care.'

'Well you know, we'd be a man down in the darts team if he croaked it. He's a bit crap at darts to be honest but he makes up the numbers. And what about you, are you all right?'

Inexplicably, Siobhan's bottom lip began to tremble. 'Oh I'm fine. You know me. Bulletproof.'

'You sure? You're not letting things get on top of you, are you?'

What was that on her face? Bollocks, it was tears. She was crying. 'Of course not. I have to go. I've a pile of work to do. Thanks for calling, Adrian. It was nice speaking to you again.'

Siobhan cut the call before she made a prat of herself. That's where softness gets you. In the end, it bites back.

36

THE CALL OF THE SEA

Frank had set his alarm to five-thirty to catch the sunrise. He slid the van's side door open as quietly as he could, aware of how much noise carried in a place like this, at a time like this. Seeming to have got away without disturbing anyone, he crept out of the campsite, wincing at every step's crunch on the gravel path.

The farmhouse's lights were on. Grace was up early too. Farmers had no choice, he supposed. A man's shape appeared on the other side of a frosted window. Not just any man but the man himself, Doogie Chambers. He must have stayed the night. Frank wondered whose face Doogie saw when he was in the throes of passion. Did he think of Netta or Grace as he reached his climax? Did he lie with Grace Buchanan in his arms and imagine he was with Netta Wilde? Frank wouldn't blame him if he did. Not that he'd ever done that. Not with Netta anyway. Come to think of it, who did Netta imagine she was making love to when she was with him? Was it the knackered old git with a dodgy back and a tendency to err on the side of the status quo? Or was it the all-round nice guy with the rock star looks who liked to plough his own furrow? He shook himself out of his stupidity with a slap on the side of his head 'Will you catch yourself on? What is wrong with you?'

The violet sky above had turned bluish by the time he got to the beach. Clouds, the colour of molten lava, hung over the horizon. Then, suddenly, a burst of white light broke them.

Frank worked quickly to capture it before it went. The faster he painted, the more his heart raced. Butterflies left a flight trail across his stomach and up into his chest. There was a momentary feeling of panic when he thought he might be having a heart attack. Then he realised it wasn't that at all. It was just something he hadn't experienced in years. Excitement. He laughed out loud. He'd finally rediscovered excitement. How about that?

The Battle of the Bands sprung to mind. The euphoria he'd felt that night, that they'd all felt. The feeling that they were part of something bigger than them, bigger than their little gang. Bigger even than the shit lives they'd carved out for themselves in those precarious times. For one night only, the future was theirs, and it had been exhilarating.

He carried on working at speed until the day was fully awake and the sun was a lemon orb in a baby blue sky. White foam crested the crashing waves and slid onto the empty beach. The sea was taunting him. It was calling to him. It was inviting him in.

Frank checked this way and that. He was completely alone. To hell with it, he was going in. He undressed down to his underpants and ran. The sun had no depth at this time of the year and the cold wind tore at his bare skin but it didn't slow him down. Fuck Doogie Chambers with his super-fit physique, Frank could run too. In fact, he was unstoppable.

He hurtled forward into the sea, roaring like a raging bull and carried on until he was up to his neck in it and the full realisation of what he'd done hit him. 'Oh Jesus. Oh fuck.' It was freezing. Beyond freezing, if there was such a thing. It was… It was … fucking unbearable. That's what it was. Every inch of him was screaming to get out, but Frank refused to give in. He had to do this one thing.

He held on a little longer, till he began to lose feeling in his hands and feet. Panting and gasping, he dragged himself out. The wind hit twice as hard this time. It was like being shot at by a thousand tiny nail guns, but Frank was victorious. He'd proved something to himself and that was all that mattered.

A while later, a little dryer and warmer, Frank climbed up the winding path through the sand dunes to the road. To reach the farm, he needed to go left but he turned right towards a cottage he'd spotted yesterday. Netta had stayed in a cottage she'd hired from Grace when came here to visit Doogie, a few years ago, and he guessed it was the same place. He knew there was no one staying there at the moment, and he remembered Netta saying there was a spot in the front garden where you could get a signal.

He wandered around the small garden, holding his phone out. When he came to a table and chairs the signal miraculously appeared. He sat down and waited to see if he had any messages. He'd had two missed calls. One from Netta and one from Siobhan. He thought about calling Netta but it was still early and anyway, he wasn't sure what he'd say if she asked where he was. While he was deliberating on this, a message popped up from Siobhan:

'Spoken to Bronagh. Call me.'

If it was too early to call Netta, it was definitely too early to call Siobhan. He'd leave it for later when he had more stomach for one of her rants.

Another message came through. This one was from Netta, telling him Adrian had called round. Shit. He'd forgotten to let Ade know he'd had to go away. He must have been worried if he'd come to the house. Ade was a good friend. The best. Frank would have to square it with him when he got back. Especially if he wanted to get him up here next year.

He rang voicemail to pick up the message Netta had left for him and replayed it a couple of times. It could have been rediscovering excitement, or his leap into the water, or even hearing her voice and those words, *I miss you*. Whatever it was, the emotion was filling him up and before he could stop it, it was flowing from him.

When he pulled himself together, he took a slow walk along the beach. Netta missed him. She loved him, not Doogie. Him. He had to keep reminding himself of that and stop all this comparing nonsense. That said. He needed to do something about his fitness. He made a mental note to talk to Finn about it, although not when Martin was around. He'd only take the piss, like he did when Frank had said Netta was nice. Okay, so it wasn't passionate, but Frank could be passionate. Couldn't he? Look at this morning with the painting, and the thing in the water. That was passion. Or was it? Did he really know what passion was these days? No, he didn't think he did. He made a second mental note, work on exuding more passion, particularly when it came to Nettta. Not teaching though. He'd pretty much wrung out as much passion as he could in that regard. Mental note number three, make a decision about work.

He went past the spot where he'd been painting yesterday, the spot where Martin had dropped the bombshell that Da was only interested in him. The more Frank thought about it, the more he realised Martin was right about the decorating. It was Da's way of bonding with him. But why him and not Martin? Frank had been racking his brains to find examples to disprove Martin's theory and he couldn't think of a single thing.

Martin's second bombshell, that he only saw what he wanted to see, was also bothering him. Typically, Martin had refused to be drawn into further discussion on it. Taking a leaf out of Bronagh's book, he told Frank to work it out for himself. It was more of his bullshit, obviously. It had to be.

37

THE LADY OF SHALOTT COMES TO LIFE – 1983

Ellen pulled Frank down onto their new sofa, in their new flat. 'Happy?'

'Ecstatic.' Frank kissed her in the hope it would distract her from his inner turmoil. He was in one of those compromise situations he was rapidly becoming used to. The flat was nice enough. Very nice, without being too grand. Ellen had spared him that much. The problem was, he'd made no contribution to it whatsoever. He was fresh out of university with no job, whereas she'd come into her inheritance and had more money than he could ever dream of. On top of that, her modelling career was taking off. Frank wasn't one of those Neanderthals who thought he had to be the provider, but there was a doctrine deeply ingrained in him that it was a man's job to be one, and he struggled to ignore it.

They were in London now, in Chelsea. Ellen wanted to be close to where her work was and London was easiest for jetting off to international destinations. Since Frank was unemployed, he could hardly argue with his soon-to-be wife. Very soon, in fact. The wedding was tomorrow. He still couldn't work out how that had come about. Ellen had been the driving force behind it, not him. He hadn't so much proposed as been led into agreeing it was about time.

His family was on their way over from Belfast. Billy and Eve weren't invited. He hadn't seen either of them since he'd found out they were a couple. Adrian was his best man. He'd stayed on in Birmingham and was training to be a teacher now.

Ma and Da had come over to meet Ellen last year and their verdict hadn't been damning which was the best he could hope for. It had been left to Ma to give the final judgement. Da probably knew better than to venture an opinion when a joint conclusion was required. 'She seems like a nice girl. You'll have beautiful children.'

Ellen's parents had refused to attend. Gavin was going to give her away. If the lack of family on her side bothered Ellen, she didn't show it. If anything, she seemed happy that they weren't coming. She filled any gaps with her odd and glamorous friends from the modelling world and old school friends who were mostly Sloanes and Hooray Henrys. It was going to be a very bizarre wedding party.

Outside, Gavin buzzed the intercom. He was here to pick Ellen up. She was staying at his tonight. They carried her bags out to meet him. Gavin made some joke about how much she was bringing with her then turned to Frank and said: 'It's not too late to run for the hills you know.'

Frank laughed to give the impression he found it funny. He liked Gavin but his constant attempts to get Frank "off the hook" were beginning to grate. At the stag night, even Adrian who was really easy going had had enough. He'd taken Gavin off to a quiet corner and had a word. Frank didn't ask what the word was. It was enough that Gavin got the message. And yet here he was again, with the same tired old joke.

Ellen opened the passenger door. 'Shut up, Gavin. You'll give him ideas.' She was smiling, but then she walked back to Frank. 'You will be there, won't you? You won't leave me.'

He let out another laugh, then realised she wasn't joking. 'Say it, Frank. Say you won't leave me.'

'Of course I won't leave you. I'll be there.'

She threw her arms around him. 'I love you so much. You're my anchor. I don't know what I'd do without you. Whatever happens with us, I want you to remember that.'

Frank waited, confused and mildly turned on, while she got in the car. Gavin closed the door behind her and mouthed: 'Last chance' at him.

He mouthed: 'Fuck off' in return.

Ironically, it was Frank who thought he was going to be left at the altar in the end. Ellen was more than fashionably late. She was so late, the registrar was beginning to look at his watch. Then, just as Frank was about to give up, she made her entrance. Her white dress looked medieval with its long pointed sleeves and gold braiding. Her only other adornment was a simple floral wreath in her hair which hung loosely down to her waist. The Lady of Shalott had come to life. There was a collective intake of breath as everyone took in the radiance of her. She walked past them all, their faces awestruck, then she turned her huge grey-gold eyes on Frank. She was ethereal. She was exquisite. She was also high as a kite.

Amazingly, they got through the ceremony without incident. How Ellen had been able to speak her lines, let alone remember them, was a mystery, but she did. As they stood outside the register office posing for photographs he leaned in and whispered: 'What have you taken?'

'Just something to calm my nerves. I've still got some if you want it.'

'No, I do not want it. My parents are here.'

'When you're ready,' said the photographer. He was a friend of Ellen's, a fashion photographer who was doing her a favour. 'Look into each other's eyes. You've just got married for Christ's sake. Let's have some romance.'

Ellen was the life and soul of the wedding party, and why wouldn't she be? Her performance was enhanced. Frank had to rely on his natural charm and charisma to get him through, and it was currently in short supply.

Somebody whose charm and charisma was even more sparse was Siobhan. She was never one for a happy disposition but for once, she had reason to be pissed off. She was heavily pregnant, too tired to move, and couldn't have a drink. Whereas Dermot, her husband, had no such constraints. He was having a great go at drinking the bar dry and dancing with as many beautiful girls as would accept him.

Frank sat down next to her. He felt unusually sorry for her but also, it was a good place to watch Ellen and Martin who were dancing together. He still didn't trust Martin. 'How are yer, Siobhan?'

Siobhan yawned. 'Tired, bored and fat, since you ask. Where's Billy Mac? After the fuss you made at my wedding, I thought he'd be the guest of honour.'

'We've lost touch.'

'Really? I heard they were living here now.'

'England?'

'London. So, you've fallen on your feet here. She must be worth a few bob. That brother of hers sounds like he's got a gob full of plums.' Trust Siobhan to notice the money. And trust her to mention it.

'I've told her to keep it to herself.'

'Oh I see. So it's your money's paying for that fancy flat, is it? Jeez, the dole's a good craic over here, so it is.'

'Obviously, I've had to make some compromises on that. Until I get a job.'

Siobhan snorted. 'Good for you. Glad to see you're sticking to your principles there, Francis.'

'And how's married life working out for you, Siobhan?'

That wiped the smile of her face. 'Pretty shite actually. But at least my husband's not a drug addict.'

'You don't know what you're talking about.'

'Probably not. My experience is pretty limited. Help me up, I'm away to my bed.' She nodded at Dermot. 'And when that twat's finished making a fool of himself, tell him I'm locking the door at twelve on the dot.'

Frank pulled her up. 'Do you want me to help you to your room?'

'No, I can manage to walk all the way to the lift on my own. You go and see to your guests. You might want to keep an eye on Finn as well. I think he's on something. Probably got it from your missus.' She waddled off, only to be stopped by Adrian who gave her his arm and walked her to the lift. That was a fella who took his best man duties seriously.

Frank couldn't see Finn anywhere, but he noticed Gavin at the bar. He'd been trying to get him alone all day. He went over and pulled up a stool.

Gavin pushed a glass of champagne over to him. 'Finishing it off before your brother-in-law does.'

It was a poor joke that Frank didn't appreciate. It was

okay for Siobhan to say Dermot was a twat. It was even okay for Frank to say it. But it was categorically not okay for Gavin to imply it. 'I can't believe you let Ellen get high today. For fuck's sake, Gavin.'

'You make it sound like I had a hand in it. It was all done and dusted by the time I came in to do my brotherly duties. It was far too late by then to do anything except brave it out. If you were so concerned about it, why didn't you check her bags before she left?'

'Why would I do that? How could I have known?'

Gavin frowned and smiled at the same time. 'Isn't it obvious? Good grief man, do you walk around blindfolded? It's not as if I haven't given you enough hints.'

38

THE EPISODE – 1984

Frank switched on the hall light, closed the door, took off his wet coat and hung it up. London was bleak and dreary in October at the best of times, but tonight was a filthy one. He was glad to get in.

He was working in a book shop now. It wasn't what he'd envisaged doing when he'd finished his degree but that was hardly surprising. While others had spent the last months of their university life working towards their future career, Frank had spent his making plans with Ellen for a future that he could see, in hindsight, was all about her. He'd entered university with all sorts of ambitious ideas about being a journalist, or a writer, or an artist, or all three. When he exited, his only ambition was to be Ellen's husband. That was sort of crap really, but at least it was an ambition fulfilled. But if you've done everything you set out to do by the time you were twenty-two, what did you do with the rest of your life? He had no idea.

The remainder of the flat was in darkness. Ellen must have gone out. He went into the kitchen, filled the kettle and switched it on. Before it had a chance to boil, he'd switched it off again because he thought he'd heard something in the living room. There it was again, a whimpering sound like a hurt animal. Instinctively, he grabbed a knife. He heard it again. His first thought was the Balaclavas had come for him, something he'd been dreading ever since the day they got Billy. Oh fuck. Had they taken it out on Ellen?

He switched the living room light on and a scream rang out that chilled his bones. 'Ellen!' Anger overtook his dread and his fear went. He was ready to slash any bastard that had touched her.

But there was no one here that he could see, except he could still hear her. He followed the sound and found her crouched behind the sofa.

She saw the knife and screamed again. 'Don't kill me.'

He threw it down. 'It's okay. There's nothing to be afraid of. I thought we had intruders. I thought they'd hurt you.'

'But we have. They've come for me. They're going to kill me.'

'Who? When did they come? What did they say? What were they wearing?' So they had found him. He was done for, and if he didn't act quick, Ellen would be too. 'Where are they now, Ellen?'

She pointed at the window. 'There. Look.'

The flat was on the fourth floor and it was a sheer drop from that window. Unsurprisingly, there was nothing to see except his own reflection. She was confused. It was the terror. He'd seen it before, back home. He knelt in front of her. 'They're not there now. It's okay, you're safe.'

Ellen edged away. 'Don't be stupid, Frank. They're right behind you. There's one on your back and he's going to kill you too.'

. . .

After an hour of trying to persuade her there was nothing there, Frank accepted something was wrong that he couldn't fix on his own. He didn't know what had happened but one thing was sure, the men in balaclavas had not called. He rang the only person he could think of that might be able to help. Gavin said he'd come straight away.

Gavin brought a doctor friend with him. 'He specialises in this sort of thing.'

'What sort of thing?' said Frank.

Gavin shrugged. 'I'm not a doctor.'

'What has she been taking?' asked the actual doctor.

Frank was confused. 'Taking?'

He looked at Frank like he was an idiot, or an accomplice. Or an idiot and accomplice. 'Your wife has taken something that has induced a psychotic episode. Do you know what it was?'

'What? No. I'm sorry, this has come as a shock. I just came in and found her like this. She doesn't do drugs. She told me she'd stopped after we got married.' He turned to Gavin, hoping his brother-in-law would back him up. 'I thought the last time she took them was on our wedding day. She promised me...' It was useless. Frank could see that now. Ellen had broken her promise and Gavin was not about to offer any words of support.

'I'm afraid Frank's a bit of an innocent in these matters,' said Gavin.

The doctor's face softened. 'Addicts can be very clever when it comes to deception. We need to get her to hospital.'

An addict? Ellen was an addict? That was just ridiculous. He'd have known. He'd have spotted the signs.

'Can we take her in the car, or do we need an ambulance?' Gavin had taken charge. Frank was still reeling.

'An ambulance would be best. Where's the phone? I'll make the call,' said the doctor.

A few minutes later he was back. 'They're on their way. Don't worry, they're very discreet.' He was talking to Gavin. Naturally. Gavin was the grown-up here. Frank was just the naive bystander, the unfortunate ignoramus who happened to be Ellen's husband.

'I'll come with you,' said Frank, trying to regain some semblance of competence.

The doctor exchanged glances with Gavin. 'Perhaps you could follow us in Gavin's car?'

Gavin drove through the busy streets, the only sound in the car being the classical music playing on the stereo. Frank had no idea what it was. He'd not been brought up to either know or appreciate classical music, but he had to admit there was something soothing about it. It helped to block out the images of the men in white coats strapping Ellen into a wheelchair while she kicked and bit them.

They drove past the hospital he'd expected them to stop at, and headed off in a direction away from the next nearest one. 'Where are we going?'

'The Richmond Park. It's a private clinic. They know how to manage her.'

Alarms bells went off in Frank's head. 'Has she been there before?'

Gavin kept his eyes on the road and his face unreadable. 'Haven't we all?'

'Actually no. We haven't all been there before. I'm an innocent, remember?'

'I'm sorry, Frank. I didn't mean to patronise you. The

place is just so well known in our circles for dealing with
these issues. I forget sometimes that—'

'I'm not from your circles?'

'Quite. She'll have to stay there for a while. It's for the
best. Leave it to the experts.'

'She's not an addict.'

'Let's see what the experts say,' said Gavin. 'For what it's
worth, I'm inclined to agree with you.'

The Richmond Park was a big house, very much in the
style of the Montagues' country home. Frank and Gavin
were shown into a plush room that could have been a
drawing room in a former life. They waited there until the
doctor returned to tell them Ellen was settled and there was
no point in them staying.

Frank went in to say goodbye to her. She was in a deep
sleep. He understood then that settled was just a softer way
of saying sedated. At least she looked peaceful.

On the drive back, he memorised the route for when he
came back to visit. The classical music was becalming his
tortured heart again. He couldn't help feeling he'd let Ellen
down, but he didn't know how. All he knew was that she
needed him and he wanted so badly to protect her.

'Will you tell anyone about this?' said Gavin.

'I don't know. Adrian, probably. He'd want to know.
You?'

'God, no.'

'Won't your parents want to be told?'

'Afraid not. They stopped wanting to be told a long time
ago. Well before you arrived on the scene. If you go to see
her tomorrow, I won't be able to take you. I have an early
flight to Hamburg. Business trip.'

'That's okay, Gavin. I can get there by myself. I am a
fully-fledged adult with a job and everything you know.'

Gavin smiled. 'Ah yes, I keep forgetting.'

Frank let himself into the flat again. The lights were still on. He went into the bedroom and lay down on the bed. Ellen had left a pile of her clothes on there. He covered himself with them and laid a blouse across his face. There'd been no men in balaclavas, although in some ways he'd have preferred it to be them, because they were something he understood. He wished his da were here. Da would know what to do. Da always knew what to do.

39

TWO WOMEN. ONE LUCKY CHARMER – 1984

Frank got off the bus by Dalston Kingsland station and walked up the High Street. Dalston was a long way from his neighbourhood but he liked it around here. The people were more like him. He was looking for a Chinese restaurant he'd found the last time he'd come here with a friend from work. They did a great chicken chow mein.

He'd just finished one of his moonlighting jobs. Recently, he'd started doing some private teaching on top of his full-time job at the book shop. The teaching had come to him through Gavin of all people. Some friends of his had a son who needed extra help with his English. He was a nice kid who just needed a bit of patience. The parents had been so pleased, they'd recommended him to others. Frank now had three pupils that he tutored. If he'd wanted more, he could have had them but three was enough to fill up his time.

He found the restaurant and ordered the chow mein. He'd been quite bad at cooking meals lately. His two jobs kept him busy, and cooking for himself had no great appeal.

Neither did staying in the flat on his own. Ellen had been in the Richmond Park for four months now and, aside from the first few days of her stay, he was only allowed to visit on Sundays. He went every week without fail. Once a month, Adrian got the train from Birmingham and came with him. Occasionally Gavin came too, although she often refused to see him, blaming him for incarcerating her. For some reason, she didn't blame Frank, even though he'd been the one who'd signed the forms.

The good news, if there was any to be had out of this, was that he and Gavin had been right. Ellen wasn't an addict, more an occasional user who'd had a very bad reaction. That was the hospital's conclusion. Their other conclusion was that she may have some underlying mental health issues that needed further investigation. In Ellen's view, that was absolute rot and the hospital was just looking for an excuse to make more money out of her. She insisted Frank made a promise not to sign any more forms. Frank was already way out of his depth. This hospital for the rich was like a top class hotel with doctors. Doctors who treated him like a fool, a bumpkin, or sometimes worse, a skirt-chasing gigolo. He didn't know how to speak to them. He lacked Gavin's authority. So he put his trust in his wife and made the promise. Anyway, as far as he could see, Ellen was her usual self again. It wouldn't be long before she was home and everything was back to normal.

He'd taken a table in the window so he could watch the passers-by rushing home to be with their loved ones. Maybe not all of them were that lucky. Some of them must be living lives as lonely as his was right now. The waiter brought his food over and he ate it greedily. The only upside to his present situation was that he wouldn't have discovered this place if Ellen hadn't been in the Richmond Park. Granted, it wasn't much of an upside but it was better than nothing.

He was about to order another beer when a woman walked past who looked awful familiar. She stopped at the kerbside and turned her head towards the oncoming traffic. It gave him a chance to see her profile properly. No doubt about it. It was Eve. Siobhan said they'd moved to London. He hadn't thought much about it at the time. London was a big place and anyway, he was over them.

Eve found enough of a gap to cross and went into a pub opposite. Frank considered the pros and cons of following her. Neither side came out on top, so he made a pact with himself. If she didn't come out by the time he'd finished his meal, he'd go over there.

She didn't come out. He paid his bill and crossed the road.

She was sitting on her own, reading a paper at the back end of the bar. Frank's plan had been to get a pint and just happen to be there for her to bump into. But the need to speak to someone who knew him, someone who was just like him, was bigger than he realised. He walked over to her table. 'How are yer, Eve?'

She looked up. Her first expression was the same as the one she'd given him when he'd last seen her. Hard. But then it changed. She almost looked pleased to see him. 'Frank? My God, it is you.'

'Aye, I just stopped by for a quick pint and saw you there. I couldn't believe it.'

She shook her head. 'That's some coincidence, what? Wait till Billy sees you.'

The smile froze on his face. 'Billy's here?'

'He's at the bar there. Billy, look who just walked in.'

Frank could not believe it. He'd been so eager to get to Eve that he'd walked straight past Billy. Bollocks.

'Well, well, Frankie Boy. It really is you. Of all the bars, in all the towns.'

Billy was blocking any chance of a speedy exit. Frank had to admit defeat and go with it. 'Who let you out of Belfast, Billy Mac?'

'Never mind me, what are you doing here? Where's your lady friend?'

'We're married now. She's away. Long assignment. She's a model.' He said that for Eve's benefit more than Billy's. He wanted her to know he had a wife who was beautiful enough to be a model, even if it made him sound like a wanker.

'Nice.' Eve looked like she was finding it hard to appear impressed which made him feel even more of a wanker.

Billy slapped him on the back. 'Let me buy you a pint, FB. It's good to see you, man.'

Frank thought of all the times Billy had his back when they were growing up. He remembered him and Billy, and those other two eejits, pogoing to the Undertones in a different time and place. He really wanted to be back in that time now. And if that wasn't possible, this was the next best thing. 'It's good to see you too, Billy.'

It was nine o'clock in the morning. Frank was woken by a call from Gavin. 'Morning. The clinic phoned me as they couldn't get hold of you last night. My sister is apparently ready to be let loose on the world again. We can take her home tomorrow.'

Frank was so happy he could hardly contain the joy.
'That's fucking ace.'

'Quite. I'll see you at one.'

Gavin arrived at one on the dot. The usual classical music
was playing on the stereo. Frank thought about asking him
if he ever listened to anything that involved a drum and
several guitars but decided he already knew the answer
would be no.

'Have you considered learning to drive? Not that I mind
acting as your personal chauffeur, but it would make life a
little easier for all of us.'

'I'll give it some thought,' said Frank.

'I can arrange lessons. I know of a very good instructor.'
Of course he did. Gavin had more connections than the
London underground.

'I can arrange them myself. But thank you, Gavin.
Thank you for everything.'

'My pleasure.' Gavin's mouth forced itself into a tiny
little smile and Frank regretted saying it straight away.

Ellen was waiting for them in the clinic's reception. She
leapt on Frank and smothered him in kisses.

'Don't I get one?' said Gavin.

'No. I still hate you.'

Gavin arched his eyebrows. 'No you don't.'

'I do. You put me in here.'

'It was for your own good. Anyway, I believe it was your
husband who signed the papers.' He held out his hand and
she took it, still scowling at him like a petulant child.

'Don't you dare try to spoil the only decent thing in my
life. Frank can do no wrong and you know it.'

'For now, at least.' Gavin kissed the top of her head.

In return she planted an almost shy kiss on his cheek. They were a strange pair. In every other way but looks they were complete opposites. Ellen was a cocktail of emotions. You never knew what you were going to get with her. Every day was a new adventure. On the surface, Gavin was a cold fish. Calm, competent, emotions never on display. Yet there was a bond between them that Frank envied. He didn't have that with his sister, and even though he spent more time with Martin than Siobhan, he didn't have it with Martin either.

Gavin dropped them home but didn't come in. As soon as they were in the flat Ellen was all over him. He wasn't prepared for it, having already scheduled in a one-to-one talk about drugs and honesty. She must have sensed he was holding back and stopped abruptly. 'You're angry with me.'

'No, I'm not angry. I just think we need to talk. Set some boundaries.' It was bullshit corporate speak, something he'd heard at work and he wanted to cringe. She'd told him once how much she hated being shackled and here he was doing that very thing. Not that he saw it that way, but he knew she would.

'What do you mean boundaries?'

'No more drugs.'

She swiped her hand across the air. 'Goes without saying, darling. That was very much a passing phase anyway. Call it a failed experiment.'

'And you've got to be honest with me. No more hiding things.' She was frowning at him, but Frank was like a freight train rolling down the tracks and he wasn't going to stop. 'If we're to have any chance of a future together, there has to be complete honesty. If there's ever a point when you feel tempted again, you must tell me. We'll beat it together.'

There was a smile on her face very like the one Gavin

had given him earlier. 'Have you been reading those pamphlets they have at the Richmond.'

'I'm serious, Ellen.'

'I know you are, my sweet. Set your boundaries. I'll do whatever you say. I never want to go in that place again. Let's go out to celebrate tonight. A meal somewhere. Your choice. I'll pay.'

He kissed her and breathed in her perfume. He'd missed her so much. 'No, wife. I'll pay.'

'Mmm. Get you, all masterful. Okay, husband, whatever you say. But first…' She unzipped his flies and put her hand down his pants. 'Still works, I see.'

He took her to the Chinese restaurant in Dalston. It was slumming for her really, but Ellen didn't mind slumming occasionally. As long as she didn't have to make a habit of it.

'I'm thinking of getting out of modelling,' she said. 'Too many temptations.'

'Good idea. What will you do instead?' Frank was never sure if it was the modelling that had got her into drugs, but he suspected it had just made it easier for her to get them.

'Not sure. I'll talk to Gavin. He'll be able to fix something up for me.'

Of course he could. Gavin could fix anything up.

'I'm thinking about a career change too. I might look at teaching. Proper teaching in a school, like Adrian. I thought I'd talk to him about it.'

'Teaching? I'm going to be a teacher's wife? How quaint.' She laughed not realising that with one word, she'd belittled him.

'Well, I haven't decided yet. Do you remember my mate Billy?'

'How could I forget?'

'He lives here now with his girlfriend. I was supposed to meet them in that pub over there tonight. We don't have to though. We can just go home.'

'No, let's go. I'm curious to see what kind of a woman would find that moron attractive.'

Eve eyed Ellen up with a certain amount of disdain. Frank wasn't clear on whether that was because of Ellen's poshness, her career choice, or her beauty. Irrationally, he hoped it was because she still had feelings for him. Judging by the way she hung onto Billy though, there was no chance of that.

'I'm amazed you're still with this eejit. I thought you'd be long gone by now,' said Billy.

'And I'm amazed an obnoxious cretin like you could have a girlfriend,' said Ellen.

Eve burst out laughing. 'She's got your number, Billy. Actually I'm his fiancée. We're getting married.'

'As soon as I can afford the ring,' said Billy.

It took a few seconds for Frank to process the information and come out looking happy about it. 'Congratulations. I'm pleased for you. I didn't realise.'

'He only proposed this morning. It must have been seeing you again, Frank. You're my lucky charm,' said Eve.

Ellen slipped her arm through Frank's. 'That's a coincidence. He's my lucky charm too.'

'Two women. One lucky charmer,' said Billy, without the slightest hint of irony in his voice.

Frank raised his glass. 'Sláinte. Here's to you both. I hope you'll be as happy as me and Ellen.'

Eve clinked her glass against his. 'Sure, that's a tall order, but we'll do our best not to disappoint.'

Frank supped on his pint and said nothing. They already had.

40

THE PRIDE OF CHAMPIONS

Frank came up off the beach by another cottage that was set back from the road. He guessed it was Doogie's. There was no sign of life in there. He was probably still at the farm. But when he got to the farm, Frank saw no sign of Doogie there either. Perhaps he'd gone for another run. Perhaps he was doing a hundred press ups, on one arm, somewhere along the beach. He looked the sort. Frank had never looked the sort, not even when he was younger. He'd always felt a touch intimidated by fit people. Especially if they were your partner's ex-lover.

Martin and Finn were up and by the looks of it had finished breakfast.

'Morning,' said Finn.

'Where have you been?' said Martin.

'The beach.' Frank held up his pad and paints. 'I wanted to catch the sunrise.'

Martin and Finn both raised their eyebrows, either in surprise or admiration. Frank didn't know which and he didn't bother asking. Instead, he pegged his damp underpants to the tent's guy ropes.

'Have you had an accident there?' said Martin, loud enough to wake any other campers who foolishly thought they could expect quiet at that time in the morning.

'Nope. I went for a swim.'

Martin did a double take. 'Did you just say you went for a swim?'

'Well it was more of a quick dip really. The water's freezing,' said Frank.

Martin snorted. 'Er, yeah. What else did you expect? This outdoor life's messing with your mind, FB. A man in your physical condition needs to be careful. You could have had a heart attack.'

'I think it's great. Well done, FB. We should all do it,' said Finn.

'Feck off.' Martin blew out a raspberry, presumably to emphasise the point.

A woman came out of her adjacent motorhome and shot them a dirty look.

'Apologies,' said Martin, not looking at all sorry.

Frank made himself a coffee. 'Where are we off to today then lads?'

'Up towards Morar,' said Finn. 'There are more great beaches to explore there, if you're up for a walk. I know a couple of spots where we can wild camp.'

'Sounds good. I'll walk with you. The exercise will do me good.'

Martin gave him a look that said too true and Frank reminded himself to talk to Finn about wellbeing, as soon as they'd got rid of Martin.

They stopped at a beach that was another silver-sanded knockout, about fifty miles from Grace's farm. Frank half-wished he'd elected to stay behind and paint, but he'd already taken time out of the road trip yesterday. Another day wouldn't have been fair on the others. And anyway, he didn't want to give Martin an excuse for not boarding the plane. He made do with taking photos and when he got a signal, sent a couple to Netta in the hope it was far enough away from Doogie for her not to guess where he'd been. He'd decided to draw a line under Doogie Chambers, or rather, his stalking of Doogie Chambers. It was best to erase it from his memory banks, seeing as it was just a blip on his part. A brief spell of ridiculousness that he'd since got under control and would never mention to anyone. Not even Netta.

He was feeling quite pleased with himself after this morning. That dip had dislodged something in him and he could sense a change coming. A good change. A positive one. He could definitely do this. Whatever "this" was. He hadn't worked that one out yet but he was prepared for it to be anything. In that spirit, he decided to send a couple of pictures to Siobhan as well, with a quick message:

'Will call when I can.'

Ellen would have liked it here. In the early days, she was always dragging him out to the country. She loved open spaces. The world was never big enough for her. Life wasn't either, it seemed. And people never met her expectations. Funnily enough though, she really liked Eve. After she called Billy an obnoxious cretin, they got on swimmingly. Perhaps that was their common ground. Frank was never sure if Eve actually liked Billy. From that night on, the four of them saw a lot of each other.

Billy and Eve didn't so much have a wedding as get married. Martin and Finn were the only ones who came over the water for the occasion. They hadn't invited their own families. Frank and Ellen were the witnesses and, aside from a few of their London friends who Frank didn't know, that was it.

If Frank hadn't loaned Billy the money to buy the ring, it would probably have been touch and go whether the marriage would have taken place. Billy and Eve were always broke, even though they both had decent jobs. She was a reporter for one of the tabloids and he worked in a recording studios. His was a relatively junior role but it paid a good wage and he was something of a rising star in those days. Billy never did pay Frank back.

In spite of announcing she was going to give up modelling, it had taken Ellen another six years before she did it. And in the end, it was only because Gavin used his inevitable connections to get her a column in one of those magazines written by the rich for the rich. She wrote about art. Real art, as she often reminded him. Not the sort Frank did as a hobby. She enjoyed picking holes in his amateur attempts. It started as a playful joke that he'd laugh off, but you can only laugh so many times before it stops being funny.

She also liked to criticise his career choice. Teaching had made everything too structured for her taste. It dictated when they went on holiday, when they went out and, the worst crime of all, it gave Frank a sense of purpose. In the space of a few years, he came to care about his pupils a little too much, in her opinion. In 1984, he'd been the man who could do no wrong. By the end of that decade, he'd turned into the man who could do no right. If it had been an overnight change perhaps he'd have noticed the deterioration sooner, but it had been a gradual drip, drip erosion of their marriage, and his confidence.

All credit to her though, she stayed away from drugs. At

least that's how it looked to Frank. If Martin was right and Frank only saw what he wanted to see, she could have been having countless drug-fuelled frenzies, right under his nose, and he wouldn't have known. He was too busy with his sense of purpose. Maybe Martin had a point.

'You're quiet,' said Finn.

'I was just thinking about when I started teaching.'

'That was a tough gig, wasn't it?' said Martin.

Finn, naturally, wouldn't remember since he'd been going through his own drug-fuelled frenzy at the time. But Martin was right. His first job had been in Leyton. For the first term, the kids had made mincemeat of him. He'd found his feet after that but it took a couple more years before they began to take him seriously. Even then, it was, as Martin put it, a tough gig. They were also the best years of his teaching career.

'I remember Ellen used to complain about it. She hated you working there,' said Martin.

Frank stiffened. Now that he had Netta in his life, Ellen had been consigned to the past, and yet he still couldn't talk to Martin and Finn about her. 'I wonder if the sea's warmed up yet.'

Martin did a fake shudder. 'Doubt it.'

Frank arched an eyebrow. 'Wanna find out?'

'You're fucking kidding me?'

But Finn already had his jacket and jumper off. 'Let's do it.'

Martin shook his head. 'No way. I am not going in there.'

Frank took off his trousers. 'Who's the boring ould fart now, Marty Boy?'

'Right, that's it.' Martin pulled off his clothes.

They ran towards the sea, Finn way ahead of them and

Martin lagging behind Frank. When the water hit them they squealed like wee girls. It hadn't warmed up in the slightest.

'How long are we supposed to stay in here?' howled Martin.

'Just until you can't take it any longer,' said Frank.

Martin got out first, then Finn. Much to Frank's delight, he lasted the longest. 'I am the champion,' he roared.

'Okay, you win. Must be all that blubber. You're like a fucking beached whale,' said Martin. But nothing could take away Frank's pride.

'Remember when we used to go to Ballycastle in the summer holidays? I'm sure the water was just as cold then. How did we not get hypothermia when we were kids?' said Martin.

'I miss those holidays when we were wee, don't you?' said Finn. 'Long days on the beach. Just the three of us and Siobhan.'

41

FRANK GOES ALL "CAN DO"

Siobhan looked at the photos Frank had sent to her yesterday. Why he thought she'd be interested in pictures of a fecking beach was anybody's guess. But that was her brother. Always in his own little headspace. People could be falling apart around him and Frank would keep soldiering on in his own little universe. Actually, that was in poor taste now that she thought about it. It was true though.

By her reckoning they were on day five of their little *Boy's Own* adventure. In two more days, Martin would be on the plane home and Ma would have someone else to harangue. Perhaps she should book the ticket. That way he couldn't get out of it.

It was five-thirty. Ma called at exactly five-forty every day. She stayed on the phone for ten minutes, tops. That left just enough time for her to make a pot of tea and settle down ready for the six o'clock news. The six o'clock news was sacrosanct as far as the parents were concerned. Siobhan provided the family news update. The six o'clock news provided everything else. It was like a religious thing for them. They didn't go to church more than once or twice a decade, but they never missed that news programme. Before Martin's so-called disappearance, Ma wanted to know all about what was going on with Siobhan and the kids. Not anymore. These days it was all about Martin.

She checked the time. Another seven minutes to go. She had stuff to do tonight. Lots of stuff. She was going on a date with some fella off a dating site and she needed to prepare. Every minute counted. Siobhan seized the initiative and called Ma.

'What are you doing calling me at this time? Has something happened?' Ma wasn't used to having the initiative seized from her.

'Nothing's happened. I have to go out, so I thought I'd call you a few minutes early.'

'Where are you going at this time of night?'

'Ma, it's twenty to six.'

'Exactly.'

'I'm going for a cervical smear test.'

'Oh.' That shut her up. If there was one thing Ma hated talking about it was medical things, especially medical things that involved down below. 'Have you any news?'

'Not really. Frank sent me some pictures of a beach. Looks like they're having a good time. I'm still waiting on him calling me.'

Ma tutted. 'I spoke to poor Bronagh again. When I get my hands on Martin I'll wring his neck, so I will.'

Ma would have to stand on a table to reach Martin's neck but Siobhan wouldn't put it past her. Not with the mood she was in, now that she'd heard the full story. There were some things even Ma couldn't turn a blind eye to.

Her phone started to vibrate. 'Ma, it's Frank. I better go. He's got this crappy ould phone that keeps losing the signal. I might not get another chance. I'll call you back.'

'Wait until after the ne–'

Siobhan cut the call before Ma had a chance to finish her instruction and picked up on Frank. 'Thanks for the pictures of the beach. I'm thrilled to hear you're having a great time.'

'I knew you'd appreciate them,' said Frank, back with the sarcasm again. 'You've spoken to Bronagh then?'

'I have and yes, she did throw him out.'

'Did she say why?'

'Where do you want me to start? There were so many reasons, we got through two bottles of wine and she was still going. But I think I can boil it down to two definitive complaints. To start with, he's been in a foul mood for about six months non-stop.'

'Ah come on, nobody can be in a foul mood for six months non-stop.'

'Bronagh's words not mine. According to her, he's been up and down like a yo-yo. One minute depressed and the next, picking fights with her for no reason.'

'That doesn't sound like Martin. Is it trouble with his business, do you think?'

'No. All good there. Bronagh thinks it's down to the second complaint.' Siobhan paused for effect, and also because she knew this wasn't going to go down well. She wasn't close in the conventional sense to Frank, but there were certain things she knew about him that he didn't know she knew.

'And that is?' Frank was sounding a bit tetchy, as if he had any right to be.

'Eve Macintyre. Bronagh says they're having an affair. He's been seeing a lot of her anyway, and Bronagh's convinced.' She stopped. That was enough for now.

Frank cleared his throat. 'She's back in Belfast then?'

Jesus. Was that the only question on his lips right now? Was that really the only thing that sprung to mind after that shocker? Sometimes Frank was such a disappointment. 'Well, obviously.'

'What about Billy?'

'Bronagh didn't mention him. You haven't seen him yourself recently then?' she said, in the full knowledge that he hadn't.

'Not in a long time.'

No of course not. How can a friendship come back from that? If you could call it a friendship. Wankers, the pair of them. 'Are you going to talk to Martin about it?'

'I guess so. Unless you think I should keep quiet in case he does another runner.'

Oh, so now he was asking her advice? *Too little too late, brother dear. You are not getting out of this one by sticking your head in the sand.* 'I think you should talk to him. Do it when you're somewhere remote, so he's got nowhere to run to.'

'Good idea. I'll do that. We're staying in the Cairngorms tomorrow. I'll do it then.'

'Oh, okay.' Frank's sudden positivity and determination was unexpected and blew her away, but only for a minute or two. 'Will you listen to yourself, five days in the wilderness and you've gone all "can do". You want to be careful there.'

Frank laughed. At one of her jokes. It was unnerving. 'Must be something in the air up here. You should try it.'

'Thanks all the same, but if I'm gonna find myself, I'd rather do it in a spa, with a bottle of Prosecco. Listen, I'm going to book a flight home for Martin. I'll send it to you. I'll send it to Finn as well, in case your ancient phone doesn't pick it up.'

'That would be great. Thank you. I'll let Finn know.

Could you give us three days? That'll be time to get back to Finn's first.'

Three days was one more day than she'd have liked, but she was in a good mood now, what with Frank laughing at her jokes and all. 'Okay. Let me know when he's on the plane.'

'Will do. Well, you have a good night, Siobhan. I'll speak to you again soon.'

Siobhan stared at the phone. What just happened there? Did her miserable curmudgeon of a brother wish her a good night? Did he say thank you? That Highland air must be one strong fecking elixir. She'd better call Ma with the latest.

She checked the time. The news would be starting right about now. Maybe later then. There were some things you didn't mess with.

42

THE CONFLICT BUSINESS

Road trip day five had been a success in Frank's eyes. Right up to the point where Siobhan had delivered her news. From that moment on, the day hadn't looked so good. So Martin was playing away. With Eve of all people. What was he thinking? What was Eve thinking? Only Finn left to go and she'll have left her mark on the lot of them. Frank wondered if Billy knew, or even if she was still with Billy. She must still be with him, otherwise Martin would have gone to her when Bronagh threw him out. Unless he had and she'd told him she didn't want him. He wouldn't put it past her.

Frank had tried Netta unsuccessfully, then called Siobhan from the harbour in Mallaig while the others waited in a pub. When he got to the pub, he made out there was no news. He didn't want Martin doing another runner. As he said to Siobhan, he'd bide his time and wait until there was nowhere for Martin to run to, except the top of a mountain. Even Martin wasn't that much of an escapologist.

Frank wasn't one for conflict. That was probably his

downfall. If he had been willing to face difficult conversations in the past, things might have turned out differently, but it had always been hard to ignore that first golden rule when it had been drummed into you from the moment you could talk. He'd been reasonably successful at staying out of trouble when others around him were up to their neck in it. He'd done that by keeping his head down and avoiding said conflict. But he could see now that hadn't always been the best strategy. In truth, he hadn't really stayed out of trouble. He'd just pretended it wasn't there. But that was before this week. This trip was forcing him to revisit the past and this time, Frank was going to take it on with his head up. Today, he'd thrown himself into the freezing cold water without fear. He was a new man now, or at least he was going to be from this day on. So that meant facing things, even if those things ended in a massive bust up. So there it was, his plan of action. Get Martin somewhere remote. Confront him about his affair with Eve and his lying. Get him back to Glasgow and on the plane home. Let the parents talk some sense into him.

Frank waited until they'd set up camp on day six. Stunning as the Cairngorms were, he wouldn't allow himself to be distracted. He was a man with a plan, and he was about to invoke it. 'So, I spoke to Siobhan yesterday. She's been talking to Bronagh.'

'How's Bronagh doing?' Martin's face was full of concern, the lying, sneaky bastard.

'She's bearing up, as far as I know. She filled Siobhan in on the details behind her throwing you out.'

'Oh aye.' Still the concerned, innocent face. It was an art with Martin. As a kid, he'd been a bona fide child protégé when it came to conveying concern and innocence, and he hadn't lost his touch.

'Yeah. According to Bronagh you've been a nightmare to live with. I believe her words were that you'd been in a foul mood for the last six months. A whole six months apparently. That's some going, six months with no let up.'

'Well I've had a lot on.'

'Have you? What is it that you've had on, Martin?'

'Is it the business, Marty? Are you in trouble?' said Finn.

Martin looked at his feet. Lost for words? Unless Frank was very much mistaken, cracks were beginning to appear in his shiny veneer. Frank was feeling very much like he had the upper hand in this conversation. Perhaps there was something to this conflict business all after all.

'Are you having trouble coping? Do you think you might be depressed, Marty?' Finn wasn't letting up in trying to give Martin a get out of jail free card.

'I think I could be,' said Martin.

Damn, the fecker was trying to worm out of it by saying he had mental health problems. Okay, so maybe he did, but Frank very much doubted it. Unless late stage male menopause was a mental health issue. 'Are you sure it's not because you've got yourself another woman?'

'Frank, that's not a very nice thing to say when Martin's obviously struggling here,' said Finn, in the kind of voice he probably reserved for his clients.

'It may not be nice, Finn, but it's true. According to Bronagh.'

'It is not,' said Martin.

Frank ignored the lying fecker. 'According to Bronagh, Marty here's been having an affair. With Eve.'

Finn's whole body jerked backwards. 'Eve Mac?'

Frank nodded, rather smugly, he had to admit. 'The one and only.'

'No. Not even Marty would do that. Not after… It can't be true. It's not true, is it?' Finn looked to Martin, his face desperate looking.

'It is not. Bronagh's got the wrong end of the stick,' said Martin.

'Of course she has, because it wouldn't be you lying would it?' said Frank.

'I'm not lying.' Martin's face went bright red. He jumped up, his nostrils flaring. The mask had finally slipped and he was bordering on rage.

Frank wasn't too far from that state himself. He got up and faced Martin. 'Come off it. Why don't you just admit what we all know? You cheated on your wife with your mate's wife.'

Martin pushed his finger into Frank's shoulder. 'Because I'm not you.'

43

WAIT FOR ME – 1991

Frank was in his office hunched over an easel. He liked to spend a couple of hours on a Sunday morning painting. It helped him wind down from the last week and prepare himself for the week ahead. Especially tomorrow. Mondays were always tough. The kids were often still hyper from the weekend and there was usually at least one fight to break up. Mostly it was just fists, occasionally it was knives. It wasn't pretty but you got used to it.

They'd moved to a larger flat a couple of years ago. It was Ellen's money again, another of those compromises. He didn't earn enough for a place like this. She'd played her face until he'd given in. She always got what she wanted in the end. The upside was, he'd been able to turn the smallest bedroom into his hideaway. He used it for marking, lesson prep, and his Sunday morning painting.

Ellen walked in, naked under her robe. The robe was embroidered turquoise silk and bespoke. It had been a gift from Gavin for starting the new job that he'd also gifted to her. The contents of Frank's pants stirred at the sight of her in it.

'Dear God, do you call that art? Give it up, darling. You just don't have it.' There'd been a time when she was full of praise for his work. She'd sit for hours while he sketched her. But that was before she became an art critic and her tastes began to lean towards the more traditional.

'You know what you are, Ellen? A snob. You're a big old art snob.'

Ellen's face sank. It was okay for her to criticise him but if he did the same to her, it knocked her off balance. He knew what would come next. She'd go from aggressive to submissive in the blink of an eye. It was a pattern that had been repeating itself for a while now. She untied her robe. It slipped off her shoulders to the floor. 'Would you like to paint me?'

He set down his brush and put his hands on her behind. 'No, I'd like to fuck you.'

Without a word, she unzipped his flies and straddled him, her bare breasts rubbing against him. The silence was erotic. Normally their sex was louder and faster, but this was something else. Contained passion, made all the more exciting because their sex life had been rocky lately. Rocky in that they generally only did it after an argument, although their arguments were frequent. It seemed to him that maybe they'd lost the ability to enjoy normal sex. There always had to be some sort of friction to instigate it. It wasn't his thing at all, but Ellen seemed to thrive on it. In fact, he'd go so far as to say she needed it.

When they'd finished she climbed off him and picked up her robe. 'I'd better take a shower before we go.'

The taxi stopped up the road from Billy and Eve's new house. They both had cars now but they'd be drinking all afternoon. They could have taken the bus or underground but that was another thing Ellen had become increasingly snobbish about.

'What a dump,' she said, as they stepped out onto the pavement.

'Will you catch yourself on. The area's fine. You know you're reverting to type? You'll be telling me how much you hate the Irish next.'

Straight away, she looked wounded. 'That's so cruel.'

'Oh I'm cruel?'

'Yes you are. And pathetic too. Grovelling around Billy like some snivelling cretin. Creeping around Eve, hoping for a few crumbs from your old sweetheart. Pathetic.'

Frank drew a breath. He hadn't told Ellen that he and Eve had once been together. He'd made a point of not telling her. But there'd been plenty of opportunities to find out, he supposed. Visitors from home might have mentioned it. Billy or Eve might even have mentioned it. Although they never did that when he was around. 'You're talking shite, as usual, my darling. If you don't want to come, just say so. We'll find you another taxi and get you home.'

'You'd like that, wouldn't you? That way you can spend all afternoon hanging on her every word. I know you prefer her to me. Is it the Irish thing? Is it the money? If I gave it all away, would that make you happy?'

Where the hell had all this come from? They'd just had the most amazing sex, for God's sake. 'What's gotten into you, Ellen? Why are you behaving like this?'

Tears welled up in her eyes. 'Because you've stopped loving me. And I'm frightened, Frank.'

Frank pulled her closer. Ellen would always be an enigma to him, it was part of her charm, but there was one thing he'd come to understand about her. Most of the time she was supremely confident, and the idea of him preferring someone else wouldn't have even entered her head. But every now and then, deep insecurities appeared from nowhere and took her hostage. He brushed a stray tear from her cheek. 'That's crazy. You drive me mad sometimes but of course I still love you.'

'Prove it. I don't want to go in there. If you really love me, you'll take me home now.'

'But they're expecting us, and Martin and Finn have come over.'

She drew back, her eyes searching him. But before either of them could speak, Billy appeared in the garden of a house a few doors along. 'About time.'

Ellen wiped the tears away and put on a smile. 'Sorry. My fault. Long story. Too boring to repeat.' She took Frank's hand and they followed Billy through the house and out to the back garden where everyone was waiting.

Eve took one look at Ellen and turned to Frank, her face full of questions. Frank shook his head and averted his eyes. There was no chance he was going to repeat that last conversation to anyone, especially Eve and Billy.

'Here they are. My gorgeous sister-in-law and the other fella,' said Martin. He'd just got divorced after a disastrous marriage that only lasted two years and he was way too happy for Frank's liking. Ma wasn't too pleased about it either. Especially as he'd managed to produce a child in that short time. A blameless baby had been left high and dry, as she'd put it when she bent Frank's ear for nearly an hour over the phone yesterday. He'd only been saved by the six o'clock news coming on the telly.

Ellen threw her arms around Martin and hugged him in a way she never did with her own brother. Finn got the same treatment. She pecked Eve on the cheek. 'I love your new place.'

'Want a tour?' said Eve.

'Yes please. Lead on,' said Ellen. She pulled Frank along with her. He noticed she wouldn't look him in the eye.

The spare bedroom was full of electronic gadgets in varying states of disrepair. Frank recognised a couple of old synthesisers. The only things that didn't look like they were past it were two electric guitars leaning up against the wall. 'Who plays them?' he said.

'Billy,' said Eve. 'Well, he can play a few chords. That's as far he got before he lost interest. You know what he's like. This is all his shit. It's not staying though. This is going to be a kid's bedroom.'

Ellen's jaw dropped. 'Are you pregnant?'

'No. Not yet, anyways. But we're thinking about it. Aren't you?'

'Absolutely not. I couldn't think of anything worse.'

It was the first Frank had heard of it. He'd always assumed they'd get round to it eventually. Although he'd never actually asked.

'You never said you didn't want kids.' He'd waited until they got home to mention it. He didn't want to bring it up in front of the others and also, he wasn't sure how she was going to react after her earlier outburst.

'Well I'm telling you now. I can't get fat. I just can't.'

Frank laughed. 'It's not fat, it's a pregnancy, and you're not modelling anymore so why should it matter?'

'It matters to me. I cannot have something growing inside me like an alien. And I hate babies.'

She ran into the bathroom and slammed the door. Frank

went to bed. Well that was that then. No children. It was going to be just him and her forever. He'd better get used to it.

He was in a light sleep and the touch of Ellen's arm tugged him out of it. He turned over and saw that she was crying. 'You understand, don't you, Frank? I can't have a child. I can't share you.'

He brushed his hand against her wet cheek. He couldn't be cross with her when she was this pitiful and sad. 'Don't cry, sweetheart. I don't mind really. I love you. You're enough for me.'

'Make love to me again, like we did this morning. It was so special.'

They did it again. She told him she'd never stop loving him and asked if he would always be hers. He said he would. 'I'll never leave you, Ellen. You're my life.' He meant it. She was mad, she was crazy, and she drove him to torment but Frank was in no doubt, Ellen was everything to him.

They slept in each other's arms, and when they woke up the next morning it was just like their first days together back in Birmingham. Things would be better now. He was convinced of it.

He went to work and the day was as tough as he'd expected it to be. Two fights stopped. One knife confiscated. Four pupils excluded. He was glad to be on his way home.

Ellen wasn't in when he got back, but there was a note waiting for him in the hall:

'Frank,
I'm sorry, I need to get away. I'll come back.
Wait for me x'

. . .

For the first seventy-two hours, Frank did nothing other than go to work, eat and sleep. He'd assumed she'd just taken off for a couple of days, like she used to when they were students. On the fourth day, with still no word, he rang Gavin.

Gavin sounded irritated: 'Why didn't you call me as soon as you got the note?'

'I assumed she'd be back in a day or two. She used to disappear a lot when we were students.'

'Have you checked the hospitals, informed the police?'

'No. Like I said–'

'Yes, yes, I heard you the first time. I'll do it. Have you tried your friends?'

'No, I've told no one except you. I'll do that now.'

He rang Billy and Eve first, then he went through the address book calling her friends. None of them knew where she was.

With no one left in London, he called Adrian. 'She phoned on Monday for a chat. Said she was going to France. I assumed it was work.'

'Did she say where in France?'

'No. I'm sorry, mate. If I'd known, I'd have asked her more, or given you the nod, but she was just like her normal self.'

Straight away, Frank rang Gavin. 'Adrian spoke to her on the day she left. She told him she was going to France. He thought it was for work.'

'That makes sense. She's not in any of the hospitals in and around London, and she's not in the morgue.'

Frank went cold. It wasn't the word itself but the casual, offhand way it was dropped in. He knew it was just Gavin's manner and he couldn't help his upbringing, but all the same.

He banished images of Ellen lying on a slab and replaced them with more optimistic thoughts that it was feasible she might be in France. 'Do you really think she could be there?'

'Yes, I do. She's always felt at home there. Mother's half French. We holidayed a lot in the south as children. I'll get someone on it. In the meantime, if you see or hear from her, contact me immediately.'

It was another two weeks before Gavin was able to confirm that she was somewhere in the south of France and that he'd spoken to her. 'She's safe and she's healthy.'

'Where is she? Can I see her?'

'She doesn't want you to know her whereabouts. She asks that you're patient. I'm sorry, Frank. I can't divulge anything else.'

'But I'm worried about her.'

'Comes with the territory I'm afraid, brother-in-law. You should have listened to me before you married her.'

'Are you saying she's done this before?'

'Yes. My sister is a serial absconder. She can't help herself. I suppose all those modelling assignments negated the need to bolt. I blame myself. I should have seen it coming, but I've been a little preoccupied lately. I've met someone.'

'You're getting married?' In all the years Frank known him, Gavin had never so much as dropped a girl's name, unless it was a relative.

'No. I am most definitely not. Not unless the laws change anyway. But I may be taking in a lodger.'

'You're–?'

'Yes.'

'Well good for you, Gavin. I hope you and your lodger will have a long and happy er, arrangement.'

'Thank you. Listen Frank, I know it's not my business but if I were you, I'd get on with my life. Ellen could be away for weeks or months. She may never come back. I've got someone keeping an eye on her to make sure she doesn't come to any harm. What I'm trying to say is don't sit around waiting for something that may or may not happen. Make the most of your freedom while you can.'

44

BILLY THE TOP DOG – 1991

Along with hundreds of others, Frank got off the train and edged away from the platform to join yet more passengers milling around Euston station. It was the October half term and he'd been to stay with Adrian. Last year, Ade had married Stella who also taught at his school. She was a great girl and she didn't mind the two of them revisiting all the old haunts. They'd had a good time, although admittedly, their favourite old pub, the Hope and Anchor was looking a bit tired now.

In the five months since Ellen had walked out on him, Frank had gone through a range of emotions. Mostly, he'd been in a dark place but more recently, he felt like he was coming out the other side. Ade was a great help. He called Frank every week and visited regularly. In the early days, his visits had been the only reason for Frank to clean the flat.

Ma had been frantic with worry when he'd told them about Ellen. The only thing that saved him from her enforced occupation was Martin's wedding. Although even that was touch and go, seeing as it was his second marriage and everyone suspected it wouldn't be his last.

Billy was another one who made sure he was okay. Of all people, Billy knew what it was like to have someone walk out on you, albeit a parent. In a funny way, Ellen's disappearance brought them closer. It was almost as if there'd never been a rift and they'd moved seamlessly from childhood to adulthood. Eve was kind too when he saw her, but she was covering stories all over the country now, so mostly he saw Billy on his own.

Gavin gave him the occasional snippet of information on Ellen's wellbeing, and she still wrote her column which he read without fail. It was actually quite good. Frank had taken Gavin's advice and got on with his life. With regard to his missing wife, he expected very little. If she came back, she came back. If she didn't, she didn't. It was the best way for him to cope with the uncertainty.

He was about to take the escalator down into the underground when someone grabbed his arm. He turned and saw Eve.

'I thought it was you. I've just come back from Manchester.' She checked her watch. 'Fancy a drink?'

'Sure. Is Billy meeting you?'

'Mr Big Shot? No, he's away in the US of A, baby.'

'I didn't realise he was doing that well.'

'You mean he hasn't been ramming it down your throat? Lucky you. He can't get enough of telling me how he's the top dog now.'

'That doesn't sound like Billy,' said Frank.

They laughed because they knew it sounded exactly like him. Billy had always been the one with the big ideas that never happened, only this time they had. In truth, he wasn't the top dog in the whole music industry, or even the company he worked for, but his skill as a recording engineer was beginning to get noticed by the right people, and London was no longer big enough to contain Billy Mac. Frank was pleased for him. If anyone deserved success, it was Billy.

'There's a pub near here we like to use when we want to get away from the high life of Canary Wharf,' said Eve.

'We?'

'Journalists, don't ya know.' She stuck her tongue out at him. She hadn't done that since the night he saw her at the Battle of the Bands.

She took him around the back streets to a pub that was pretty full considering it was only mid-afternoon. A few of the drinkers acknowledged her and invited her to join them. She turned them down. 'I'm with an old friend. We've some catching up to do, and you'd bore the life out of him.'

Frank was equal parts amused and amazed by her easy banter. She was that same cheeky girl who used to be his girlfriend, but that had been ten years ago and she was so much more sure of herself now. He couldn't imagine this Eve meekly getting in the car after her daddy had just arranged for her future husband to be dealt with.

'So we have some catching up to do, do we?' He heard himself say it and immediately felt like an idiotic kid. It was the kind of thing he'd have said to her back when he'd been trying to show her how funny he could be. It seemed he hadn't grown up, even if she had.

'Don't we always?' Her eyes lingered on him for a few seconds longer than was necessary. Frank's mouth went dry. He reached for his pint and she looked away. 'Anyway, I've hardly seen you since Ellen left. Billy's been keeping you all to himself.'

'I thought you were busy.'

'Is that what he told you? Oh Billy, you false bastard.'

'I probably just misunderstood. I guess he thought I was too delicate to be in the company of women.' He grinned at her to show that he really wasn't that delicate.

'Yeah, he's all heart like that. Anyway, we're here now and you don't look like you're about to have a breakdown.'

'Can I ask you something? That day Billy was taken by the Balaclavas. Was that down to your ould man?'

She seemed surprised by his question. Frank was surprised too. He didn't know why he'd asked it. Although, truth be told, it was a question that had been bugging him since the day it happened.

She frowned. 'Don't be ridiculous. Why would he do something like that?'

'What was he doing there then?'

'He got word. News flows down the line, comes through the cracks. It's a complicated process. You have no idea.'

She was right, he really did have no idea. His parents with their rules and no-go zones had done their best to keep him away from all of that shady stuff that went on. He'd known it was there but it hadn't been part of his day-to-day life. Until that one day.

'Was it the guns then? Did Billy grass about the guns?' Frank didn't believe he'd be that stupid but he was clutching at straws here. He'd tried asking Billy a couple of times since that day in the hospital, but he'd always refused to talk about it. As far as Billy was concerned, the past was dead and buried.

'Billy's no grass. It wasn't you then?'

'What? Of course it wasn't me. How could you think that?'

'I don't think it,' she said, thus implying someone else did, and that someone was Billy.

'I would never do that. Jesus, it would have been the kiss of death.'

She shrugged. 'He was just unlucky then. It was always on the cards with Billy anyway. If it wasn't for that, they'd have got him for something else.'

'What were you doing there with him?'

'What does Billy say we were doing?'

'I haven't asked him.'

'Why not?' Her face softened into a smile. 'I don't remember. I think we just bumped into each other on the way to Good Vibes.'

'And why didn't you come to Birmingham?' he said, surprising himself again.

'I couldn't.'

'I thought we agreed. I only came over because of you. I waited for you.'

'Come off it, FB. You only waited until a better offer came along. Don't tell me you're sorry you left Belfast.'

'No, but I just need to know. Was it your da that stopped you coming?'

'Yes. Enough now, Frank. Let's have another drink.'

They changed the subject and talked about those Saturdays in Good Vibes and the Harp Bar. Great days. They downed a few more drinks and left in search of food.

'Let's go to that Chinese you like. I can get home easily from there,' said Eve.

They took the Victoria line from Euston and then the overground. As they approached Dalston, she said: 'I'm shattered. Why don't we go back to mine instead? There's a decent takeaway up the road and I've beers in the fridge.'

What was she suggesting? Her eyes lingered on him again and straight away he knew exactly what she was suggesting. 'Is that a good idea?'

'I think so. Don't you?'

A memory of Billy telling him to embrace the danger burned into him. Billy, the top dog. Billy, the best mate who thought he'd been a grass. Billy, the guy who stole his girl. 'Yes, I do.'

45

HELLO, MY LOVE – 1992

Frank was an adulterer. Or was he? If your wife had already
left you, were you still classed as an adulterer? He didn't
know. If you were having an affair with your oldest friend's
wife, were you a dirty, lying, cheating bastard? That was a
question he did know the answer to. Yes he was. How had it
come to this? How had he stooped so low? More questions
he couldn't answer.

Ellen's continued absence and Billy's frequent trips to
America made it easy for him and Eve to have their illicit
meet ups. The hard part was behaving as if nothing was
going on when Billy was around. It was almost impossible
not to steal a kiss when they thought they might get away
with it. Even when they were trying to behave normally, the
slightest touch, deliberate or otherwise, would set Frank's
pulse racing. They daren't even look at each other, in case
the wrong kind of glance gave away their secret. It was
immoral, so very wrong. Frank appalled himself. And yet he
couldn't walk away.

Back in Belfast, when Eve had been his girlfriend, he'd
spent a lot of time imagining what sex with her would be

like. It turned out his imagination was way off. Sex with Eve was sometimes glorious and abandoned and other times, tender and loving. Crucially, it was nothing like it was with Ellen. Most of the time with Ellen, he was putting in a performance that she was in control of. But with Eve, it was just two people enjoying each other and doing whatever they pleased. It was liberating, and unusually comfortable.

He'd given up on Ellen returning now. It was almost a year to the day he'd come home and found her gone. He'd been desperate to have her back, even after the beginning of his affair with Eve. But lately, he was starting to consider the possibility of a permanent life without her and whether that life might include Eve. Tonight he was going to bring the subject up. They were at his flat. The evening had started well with an hour in bed. Now, Eve was in the shower and he was cooking dinner. The table was set for a romantic meal for two and Frank was mentally rehearsing his speech.

Eve walked in wearing Ellen's turquoise silk robe. He tried not to think about the last time he'd seen Ellen wearing it. She snuggled up against the back of him. 'It's nice, you cooking for me. I'm not used to it.' She hardly ever mentioned Billy by name when they were together these days, just as Ellen rarely dropped from Frank's lips. It wasn't a pre-agreed rule but they did it all the same.

The intercom buzzed and mild panic invaded their domestic bliss. 'Ignore it. Probably just someone got locked out,' he said.

It buzzed again.

Eve was on her way to the bedroom. 'I'll get dressed. Just in case.'

He pressed the intercom button. 'Hello.'

'It's Gavin. Let me in. I have news.'

Frank closed the dining room door before he let Gavin in.

Gavin breezed straight past him, grumbling about the lack of parking and only stopped when he saw Eve. 'Ah. Gavin Montague. I don't believe we've met.'

Eve shook his hand, very businesslike. It was a side of her that Frank hadn't seen before. 'Eve Macintyre. You might know my husband, Billy. Frank's an old friend to both of us.'

'I think I've heard the name, but I'm not familiar. Apologies.'

'Well, if you stick around you might meet him,' she said, cool as a cucumber.

'Alas, I can't.'

'Are you sure, Gavin? There's enough food to go round. I even have decent wine,' said Frank, putting on a good show of pretending his presence was welcome.

'Thank you, no. Roger's waiting in the car.'

'Roger?'

'My lodger.'

Frank's face contorted into an enormous smirk.

Gavin arched an eyebrow. 'What?'

'Your lodger is called Roger?'

'What of it? Oh for God's sake, Frank. I do wonder sometimes what my sister sees in you. Which brings me to the reason for my visit. Sorry Eve, it's a little private. I hope you'll excuse us.' He dragged Frank into the dining room, gave the table a cursory once over, and closed the door. 'Ellen wants you to call her. She's coming back. Here's the number. I have to go. You will call her, won't you?'

Frank held onto the back of a chair. All of a sudden, his world was spinning on its axis and in the space of five minutes, it was reshaping.

'Frank?'

'Yes. I'll call her. I ... it's just come as a shock. I'd assumed she wasn't coming back.'

'Ellen is full of surprises. I have to go. Roger.' He shot Frank a glare that told him not to even contemplate trifling with Roger's name again, but Frank was past that now.

Gavin held the door handle. 'Ring her tomorrow perhaps, when you've had time to take it in, and you don't have any guests. By the way, I'm glad to see you took my advice. Time to concentrate on your wife now though.'

'What is it? What's the news?' said Eve.

Frank went over to the window and watched Gavin get into his car. He felt dizzy, like he'd just been punched in the head. 'Ellen wants me to call her. She wants to come back.'

'The cheek of her. She fucks off and leaves you in the dark for a year, and then expects you to just take her back.'

'That's about the gist of it, yes.'

'You're not going to though, are you? My God, you are, aren't you? You're going to have her back.'

'I don't know what I'm going to do. I'll call her tomorrow. I owe her that much.'

'You owe her nothing. Frank, grow a pair of balls will you? She just walks all over you and you lie there begging for more.'

'Sure, and don't you do the same with Billy? You think I don't know how he treats you? No, Billy doesn't cook for you because he expects you to do everything. Just like he expects you to spend all your hard-earned money on keeping the two of you afloat while he blows his on drink and fuck knows what else.' Frank stopped before it was too late, but then he saw her face and realised it was already too late. Just like that day he'd stormed up to their place in Belfast to have it out with them, Eve was giving him the hard stare. He'd blown it.

She grabbed her things. 'This was a mistake. One huge, fucking mistake. Bye, Frank.'

It had been three days and Frank had still not called Ellen. Neither had he heard from Eve. He'd managed to hold it together for work but he'd spent the evenings full of agitation. The night after Eve had walked out, he'd gone round to her house but there was no answer. He'd tried calling her but each time, it clicked over to their answerphone so he put the phone down. Billy was back home now. There was no point in trying her again.

He didn't know what finally made him call Ellen. He'd all but decided not to after Eve had laid bare how their marriage looked to the outside world, but he was so desperately lonely that he succumbed.

It rang out for such a long time he thought she wasn't going to answer but now that he'd committed to the call, he couldn't put the receiver down. He waited in a trance-like state until the tone changed and he heard her voice on the other end of the line.

'Ellen.' He was aware that he was croaking rather than speaking.

'I thought you weren't going to call.' How strange it was to hear her again.

'I nearly didn't.' There was a whooshing sound inside his head, as if every drop of blood was firing at his brain. It was too much. His legs went from under him and he slid down the wall onto the floor.

Ellen, of course, was unaware of the effect she was

having on him. 'I understand. I've hurt you. I'm sorry. I
haven't been myself for a while. Can you forgive me?'

'I, I don't know. It's been so…' So, what? His mind
finished the words he couldn't speak So long. So tough. So
lonely. So utterly confusing. All of those things rolled into
one giant ache.

'I've missed you so much, my darling. Will you let me
make it up to you?'

'I think we may be too late for that, Ellen.'

'Please don't say that, Frank,' she sobbed. 'I beg you,
give me another chance. I'll make it right, I promise. Surely
our marriage is worth another try?'

Was it worth another shot? Frank wasn't sure. He knew
he still loved her but did he love her enough to go through
the torture that inevitably came with Ellen? Then again, he
had nothing left to lose, and maybe this time things would
be different. 'Okay. We'll try again.'

Eve had finally agreed to see him the day before Ellen's
return. They'd met up at the pub they'd gone to when
they'd bumped into each other at Euston. She wasn't
surprised when he told her Ellen was coming back. She said
she knew he wouldn't be able to say no to her. She didn't say
she was disappointed in him but it was written all over her
face. It was probably written on Frank's face too, because he
was just as disappointed in himself.

'So what do we do now?' He was hoping she'd suggest
they carried on the affair, even though the realist in him
knew he was expecting the moon on a stick.

She sighed. 'What do you want me to say? There's
nothing we can do, except pretend we never happened.'

'Do you think that's possible?'

'We have to make it possible. If it were just us, we could walk away and never see each other again, but we can't. Not unless we want to tell Billy and Ellen, and I don't think either of us is ready for that. We're not kids anymore, Frank. We've got to be grown-up about this.'

She was right. They had no choice. 'We'll do it.'

'Me and Billy. We're not the same as you and Ellen.'

Maybe not in her eyes, but there wasn't a lot of difference as far as Frank could see. If he'd told her that, she'd have flared up, so he tried another tack. 'Back in the old days, I always thought you hated him. I've never understood why–'

'Love, hate. It's a fine line isn't it? Billy gave me freedom. He still does.'

Freedom? Was that all it was? 'I could have given you freedom.'

She smiled. 'No, love, you couldn't. You're not like Billy. No one is. Your freedom is not the kind I need.'

'Well, if it's so great, how come you've been fucking me?' There, he'd snapped. He didn't mean to, but it had happened and all he could do now was wait for the shit to hit the fan.

But it didn't. She just shrugged. 'Because freedom can be lonely.'

She picked at the skin around her thumbnail. Frank noticed for the first time how sore it looked. He put his hand on hers to stop her making it worse. She looked up at him. 'It would kill Billy if he found out about us.'

'Ellen too.' It sounded like a pathetic game of adulterers one-upmanship, who could hurt their spouse the most, and Frank immediately felt like a heel.

Eve pulled her hand away. 'You have got to be kidding me? Sometimes Frank, you are one first-class idiot.'

.   .   .

Frank was waiting in arrivals for the flight from Paris, still wondering if he'd done the right thing. When he'd spoken to Ellen, it had all seemed so simple. He'd take her back, forget Eve, and make a fresh start. But seeing Eve again had sent his emotions all over the place. He didn't know how to describe what he felt for her. He didn't know if it was love. Not that it mattered, because it was clear she wasn't ready to give Billy up.

And if he was unsure about Eve, he was even more so about Ellen. She'd left him. Unlike Billy, she wasn't exactly an innocent party in all of this. But for all the havoc she wreaked, for all her haughty exterior, Ellen was fragile and he couldn't bear the thought of damaging her.

The first passengers began to file out of arrivals. Frank felt a wave of nausea rush over him. He wanted to run away. And then she appeared, her tanned face framed in a pair of big dark glasses. She looked like a movie star shunning the paparazzi.

She threw herself at him, covering him in kisses. 'Oh my darling, you came for me. I was sure you wouldn't. I love you so much. I'm so sorry. So very sorry.'

She tipped back her glasses, her eyes searching him. He saw then how red they were and how breakable she was, and in that instant, he knew who needed him most. She'd once said he was the most decent person she knew. It was time to be that person again.

He put his arms around her. 'Hello, my love.'

46

SHOULDERS TO CRY ON

Because I'm not you.

Martin was gone. He'd stormed off into the mountains half an hour ago, but his words were still ringing in Frank's ears. How was it that Martin, serial philanderer, got to act all holier than thou over Frank's one indiscretion? Everyone knew he'd cheated on his first two wives. Not to mention the other business, which Frank refused to even think about right now. And didn't he always want what Frank had? He wouldn't put it past Martin, the cheating fecker, to jump into Eve's bed as soon as he had the chance. And anyway, how did they know about him and Eve? Because it was plain to see, Finn knew as well.

'Are you all right there, Frank?' Finn had been watching him ever since Martin had left in a strop.

'I'm good, Finn. Don't you be worrying about me. While I've got you alone, Siobhan said she'd book the eejit's plane ticket. She's going to send it to both of us. And one other thing. I've realised I'm a bit out of shape. I'd like to change that. Do you think you could help me?'

'No problem. I can put together a programme for you.

We can have one to ones online to keep track. I've other clients I do that with.'

'I'll pay you the going rate, obviously.'

'No way. I wouldn't charge. It'll be my pleasure to help you.' Finn looked like it really would be a pleasure to help Frank. Beyond his wildest dreams in fact.

'Don't say anything to Martin though. He'll only take the piss.'

'You know, it wouldn't hurt for you to give Marty a chance, Frank. He's not as bad as you think he is.'

Frank didn't answer. He figured Finn probably didn't want to know how bad he thought Martin was.

'I wonder if he's okay,' said Finn.

Again, Frank didn't answer.

'I'll go look for him. It'll be dark soon. It's easy to get lost when you're not used to it.' He gave Frank a pointed look.

It took him a while to catch Finn's drift. He was, of course, referring to Frank's own storming off, when Martin had rescued him and for a short while, they sat together like proper brothers. He should help find him. Martin was infuriating, but he was his brother. Besides, Ma and Siobhan would be incandescent with rage if anything happened to him. 'You're right. Let's go and find the dozy prick.'

It didn't actually take them very long to find him. Once they followed his path for a few hundred metres, they practically fell over him. He was sitting near a lochan watching the sun go down. 'It's so tranquil. It gets you right here, doesn't it?' He punched his heart.

'Aye, it does,' said Finn. 'Sometimes it's all you need.'

'I know you don't think much of me, Frank but I have never cheated on Bronagh. The other two, yes, but never Bronagh,' said Martin.

'You need to go back home and tell her that. You can't

just run away, Marty,' said Finn.

'I will.'

'Siobhan's booked your plane ticket for the day after tomorrow,' said Frank.

'So soon.' Martin looked defeated.

Finn put his hand on Martin's shoulder. 'They're all worried about you, Marty. They want to help you.'

'They don't need to worry about me.'

'Bronagh might think otherwise,' said Frank, sounding more sympathetic than he actually felt. 'Even if she's wrong about you and Eve, she can't have been wrong about the moods.'

Martin put his head in his heads. 'She is wrong about me and Eve. It's true I've been seeing her, but not in that way. She came to me to help fix up her parents' house. Her ould fella's moved into a care home.'

'There you go then,' said Finn. 'That explains it.'

'And she needed someone to talk to. A shoulder to cry on. That's it. We're friends. And none of that friends with benefits shit either. Proper friends.'

'Has she left Billy then?' said Frank.

Martin shook his head. 'Billy's dead.'

Frank's mouth dropped open. Billy, dead?

'Not Billy?' Finn's voice cracked. 'How?'

Martin sniffed. Great tears ran down his face and dropped onto his hands. 'He killed himself. Eight months ago.'

Frank's stomach twisted. He staggered up and ran for the water. It twisted again and this time, he threw up. Still reeling, he stumbled on. Everything was swirling and bending out of shape and he thought he was going to black out. He sank to his knees. Billy Mac was gone. He was dead. How could that be?

47

WHO TOLD YOU?

Darkness was taking hold of the day and they were yet to make a move. Martin was still weeping. Frank was in shock. Both were paralysed. Frank, on hearing those words. Martin, on saying them out loud.

'We have to go back to the van. Get up and follow me.' Finn spoke with the calm authority they needed to jolt them into action. They did as he said and he led them through the heavy mist that had begun to surround and settle on them. All was quiet, save for the occasional call of a wild animal and the sound of Martin's sobs.

When they reached the van, Finn made them sit down. He wrapped a blanket around each of them, lit a fire and poured them whisky. Finn, the one-time waster, was saving them from themselves. He'd come good again.

The flames crackled, Martin wept on, and no one said anything. The fire began to die. Finn rebuilt it, refilled their glasses and Martin's tears finally dried up.

Finn broke the silence. 'Poor Eve. No wonder she needed someone to talk to.'

Martin wiped his eyes. 'Aye. She has no friends in

London anymore. She must have been desperate to choose me, what?'

'Don't do yourself down like that, Marty. You've always been great to talk to. You've a lot of empathy skills,' said Finn.

Empathy skills? The only time Frank had ever seen Martin use any empathy skills was when he was trying to get something out of someone. Or to get into their bed. He was great with the old empathy skills then. He stopped himself. This was getting out of hand and just a little bit petty. Wasn't he a new man now, after all that shedding his old skin in the freezing cold water? New man Frank wouldn't sully himself with such behaviour. New man Frank would strike while the iron was hot and ask the difficult questions. 'Why has she no friends in London?'

'Billy drove them away. He's been bad since … but he's been getting worse over the last five or so years.' Martin was still speaking about Billy in the present tense, as if he still existed.

'Do you know how he…' Frank couldn't say it. He couldn't even think it.

'Usual way. Pills and a bottle of this.' Martin held up his glass. 'He never did have a big imagination.'

Finn smiled. 'Oh I don't know, he was always coming up with big ideas about how he was going to make it.'

'Yeah, but they were never the best ideas,' said Frank. 'Lacked imagination.'

'That does sum Billy up, right enough,' said Martin.

'Did he leave a note?' said Frank.

Martin shook his head. 'No. Probably couldn't think of anything to say. You need imagination for that.'

They laughed so much it could have been the funniest thing they'd heard in ages.

'Does anyone else back home know about Billy?' said Frank.

Martin shrugged. 'I don't know about the rest of the family, but Da knows.'

'Sure, your da knows everything. He probably knows who really killed Kennedy,' said Finn.

They laughed again at the ridiculousness and faint possibility of Da being in on that particular conspiracy theory.

'Did Eve tell you about me and her?' It was new man Frank that had pushed him to ask that question. Old man Frank almost didn't want to know the answer.

'No.'

'How'd you find out then?'

For the first time since their fight, Martin looked Frank in the eye. 'How d'yer think?'

Billy then. It must have been. 'When did he tell you?'

'Years ago. Before Ellen died,' said Finn. 'We were staying with them. We went to a bar with Eve. Billy was working and met us after. He was already tanked up when he got there. He was sniping at her straight away, and she was having a go back. It ended in a big row and we got thrown out. Eve was really mad at him and walked off. Billy took us to some back street drinking club. One of those really seedy ones, you know the sort. We had a few more drinks and that's when he told us. We never let on to Eve that we knew though, did we Marty?'

'No, we've kept your secret, Frankie Boy.'

The way Martin said it made Frank feel dirty. 'So no one else knows?'

'I didn't say that. I just said we didn't tell them.'

'Who else knows then?'

'Well Da, obviously.'

Of course he did. Da knew everything. Finn was probably right about that Kennedy thing too.

Finn topped up their glasses. 'Come on now. Let's take a dram for Billy before we run out. To our ould friend Billy Mac. Wherever you are now Billy, may your drinks be plentiful and your imagination never be lacking.'

They raised their glasses and drank the whisky back in one go.

'Good luck Billy, you crazy fecker,' said Martin. He began to laugh again. They almost joined in, until they realised he wasn't laughing at all. He was crying.

Frank would have liked to have cried. He would have liked to have screamed, and yelled, and ranted. But he couldn't. Not because he didn't need to, but because he didn't have the right to. Because the more he thought about it, the more he was convinced, he'd played a part in Billy's death.

48

FOOTSTEPS ON THE LANDING – 1995

When Ellen came back to Frank, she'd been full of remorse and desperate for his forgiveness. Nothing was too much trouble when it came to regaining his love. Not that Frank had fallen out of love with her. It was just that he'd resigned himself to living without her and had settled for someone else. He'd realised that within the first month of her return and was thankful Gavin had called that night and stopped him from ruining both his own life and Eve's. That was what he told himself almost every day until he was convinced it was true. But when the cracks in their sticking-plaster marriage began to reopen, Frank knew he'd been kidding himself.

It started as it always did, with the snipes and digs, the pointed remarks about his job, his appearance, and his paintings. They were tiny little things at first, building up layer by layer until it was unmissable. That's when it dawned on him that the honeymoon period was over and they were back to square one. In the space of two years, he was in exactly the same place he'd been in before she'd walked out on him.

Tonight, the griping began as soon as he came in from work. She could have got the dinner started, or done last night's washing up, but that kind of thing was beneath her. She was lying on the sofa, reading that hideous magazine she wrote for. 'At last. I'm starving.'

'If you want me home earlier, we should move closer to my work.' He'd given up apologising for the traffic long ago.

'Or you could just give up your job in that horrible school. Gavin could get you into somewhere much nicer and closer to home.'

Frank didn't bother to answer. He went into the kitchen and switched on the radio. The Happy Mondays were playing back-to-back. He turned it up, took a beer out of the fridge, and danced to 'Step On' as he pulled together the ingredients for a vegetable chilli. Ellen was going through her 'Meat is Murder' phase. Or at least she would be, if she actually liked The Smiths. She'd grown up with the hunting, shooting and fishing set, so it wasn't that she thought it was murdering the poor wee animals. It was more that she thought it was murdering her. She had some weird ideas sometimes.

She appeared in the doorway, having managed to extricate herself from the sofa. 'You look ludicrous. Has no one ever told you, you can't dance?'

'Nope. And I wouldn't give a toss if they had.' He turned the radio up a notch. The Stone Roses were on now, 'Sally Cinnamon'.

'You're so pitiful.' She trounced off, back to the sofa.

Frank congratulated himself. He'd won that round.

She stayed away from the kitchen, never her favourite room, until he called her in. He was in a good mood now. He'd successfully batted away her jibes, had a couple of cans and the food was smelling pretty good.

Ellen reappeared, her face set like a sulky teenager. 'What is it?'

'Dinner's ready. Do you want to try it?'

She peered into the pan. 'I can't eat that slop.'

That was it. Frank snapped. 'If my cooking's so bad, why don't you get off your arse and take a turn for a change.'

'Because I don't need to. I can buy someone to do it for me.'

'You know what, Ellen? I've had it up to here. You're just not worth the effort.'

'Oh for God's sake. I was just joking.'

But Frank was already on his way out the door. For once, he was going to be the one that walked. Although he wasn't one hundred per cent on where he was walking to.

An hour later, he arrived at Billy's usual pub. Billy practically lived there these days. Eve would often joke the only way she knew she'd see him was if she went there. They were friends again now. Out of necessity more than anything. It was too tricky to make excuses not to see each other when your partners were all for it. At first it had been awkward but they'd got over it.

Billy was at his normal table holding court over a couple of mates from work. They might even have been the newest pop sensations. Frank wouldn't know. He was too busy trying to stop himself drowning in misery and self-pity to be keeping up with the latest chart-toppers.

He got a couple of pints, with a whisky chaser for Billy. Beer didn't touch the sides for Billy these days. He drank it like normal people drank tea.

When Frank reached the table, Billy patted an empty seat next to him. 'FB, how are yer? Am I glad to see you. These lightweights were gonna leave me here on my own.'

The others looked relieved to have someone to hand the baton over to. They were soon gone and it was just Frank and Billy.

'Where's Lottie?' Only Adrian called Ellen that and it took Frank by surprise to hear it from Billy. Especially since Billy's opinion of Adrian was a pretty poor one, although Frank never got why Billy didn't like him.

'Fuck knows. I left her at home, but she's probably had her brother whisk her off to an expensive restaurant by now.'

'Ouch. Somebody's a little annoyed there.'

'We had an argument. Over my cooking, would you believe? I walked out.'

'Remind me not to criticise your lemon souffle. I'd hate for you to walk out on me.'

'Very funny.'

'C'mon, drink up. You need to get pissed.'

Billy was already pissed and Frank was never going to catch up. He tried but it soon became clear that one of them had to be relatively sober to get them home, and it wasn't going to be Billy.

There was a look of revolted resignation on Eve's face when she let them in.

'Frank's walked out on the lady,' slurred Billy.

'Ellen? You've left her?' said Eve.

Billy started to giggle. 'No, he hasn't left her. He just walked out in a huff. He'll be back there in no time, ready for another kicking.'

Eve rounded on him. 'Shut up, you. The fucking state of you. Do you want to stay here tonight, Frank? You can sleep in the spare room.'

'Would that be okay? I've nowhere else to go.'

'No bother at all. I'll make up the bed, then you can help me get that one upstairs.'

Eve's anger with Billy had fizzled out by the time she came back down. She was even laughing as they dragged him up the stairs, one step forward, two steps back. She pulled Billy's jacket off before they lay him down on the bed. Frank helped to take off his shoes.

'I can take it from here. I'm a dab hand at it,' she said.

'I'll go to bed then. Thanks for being so decent about this.'

She started unbuttoning Billy's shirt and wasn't listening. Frank hoped she wasn't anyway. It was a dumb thing to say and he already felt bad enough about the whole situation.

He undressed in the spare bedroom. This room was supposed to have been for Billy and Eve's kids but they hadn't happened yet. He'd asked her why not, back when they were having their affair and she'd said they were too busy with work. A while later, she let it slip that they'd been trying for years.

Frank switched off the bedside lamp and lay in the dark thinking about what Billy had said about him going back for another kicking. He was tired of being kicked. Maybe it really was time to walk away.

The door opened and light from the landing filled the room. Eve stood in the doorway wearing a dressing gown. An image of her in Ellen's robe flashed in front of him and he silently cursed Gavin.

She closed the door gently, walked over to him and took off the dressing gown to reveal bare skin. Frank thought of Billy, sleeping it off in the next room. He should tell her to go. He should get dressed and go back to his wife. He should do both those things, but he couldn't. He reached out and touched her softly rounded body. There was nothing hard about Eve. Everything was softness. On the outside anyway. She was the exact opposite of Ellen.

'What about Billy?' he whispered.

She slipped into bed. 'He's comatose. He won't resurface till tomorrow afternoon.'

'Eve–'

She put her finger on his lips. 'Shh.'

He was going to tell her how much he'd missed her, how sorry he was, but he just held her in the dark and made love to her, all the time listening for the sound of Billy's footsteps on the landing.

49

AS LONG AS IT'S NOT YOU – 1995

From the moment he woke up, Frank was riddled with guilt. The affair had been bad enough but last night, he'd hit an all-time low. He still couldn't believe he'd done it. He blamed Ellen for pushing him into it. For about ten seconds. Then he gave himself a good talking to. No one could say his marriage was an easy one, but it was no excuse. There was only himself to blame.

He was alone. Eve must have slipped out during the night and gone back to Billy. Another wave of guilt crashed over him. What the hell was he thinking, taking advantage of Billy's generosity like that? He'd never be able to face him again. He got dressed and tiptoed out onto the landing. The main bedroom's door was closed. He crept downstairs and stole out of the house like a thief, glad he didn't have to face either Billy or Eve today.

Frank found the flat empty. On the way home, his guilt had expanded to include Ellen. For all their ups and downs, he was in no doubt that she loved him and he didn't want to hurt her, but he'd made up his mind to go. Perhaps he didn't need to worry about that if she'd left him again. She might have made it easy for him. He sank down onto the sofa and put his head in his hands. God, it was a mess.

When he caught sight of a note on the coffee table, he almost smiled at the futility of his strike for freedom. He couldn't even leave his wife properly. That's how shit he was. He wondered if this one would be longer than the last. Less, it's not you it's me and more, it's definitely you this time. There was only one way to find out. He picked up the note and read it.

'Daddy's had a heart attack. Gavin's taken me to the hospital. I'll call you when I can.

I love you x.'

A heart attack? The Brigadier wasn't indestructible then. The note suggested a fondness between Ellen and her parents, but she'd pulled up the drawbridge when they refused to attend the wedding and as far as Frank knew, she'd made no attempt to reconcile with them. And yet her words on paper told a different story. Then there were those three words solely for his benefit. *'I love you'.* He despised himself all over again.

He checked the answerphone. Ellen had left a message that morning: 'Hello darling. Sorry to have missed you. The doctors have stabilised Daddy but he's still critical. I'm at the hospital. I'll call again this evening.'

She sounded normal. As if they hadn't had a row the night before that had resulted in him walking out on her. Perhaps someone else had been there. Her mother maybe. That would be it. Ellen wouldn't have wanted her mother to know things were strained between them.

He went into the kitchen. The veggie chilli that had caused so much trouble was still in the pan on the hob, looking a bit dry around the edges but otherwise okay. It would do for tonight's dinner. For now, he was desperate for coffee and a shower. He needed to wash all traces of Eve away.

It was late by the time Ellen called. She'd been at the hospital all day and had only just returned to her parents' home. She sounded worn out. 'He's no longer officially critical but he'll have to remain in hospital for some time. They're saying he'll need an operation. Daddy's not too happy about it. You know what he's like.'

No, Frank didn't know what old man Montague was like. His only face-to-face experience of him had been that one cut-short visit. If that was anything to go by, then it was highly possible he'd be unhappy. Especially if any of the doctors were Johnny Foreigners. Not the Brigadier's cup of tea at all. Even if it did mean they were saving his life.

'I'll have to stay here for a while. You don't mind, do you darling?' She was still pretending all was well with them. Sometimes Frank wondered if Ellen had this internal switch that enabled her to turn things on and off when it was convenient.

'I don't mind at all,' he said, dutifully. 'Do you need me to bring some clothes over?'

'Would you? That would be awfully good of you. Thank you, darling.'

Frank was approaching the Montagues' home in his car. He'd been married to Ellen for twelve years and this was only the second time he'd been here. If that didn't tell him something, he didn't know what did.

Ellen ran out and treated him to the kind of over-the-top greeting that usually followed one of her absences. She took his hand. 'Come inside. Gavin's here with Roger.'

Mrs Montague was also there. Her stony eyes did a quick and brutal assessment of him. Judging by the sour face, his best T-shirt and jeans were not deemed satisfactory attire. Roger the Lodger, who had the look of a toned down Andrew Ridgeley, had obviously nailed the off-duty but still classy look, since Mrs M was all over him. Frank wondered if she knew that he and Gavin were more than just friends. Even if Gavin was still maintaining the pretence, the Montagues must have guessed by now. Maybe Ellen wasn't the only one with a convenient internal switch.

Gavin at least, was pleased to see him. 'Will you stay for lunch, Frank?'

'Thanks but I have to get back. I've a pile of marking to do.'

'Frank's a teacher, Mummy,' said Ellen to a bewildered Mrs Montague. By the look of her, it was the first she'd heard of her son-in-law's profession.

Ellen walked him out to the car, her arm in his. Once again he'd couldn't escape the feeling that it was all for her mother's benefit. When they reached the car, she turned to face him and held both his hands 'I don't know how long I'll be away for. Will you be all right without me?' It was quite endearing really, if you believed any of it.

'Take as long as you like. I'll be fine.' He let her hands slip from his. 'I'll be here for you while you need it. But afterwards, I think we should call it a day.'

Her mouth parted slightly and her beautiful brow furrowed. Frank expected her to say something, maybe shout, or cry. But she just nodded and took a step backwards.

He got in the car. Through the rearview mirror he saw her standing, tall and magnificent, watching him drive all the way down the long driveway.

He went straight to Billy and Eve's house. Eve had called him yesterday to arrange it. 'We don't need to worry about interruptions. Billy's gone to New York for a couple of weeks,' she'd said. It seemed their relationship was back on.

As soon as she shut the door on the outside world, Eve began to undress him. Frank pulled away. There was something he needed to say: 'I've told Ellen I'll support her while her dad's ill but after that, it's over.'

Eve frowned. 'How did she take it?'

'Very calmly. She might need time to process it.'

'I bet she will. It's probably the first time she won't get her own way. What'll you do? Where will you live?'

'I dunno. I haven't thought that far ahead. I thought maybe…' He let it tail off, scared to put a voice to his hopes.

'Maybe what, that I'd leave Billy? Is that what you think this is all about?'

'I haven't a fucking clue what this is all about. I thought we'd agreed to stop three years ago and the next thing I know, you're climbing into bed with me again. Maybe I'm being an idiot, but I thought maybe you'd changed your mind.'

She cast her eyes over him and, for the second time that day, he felt like he was being assessed. He couldn't help thinking the conclusion would be just as savage as Mrs Montague's.

'You need to understand something about Billy and me. There are things we've shared that keep us together, no matter what. Whatever happens, we will never leave each other. We're too … invested.'

Frank felt small and pathetic. He'd made the wrong assumptions about her, jumped to the wrong conclusions. She didn't want him instead of Billy. She wanted them both. On her terms.

But Eve hadn't finished. She had more to say: 'The other thing you need to know is that Billy doesn't care who I sleep with. As long as it's not you.'

And that's when he realised, he wasn't her only indiscretion.

50

THE MAGIC OF PARIS – 1996

You'd have expected a man with the will and ego the size and strength of the Brigadier's to have made a speedy recovery. Apparently not. If anything, it worked against him. It seemed the will to get well was outmatched by the ego that said he knew better than the health professionals responsible for his care. Ironically, having spent a lifetime barking out orders, old man Montague had difficulty in following doctor's orders and was regularly pushing himself into a relapse. Frank knew this because Ellen told him on her weekly visits home.

Six months had passed since the Brigadier's heart attack. At first Ellen had stayed with her mother permanently, her only contact with Frank being a phone call every few days. But when her father left hospital, she settled into a routine of coming home at the weekend, and Frank's weekly pattern was set. In the week he saw Eve, whenever she could get away. Weekends were reserved for Ellen. It was like he had two very separate lives, requiring two very separate personalities. With Ellen, he was the caring supportive husband, albeit one that was not being wholly intimate with her. He'd made it clear their marriage was on notice and that at some point in the near future they'd be going different ways.

Being with Eve was just pure hedonism. The knowledge that she wasn't going to leave Billy for him had released Frank from any lingering pretence that it was anything more than mutual attraction and sex. If it ended tomorrow, that would be it. He could walk away without looking back.

Frank drove up to the Montagues' mansion and stopped outside. It was Saturday morning and he was here to pick Ellen up. He didn't always do the drive. Sometimes Ray, the Brigadier's man, brought her to London. Sometimes it was Gavin. This week, Ellen had asked him to come himself.

She came straight out, probably because she didn't want to risk further setbacks to the Brigadier's health, caused by close proximity to his Irish son-in-law. She kissed his cheek. That was as close to sex as they got these days. 'Good news. I've managed to get time off for good behaviour. I've booked us a little holiday.' She laughed then caught the look on his face and her expression changed. 'It is the spring holiday, isn't it? Don't tell me I've got the dates wrong.'

'It is. But you shouldn't have just booked something up without asking. I might have had plans. I was thinking of going to see Adrian.' It was a lie. Ade and Stella had taken their kids camping. The truth was that Eve had booked a couple of days off work and they were going to spend much of that time together.

'I'm sorry, darling. I wanted it to be a surprise. Adrian won't mind. It's just a few days in Paris. I thought you'd enjoy the museums. It's my way of saying thank you.'

'What for?'

'For putting up with me and all of this, for a start. You will come won't you, Frank?'

Her eyes were brimming. Even though he knew it was all an act to get what she wanted, his heart still tugged. 'Well, I suppose I've always wanted to see the Mona Lisa.'

She squealed with delight. 'Sometimes, my darling, I love you so much I can't contain myself.'

Frank laughed. Ellen beamed at him, her face questioning. It would have been a good moment to tell her he loved her too, and he did still love her, but it would have been a cruel kindness. One that filled her with false hope. Her face dropped. She got in the car and wiped away a tear that had escaped and was trickling down her cheek.

Paris was all Frank had expected it to be. If he'd been here with Eve, he'd have had the most amazing time. Sure, they'd have visited the museums but they'd have eaten bucketloads of food, got drunk, and had a great craic. But he was here with Ellen and her exacting standards. They couldn't just look at a painting and admire it for its beauty. She had to give him a running commentary on it. They just couldn't neck a bottle of vin de la maison. It had to be top notch and savoured. Food had to be respected. Laughs too were thin on the ground.

Ellen came in from the bedroom. She was wearing a black dress that skimmed her curves and her hair was up, revealing simple diamond studs in her ears. 'How do I look?'

'Stunning,' said Frank, and he meant it. Except looks weren't everything, were they? You couldn't build a lifetime together on looks alone. Once upon a time there'd been some substance to their marriage. That seemed like a long time ago. Frank consoled himself with the knowledge that this would be their last holiday together. Soon, all of it would be nothing more than a sad memory.

'Thank you, kind sir.' She reached out and fixed his tie. It didn't need straightening. 'I've booked a table at my most favourite restaurant in Paris. I used to go there all the time when…'

'When you left me.'

She grimaced. 'I'm sorry Frank. I've not been the best of wives, have I? I don't blame you for wanting a divorce.' It was the first time either of them had actually said the word. It felt like progress.

'I'm sorry too. I haven't always been the husband you want.'

Ellen laughed. 'Frank, my love, you have always been the husband I want. You know what, forget the restaurant. Let's do something else.'

Some time later, they were strolling around Paris, their finery cast off and replaced by jeans and T-shirts. They'd eaten in a bistro that Ellen would normally bypass and were following it up with an impromptu bar crawl. It was like the old days, but they were different people now. All the same, they were enjoying themselves. It was a good way to bow out of a failing marriage.

They got back to their hotel and retrieved the key from a sour-faced receptionist which made them laugh all the more. Giggling hysterically, they unlocked the door and fell into their room. Then, they tore each other's clothes off and had sex like they used to, back when she rode him like he was one of her daddy's stallions.

51

CRUNCH TIME – 1996

In the cold light of the next morning, Frank knew he'd made a stupid mistake. He'd been a fool to lose control like that. He'd drunk too much and let himself get overtaken by memories of what had once been, instead of remembering the reality of his situation. He had to pull this back.

Ellen had arranged breakfast in their room. Sitting opposite, she was wearing the turquoise robe. It had been left loose, purposely he guessed, so that he could see her pert breasts and perfect frame in between a basket of croissants and a pot of coffee. It would have made a good painting. *Nude with Pastries*, maybe. Or perhaps, *A Woman's Guile*. That last one was a bit sexist of him. He knew most women weren't like that. Just the ones he got involved with.

'Coffee?' She poured it into his cup. It came out a little too fast, causing a splash to land on her bare nipple. She flinched slightly, then looked at him, eyebrows arched.

Much as he would have liked to have licked it off, Frank resisted the urge. 'I think we got carried away last night. I'm sorry. I drank too much. I don't want to give you the impression everything's back to normal with us.'

Ellen drew the robe together and tightened the belt. 'No, you wouldn't want to give that impression, would you? God forbid.' She picked a croissant out of the basket and dropped it onto her plate. 'I suppose you have your new life all mapped out.'

'I haven't made any plans,' he said, realising that he really should be making them by now.

She tore the croissant apart and dabbed jam on it. 'You can't have the flat.'

'I don't want it. It's yours, you bought it.'

'Quite.' She stood up and made for the bedroom, slamming the door behind her.

Frank let out a long breath, glad that this was their last day. They'd be home by this evening. She'd be back with her parents soon enough and he could relax. At least she hadn't asked him if there was someone else. He would have asked it, but then he wasn't Ellen. She probably hadn't even considered that he would want anybody else. Or that anyone else would want him.

Unlike Ellen, it was the first question Adrian asked. He and Stella were back from their camping trip and Frank had gone to stay with them on his return from Paris. Ade didn't seem surprised when Frank said he was leaving her. 'I love Lottie to bits, but I know what she's like. Is there someone else?'

Now that the question was out there, Frank didn't know how to respond to it, because he really didn't want to lie. But Adrian knew him too well and made the correct assumption without him needing to speak. 'Anyone I know?'

'Eve.'

Adrian nodded. 'Is she planning to leave Billy the Wanker for you?'

'I don't think so, no. She likes the arrangement as it is.'

'I imagine she does.'

'What do you mean by that?'

'Best of both worlds, isn't it? Although I'll never understand what she sees in that loud mouthed twat, if I'm honest. Mind you, I've never understood what you see in him either.'

'I've known Billy since I was a kid, he's my oldest friend.'

'And yet you're screwing his wife.' Adrian held up his hand. 'I'm not judging you, mate. I'm just saying, don't kid yourself there's anything between you and Billy, other than having the bad luck to be born in the same place and finding the same woman attractive.'

Frank wasn't entirely convinced that was true but one thing was sure, he couldn't go on like this. While he was with Ellen, he could kid himself it was all right to have this fling with Eve, just as long as he ignored the guilt over Billy. But when he and Ellen split, what would he have then? A part-time fling and one hell of a guilty conscience. 'I need to get out of all this madness. It's not me, Ade. It's too much.'

'I know, mate. I know. If you want a completely new start, one of our English teachers is retiring at the end of the school year.'

It had been two months since the Paris trip. On his way home from work, Frank bought a bottle of gin and some tonic water from the off-licence. Eve was coming over and it was her preferred tipple. He'd gone back to the same arrangement of seeing her in the week. Ellen had stayed away for a while after the trip, but then she'd started coming back at the weekends.

Frank had applied for the job at Adrian's school while the memory of Paris was fresh and the need to get away was keenest. Not quite a spur of the moment thing, but not fully thought through. Somewhere in the recruitment process, he'd grown used to the idea. His interviews had gone well, he thought. He liked what he saw of the school, and the idea of being near Adrian and Stella was a draw. All in all, a fresh start in a city he'd always felt at home in was becoming increasingly appealing.

He'd told Ellen about the job. She'd taken it remarkably well. There were no tantrums or tears, just quiet acceptance. In fact, they were getting on pretty well. That made him nervous. It was only a matter of time before something blew. He hadn't mentioned the job to Eve. If he got it, he'd tell her. Then he'd leave it up to her to decide what she wanted to do. Although in his heart, he already knew what she would do and he was preparing himself for the end of their affair.

The letter was waiting for Frank on the doormat. He ripped the envelope open with shaking hands. When he read the letter, he shook even more. The job was his. They wanted him to start in September. It was crunch time.

Eve pressed the downstairs intercom. He let her into the building and poured her drink so that he had it in his hand as he opened the door. She took it from him, had a sip and gasped. 'Boy, did I need that.' It was a little joke of theirs that they did every time, a private ritual that added some legitimacy to what they were doing.

She dropped her bag in the hall and took her drink straight into the bedroom. 'I've two hours. Let's make the most of it.'

Frank undressed. He'd tell her later about the job.

When they were done, they lay next to each other on the bed. Eve rolled onto her side to face him. 'That was just what I needed. You know when we were going together in Belfast, I used to fantasise about having sex with you. I knew you'd be good at it.'

He ran his fingers along the length of her body. 'I used to do the same about you. Although I thought you'd be crap at it.'

She slapped him. 'Cheeky fecker. Go on and make me another drink. And have you any nibbles? I'm starving.'

Frank went into the kitchen and made two more drinks. He found a large bag of peanuts in the cupboard, gripped it between his teeth, and picked up the drinks.

He reached the hall just as the front door opened. Ellen stood in the doorway and stared at him. He must have been some sight, stark naked, a big bag of nuts in his mouth and a drink in each hand. His teeth let go of the peanuts and they fell to the ground. She released her grip on the door. It clattered against the wall. Behind her, the door of the flat opposite opened. Their elderly neighbour came out, took one look at Frank's tackle, and swiftly went back in again.

Ellen's eyes flitted from one drink to the other, then to the bag of nuts at Frank's feet. She closed the door, pushed past Frank, and marched into the bedroom.

Eve pulled the sheet up to her neck. Ellen snorted. 'Don't be so fucking ridiculous.'

'Ellen.' Frank was still in the hall. He'd imagined this scenario a number of times. Well, not this particular scenario, but something like it. In all his imaginings, he'd been the cool one taking control of the situation. He'd never been the naked eejit, tongue-tied and glued to the spot in his own hall, with a pair of redundant gin and tonics in his hands.

Ellen came up close to him. 'You've dropped something, darling.' She picked up the nuts and shoved them with such force at his dick that he could feel them crunching against his balls. Then she swung the door open again and walked out.

Frank put the drinks down and went to shut the door. The neighbour was treated to another glimpse of his private parts as she made a second attempt to leave home, unfettered by lewd images. He gave her an apologetic look. She returned it with a scowl and scurried off towards the lift.

'Fuck. Are you all right?' said Eve, still under the sheet.

'Aye. I think perhaps–'

'Yeah, you're right. I should go. You don't think she'll do anything stupid, do you?'

'I don't know. I'll see if I can find her.'

Eve was dressed and gone within minutes. Frank went to all the local places Ellen liked to go to but he couldn't find her. He went back to the flat and called Gavin. If anyone knew where she might be, it would be him.

'She's here. Just a minute.' Gavin went away for a few seconds. 'Just closing the study door. Ellen's in the sitting room, drowning her sorrows with Roger. I take it you didn't follow my advice when she came back to you? Really, Frank. I'm rather surprised and more than a little disappointed in you.'

It was rather like being told off by a richer, better educated version of Ma. But Gavin wasn't Ma and so Frank felt no inclination to take the telling. 'Actually, I did follow your advice until life with your sister became intolerable again. I'm sorry for what Ellen saw, but our marriage was over some time ago. She knows I'm looking for a divorce. She must have told you that.'

'No, she did not. Quite the contrary. Look, I think it's best if she stays here for the time being. We'll keep an eye on her. I'll call you tomorrow.'

The next day was a pain in the arse. The worst pupils were worse than usual and even the better-behaved ones seemed to have made it their mission to wind Frank up. It was as if they knew he was leaving and were punishing him for it. It was a relief when the end of day bell went and he was left in the peace and quiet of the classroom.

It didn't last long. A couple of the boys from his form pushed the door open. 'Sir, you'd better come outside.'

Frank tutted and followed them out to the car park. 'What is it now?'

'That,' said one of them, pointing towards what was left of his car. Every window and light had been smashed. There was a huge dent in the bonnet.

Frank's first thought was that it was Ellen, but then he saw Billy coming his way, with a baseball bat. 'You bastard. You think you can fuck my wife and get away with it?' He was drunk, but that didn't make him any less dangerous.

Frank turned to the kids, their safety his most immediate concern. 'Boys, get inside the school. Go to the secretary's office.'

The boys, hyped up on the excitement, stayed where they were.

'I said inside. Now!' That did it, they reluctantly slunk back into the building.

'Oh you're the big man, so. Shouting at kids. Let's see how big you are now, Frankie Boy.' Billy swung the bat straight at Frank. It hit him square in the stomach and he went down.

Winded, Frank sucked in air and tried to form some words: 'If you've hurt Eve, I'll–'

'What? Kill me? You haven't got the guts. You've always been soft. Don't you be worrying yourself about Eve. I wouldn't lay a hand on her. But I'll tell you what, FB. If you go near her again, I'll have you gone just like that.' He snapped his fingers. 'I know people. You know what I'm saying? I could make you disappear, and not even your da would know where to find you.'

To Frank's relief, the Head came out of the building. 'We've called the police. They're on their way.'

'And there was me just gonna knock his head off.' Billy turned to leave. 'I'm not done with you yet, Frank. Keep looking over your shoulder. Because one day, I'll be behind you.'

Frank had been given the rest of the week off. He'd managed to persuade the Head not to pursue things any further, but they'd both agreed it was a good thing he was moving on. He lay on the sofa, bruised and tender but otherwise still intact.

Eve had called him earlier to say it was over between them. 'We can't do this anymore. It's killing Billy.'

If anyone was close to being killed it was Frank, not Billy. He hadn't told her that, but he had asked how Billy had found out. Eve said Ellen had told him. It hadn't come as a surprise.

Ellen let herself in. Gavin had phoned to warn him she was on her way, so Frank was expecting her. She sat down in an armchair. 'Well you look dreadful.'

'Thanks. It turns out Billy's quite handy with the baseball bat.'

'Oh. I'm sorry about that, but he had a right to know.'

'Well he knows now, so good job you.'

'Aren't you going to ask me why I came back early?'

He shook his head. Whatever it was, he didn't want to hear it. He'd waited for her to come just so he could tell her to her face how much he hated her. Because right now, that was exactly how he felt. Once he'd adored her, worshipped her even. But she'd beaten anything resembling love out of him and now he loathed her. His bags were packed. He was going to tell her exactly that and then he was leaving.

'I wanted to give you some news personally. I'm pregnant.'

Frank's need for vengeance came to an abrupt halt. Had she just said she was pregnant? 'But you're on the pill.'

'I haven't bothered for a while. It didn't seem necessary as we weren't doing anything. It was that night in Paris.'

'I got that job. I'm moving back to Birmingham.' It was a stupid response, but it was the shock. They were having a baby. What the hell was he going to do now?

52

YOU'VE STILL GOT ME

When Martin was a kid he used to have nightmares about men doing bad things to him. Sometimes those men were the soldiers. Sometimes they were the Balaclavas. When it happened, he'd come into Frank's bed and cling to him until a peaceful sleep claimed him. Frank had forgotten that until now, forgotten how he used to soothe his wee brother to sleep with tales of big adventures they'd have together when they were older. They'd go over the water and catch criminals, just like the Famous Five. Or go the other way, to America, and be like the Hardy Boys. Always one for the reading, Frank had been very into those sort of books at the time. Martin's main concern was whether their adventures came with a four-legged friend. 'And will we have a dog like Timmy, Frank?' he'd say. It always seemed to be important to him.

'We will.'

'What would he be like, Frank?'

'Big. With lots of hair. A bit dopey, but loyal and steadfast.' The reply was always the same, because that was what Martin wanted to hear. Funny. He could have been describing Fred, the dog he finally did get. Perhaps that's why he and Fred clicked. It was destiny.

From behind him, Martin sniffed. They were sharing the bed in the campervan. Finn had suggested it, although he had sensibly opted for the tent.

'Do you remember how you used to come into my bed after a bad dream, Marty?' said Frank.

Another sniff. 'Aye. We'd make up stories until I fell asleep.'

Not quite how Frank remembered Martin's input, but it wasn't the time to split hairs. Although, now that he thought about it, it was Martin who came up with the name Balaclavas in the first place. 'Do you remember how you'd always ask for a dog?'

'I do. I was mad for dogs. I thought I'd have a dozen of them when I grew up.'

'I have one. His name's Fred.'

'No. Really? What's he like Frank?'

'Big. With lots of hair. A bit dopey, but loyal and steadfast.'

'You got yourself a Timmy.'

'I did. What about you?'

'Nah. No dog to keep the bad guys away. Just me.'

'You've still got me,' said Frank. But Martin had already been claimed by sleep. Whether it was peaceful or not, Frank didn't know.

In the absence of any rest of his own, Frank thought about those few days in 1996 when he was certain his life was about to end. He didn't doubt for a minute that Billy would either kill him, or have him killed. He was the kind of mad bastard that would do just that. It was some years before he stopped looking over his shoulder and under his car, or before the sight of an unusual looking package through the letterbox didn't leave his mouth dry and his stomach lurching.

Ellen's pregnancy changed everything. At first she punished him with talk of an abortion but when Frank said they should try again for the sake of the child, she agreed to keep it. Looking back on it, he could see the baby had been her bargaining tool. He wouldn't be surprised if she'd organised the Paris trip for the specific purpose of conceiving a child. And if Paris hadn't worked, perhaps she'd have tried something else. Because regardless of his feelings for her, he would never have left a child. He was no Martin, and Ellen knew that.

He wondered whether she'd already known about Eve before that night, because her reaction had been so measured. For Ellen, anyway. After those first few days, she never mentioned Eve or Billy again. It was as if they'd never existed and all that mattered was that she kept him.

Frank's only stipulation was that they moved to Birmingham. It had been a fight but Ellen eventually agreed to it, only because he'd made it clear his life might depend on it. When they moved into a rented house near Adrian, she was already beginning to show. Adrian and Stella talked them through everything and were much more helpful than the hospital. By the time Robyn arrived they were ready, physically at least.

Frank fell into sleep, his mind replaying the moment his darling daughter first came into the world. It was the one thing that gave him peace.

The morning light shone through a crack in the blinds directly into Frank's eyes. With all the drama of last night, he hadn't closed it properly and now he was paying the

price. Martin was curled up around him. For some reason
that made Frank smile.

Breakfast was a subdued affair. The news of Billy's death
hung over them, and this was the day their road trip ended.
None of them seemed ready to come to terms with either of
those things.

'Eve told me that Billy was on the way out anyway. His
liver. You know how he was with the drink. He's been killing
himself with it for decades. I guess he didn't want to hang
around to the bitter end,' said Martin.

'Do you think the drinking was because of me and Eve?'
said Frank.

Martin shook his head. 'He was already on that track
well before then.'

Something approaching relief found some light in
Frank's mood. His conscience could rest easy. For now, at
least.

'I'm sorry I left it so late to tell you he was dead.'

'I guess your timing could have been better.' Frank said
it without malice. 'Is that what this was all about?'

Martin nodded. 'It was the only way to get you here. I
knew Ma and Siobhan would have you come after me.'

'And Bronagh?'

Martin began to crumble. When did his brother get so
soft?

'Marty, do you think you might consider counselling? It
helped me, and I think you've a lot going on up there.' Finn
tapped the side of his own head.

Martin shrugged.

'I know someone who saw a therapist because she had a
lot of historic trauma. It really helped her. She's a changed
woman now.' Frank was thinking of Geraldine, Netta's

mum. He wished Geraldine were here now. She had an uncanny knack of knowing what to say in these situations.

'I'll think about it. What time is this flight Siobhan's booked for me?'

Finn checked the email. 'It's tomorrow at ten. We've one more night in Glasgow. Let's make it a proper farewell. Not too mad though. You've an early start.'

Martin laughed. 'Finn Meister, the voice of reason. What happened to you, man?'

'I grew up.' Finn was looking a tad pleased with himself in Frank's opinion. Probably because he knew that against all odds, he'd turned out to be the most grown-up of them all. Certainly the most well balanced.

53

GUILT, REGRETS, AND FRILLY KNICKERS

Netta had stopped off to see her mum and dad on the way home, so she was a little later than usual. Hence the ensuing madness coming from the two younger dogs in her charge. She let them out into the back garden and they tore around in circles, leaving nothing but carnage behind. They fed off each other. Alone, each dog was something approaching normal. Together, they were quite mad.

Her mum and dad had been keen to hear all about Frank's trip, and Netta had dredged her memory banks for information she'd gleaned from Frank in an effort to give them as much detail as possible. That was when she realised just how scant the information was. The calls had been few and far between. He'd sent messages and photos too but even when pieced together, they didn't add up to a fat lot. For an English teacher, Frank was extremely brief with his prose. Not that she was expecting a travelogue or anything, but it would have been nice to have had a little more material to work with. And if she was being really picky, a little more honesty wouldn't go amiss.

It had been a funny week. With the kids off doing their

own things, she'd started it thinking she was going to be spending a quiet week with Frank. In her mind's eye, she'd have been coming home from work, or the foodbank where she volunteered, to romantic meals lovingly prepared by her man. They'd have shared a bottle of wine and talked about their day. They might even have had sex. She'd been looking forward to it. Although, she reminded herself, not enough to return from Brighton when she was supposed to.

When she'd gone to Claire's, Netta had known Doogie might be there too. As usual with Doogie, there was a will he-won't he element involved. Although, to be fair, this time it was because he was helping Grace with the lambing season. Quite a change from the excuses he used back when they were a couple.

She'd like to think it was the lack of certainty that had stopped her mentioning Doogie's possible visit to Frank beforehand. But while she was thinking about honesty, she might as well be honest with herself. It was because she felt a bit uneasy talking to Frank about Doogie. In the present tense anyway. When it came to conversations about Doogie in her past, Frank was there all the way with her. When she mentioned him in the here and now, Frank made the right noises, but there was something in the way his body tensed slightly that gave away his true feelings. Not jealousy. Frank wasn't like that. Vulnerability. That was it. Netta sensed vulnerability. So she didn't say anything to him, and when Doogie did actually turn up, she pretended it was a surprise. She hadn't exactly lied, just skewed the truth a little.

To her shame, not only had she stretched the facts, she'd also decided to stay on for an extra day, and the reason for that was probably the hardest shame to deal with. It was because she still got a thrill from being with the man who had been her first love. They were great friends now and that was all, but you never really lost that buzz when you loved someone intensely, did you? And so she'd weighed up one more day with Doogie against an extra one with Frank, and Doogie won. It had been an easy choice because things had got a bit too comfortable of late. She liked comfortable. She liked that she didn't have to be anything other than herself with Frank. But there was a fine line between comfortable and boring, and lately she'd begun to wonder if they weren't a little too – dare she say it – boring. Besides, she'd been expecting to spend the rest of the week with Frank. Unfortunately, Frank had raced off to Scotland, leaving her alone in the middle of England with her guilt and regrets. More fool her. That would teach her to go for the cheap thrill. And anyway, Frank didn't seem quite so boring now.

She listened to the message he'd left her while she'd been driving home: 'Just letting you know we're back in Glasgow. We'll be putting Martin on the plane home tomorrow, and I'll get one a bit later. I'll be back in the afternoon.'

Back in the afternoon? All was not lost then. There was still time for a little relationship jazzing up and for easing her guilty conscience. She replayed the message. She loved to hear his voice, and if she wasn't mistaken, his accent was stronger than normal. It was actually quite sexy. Being with his family must have brought it out. Tomorrow suddenly seemed a long way off and she longed to hear him say something other than I'll be back in the afternoon.

He answered after a few rings. 'Hello, gorgeous woman.'

Yes that was the kind of thing she wanted to hear. 'Hello. I was driving when you called. I thought I'd try you.'

'I'm glad you did. It's so good to hear your voice. I've missed it. I've missed you.'

'I've missed you too, Frank. I'm looking forward to

seeing you tomorrow.' The word 'boring' popped into her head, bizarrely in a weird American accent. 'Sorry, I appear to have turned into Miss Jean Brodie. What I meant to say was, I can't wait to see you tomorrow. No one else is here so it'll be just the two of us. I may even buy some frilly knickers.'

'Wow! Now there's a treat I'll be holding you to. Hang on a minute. I'm just committing to memory an image of you in nothing but frilly knickers. It might just keep me going until tomorrow.'

'You naughty man. How has your trip been anyway?'

'Eventful.'

'Good eventful or bad eventful?'

'Haven't worked that out yet. I'll tell you more about it tomorrow. There are some things I'd like to share with you.'

'Should I be worried?'

'No, it's nothing like that. Honestly, it's … oh the taxi's here. We're going out for a meal and a quiet drink. All very grown-up. Finn's orders. Sorry about the Adrian thing, by the way. I thought I mentioned we were old uni friends. Stupid of me. Anyway, I'll see you tomorrow. Looking forward to those knickers.'

Netta sat in the breakfast room with a cottage pie for one that her mother had insisted on making for her, musing on what Frank might want to talk about. Had something happened on the trip that had triggered this need to share, or could it be about them? He could have been doing some thinking of his own and decided he was bored too. She momentarily entertained the idea that Frank was going cold on their relationship, then dismissed it as rubbish.

It could just be that he was going to tell her he went to the place where Doogie lived. She'd recognised the photos he'd sent her. She had some very similar ones on her phone from the time she'd been up that way. But just to be sure, she'd called Doogie. She hadn't asked him directly, instead choosing to amble around gathering this fact and that until her loose questioning led to one conclusion. Yes, there had been three Irishmen staying at Grace's campsite at around that time. Doogie had seen one of them painting on the beach. They'd even spoken.

Netta could understand why they'd want to go there. The place was stunning. What she couldn't understand was why Frank was hiding it. Perhaps she'd find out when he did his sharing. In the meantime, she had to work out where she was going to get some frilly knickers from before tomorrow afternoon.

54

HOME AT LAST

The Mini would have been too tight a squeeze, so Finn took them to the airport in the campervan. It was a fitting end to their trip.

Frank and Martin left it as long as they could to go through to departures. Finn gave them each a manly hug. 'We should definitely do this again next year. With better planning and less drama.'

'Agreed,' said Frank. Despite his keenness to get home, a sense of loss was already creeping over him.

'I'm up for it. Sorry again for stealing your van there, Finn,' said Martin.

'That's okay. You take care of yourself, big fella. I'll be in touch with both of youse.'

'Will you come back over, now that Billy's dead?' said Martin, after they'd gone through.

'I'll see. It was never about Billy.' Well maybe part of it was about Billy, or at least the worry that his contacts had more chance of doing away with him on their home turf. Although, Billy had never actually said where his so-called contacts were, and Frank was beginning to question whether they ever actually existed.

'What was it about then?' said Martin.

'It doesn't matter now.'

'You'll come then?'

'I don't know. Maybe.'

'Please come. Eve would like it. She wants to get the boys together again to scatter Billy's ashes. You will come, won't you?'

'They're calling your flight.'

Martin picked up his bag. 'You didn't answer me.'

Frank gave his brother a clumsy hug. 'Go on now. The plane's waiting.'

He watched Martin walk to the gate and join the queue. A message pinged on his phone from Siobhan, checking all was going to plan. He tapped out a quick reply to say Martin was on the plane. When he looked up, the queue was gone. That was it then. He was on his way to Belfast. Siobhan would be meeting him at the other end, no doubt with their parents in tow in case he needed further persuasion. Poor Martin.

It came as a shock to realise it had been a long time since he'd had any sympathy for his brother. Back in those days when he made up stories to get rid of Martin's bogeymen, he'd been fierce in love with the wee man and would have done anything to protect him. Something changed as he got older. Something that made him fall out of love with his brother. It was the teenage years to some extent, but there was more to it than that. Billy didn't want Martin hanging around. He wanted it to be just the two of them.

Frank looked around him. His plane wasn't due in for over an hour. He needed a distraction. Some mindless retail therapy maybe.

. . .

Frank closed his front door behind him. He was home at last. He did a quick reccy of each room, noticing someone had tidied up his records. It could only have been Netta. His canvases were just as he'd left them a week and a half ago, although it felt longer. Maybe not a lifetime, but certainly months or years. He got freshened up and changed. He didn't have a lot of clothes but he was sick of the sight of the few he'd taken with him, and he wanted to look his best for Netta. Best for a man with a body like his anyway. There was no denying he'd let himself go, but he was determined to change now that he was new man Frank.

He unlocked Netta's door. She was still at work but he wanted to see his doggy pal. Fred leapt up at him, whining with excitement. Betty followed suit. Maud less so. He rattled their leads. 'Will we go walkies, dogs?'

They were soon at the park. Thankfully, there was no sign of that former pupil. Frank would have been quite new at the college then. It had been a necessary move, fitting in well with looking after Robyn. The place had been good to him. He'd be sad to leave, but it was time to let go. He'd been in denial about it before the trip but Rebel had helped him come to the decision. Rebel, the quiet man at peace with himself. Frank was not at peace with himself. That was the truth of it. He had never been at peace with himself. He just hadn't seen it until now. It wasn't the Troubles. They'd been hard times to live through but they hadn't beaten him. It was Ellen. But she was dead and so was Billy. Robyn was all grown up and happy, and while he was out of shape and a bit too inclined to inaction, he wasn't exactly ancient. Surely his time was now? Surely it was his turn to do what he wanted?

He checked his phone for messages, but there were none. They were probably too busy fussing around Martin, trying to put his life back on track. He hadn't been to Belfast in thirteen years? He'd tried to keep going after Ellen left but the anger was too much for him. Ma and Da did their best to get him over there but eventually they stopped asking. Frank wondered if they knew the reason for the anger that even now sometimes threatened to boil over.

Fred dropped a stick at his feet. Loyal, steadfast and somewhat dopey Fred. Without thinking, he'd got himself a Timmy. 'Last one, then we go home.' He hurled the stick and the two dogs flew off in hot pursuit. Robyn would be back from her holidays soon. He'd go up and see her. Maybe take her over to see Finn and ask her to keep an eye on him. He tapped out a message and sent it to her:

'Hello darling girl. I hope you're having a great time. Give me a call when you get back xx.'

A message came back from his darling girl, just as Frank and the dogs were leaving the park.

'Hi Dad. Will do. We're having the best time. Everyone sends their love. Especially me.'

Frank smiled. He loved his daughter with a ferocity that was incomparable to any other emotion, and he always would. Was that normal for a father, he wondered, or was it just because of the way they'd been thrown together?

55

A FUZZY RED-TOPPED MIRACLE – 1997

It was love at first sight. Frank held his newborn daughter in his arms, tears running down his cheeks. This tiny, mewling thing, this fuzzy red-topped miracle was his little girl and he would rather die than let anything bad happen to her.

'Why are you crying?' Ellen had just given birth and yet there was no emotion in her voice. She seemed genuinely puzzled.

'Because we have a baby, and she's wonderful.'

'I suppose she is, but I didn't expect you to be quite so emotional about it.'

Frank laughed. 'Well if a man can't get emotional when he's welcoming his beautiful daughter into the world, when can he?'

'I do hope you're not going to be like this all the time, Frank. You'll be no use whatsoever.'

He ignored the look that passed between the midwife and the nurse. 'Can't make any promises. She has your hair, but she has my stamp on her too. Did you notice the birthmark on her back?'

'Yes I did. But hers is a heart shape. Yours is more like a squashed tomato.'

'Siobhan's is shaped more like a heart. So is Ma's. It comes from her side of the family really. God, she's just gorgeous. I can't believe we made her.'

When Frank arrived at the hospital the next day, he found the Montagues had graced them with their presence. The Brigadier was back to near full health now and Gavin had driven them up from Surrey.

The best Mr and Mrs Montague could give Frank was a curt nod, but Gavin more than made up for it. 'Congratulations, Frank. She's adorable.'

Frank considered pointing out that he'd done very little to warrant congratulations, aside from allowing himself to be duped into impregnating Ellen, but that would have been ungrateful. At least the Montagues had swallowed their pride and come to see their granddaughter. He lifted the baby out of her cot. This child had reconciled him and Ellen. Perhaps she would reconcile the rest of this dysfunctional family. 'Would you like to hold her?' He directed his words to his mother-in-law.

'I think not,' said Mrs Montague.

'May I?' Gavin held out his arms. The Brigadier muttered something under his breath.

Frank handed her over. Gavin rocked and cooed the little bundle in his arms, his eyes damp and twinkly. A tiny chink in his armour had just been revealed.

'Oh for God's sake, man. Pull yourself together,' said the Brigadier.

'If you'd chosen to marry the girl we suggested, you'd have had plenty of your own by now,' said Mrs Montague.

'I'm quite happy with my niece, Mother.' Gavin smiled, leaving Frank marvelling at the infinite patience of the man.

'What's that on her back,' said Mrs Montague.

'It's a birthmark, Mummy. All of Frank's family have it,' said Ellen.

'Well, I'm sure there are treatments. There are some very good clinics.'

A flashback carried Frank through time to the day the Balaclavas took Billy. That look Eve's dad had given him. Suddenly he understood it. 'There'll be none of that. Our daughter doesn't need any treatments.'

Mrs Montague gave him one of her steeliest stares. That would be a no on the reconciliation then. 'We must be off. Ellen, think about what we discussed earlier.'

Gavin kissed the top of his sister's head. 'Goodbye, my darling. I'll come and see you next week with Roger.'

Mr and Mrs Montague did not kiss any part of their daughter. They merely tutted at the mention of Roger's name, leading Frank to assume that he was no longer to be referred to as Roger the Lodger.

He sat down in one of the recently vacated chairs. 'What was she talking about?'

Ellen waved her hand. 'She wants me to go home for a while. She thinks it's best for me and the baby.'

'Do you want to?'

'Couldn't think of anything worse. And there is more chance of a second coming than my mother knowing what's best for a baby. No. Robyn and I are going to stay in our own home, thank you very much.'

'Robyn?'

'Yes. Do you like it? I know we'd considered other names but it came to me this morning and it seemed to suit her.'

Frank squeezed Ellen's hand. It was good that she was

thinking positively. After the birth yesterday, he was beginning to worry. 'I love it. Robyn O'Hare. Sounds perfect. A perfect name for a perfect darling girl.'

'Except she's not perfect, according to my dear mother. Not with that mark on her back.'

The first clue Frank had that something was wrong came from Stella. She worked part time these days and had been stopping by each day while Frank was at work. It was actually Adrian that caught him on their lunch break. 'Stella thinks Lottie might be suffering with post-natal depression. Apparently she's not really looking after the baby properly. I don't mean silly things. Stell's not trying to pick holes, but she's not interested in feeding her, or changing her nappy. When she went round yesterday, the poor little mite was screaming at the top of her lungs and Lottie was just reading a magazine and ignoring her.'

Frank went home as soon as the end of day bell went. He could see Ellen sunbathing in the garden but there was no sign of the baby. He checked each room and found Robyn lying in her cot, wide awake. Her nappy was soaking. He changed her and took her out into the garden.

Ellen looked up from her magazine. 'Home time already?'

'I've changed Robyn. Her nappy was wet.'

'Really? It's hardly been any time since Stella put a clean one on.'

'Ellen, you need to be doing these things.'

Her jaw clenched. 'What are you implying? Has Stella said something?'

'No. I'm worried that you might be a bit down. I think maybe it's worth seeing a doctor.'

'A bit down? How very patronising of you, Frank. I think you'll find it's called post-natal depression, if I were suffering from it that is. In actual fact there is nothing wrong with me. It's the child that's the problem. She's so damn needy.'

'She's a baby. Babies need a lot of looking after. You can't just ignore her. Before we know it, we'll have the social services round here.'

Ellen's face softened 'You're right. I'm sorry. I promise you I'm not depressed. I'm just bored. I need more than this.'

'Okay. What about going back to work? Could Gavin help with that?'

'You wouldn't mind?'

'Of course not. We'll make it work.' Frank was thinking of a childminder or nursery. Anything would be better than the care their baby was probably receiving now. 'Or there is something else that might help, if there's nothing forthcoming on the work front. I spotted a house for sale the other day that might be worth looking at. It needs doing up. It might be a good project for you to get your teeth into.'

56

A NEW NEIGHBOUR AND AN OLD
PROBLEM – 1997

The removals men brought in the last of the boxes. Frank cleared a space for a rug and put Robyn down on it. She was six months now. That's how long it had taken to look at the house, buy it, and turn it into something Ellen thought suitable. He'd taken out a mortgage to buy it in his name. Ellen could have bought it outright but he'd insisted on it. If anything went wrong between them, he didn't want to be left homeless. Not now that he had Robyn to think of. As a compromise, he'd allowed Ellen to spend her own money on the refurbishments. He didn't ask how much it had cost but he guessed it probably wasn't far off what they'd paid for the house.

He sat down on the rug next to Robyn. 'What do you think of our new house, Baba? Isn't Mummy clever?' he said.

Ellen's face lit up. 'You like it then?'

'Very much. You've made it into a lovely family home.' He'd half-expected the place to be completely child unfriendly but it had turned out comfortable, cosy and very much for all three of them.

'Come and have a look at the garden.'

Frank picked Robyn up and followed Ellen out through the kitchen. The last time he'd seen the garden it had been a dumping ground for everything that had been ripped out of the house. Now it was all clear, he could see the rolling lawn with mature fruit trees and borders. Those things had been there before, but Ellen had added a new patio and a play area for Robyn, when she was old enough.

'You've made an excellent job of it, if I may say so.' Their new neighbour, a little, round old lady was on the other side of the hedge. 'Edith Pinsent. How do you do. Friends and neighbours generally call me Edie. Oh what a charming child.'

'Thank you,' said Frank. 'This is Robyn. And we're Frank and Ellen O'Hare.'

'I hope you'll be happy here. I say, do you like jam? Of course you do. Who doesn't? Hang on a tick.' Edith Pinsent scurried off, returning a few minutes later with a jar of homemade jam. 'I only made it yesterday. Please consider it a welcome gift. Anything you need, don't hesitate to pop round. Can't stop. Things to do.'

'I think our new neighbour may be a little eccentric,' said Frank.

'She seems rather nice though,' said Ellen.

Frank parked up on his new drive. He still couldn't believe he was a man with a drive now. He was also a man who was back at work after the long summer break. The start of term had been a week ago and he'd just about got back into the habit of the school routine. He had some prep work to do for tomorrow's lessons but he'd save that until after they put Robyn to bed. Before she was born, he'd do that work in

school and then come home but these days, he got back as
quickly as he could.

His parents had come over for a week in the holidays to
spend some time with their new granddaughter and to see
the house. Da had been very impressed by the decorating
but Ma had let on that he'd been a bit hurt Frank hadn't
asked him to do it. Frank had to make some excuse about
not wanting to eat into Da's time. He didn't want to say that
neither Ellen nor he had considered it.

The house was silent and empty. He was about to call
Adrian and Stella to see if Ellen was visiting them when
there was a knock at the door. It was Edie with Robyn
perched on her hip. Considering she didn't have children,
she looked quite well practised. 'Hello, Frank. Ellen asked
me to have Robyn. An emergency dash to London apparently. She said she'd call this evening.'

'Ah! She has a brother in London and parents in Surrey.
Hopefully, nothing bad.'

'Yes indeed. Come along my dear. Time to go to Daddy.'
She kissed Robyn's cheek and passed her over to Frank.
'She'll be wanting her usual feed in an hour.'

'That's very kind of you, Edie. Thank you. I'm so sorry
for the inconvenience.'

'Nonsense. I adore this little cherub. Couldn't be happier
when spending time with her, and she loves the dogs. I'm
around all day tomorrow, if you need a babysitter. I'm
usually up at six, so any time after then. Cheerio.'

Frank closed the door and checked Robyn's nappy. It
was dry. She looked clean and perfectly happy. Aside from
some embarrassment on his part, no harm had been done,
but where the hell was Ellen?

He called Gavin who assured him she wasn't there and
there were no emergencies on his side of the family. He

tried the old flat. Ellen had kept it on in case they changed their mind about Birmingham. That was the excuse she gave anyway. There was no answer there. So he rang Adrian's, on the off chance that Stella might know something, but they were equally clueless. He'd run out of ideas. There was nothing else to do but wait for her to call.

She rang after he'd put Robyn to bed.

'Where the hell are you?'

'I'm at the flat in London.' She said it as if it was obvious.

'Why? I know there's no emergency with your parents. I called Gavin.'

'It was a work emergency. I got an assignment but I had to be here immediately. My old editor called me this morning. The columnist they'd engaged was taken ill.'

'A work assignment? You left our daughter with a stranger for a work assignment?'

'Edie is not a stranger. Robyn and I see her all the time. And I thought we agreed I'd go back to work when the house was finished.'

'Yes, but you can't just take off like that without any discussion.'

'Well I did. The assignment's in New York. I'll be away for a couple of weeks. You'll hardly know I'm gone.'

'And how am I supposed to arrange childcare with no notice? You know I don't have the kind of job I can take time off from.'

'You'll sort something out. Speak to Stella. And there's always Edie.'

57

MADONNA AND CHILD – 1997

Frank woke to the sound of baby gurgles. It was six forty-five. Not bad. Fifty minutes later than yesterday. Robyn must know the holidays had started. He switched off the baby monitor and dragged himself out of bed.

Robyn was sitting up in her cot. She greeted him with a big smile. She was crawling now, in a fashion, and into everything. Yesterday, she'd got her hand stuck in the video slot, the little monkey. So much for a child-friendly house.

'Morning, Baba. How are you today?' Frank lifted her out. 'Wet, I see.'

'Ba-ba-ba-ba.'

'Yes, you clever girl. And who am I? I'm the dada, aren't I?'

'Da-da-da-da.'

Frank kissed his little girl. Even when she was bawling her head off, she never failed to cheer him up. 'Come on sweetie, let's get you cleaned up. You smell like a sewer.'

He gave her a quick wash and put on a clean nappy and pyjamas. Experience had taught him that the proper cleaning operation was best left until after breakfast, which could be a messy affair for both of them.

In the kitchen, he let Robyn crawl around on the floor while he made breakfast. They were currently experimenting with porridge, with mixed results. Some days Robyn loved it. Other days, Frank had more of it on his face and in his hair than his darling girl had in her stomach. But he was not one to be put off. Edie had suggested mashing some banana in it. She was a mine of useful information. Since Ellen had gone, Edie and Stella had been invaluable. They were his little support network, taking care of Robyn while he was at work until he could organise more formal childcare. In the new year, they were going to trial a couple of days at a nursery, with Edie and Stella taking up the slack when he couldn't.

If he'd been honest with the parents, Ma would have been straight on the boat over. But he couldn't tell them. He was too ashamed. So instead, he told them everything was rosy each time they called.

Ellen rang every week, always finishing with a promise to be home soon. She was in Europe now. The New York assignment had moved on to other things.

'Da-da-da-da.' Robyn had crawled into the breakfast room. Frank took in her porridge and found her standing, holding onto a chair. Edie had told him she'd pulled herself up the other day so it wasn't the first time, but it was the first time he'd seen it. Ellen was missing all of this. But that was her choice. Frank was a modern man. He had no problem with working mothers whatsoever, whether through choice or necessity. He just had a problem with parents who deserted their children.

· · ·

It was a sunny morning but cold with it, so Frank wrapped Robyn up before wheeling her round to Edie's. It was Christmas Eve and Edie was taking her so that he could do some last minute Christmas shopping.

Edie opened her front door, dressed for the outside. 'That looks like a young lady who's ready for a walk in the park.' The sun caught her eyes and Frank couldn't help noticing how like sapphires they were. Quite arresting. She must have been a beauty in her day.

She called back into the house. 'Are you coming with me?' Her two dogs, some sort of terrier mix, skittered along the hallway. 'I should think so too. You both need the exercise.'

'I'll walk part of the way with you. I'm taking the train into town,' said Frank.

As they went they discussed their Christmas arrangements. She was spending it with her dearest friends who lived in Kings Heath. He was going to Stella and Adrian's. Conversation was always easy with Edie. Frank never needed to try too hard. He liked that about his neighbour.

'Have you heard from Ellen?' she said.

'Other than a Christmas card, not since last week.'

'Such a shame that she's missing so much.'

'I was thinking the same thing this morning. But she prefers it this way.'

'Do you think so, Frank? Pardon me, I don't wish to speak out of turn, but do you think there's a possibility that Ellen might be ill? Mentally, I mean.'

'I tried that one, Edie. We talked about post-natal depression after Robyn was born but she refused to see a doctor. To be honest, I'm not sure if it's just the way she was brought up. She's always behaved like a spoilt child. I'm sorry. I shouldn't…'

Edie touched his arm. 'Nothing to be sorry about. You know Ellen better than anyone. Take your time this morning, Frank. Have a few hours to yourself. You deserve it.'

He went on to the station lost in thought. Edie wasn't the first person to raise the subject of Ellen's mental health. Ade and Stella had done so too. And of course there had been the doctors at the Richmond Park not long after they'd married. But Ellen wasn't mad. Selfish, impulsive and careless with other people's feeling, yes. But mad? No.

Frank walked up Edie's path. He'd done as she'd suggested and had a reasonably leisurely morning, despite the busy shops. He'd even treated himself to a pub lunch. He was feeling chilled.

Edie met him along the path, a picture of concern. 'Ellen's here. She was waiting for me when we got back from the park.'

Ellen was sitting on Edie's sofa with Robyn asleep in her lap. Her hair was tied loosely and she had on a cobalt blue dress that he hadn't seen before. A Pre-Raphaelite painting, *Madonna and Child*, immediately sprang to mind. History's most perfect mother. Frank almost laughed out loud.

She looked down at her sleeping daughter, then at Frank and smiled. 'Hello darling. Shall we go home?'

As soon as he closed the front door, Frank asked the question that had been on his lips from the moment Edie told him she was back: 'How long are you staying?'

'For good. I'll have to go away for work now and then but I'm back now.'

She was so casual about it that it really riled him. 'You know if I didn't want Robyn to know her mother, I would quite happily tell you to just fuck yourself right back off again.'

'Oh, have you got yourself another lover?'

Frank's jaw dropped. The woman was completely devoid of empathy or guilt. 'No, I have not. You're unbelievable Ellen, you know that? Fucking unbelievable.'

She frowned. 'Should I go then?'

Robyn stirred and began to cry.

Frank chewed on his lip. He should tell Ellen to go and never darken their doors again, but he couldn't do that to his darling Baba. 'Stay.'

58

THE SCARLET PIMPERNEL DOES IT AGAIN

Netta shut the front door and called out: 'Honey, I'm home.'

'In the kitchen. I'm making dinner.' Frank wiped his hands and met her in the doorway.

She gave him a long, tender kiss. 'Well hello, Mr O'Hare. Long time no see.'

'Too long, Ms Wilde. Let me look at you.' God but she was the most incredible, beautiful woman. And the wonderful thing about Netta Wilde, the most amazingly wonderful thing about her, was that she was as incredibly beautiful on the inside as the outside. 'That's a sexy number you're wearing if I may say so.'

She looked down at her jeans and T-shirt and her mouth turned up in one corner. 'Thank you. I find haute couture lends itself so well to jam making. And look, I've even added a few splashes for that extra special elegance.'

Frank dabbed a spot of jam stuck on her top and licked his finger. 'Hmm, strawberry, if I'm not mistaken. There's only one more thing this outfit needs, and I have it right here.' He reached for the bag he'd left on the dresser. 'Ta-da.'

Netta pulled out its contents. 'Frilly knickers! How did you manage that?'

'There was an underwear shop in the airport and I figured you wouldn't have time yourself.'

She laughed with that gorgeous tinkling laugh of hers and held the knickers against her hips. 'Over the jeans or underneath?'

'Oh underneath, I think. Or without. Yes. Definitely without.'

She kissed him again. 'Wait here.'

'I'll stick the dinner in the oven.'

She waved the knickers in the air. 'Make sure you put it on a low setting.'

Frank put the lid on the casserole dish, popped it in the oven, and turned it down low. This was the sort of thing he'd envisaged doing at the start of the Easter break, but things don't always turn out as planned, do they? Anyway, today's plans were as follows. Make love to the most incredible woman in the world. Have a nice dinner with a good bottle of wine. Share some stuff. The plans hadn't yet got as far as deciding how much stuff he was going to share. Probably not the bit about stalking the most incredible woman in the world's former lover. He would tell her about Eve and Billy though. When they were not long into their relationship, Netta had told him all her secrets and he'd told her about Ellen. After that, they'd promised each other no secrets. Frank hadn't meant to keep quiet about Billy and Eve, it was just something he didn't want to think about. Hiding from things again. But he was new man Frank now, and it was time he stopped.

'Just having a shower.' Netta's voice floated down from the landing.

He remembered another thing new man Frank was

going to do. Exude passion. 'Okay. Dinner's on low. I'll come up.' He smoothed down his hair, undid a few shirt buttons, and pulled his stomach in. Make way for the all new passionate Frank.

He went up to the bedroom he'd helped Netta decorate. They'd made a decent job of it. Da wouldn't be displeased with it. It had been Edie's room once. She'd been a good friend to him over the years. He liked to think he'd repaid her in kind.

The first time he saw Netta she'd come to view the house after Edie had died. She was Annette Grey then. Quite a broken thing, her ex-husband's doing. He'd liked her immediately, but when their friendship turned into more than that, he couldn't have been more surprised. He'd made a complete mess of their first date, gabbling on about Ellen as if they'd had the perfect marriage. In spite of that, they'd ended up having the most amazing sex in his kitchen. Frank had yet to work out how it had happened, other than they were very drunk. He'd woken the next morning in full panic attack mode and nearly ruined everything. He'd never really understood why until this week. Driving through those long, empty roads and replaying the past in his head had helped him work it out. Ellen had once said she'd scarred him for life. She had. Almost. It took a very special person to show him that love was not something to fear.

That person came in wrapped in a towel. 'You look miles away.'

'I was just thinking about the first time we made love.'

'As I recall, I frightened the pants off of you.' She dropped the towel to reveal herself in her new knickers.

He pulled her closer. 'Well I'm a big strong boy now.'

Her eyes moved downwards. 'So I see.'

·   ·   ·

Frank propped himself up on a pillow and put his arm around Netta. He didn't want to sound arrogant but he'd been pleased with his performance. Passion had been undeniably exuded.

The casserole's aroma wafted up the stairs. Netta sniffed the air. 'Mmm that smells good. I'm embarrassed to say, I've rather gone back to bad old ways when I've been on my own. Beans on toast and ready meals, except when Mum took pity on me.'

'Also guilty. How many days do we have the house to ourselves?'

'Two or three.'

'I'm sorry to have run off and left you.'

'Never mind. Family's important. Talking of which, tell me more about Martin and Cousin Finn.'

Frank kissed her head. She was quite right, family was important. He'd let himself forget that. 'We've not always hit it off, me and Martin. He's only a bit younger than me. When we were kids I guess he looked up to me. That was fine when we were kids, but him always wanting to tag along got in the way when we were teenagers. Finn's a bit younger than Martin. His mum and my mum are sisters. They lived a couple of doors down from us. His dad was killed in the Troubles so my dad became his proxy dad.'

'Poor kid.'

'Aye well, it wasn't exactly common but it happened. So Martin tagged along with me, and Finn tagged along with Martin.'

'That's sweet. Like the Three Amigos.'

'Actually, there were four of us.'

Frank was interrupted by his phone ringing. He rustled around in his jeans pocket and found it. 'It's Siobhan. I'd better take it.'

'Where is he?' Siobhan hadn't even bothered to say hello.

'What?'

'Martin. Where is he?'

'He should have been with you hours ago.'

'I know that. We thought maybe he'd given us the slip at the airport and gone straight to see Bronagh, but he's not there. We've looked all over the city for him. Are you absolutely sure he got on that plane.'

'I watched him go. I…' Frank ran his fingers through his hair. That sneaky bastard had done it again. 'I didn't see him go through the gate.'

'You didn't see him go through the gate.' Frank could literally taste the disgust coming off of his sister right now.

'I was reading your message.'

'Well aren't you just the prize eejit? Martin, the Scarlet fucking Pimpernel has done it again.'

Frank saw Netta slip the frilly panties back on and step into a clean pair of jeans. It seemed a second go was off the cards. 'What do we do now?'

'Find him,' hissed Siobhan. 'Find him now.'

59

HER OFF 'THE EXORCIST'

Siobhan hung up. Stupid eejit. Stupid, fecking, useless eejit. Men! Hopeless the lot of them. Except for Da, obviously. He was the one shining light in a sea of useless feckers.

She called Cousin Finn. Maybe she'd have better luck with him, now that he'd gone sensible.

'Siobhan. How's it going?'

'Very badly, Finn. Very badly indeed.'

'Whatever's the matter?'

'Martin has not come home.'

'Are you sure?'

'Of course I'm sure, and before you ask, he's not with Bronagh, or Frank, and he can't be found in the whole of Belfast. I take it he's not with you either?'

'He's not. He promised us he'd go. Frank was going to stay with him till he got on the plane.'

Siobhan heaved a massive, overwhelming sigh. She could feel tears edging themselves out of every one of her facial orifices. 'Frank might have said that, but he didn't. He took his eye off the ball which, as we both know, is all Martin needs. Typical of that selfish pig not to keep to his word.' She meant Martin, but the words could have equally applied to Frank.

'You sound a little upset there, Siobhan. Can you try to breathe slowly?'

Breathe slowly? Fucking breathe slowly? She was lucky she could breathe at all, what with the snot and the tears. 'Of course I'm upset. I've spent all week talking Bronagh round. All week assuring Ma that Martin's third marriage was not about to end badly. All week trying to get hold of you bunch of fucking feckers while you've been swanning around, admiring scenery and having a full scale bromance. And what for, Finn? What for? Da hasn't got a clue. Did you hear that Finn? Even Da doesn't know what Martin's up to. And Ma's gone to church! She hasn't been there in years. And look at the time, Finn. It's six o'clock, and she's at the church.'

'She missing the news?'

'Exactly.'

'Okay. Siobhan, I know this is hard but it's important to stay calm. Light a candle and relax.'

'Light a fucking candle. Is that the best you can do, Finn? I'm about to explode here. I could probably light a candle with my own flames, the heat that's coming off of me.'

'I'm going to find him. I give you my word. Just try to stay calm.'

'Well do it quick. And stop telling me to stay calm.' Siobhan pressed the button. Cutting people off was surprisingly satisfying. She eyed the candle that was collecting dust on her shelf. Couldn't do any harm she supposed.

After five minutes of sniffing the candle's scent, she was no calmer. She tried Martin's phone again, now that he'd apparently been reunited with it. Naturally, it went straight to voicemail. He hardly ever answered her calls at the best of times. 'Where are you, you bastard?' Jesus, she sounded like her off 'The Exorcist'.

As if her week hadn't been bad enough with that shite date. She would not be trying that dating site business again, thank you very much. She'd get a hobby instead. Or maybe a dog. Frank said he had dogs. She'd have to ask his advice. She caught herself on. Ask Frank for advice? Ha! Never in a million years.

She called Da's mobile. 'I've no news. I just thought I'd try you in case you'd heard anything through your feelers.'

'None whatsoever. If he was back over here, I'd have found him. He must still be over the water.'

'Are you in the car, Daddy?'

'Aye. I'm after picking your mother up from the church.'

'Tell her,' said Ma in the background.

'Your mammy thinks we need to take drastic action.'

'You mean–?'

'I do. Can you make the arrangements, Siobhan? Soon as possible.'

Siobhan closed the lid on her laptop. All done. There was a quickening in her chest. She tried the slow breathing thing again. Finn seemed very fond of it. No. The quickening was still there, and the candle's smell was making her want to boke. She blew it out and went to the fridge. Fuck the breathing. Fuck the candle. Siobhan had her own relaxation trick and it was called Sauvignon Blanc.

60

GUESS WHO'S COME TO DINNER

'Did I hear right? Did your sister say Martin wasn't on the plane?' said Netta. She'd heard the conversation playing out over the phone and had to stop herself laughing when Siobhan had said that thing about their brother being Martin, the Scarlet fucking Pimpernel. Siobhan was someone she'd really like to meet.

'Sounds like it. He promised us. He promised he'd go home. He was in the queue for the plane. I only looked away for a minute. Less than a minute. I will kill the fecker when I get my hands on him.'

She'd never seen Frank angry before. Maybe angry was too strong a word. Annoyed. He was definitely annoyed.

He put the phone to his ear. 'Sorry, I have to make some calls.'

Netta heard the familiar sound of voicemail asking him to leave a message.

'Martin, where are you? Call me.' He tried another number. This time he got through. 'Has Siobhan called you? So you know then. I watched him go. No, I didn't walk him right up to the gate. I took him at his word and thought I could trust him to manage that much himself. Foolishly, obviously. I am calm, Finn. Yes, I'm breathing slowly. Listen.' He rolled his eyes at Netta and breathed slowly and loudly down the phone. This time she allowed herself a smile.

The door knocker went, setting off a cacophony of barks downstairs. 'I'll go and answer it,' she whispered.

The man on the doorstep looked like a slimmer, smoother version of Frank. He smiled at her showing a set of near-perfect white teeth. He had to have had them fixed. 'Netta?'

'I'm guessing you're Martin.'

He smiled again. 'You guessed right. I'm looking for Frank. There's no answer at his house.'

Netta opened the door wider for him. 'Come in. I hope you like dogs.'

'I love them. Does one of these belong to Frank?'

She pointed to Fred. 'Yes, that one.'

He called Fred to him. 'I'd have put my money on it being him. He's just like Timmy.'

'Timmy?' The only Timmy Netta knew of was the dog in the Famous Five books and if memory served her right, he was a bit smaller than Fred.

'Ignore me. It's just a thing from when we were kids,' he said.

Maybe it was something to do with the Famous Five then. 'Frank, you have a visitor. It's Martin,' she called up the stairs.

'Have I interrupted something?' Martin's smile turned into a sheepish grin.

'Oh no. We were just about to have dinner. Knowing Frank's cooking, he'll have made enough for a whole family, so there'll be plenty for you too. Come into the lounge.'

Frank came down, fully dressed. 'What the fuck are you playing at? I've had Siobhan screaming down the phone at me.'

'No change there then,' said the prodigal brother.

Frank stuck his finger inches away from Martin's nose. 'Don't piss about. I am this close to battering you.'

'I've invited Martin to stay for dinner.' Netta blurted it out in the hope of cooling the situation down. Frank was definitely angry now and, although she'd never imagined him battering anything other than a piece of fish, there was every chance a battering was on the cards. That said, as she sized the two men up, she wasn't convinced Frank would come out on top.

'Oh he's staying for dinner. He's not going anywhere until I have personally made sure he's in Belfast.' Frank folded his arms. It was like watching one of those boxing weigh ins. 'And Finn's on his way down. I've told him I'd take care of it, but he's made a promise to Siobhan.'

Martin took three steps back, possibly to avoid anything swinging in his direction. 'God help us if we break a promise to Siobhan.' He winked at Netta. 'Our sister is a bit of a tyrant.'

She thought she saw Frank flinch. Probably her imagination. 'I'm not surprised. I'd say she has her hands full. I'll lay the table.'

Dinner was more than a little awkward. Netta started off trying to make polite conversation until she realised it was futile. In the end she settled for amused detachment, letting the drama unfold before her.

'You've a nice house,' said Martin.

'Thanks. It's a bit tatty around the edges but I like it that way. Frank helped a lot with the decorating.'

'He would do. He gets that from our da. It was Da's

paying hobby. He's probably decorated every house in the street at some time.'

'I didn't know that. And you both used to help him?' said Netta.

Martin shook his head. 'Only Frank. I was never asked. It was their thing.'

'It was not our thing. It was just because I was the oldest.' Frank slugged his wine back. He'd been drinking it a lot faster than he normally did. Netta thought of the empty bottles she'd found in his lounge. The mystery behind them was becoming clearer with every passing minute.

'No. Siobhan's the oldest. Age had nothing to do with it.' Martin turned to Netta. 'Wasn't there an old lady who used to live here before you?'

'Yes, Edie. You've been here before then?' said Netta.

'Not for a good while. I think the last time I was here was… When was it, Frank?'

'2007.' Frank emptied his glass. 'It was the summer of 2007.'

61

IS IT EVE?

Frank kissed Netta goodnight. 'I'm sorry, our plans have been ruined again.'

'It's okay. We'll sort things out tomorrow and we'll have time left for us.'

'I had so many things to share with you.'

'Another time.' She closed the front door.

Martin was waiting on the pavement with Fred. Frank glared at him. 'Come on you.'

Frank switched on the light in his hall. Martin closed the door behind him and cast his eyes up and across the wide hall, then wandered around opening doors and looking into the rooms. 'It's hardly changed. Did you not think of giving it a lick of paint?'

'No, I did not. I've been too busy.' It was the truth. In part. He had been too busy when it was just him and Robyn. When Ellen went for the final time, he'd been intending to make a start, but it was only after Netta arrived that he'd been forced out of his inertia and begun to clear Ellen's things. One of these days he'd get round to decorating and make the place his own.

'Still, you've a nice set up here with your woman next door.'

Martin had just made his relationship sound like some sordid business arrangement and for that reason alone, Frank refused to dignify the observation with an acknowledgement.

Unperturbed, Martin continued: 'I like her, by the way. She's not what I expected her to be.'

'And what exactly did you expect?' said Frank, finally giving in to bitter sarcasm.

'Somebody quieter. Less funny. Less quirky.'

'Quirky?'

'You know. Different. In a good way. Not like…' Like Ellen, he meant. Not like Ellen. 'You didn't mention she was a stunner either.'

'Because I'm not fifteen. It's not something an adult brags about. Anyway, her looks aren't important.'

'I know. I was just saying, she's a looker.'

'Keep your hands off her.' Frank was snarling now. It wasn't a good look but he wasn't going to stand by and say nothing. Not this time.

'Jesus, Frank. I was just saying. Have you any whisky? I could do with a nightcap.'

Frank poured him a whisky. He poured himself one, in the hope it would calm him down. On the phone earlier, Finn had given him some shite about breathing and candles. Forget that. He needed alcohol. 'Why are you here, Martin? Why didn't you go home as promised?'

Martin drank the whisky straight down, then held out his glass for more. 'I was all set to go. I was nearly through the gate, and then it hit me. Unfinished business.'

Frank topped him up. 'What do you mean, unfinished business?'

'You won't come back over to scatter Billy's ashes.'

'I said I'd think about it.'

'And we both know what that means. Finn wants to do it. He thinks it'll help us all to move on.'

Frank winced. Move on was it? That would be convenient.

Martin frowned. At the same time, the corners of his mouth turned up slightly. 'What was that? Did you just wince? What's going on with you, FB? Do you not want to move on?'

'I moved on a long time ago.'

Martin shook his head. 'That's shite and you know it. Something's holding you back. Something that you're still mightily pissed off about. Is it Eve? You resent her picking Billy over you. Is that it?'

Frank laughed. Was Martin being deliberately obtuse? 'I always knew the score with Eve. I never expected anything different, and I never really wanted anything different.'

'What then?'

'Summer 2007.'

62

SUMMER BEGINS – 2007

Sometimes, Frank wished he could go back in time and rewrite his own history. He'd almost certainly erase the part where Ellen found out about him and Eve. Not the times with Eve. They were all too brief spells of something approaching happiness, even if they were the cause of his break up with Billy. His break up with Billy? He made it sound like they were a couple instead of friends which in itself was an ironic description, because he'd hadn't been much of a friend to Billy at all.

If he could take a pen to his back story, there was no way he'd stop himself from marrying Ellen. Because if he did that, he wouldn't have Robyn, and all the misery in the world wouldn't keep him from being her daddy. But there was absolutely no doubt in his mind that if he could, he'd go back and change his answer to the question Ellen had asked him on Christmas Eve, 1997. He would have said go, and never darken our doors again.

It wasn't that the last ten years had been complete hell. There had been some bright spots, but most of them had been when Ellen wasn't here. Her trips to London and abroad began again in 1998, and became more frequent as the years rolled on. In fact, if Frank added up the amount of time she'd spent at home since then, it was probably five years at the most. Even then, it was too much time. When she was home there were moods to endure, tantrums to deal with that were worse than anything Robyn had to offer. And pandering, so much pandering, to her whims. The number of house redecorations was astonishing. Nothing was ever good enough. They seemed to be living in the residential equivalent of the Forth Bridge.

Worst of all, the relentless carping had come back with a vengeance, and he was finding it increasingly hard to fight off. She was grinding him down and he had nothing left to fight back with. Friends were beginning to notice. Adrian had sat him down and said he should either divorce her, or get her committed. Edie had hinted on numerous occasions that it couldn't go on. Even Gavin had offered to get it sorted. But Frank couldn't. Not because he didn't want to, but because he was too busy trying to keep everything normal for Robyn. And because he was slowly dying inside.

Ellen came in from her routine inspection of the house. On her insistence, they'd hired a cleaner, but it didn't stop her checking that the cleaner had done her job properly. It occurred to him that Ellen was turning into her mother. The thought would have appalled her, but the superior attitude, the chill that emanated from her, it was carbon copy Mrs Montague. She still saw her mother occasionally. Several years ago, the Brigadier had not so much shuffled off the earth as blasted his heart into space by once again refusing to believe the doctors knew best. When Robyn was small, Ellen had taken her along to see her grandmother, but more recently Rob had put her foot down and rejected all attempts to make her change her mind. Frank may not have any will left but Robyn had mettle enough for both of them. He took great pride in that.

'Next time the cleaner comes, remind her we pay her for a full morning's work. There is dust on the stair rail.'

Frank looked up from the drawing he was helping Robyn with. 'I doubt our visitors will notice.'

Ellen fixed him with an icy stare. 'I notice.'

'They're here.' Robyn jumped down off her chair and ran out to the hall, throwing the front door open. Martin and Finn barely had a chance to get out of the car before she launched herself on them.

Martin picked Robyn up and swung her round. He had two kids of his own now, one with his first wife and another with his second. He'd left both wives. According to Siobhan, he was sniffing around one of her friends, Bronagh.

Finn stumbled onto the pavement. He was looking beyond rough.

'Are you all right there, Finn?' said Frank.

Martin slapped Finn on the back and nearly sent him flying. 'He had a big night last night and the crossing was a bit ropey. He'll be right as rain after a cup of strong tea.'

Ellen looped her arm through Finn's. 'Come on, darling. Let's get you a nice tea.'

Martin waited until Ellen and Robyn had escorted Finn into the house. 'How are yer?'

'Grand. Yourself?'

'Grand. Thanks for putting us up.'

'Ma would have my arse if I didn't.'

'True enough.'

'How long are you here for?'

'We'll be done by the end of summer.'

Frank's main concern about Martin and Finn staying for the summer was that the holes in his carefully constructed web of deceit would soon become apparent. As far as his family was concerned, his marriage was mostly a happy one. That lie was easy enough to maintain when the family was over the water, but then Martin had messed up yet another job and taken Finn down with him. Cousin Eamon had finally forgiven Martin for making a pass at his daughter and found them some work on a building project over here. That said, he refused to let them stay under his roof. So Martin and Finn needed somewhere to live and Ma had reminded Frank he had two spare rooms. Frank had no choice in the matter. He just hoped Ellen wouldn't humiliate him in front of them.

It had been three weeks since Martin and Finn's arrival and things were going reasonably well. Finn was on his best behaviour and wasn't getting too drunk or stoned. Mainly because Frank had threatened to throw him out if he was either of those two things in Robyn's presence. Martin was on good form, charming the pants off everyone. Edie had taken a particular liking to him. And best of all, Ellen was being nice. It was a Saturday and the weather was glorious. They were having a summer party in the garden. Edie was here. So were Adrian and Stella, and some of Frank's other friends from work.

As evening drew in, the guests moved indoors and the music went on. Ade and Frank stayed in the garden, talking about the usual nonsense. It was all daftness but it was a humour they'd nurtured over the years.

'Lottie's in good form,' said Adrian.

'I'm hoping she'll stay like this for the rest of the summer.'

'You should tell the family. I'm sure they'll understand.'

'Maybe.'

'Stell and me are getting a divorce.'

Frank put his hand on Ade's shoulder. 'I'm sorry, mate. I didn't realise.'

'You've had other things to deal with. It's very friendly. We're still mates but we're both agreed, it's run its course. The kids are older now so it's a good time. She'll stay in the house and buy me out.'

'Where will you live?'

'I'll find somewhere to rent for a bit, until Stella's money comes through, then think about getting somewhere.'

'If you can wait until after the summer, you can stay here. Martin and Finn will have gone back and Ellen's hardly here. We can console each other.' What Frank wasn't saying was Ade could be his back up man. Maybe he'd be braver with him around.

'Cheers, mate. I appreciate that. I'll talk to Stell. Shall we go in? I might have a dance with my wife while she's still my wife.'

Frank leaned on the wall and watched his guests. Martin and Ellen were dancing. Finn had picked on one of Frank's friends from work to have an in depth discussion with. She didn't seem to be too put off by the fact that he could hardly stand. Adrian and Stella were smooching. If he wasn't mistaken they each had tears in their eyes. He felt like crying himself. Ade and Stell had been a constant in his life for such a long time, and they'd always seemed so good together. It was so sad.

He looked back to Ellen and Martin. They made a handsome couple. Ellen said something in Martin's ear. It was the intimate way she brushed her cheek against his as she leaned in that made the hairs on the back of Frank's next stand up. Now that he thought about it, they were dancing very closely.

Frank pushed himself off the wall and tapped on his brother's shoulder. 'Okay if I cut in?'

'Sure.' Martin let go of Ellen and smiled. He didn't even look embarrassed.

63

SUMMER ENDS – 2007

Frank was convinced Ellen and Martin were having an affair. He was becoming obsessed with it. Every time they were near each other Frank watched them like a hawk. She was flirting with Martin. That much was obvious. She looked at him the way she used to look at Frank. Occasionally she'd graze Martin's arm, or rest her hand on his shoulder. Or she'd stand a bit too close. Martin was playing it cool. Other than a blink or a jump, he did nothing to reciprocate. Nothing that Frank could see anyway, but Martin always was a devious bastard. You could never trust him.

She was all over Finn too. More so than Martin, but that was a bit too obvious, like she was trying to throw him off the scent. Finn was lapping it up. He idolised her. If she'd told him to roll over so she could tickle his tummy, he'd have done it.

Sometimes, Frank could swear, she saw him watching and did it all the more. It was her new torture. What surprised him though was just how much it bothered him. You'd have thought his feelings for Ellen were spent, but she'd somehow managed to resurrect his passion. Not the same passion he'd loved her with before everything began to crumble, but something vicious. It was hatred, loathing and jealousy all rolled into one. It was dark and ugly and revolting but he fed off it. Every day he looked for reasons to stoke it and the tighter its grip became. And every day he despised Ellen, Martin and Finn a little bit more.

They were almost at the end of the summer holidays. Frank had taken Robyn out for a day trip to a theme park. When they returned home, Martin and Finn were already back from work. Robyn was straight into the living room to watch the TV. Frank could hear the shower running in the bathroom. He concluded it was Finn when he saw Ellen and Martin in the garden through the kitchen window. She was wearing a bikini. They were sitting talking on her sun lounger, their knees practically touching. She grabbed Martin's arm. He pulled away, and that's when he saw Frank. He stood up and for once, looked as if he'd been caught with his hands in the till. 'You're back. Did Rob have a good day?'

Frank really wanted to slap Martin right now but his daughter was here. He had to maintain some order. 'She did. She's watching her favourite programme now.'

'She watches too much TV,' said Ellen. She had her back to Frank so he couldn't read her expression, but he noticed how low and cracked her voice sounded.

'What else are the holidays for, eh?' said Martin. 'I was just telling Ellen, we've been finished today. We'll head back home tomorrow morning. How about we go for a curry tonight and stop off at the Hope and Anchor. What do you say, FB?'

Frank let his coiled spring unwind slightly. Martin was going home. If anything was going on between them it had to come to an end now. 'Sure, why not. I'll ask Adrian and Stella if they want to come along.'

Martin nodded, a little too eagerly. 'That'll be grand, won't it Ellen?'

'Marvellous, darling. I'll see if Edie will have Robyn.' She got up and strode through them without looking at either of them.

Edie was happy to have Robyn stay over for the night, and Adrian and Stella were just as happy to give the boys a send-off.

If Ellen had been upset about her lover leaving, she wasn't showing it. She'd come out with all guns blazing on the charisma front. She breezed and charmed her way through the meal and was equally delightful in the pub, despite it being well below her acceptable standards. There wasn't much she and Stella agreed on, particularly when it came to motherly duties, but one thing they had no disagreement about was the Hope and Anchor.

'I don't know what you see in this place. It was a dump in its day, and it's an even bigger dump now,' said Stella.

Ellen raised her glass. 'Hear, hear. I don't ever want to come to this place again.'

'It's a bit scruffy but it's got its own charm,' said Adrian. 'And the beer's cheap.'

Stella rolled her eyes. 'Ade, my love, that's you in a nutshell.'

Frank laughed along with everyone else, but in his heart he was screaming. Stella and Adrian really cared for each other and they still couldn't make things work. What hope did he have?

. . .

They were up early in the morning to see Martin and Finn off.

Finn threw his arms around Frank. 'Bye, FB. Thanks for having us.'

'Take care of yourself now, Finn. Take it easy on the…' Frank tapped his nose. He didn't want to say the words because Robyn was here. He couldn't even spell them out these days. She was way too good at reading and writing.

Martin went to give him a hug but Frank held back. He didn't have it in him to be anything other than civil. Martin tensed and gave Frank a sideways glance. 'Will I tell Ma you'll be over for Christmas?'

Robyn jumped up and down. 'Oh yes. Can we, can we?'

'We'll see. Don't say anything yet,' said Frank.

Martin nodded. He gave Ellen a subdued peck on the cheek. She responded with a tight smile. After final hugs from Robyn, they drove away.

Frank put his arm around his teary-eyed daughter. 'Coming in for some breakfast, Baba?'

Robyn threw him off. 'No. I'm going back to Edie's. She's making me pancakes, and then we're going to the park.'

'Sorry,' said Edie who was also there to wave them off. 'I thought she might need cheering up.'

Ellen was already up the path and on the way back to the house. She was flouncing. Flouncing usually meant trouble. Rob was best out of it. 'No bother, Edie. If you don't mind Robyn staying with you this morning, I think it'll help immensely.'

Edie gave Ellen a cursory glance. She was well versed in her moods and easily got the hint. 'Of course. She can stay as long as she wants to.'

Frank followed Ellen up the path and closed the front door. 'Did you have to be so rude to Edie?'

'The woman's trying to take our daughter away from us, why shouldn't I be rude?'

'Don't be ridiculous. Robyn goes there because she likes Edie. And you're quite happy to use her as a free babysitting service when it suits you.'

'Well you won't let me get a nanny.'

'No child of mine will have a nanny. She didn't need one when she was a baby and she doesn't need one now.'

Ellen stomped over to him. 'How predictably working class of you, FB. Frankie Boy. How utterly common.'

'I thought that was what you liked, being with someone you could feel superior to.'

'Ordinarily yes, but you are so far down the food chain these days, I've had to resort to other entertainment.'

A coldness came over him. This was the real face of Ellen. The face few people saw but him. 'Is that why you've been screwing my brother?'

'Oh you noticed, did you? Yes well, he's very good at it, and you've only got yourself to blame. If you weren't so fucking boring with your little teacher's job, and your ridiculous provincial friends. And as for the way you allow that child to walk all over you, it makes me sick.'

'That child is our daughter.'

Ellen's eyebrows arched. 'Really?'

No. Frank absolutely refused to take the bait. 'You know Ellen, you're not right in the head.'

She punched him in the chest. 'Take that back. Take it back or I'm going, and this time I won't come back.'

He pushed her fist away. 'I think that would be the best thing, don't you?'

'You really want me to go? You do understand you won't see me again, and neither will Robyn.'

'Yes. It's what I want.'

She stared at him, her face cold, hard and full of contempt. He held his nerve refusing to look away. He'd had enough. Their time was up.

They remained locked in that position until she said: 'I don't know what I ever saw in you. Martin is twice the man you are.'

Frank opened the front door and went over to Edie's before he did something he would always regret.

He was on his way home from work. The last few days of the holidays had been awful. Ellen had been back to her usual venomous self, but something had altered in him. He wasn't prepared to take it anymore. He was careful not to say anything in front of Robyn but when she wasn't around, he gave as good as he got. That was all very well, but Frank didn't know how long he could keep it up, or what Ellen might do next. They'd never come to blows before and he was worried that punch of hers signalled a new phase. And if she hit him, there was a possibility she might also hit Robyn. On top of that there was his very real fear that he too might lash out. The thought of it horrified him, but he'd nearly lost it the other day. He made up his mind to speak to Gavin. He was the only one who could persuade her to seek help.

Ellen's car wasn't in the drive. She was supposed to have picked Robyn up from school. He felt the panic rising, until Edie and Rob appeared from the back of her house.

'Ellen asked me to collect Robyn. She had to go away.'

Edie raised her eyebrows at him, her head turned away from Rob so she couldn't see.

When they got inside, Robyn settled herself in front of the TV. It was business as usual for her. She was used to her mother disappearing at a moment's notice. Frank went into the kitchen to start on dinner and found another of Ellen's farewell notes.

Robyn was engrossed in her programme and didn't notice him creeping past her and up the stairs. He closed the bedroom door and opened the letter:

'As you can see, I've gone. It's what you wanted, isn't it? You now have your princess all to yourself. Don't worry, I'm not coming back this time. You're really not worth the effort.'

Frank dropped down onto the bed. Gone at last. Enormous relief flooded him and unable to hold it back any longer, he buried his face in his hands and wept.

He heard the door open and tried to bring the sobs to a halt. Robyn lifted his arm and sat under it. 'Has she gone again?'

He wiped his eyes. 'Yes, Baba. I don't think she's coming back this time.'

'Good. I don't want her to. I hate her.'

Frank blew his nose. 'Hate's a strong word, darling. Are you sure that's how you feel?'

'Yes. She's horrible to you. Now that she's gone, can my friends come round?'

'Of course they can. Mum didn't stop your friends from coming round, did she?'

'She was spiteful about them. It was embarrassing.'

'I didn't know that. I'm so sorry, darling.' Another sob found its way out of Frank.

Robyn squeezed her arms against him. 'Don't cry, Dad. I'll look after you.'

Frank held on tight to his darling girl. 'I know you will, Baba. And I'll look after you, I promise.' The first thing he'd do after Robyn went to bed was call Gavin and tell him to make it clear to Ellen not to come back. Then he'd think about divorce.

Robyn looked up at him, her eyes pleading. 'Does this mean we can go to see Granny and Grandda at Christmas?'

'We'll see.' He didn't want to let her down after all she'd been through but before he could go over the water he'd have to admit to his parents what was really going on. The other thing he'd have to do was face Martin, and that was going to be the hardest thing, because right now all he wanted to do was batter him.

64

THE SCALES HAVE FALLEN

Frank was balanced on the edge of the sofa. His right knee was jiggling and no matter how hard he gripped it, he couldn't make it stop. That, along with the flashing eyes and the hard, heavy breathing probably made him look like an angry old grizzly bear, but he couldn't care less, because that's exactly how he felt. After all those years of suppressing it, he'd finally blown. And in the heat of his rage, he'd put a voice to his suspicions and told Martin exactly what he thought had happened in the summer of 2007.

Martin paced up and down in front of him. 'I can't believe you'd think that of me.'

'Well one of you feckers slept with my wife, and since she pointed the finger at you and Finn could barely stand most of the time, I'm guessing it was you.'

'I did not sleep with Ellen, you crazy bastard.'

Frank jumped up and slapped him. 'You did. You know you did. Admit it.' He gave him another slap for good measure. It felt good. Not as good as beating the living daylights out of him would have felt back in 2007, but near enough.

'Ow. Would you cut out the slapping.'

He hit Martin again.

Martin jabbed him in the chest. 'Do that again and I'm gonna slap you back.'

Well that was an invite right there. Frank gave him another smack, even harder this time.

'Right. You asked for it.' Martin's hand landed on the side of Frank's face. It was so light, he hardly felt it.

'You call that a slap? You big wuss.'

'I was trying not to hurt you. Ow. You did it again! That's it now, Frank. Gloves off. Prepare to be whacked.'

Frank was not having that. He was the injured party here. If anyone was going to be doing any whacking, it was him. He pulled up both hands and boxed Martin's ears.

Martin jumped back in shock. A split second later he lashed out, but Frank ducked down and shouldered him in the stomach. Winded but not immobilised, Martin got Frank in an armlock. But Frank would not be bested. He grappled Martin to the ground. They rolled around the floor, arms, legs and heads tangled together. It wasn't long before he was hot, sweaty, and out of breath but he wasn't going to admit it so he carried on rolling, slapping and punching.

'Frank, can we stop now. I've the stitch something bad,' panted Martin.

Relieved but triumphant, Frank let him go and they scrambled back up onto the sofa.

Martin clutched his side. 'Have you any more of that whisky?'

Frank wiped the sweat from his brow and poured two out. 'I saw you that summer. I saw the way she kept touching you, the way she looked at you.'

'She was winding you up. Trying to throw you off the scent.'

'And I saw you talking in the garden, the day before you left. She was angry. It was because you were going back, wasn't it? She didn't want you to leave.'

Martin took a swig of his drink. 'Are you not listening to me? She was doing all that stuff for your benefit. She wanted to hurt you. She was cruel like that. But it wasn't me, and it wasn't Finn either. It was Billy. She'd been seeing him on and off for ages. That day you saw us talking, I was threatening to tell you if she didn't stop. She was upset, but not because she wanted me. She didn't want to stop seeing Billy.'

No, that was wrong. They'd stopped seeing Billy after he came for Frank with a baseball bat. And she didn't even like Billy in that way. 'I don't believe you.'

'No surprise there. You haven't believed a word I've said since we were kids.'

'Because you've always been a lying, sneaky fecker.'

Martin laughed and shook his head. 'That's Billy talking now.'

'Leave him out of this. He was a good friend to me, until I fucked everything up with Eve.'

Martin threw his hands up in the air. 'Will you catch yourself on? Billy was never a good friend to you. He was the worst kind of friend. God knows we all loved him, but he only ever thought of himself. All that bullshit about you stealing his missus when he'd been stealing from you for years.'

'What the hell are you talking about?'

'Him and Ellen started sleeping together not long after he hooked up with you in London. But he was doing the dirty on you well before that. He was seeing Eve when you were still with her. She was never gonna follow you to Birmingham. Billy already had his claws in her by then.'

It was all lies. It had to be. Billy wasn't like that. Frank was the one who'd betrayed him, not the other way round. That was the truth of it. Except. Except he'd never got a believable answer from Billy or Eve on what they'd been doing that day the Balaclavas took Billy away. But this was Martin telling him, and Martin was a dab hand at twisting the truth to suit him. 'If it's true, how come you knew about it and not me?'

'Siobhan told me. Not sure how she knew. Maybe Da told her. Me and Finn kept an eye on them after that. They weren't that good at hiding it. It was almost as if they wanted to be found out. Well, Billy anyway.'

'And Ellen. How did you know about her?'

'Billy, of course. The big-headed twat was bragging about how he had the sweetest revenge on you for shagging his wife. He couldn't see the irony. Like we said before, no imagination. It was always all about him. I know you're not even thinking this right now but just in case you're lying in bed some night in the future killing yourself over it, Robyn is definitely yours. They'd stopped seeing each other when her old man got sick, and didn't get back together until after Robyn was born. In New York, I think he said it was. Anyways, she has our birthmark, doesn't she? And she absolutely did not get that from me.'

Of course Robyn was his. Frank had no doubt in his mind whatsoever about that. He knew it the first time he held her, and he'd never for one minute considered that she wasn't his daughter. Not even in their darkest times when Ellen had implied that she wasn't.

Martin was back on his feet again. 'That's why we stopped seeing Billy, me and Finn. We'd had enough of him.

Look, I'm gonna hit the sack. You need some space to get
your head round all of this. Do you still keep the bedding in
the same cupboard?'

Frank nodded. His head was spinning and bed linen was
not something he could even contemplate right now. Martin
put his hand on Frank's shoulder. 'We can talk more in the
morning. Sorry it's all come out this way.'

'Uh huh. Martin. That day the Balaclavas came for
Billy.'

'I knew he was meeting Eve there. I had this plan of
taking you that way so's you'd see them together. I knew you
wouldn't believe me if I told you.'

'I might have.'

'Nah. Billy had already turned you against me. That
thing we had, you and me, Billy broke it. He ruined us all in
different ways. We just didn't know it then.'

'Did you know about the Balaclavas, or why they came
for him?'

'No. It was as much a shock to me as you. You fight like
a girl, by the way.'

'Go fuck yourself, Martin.'

'You too, brother. Goodnight.'

It was after three. The whisky bottle was empty. At one
point Frank had switched off the light with the intention of
going up but he'd ended up back on the sofa. As he recalled,
it was one of the last things Ellen had bought for this house,
just before the summer of 2007. He really needed to change
it. There were a lot of things he needed to change.

In the last few hours he'd reassessed his relationship with
Billy. With the blinkers removed, Frank was beginning to see
it as others might. When they were kids, Billy had been the

cool one that everyone wanted for their best friend. But being Billy's best friend could be a scary business, because trouble always seemed to be just around the corner. The thing with the guns was one of many scrapes he'd gotten them into. It wasn't that he loved danger, it was that he always had to be top dog. And if you were the top dog's best friend, no one else was allowed to get close. That would be why he poisoned Frank against Martin, making out it was Martin who was the sneaky fecker when all the time it was him. Maybe that was why he'd stolen Eve when she'd been his girl.

He remembered Eve once telling him that Billy didn't care who she slept with, as long as it wasn't him. He'd thought that meant she'd had other affairs. She may have done, but that wasn't what she was saying. She was saying Billy had no intention of letting Frank be top dog. She was saying, Billy despised him.

Then there was Ellen. Much as Frank wanted to turn away from it, he had to face the overwhelming possibility that Martin was telling the truth. Because the clues were there if you looked for them. The time Billy had called her Lottie. The way she went straight to him after she walked in on Frank and Eve. The amount of time they'd both spent away from home. And yes, Ellen had been in New York when Robyn was a baby. There were other little signs too. Now that the scales were falling, he remembered scenes differently. There were looks that passed between Billy and Ellen sometimes that Frank had ignored. Looks like the kind that passed between him and Eve when they were mad for each other.

So there you go then. Billy Mac was beating Frank with a baseball bat for screwing his wife when all the time he was doing the exact same thing with Frank's wife. That was the real Billy Mac. He wanted you all to himself, and then he wanted what you had. And if he couldn't have it, he ruined it.

Something else occurred to him. Did Eve know about Billy and Ellen? Is that why she took up with Frank in the first place? The words she spoke that day the Balaclavas came rang in his ears. *He's no one.* Frank put his head in his hands. Christ, he was one big fucking dummy.

He was woken up by Fred's soft nose nuzzling under his chin. When he opened his eyes he realised the dog was nestled beside him on the sofa. One of them had been dribbling. Most likely him since his left cheek was embedded in a damp patch. It would probably leave a water mark. Ellen would be outraged. That made him smile. He rubbed his eyes and looked around the room. It was still very much Ellen and not his style at all. Not that he actually had a style to call his own. One thing was certain. It was looking a bit tired and shabby. Ellen had said that herself when she came back for the last time.

65

ROBYN THE DESTROYER – 2015

Frank was standing over an easel in the breakfast room. He'd only recently started painting again. After Ellen left, he'd had no spare time what with working, taking care of Robyn, and hanging out with Adrian. Ade had moved in after that summer of 2007. He'd stayed three years, only moving out when he decided to give up teaching and buy the Hope and Anchor. Stella had accused him of having a typical Adrian mid-life crisis, but Ade was happy. The Hope and Anchor had always been his spiritual home.

They'd supported each other during those years, him and Ade, as they each adjusted to their new lives. The house had been an alternative home for Ade's kids and their presence enriched Robyn's life. Stella and Edie were also a great help and so were Ma and Da, after Frank finally disclosed the situation to them. Surprisingly, the most invaluable support came from Siobhan. Most of the time her relationship with Frank was antagonistic at best. But of all the people she could have chosen, Rob picked Siobhan to be her mother figure. They spoke at least once a week, talking about things girls couldn't talk to their dads about. It was

Siobhan who took Rob to buy her first bra, and it was
Siobhan she cried down the phone to whenever her heart
was broken. Siobhan would give him advice too. Really
useful stuff, not just her usual nagging. If she rang when
Frank wasn't there, she'd leave lists of things he needed to
do with Adrian. She'd been amazing really. Not that Frank
would tell her. She'd only accuse him of being sarcastic.

Robyn was at university in Edinburgh now. In 2008,
Frank had moved to a part-time position at a sixth form
college so he could be around more for her. But Rob was
starting out on her own adventure now and he was alone in
this big old house with hours to spare. He needed something
to occupy him, so he'd picked up painting again.

It wasn't just the lonely hours he needed to take his
mind off. Ellen had been in touch. It started a year ago with
a birthday card for Robyn which she'd binned without even
opening. Next came a Christmas card for them both. Frank
had opened that one. It had simply said:

'To Frank and Robyn,
Merry Christmas, my darlings,
Ellen xx'

Robyn had trashed it as soon as she saw it. She did the
same with this year's birthday card. But three weeks ago,
Ellen had sent her a letter. Frank had taken it up to Edinburgh in person but she'd refused to take it. 'If you get any
more of these, Dad, just bin them. I'm not interested.
End of.'

Frank hadn't binned it. He'd kept it in his office drawer,
in case she changed her mind at some point in the future.
Right now though, he was regretting it, because every day
since it had arrived, Frank held the package in his hands
and feared what might be inside.

The package had a French postmark, just like the others.

She was probably living there permanently now. Gavin knew where she was but Frank had told him never to speak of her again. All credit to him, he abided by that. He and Roger visited every month, primarily to see Robyn. He was the only Montague to ever show any warmth towards her. Robyn loved her Uncle Gav, and even though he rolled his eyes every time she shortened his name, it was obvious Gavin was touched by the level of intimacy he'd never achieved with his own family. It was highly likely that he kept Ellen abreast of what was happening. That was acceptable, as long the flow of information was only one way. But Ellen was up to something. Why else had she started with the communications?

Frank put down his brush. It was hard to concentrate today. Too much on his mind. Too many memories, doubts and fears. He really needed to speak to a solicitor about a divorce again. He'd done it after Ellen went, but got cold feet when the solicitor suggested she might file for custody of Robyn. He knew that no matter how much he argued she was an unfit mother, she had the money to buy the best solicitors in the country. It was a risk he hadn't been prepared to take. But now that Robyn was of age, it was time to think about himself. Not that he was interested in finding another partner. Who'd want him anyway?

He heard the front door opening. Edie had a key and she usually let herself in. 'Perfect timing, I was about to have a coffee.'

Then he saw who it was and his smile dropped.

Ellen took off her coat and shook the rain from her hair. It was shorter and streaked with silver now. 'Coffee would be very nice. The rain's getting quite heavy. I was in danger of a soaking.'

Frank remained frozen in the same spot, unable to believe what he was seeing.

She pecked him on the cheek. 'Shall I pour?'

'What are you doing here?' Her kiss had broken the spell but he was struggling with an overwhelming urge to vomit.

'You seem surprised to see me. Didn't Robyn tell you?'

'Robyn?' The letter, of course. 'She doesn't open your letters.'

'I see. You turned her against me.'

'No. You did that all by yourself. What are you doing here, Ellen?'

She opened the cupboard, took down two clean mugs and poured the coffee. 'Shall we talk in the lounge?' She handed Frank one of the mugs. Up close he could see she had a few wrinkles. They didn't diminish her beauty.

Still in shock, he followed her trail, spotting two suitcases by the stairs on the way into the living room.

She sat in an armchair, the picture of elegance. 'The place is looking a bit shabby, Frank. It wouldn't hurt to get the decorators in.'

'I hope you're not expecting me to take you back.'

'I'm expecting nothing. I came to put things right. Think of it as an atonement. For my sins.'

Frank frowned. 'You've found religion?'

'Absolutely not. I've found medicine. I have an illness. A condition.'

'Oh.' Frank didn't know what else to say. As an afterthought, he added: 'I'm sorry.'

Ellen waved her hand. 'I've learned to live with it. The only thing I can't live with is the way I treated you. Robyn too, but particularly you. I put you through hell. I'm so sorry. Will you let me make it up to you?'

Let me make it up to you. How many times in the past

had he heard those words fall from her lips? Too many to count, and too many to add to. 'There's no need.'

'There is. There really is. You see, Frank, when I said I can't live with it, I really meant it.'

Frank looked into her eyes. Was she saying what he thought she was saying? Or was she just messing with his head and his conscience? 'I … I don't know what it is you want from me, Ellen.'

'I want you to give me a chance to put things right. Let me come back, just until you can honestly say you've forgiven me. I'm not expecting anything. My only hope is that you'll allow me friendship and forgiveness.'

The nausea was becoming stronger. It had nearly reached his mouth. Frank took a gulp of coffee to wash it back down. 'I don't think I can go through all of that again.'

She stretched out for his hand. 'I understand. But I'm a better person now, Frank. That destructive part of me is under control. I just need a little time.'

Frank tore himself away from her beautiful grey-gold, pleading eyes before they sucked him in too far to get out. 'I need to speak to Rob.'

'Poor, darling Robyn. She's at Edinburgh now, I hear. Doing art history. Some of me must have rubbed off on her then.'

'Why didn't you just tell her to go?' Robyn was furious. Frank had picked her up from New Street Station. As soon as he told her that Ellen was back, she'd jumped on the next train down.

'I honestly don't know. I think I felt sorry for her.' Now that he'd said it, Frank realised it was true. On the surface, Ellen seemed like her old self on a good day, but there was something about the way she carried herself, something in those eyes. A sadness. It was that alone that had melted his heart and made him consider giving her a chance to find peace with her past, before he divorced her. Perhaps they'd be able to split amicably and stay friendly, the way Ade and Stella had done. Wouldn't that be best all round?

Robyn shook her head slowly and let out a long, loud breath. 'I really don't believe you sometimes, Dad. It's like you can't get enough of being shat on.'

He glanced over at her and saw that her eyes were glistening. They were tears of anger. Anger on his behalf. He reached for her hand and squeezed it. 'I know, Baba.' He rarely called her by that name now that she was an adult, but today she was his baby girl again. 'It's not like that this time, I promise you. She wants to put things right. I think we should let her try to do that. Then we'll go our separate ways. Officially.'

'Does she know that?'

'I haven't told her yet, but I will. Trust me, I am so over her.'

Robyn managed a weak smile. 'You know you're way too ancient to be saying stuff like that, don't you?'

'What? Don't tell me you're shitting on me as well?'

She tapped his arm. 'I would never do that.'

Ellen was waiting in the living room for them. Frank let Robyn go ahead of him. Ellen stood in front of the window, her hands clasped in front of her. She was trembling.

Robyn came to a halt in the middle of the room and faced her mother, hands on hips.

Ellen pushed a loose strand of hair away, then returned her hands to their former grip. 'Gavin told me how beautiful you were. He'd sent me photos, but they don't do you justice.'

Robyn looked to Frank, her eyebrows sky high, then turned back to Ellen. 'What the fuck has that got to do with anything? Do you think I care whether you judge me to be beautiful or not? Do you really think I give any kind of shit about your opinion of me at all? I don't know what you're playing at coming back here, but I tell you this, if you ever hurt my dad again, I will destroy you.'

'I don't want to hurt him. I never wanted to hurt you either, my darling. I just couldn't help myself.'

'I'm not your darling. I'm just the person you happened to give birth to. There's a big difference.'

If that was a demonstration of just how easily Robyn could destroy her mother, Ellen's expression suggested it had done the trick. She gripped the back of the armchair as if it were a crutch.

Frank went over to Robyn and put his arm around her. 'Rob, will we let Ellen explain why she's come back? Then we can decide between the three of us what to do.'

Robyn eyed her mother with a look of disdain. 'Okay. But know this. I'm only doing it for Dad.'

66

THE BEST CHRISTMAS – 2015

'I've been receiving treatment for several years now. It seems you were correct all along, Frank. What was it you once said? I wasn't right in the head. I think those were the words you used. It turns out your insight was spot on. I was indeed not right in the head. I have a disorder.' Ellen moved away from the window and sat, ramrod straight in the armchair.

'What kind of disorder?' said Frank.

'Bipolar. Sort of.'

'Sort of? You either are or you aren't bipolar. Which is it?' snapped Robyn.

Ellen sighed. 'I am. I suppose you could say the treatment has been both a help and a hindrance. I'm the closest I'll ever be to normal which is the helpful part. However, it's given me a clarity that I've found very distressing. I can see now how monstrous I was. It's quite an unbearable burden.'

Robyn crossed her arms. 'A monster is exactly what you were.' Clearly she wasn't ready to give in to sympathy just yet.

Ellen nodded but said nothing.

'I'm going to see Edie,' said Rob. She went out the back

way, through the gate Frank had made between the two gardens when she was a little girl.

Ellen looked as if she was about to cry. 'Well that went–'

'Better than I thought it would,' said Frank.

It took two days for Robyn to agree that Ellen could stay. Much of that was down to Edie who'd suggested Rob might regret not trying. Even then, she did it reluctantly and made it clear that one swipe at Frank and Ellen would be out the door.

When Rob went back to university, Frank and Ellen started doing the kind of things they might have done if they'd had a long life together with a half decent marriage. They talked, went to museums, the theatre, restaurants. She took him shopping for new clothes, gently teasing him that he dressed like a tramp. From the outside, they appeared to be repairing their relationship but appearances, as always, were deceptive. There was nothing left of that tired, fractious relationship to repair. Instead, they were building a friendship that was platonic and entirely without passion. It was comfortable. An altogether new experience for them both.

Frank poured two glasses of sherry. Ellen was dressing the Christmas tree. She stepped back and took a glass from him. 'What do you think?'

'Looks great. You've managed to ignore your aversion to tat and put all of Robyn's favourite decorations on.'

She giggled. It made Frank think of the girl he'd fallen for all those years ago. He began to wonder if he shouldn't have been stronger back then and if that strength could have made her seek help earlier. Perhaps if he had been, their lives would have been very different.

'Do you think she'll like it? I don't want her thinking I'm trying to do Christmas my way.'

'She'll be more than happy with it. What kind of Christmases did you have while you were in France?' It was funny how easily he could talk about Ellen's other life now.

'Oh very French and sophisticated. Quiet too. I have a feeling this one will be pleasantly different.'

'You didn't have anyone special to share it with?' Frank wanted to ask if she'd ever spent it with Martin, but that was the one thing that didn't come so easily. He'd stopped talking to Martin and Finn now. Well, not so much stopped as avoided any chance of it happening. It was the only way he could deal with the betrayal and maintain the status quo with the rest of the family.

Ellen smiled. 'Sometimes. I had friends you know. What about you?'

'Someone special? No. Not unless you count Robyn and Adrian.'

'I've scarred you for life.'

Frank shrugged. 'Maybe one day.'

She sat down on the sofa and held out her hand to him. He took it and sat next to her. 'You're going to divorce me, aren't you?'

Frank kissed her hand. 'Yes.'

She sighed. 'It's as I expected. Give me a little longer though, please.'

'Of course.'

'You did a wonderful job with Robyn. I knew you would. I wish I'd been as decent as you. I wish I could have stayed, but I did it for her sake. I couldn't trust myself. You see that, don't you?'

· · ·

It had been the best Christmas he and Ellen had ever spent together. Even better than that first one when they hid out in the Montagues' London flat and trashed the Brigadier's wine cellar. Gavin and Roger came to stay. Old lady Montague had not been invited but wouldn't have come anyway. Apparently she'd opted to spend it with friends in warmer climes. Edie had also popped over, in between visits to family and friends, and so had Adrian and Stella. In the interest of harmony, Rob put her feelings to one side and put on a happy face.

On Christmas morning, Ma and Da had called from Siobhan's. Rob had spent a long time talking with Siobhan and afterwards, Siobhan had bent Frank's ear about neglecting the parents and not letting Ellen fool him. He'd let it wash over him in the spirit of Christmas goodwill to all men and women. Except for Martin. Frank still couldn't forgive him for what he'd done.

Today, Frank was driving Robyn back up to Edinburgh. He'd thought about suggesting Ellen came too but guessed that might be a step too far for Rob. She did however manage a smile and a wave as she said goodbye and strapped herself into the passenger seat.

He gave Ellen a peck on the cheek. 'I'll call you this evening.'

'Are you still getting a divorce?' said Rob as they drove away.

'Yes. She knows. We talked about it. Do you mind?'

'Er, no!' She eyed him as if he was mad, then her face softened. 'You need to do what's best for you, Dad. You've spent too long thinking about everyone else.'

Frank called Ellen from his hotel room. 'I thought I'd call

before I meet up with Rob for dinner. She's all settled back at hers now. Are you doing okay on your own down there?'

'Yes. I'm fine. I've been out shopping and had tea with Edie. I even popped in to see Adrian in that abominable place he calls a pub. I didn't stay long. He was busy with the lunchtime crowd and to be honest, the place looked like it needs a thorough deep clean.'

Frank laughed. 'I hope you told him.'

'Naturally. I am never anything but honest with Adrian. What time do you think you'll be back tomorrow?'

'I'll set off early so I'm hoping for around two. Have a good night.'

'You too. Tell Robyn I love her.'

'I will. Bye Ellen.'

'Goodbye Frank.'

The house was empty when he returned home. Frank went straight up to the main bedroom where Ellen had been sleeping. The clothes she'd brought with her had gone, as had the suitcases. As he went through the drawers and wardrobes, he realised she'd bought him more new clothes and underwear. There were new towels in the bathroom and new bed linen. There was no note, no email, no message, but he knew it would be the last time he'd see her.

He tried Ellen's mobile. It was switched off. Then he called Robyn. 'She's gone.'

'I guess it had to happen sooner or later. How do you feel?'

'I think I'm okay. I was expecting it.'

67

SAINT-GERMAIN-EN-LAYE – 2016

When the police officers knocked on his door, Frank instantly knew it would be about Ellen. She was dead. Suicide, according to the French authorities. They left him with the details of who to contact, along with their sincere condolences.

The first person he called was Gavin who had also just been told. Gavin was his usual controlled self, regardless of what might be going on inside. 'I'll call France. I speak the language, it'll be easier. Unless you'd prefer to do it yourself?'

'No. Thank you. I need to go and see Robyn. I can't tell her over the phone.'

'Yes, of course. I'd better do the same with Mother. I'll be in touch.'

Frank went straight to Robyn's house from the plane. He hadn't pre-warned her he was coming, that would have required an explanation. He just hoped she was in.

Her housemate answered the door but Rob wasn't far behind: she'd heard him asking for her. 'What is it?'

'It's Ellen.'

Rob's hand shot to her throat. 'She's dead, isn't she?'

Frank flew in to Charles de Gaulle airport. Robyn was coming in separately from Edinburgh in a few days. There were things he needed to do before that, papers to sign, that sort of thing, because he was still Ellen's next of kin.

Gavin had organised the funeral which would be in Saint-Germain-en-Laye, a small town about an hour away from Paris. Ellen had lived there for years. A few months ago, she'd been in a French restaurant in Birmingham with Frank, very much alive, when she'd told him all about Saint-Germain-en-Laye and how she'd found contentment there. He'd taken that to be a sign that she was ready to give him up. He hadn't realised at the time she was ready to give everything else up too.

Two days after his dash to Edinburgh, he'd received a letter from Ellen. There were actually two letters inside. One for him and one for Robyn. His was short, typical Ellen. She said she loved him and asked for his forgiveness for what she was about to do.

Frank had gone back up to Edinburgh to deliver Robyn's letter personally. Rob had read it and shown it to him. It was pages long and talked mostly about the future. Ellen had left a lifetime of love and advice in that letter. All the things she hadn't been able to do when she was alive.

'Do you think if I'd been nicer to her, she'd still be alive?' said Robyn.

Frank put his arm around her. 'No, Baba, I don't. This had nothing to do with you. Ellen understood why you didn't trust her. For what it's worth, she didn't trust herself either. I think she'd planned it before she came back. She just came home to make peace with us.'

Gavin was waiting for him in arrivals. He looked tired and much less polished than usual. He met Frank with a grim nod. 'How's Robyn?'

'Hard to say. She seems okay. I don't think she ever felt close to Ellen.'

'Sadly, I think you're right. I've put you up in a hotel near our apartment. It's not far from Ellen's house. I would have you stay with us, but Mother's there. I thought you'd prefer the distance.'

'Yes, that would be best. You're not staying in Ellen's house then?'

Gavin shook his head. 'There are complications in that regard. I'll explain later.'

It must be old lady Montague. It must be too upsetting for her to be near Ellen's things, thought Frank. 'How's your mother doing?'

Gavin gave him a faint smile. 'Mother has always had what Roger likes to call attachment issues. I have no idea what's going on underneath the bonnet but on the surface, she is as she always is.'

Poor Gavin. Poor, poor Ellen. Frank was so glad he had a mother like his own. She might have been hard on him as a kid, she might be a huge pain in the arse sometimes, but he was in no doubt she loved him.

They got into Gavin's car. Gavin didn't switch the engine on straight away. 'I hope you didn't mind about the funeral. As her executor, I have to make sure I carry out her final instructions.'

He put his hand on Gavin's arm. 'I know. It's fine. She loved this place. She had everything she wanted here.'

Gavin sighed. 'Perhaps not quite everything. You did your best, Frank. No one could have asked you to do more.'

'Thank you.' Frank knew that, but it was good of him to say it.

'She seemed so happy over Christmas. I'd thought she'd found some comfort at last.'

'I think she had. She was the happiest and most content I've ever known her to be. Perhaps that was enough.'

Gavin smiled another faint smile. 'Leaving on a high.'

'Exactly.'

'Frank, there's something I have to tell you. Ellen was living with someone here. A chap called Benoit. From what I can make out, they'd had something of an on-off relationship until the last time she left you and she moved to France permanently.'

Ah. So those were the complications. 'You didn't know?'

He grimaced. 'I knew about him. I didn't know it was as serious as it was. Benoit was the one who found her. He's taken it rather badly, as you can imagine.'

'Can I meet him?'

'I was hoping you'd say that. Better to get it over with before the funeral.'

Benoit was good looking, clean shaven and well dressed. Exactly the kind of man Frank would have expected Ellen to have gone for. He was as polished as his nails, if you ignored the haunted look in his eyes. He shook Frank's hand tentatively. 'I am so sorry. You must think me a very bad person, but your existence was news to me. She never told me she was married. Or that she had a daughter.'

'Don't worry about it, your existence was news to me too,' said Frank. They were in a bar, a few streets away from his hotel. Gavin had introduced them and left them to talk.

'She was some woman,' said Benoit.

'Yes she was.' Frank couldn't argue with that sentiment. There truly was no other woman like Ellen. 'Did she tell you where she was last year?'

'No. And I had learned not to ask.'

'Me too. I don't think she meant to be the way she was. I guess it was her condition.'

Benoit frowned. 'Condition?'

'The bipolar.'

'Bipolar?' Benoit muttered something in French that Frank didn't catch. 'I was not aware of this. Perhaps you made a mistake?'

'I…' Frank saw the confusion playing out on Benoit's face. The poor guy had been through enough. 'Yes. Perhaps I did.'

'Christmas was so miserable without her. When she called to say she was coming home, I was overjoyed. We had two wonderful weeks and then, and then this.' Benoit began to cry. 'Apologies. I can't believe she is gone. But I know it is true. I saw her. I felt her cold skin. Again, I'm sorry. You do not want to hear this.'

'It's okay. I understand.'

'You're very kind. I don't think I would be so generous if I were in your shoes.'

Perhaps not, but Benoit wasn't in Frank's shoes. Benoit had probably seen the best of Ellen. Frank could have envied that in him, but all he could do was pity him for his suffering. 'Was she happy with you, Benoit?'

Benoit blew his nose. 'I think so. Was she happy with you, Frank?'

'Only at the end.'

.   .   .

Robyn was not at all surprised that her mother had another man on the go, but Frank saw her sneaking a glance at Benoit at the funeral. For his part, Benoit looked astounded when he saw Robyn walking on Frank's arm. She was so like Ellen, it must have been a shock. He caught Mrs Montague casting an eye over her too. The old woman sat rigid and unyielding throughout the service, completely dry-eyed. Benoit was distraught. The only person to match his emotions was Adrian.

The wake was held in one of the smaller rooms of a grand hotel. Mrs Montague sat by a window looking out to a lake in the grounds, accepting and responding to condolences in perfect French.

The British contingent of mourners huddled around Frank and Robyn.

Adrian proposed a toast. 'To Lady Lottie. One of a kind. We loved her regardless.'

'So true,' said Gavin. 'Would you excuse me?' He left the room and a few minutes later, Frank saw him through the window, on his way to the lake.

Frank followed him out. The setting reminded him of the first time he and Gavin had met, the one and only time he'd stayed at the Montagues' house. It was also the first time Gavin had warned him about Ellen, although Frank hadn't realised he'd been serious at the time.

Ahead of him, Gavin stopped by the lake. He had his back to Frank and it was only as he got closer, Frank realised he was weeping.

Gavin turned to face him, tears streaming down his face. 'Ah, the mask has slipped I'm afraid. You've rather caught me at a bad time. Would you mind leaving me to it?'

Frank nodded and walked back up to the hotel. Mrs Montague was watching them through the window, her face as impassive as ever.

The next day, Robyn and Adrian flew home. Frank was staying for another day to go over some points from Ellen's will.

'Most of her money goes to Benoit. She didn't think you'd want it,' said Gavin. 'She has left the London flat to you though.'

'She was right, I don't want it. I don't want the flat either.'

'I could arrange a sale. You could put the money away for a rainy day.'

Frank nodded in agreement. He was too tired to fight it. 'What about Robyn?'

'Ellen didn't think the money did her any good whatsoever. She wanted better for Robyn. She's left something in trust for her but she won't get it until she's thirty. She was very keen not to have her young life spoiled by wealth. You know it will all come to Robyn eventually, the Montague money. She's the last in line.'

'We'll cross that bridge when we come to it,' said Frank. There was always the chance that old lady Montague would leave everything to the National Trust or something. Not for philanthropic reasons, obviously. More to make a point about how disappointed she was in her children and their choices.

68

OLDEST AND DEAREST FRIENDS

Two things happened not long after Ellen died. The first was that sour-faced old Mrs Montague finally popped her clogs. Out of respect for Gavin, Frank and Robyn went to the funeral but it was fair to say, no tears were shed by either of them. The old woman would have expected nothing less.

The second was a happier occasion. Gavin and Roger got married. At the wedding, they spoke about adopting. They were probably too old for it really but Gavin, with his connections, could arrange anything. During the reception, Gavin told him he'd found out that Ellen had been seeing a psychiatrist towards the end of her life. Frank had asked him about Ellen being bipolar. Gavin had been as surprised as Benoit had been. He'd suggested something closer to borderline personality disorder. Apparently, that was what the doctors at the Richmond Park suspected all those years ago. If only Frank had listened to the experts instead of Ellen, he could have spared her and others years of suffering. The guilt of that still haunted him.

He hadn't seen Gavin since that day, but Robyn gave him updates every now and then. He and Roger did manage to adopt three children and, judging by the reports from Rob, all five were happy and thriving. Of course, that meant Rob was no longer the sole heir to the Montagues' estate which was a definite plus in Frank's eyes. It was a shame he'd lost touch with Gavin. He really should do something about that.

He opened the living room curtains and saw Finn's campervan parked up on the road outside the house. He had a headache and it felt like a badger had scraped its arse along his tongue, but the sight of Finn's van lifted his spirits. Fred, his other loyal friend, was at his side. He put his fingers behind the dog's right ear and scratched it. 'Come on and meet Cousin Finn. You're gonna love him.'

Frank tapped on the campervan window and heard the sound of movement coming from inside. A bleary-eyed Finn slid the door open. 'Morning. I got here early and didn't want to disturb you.'

'Have you had any sleep?'

'Yeah. A couple of hours in the motorway services and the same after I arrived. I'm grand. Martin inside?'

'Still in bed. I think. Shit, I haven't checked.' He looked up at the closed curtains in one of the spare rooms. He wouldn't do it again, would he? At that moment Martin drew the curtains open and Frank's heartbeat slowed down to its normal pace.

Finn put his hand on Frank's back. 'It's gonna be okay, FB. We're gonna sort this. Now, who's this fine-looking fella?' He crouched down and petted Fred who was loving the extra attention.

'This is my main man, Fred. You go inside and help yourself to whatever you want. I have to pop next door to see Netta before she goes to work.'

. . .

Netta was already up. 'How did it go last night?'

Frank thought of him and Martin girl-slapping each other and rolling around the floor. Thank Christ she wasn't there to see that. 'It was revealing.'

'That sounds ominous.'

'That's not an entirely incorrect description. Finn's arrived.'

'Cousin Finn?' The fact that she took great delight every time she used Finn's full title had not escaped Frank.

'The one and only. I just wanted to apologise again for last night. And for Martin turning up. And for this whole mess. It's really–'

'Interesting. It's really interesting. To me anyway. I'd like to know more.'

'Oh.' He wasn't expecting that. She'd stumped him.

'Perhaps we can talk about it soon?'

'Yes. There's quite a lot.' He left it at that. No need to say any more. Although there was that thing they'd promised each other about no secrets. Should he? Could he? He would. 'I haven't been entirely open with you.' He held his breath and waited for his admission to sink in.

She smiled. 'I know.'

He hadn't been expecting that either. 'You do?'

'Yes. It's all right. I don't mind.'

'You don't?' he said, although he wasn't sure what it was exactly that she didn't mind. He just hoped it had nothing to do with Doogie Chambers.

She shook her head. 'I don't. But I have to go to work. We've got a big order to get out this morning. Let's talk about it when things have calmed down.'

'Of course. When things have calmed down. Shouldn't be long now.'

.   .   .

Frank went out the back way, through the gate into his garden. He could see Finn and Martin in his studio. They let him in through the French windows.

'We were admiring your work,' said Finn. 'Are you selling it now?'

'I am.'

'That's great, Frank. How's it going?' said Finn.

Normally he would have shuffled his feet and muttered something like, 'I get by' but he was back to thinking about the differences between old Frank and new Frank. 'It's going well. In fact, I've decided to give up teaching and focus on doing it full time.' There. He'd said it now. It felt right, but he couldn't help thinking he should have said it to Netta first.

Martin coughed and shoved his hands in his pockets. 'They're pretty amazing. I didn't know you were that good.'

'Thanks. I've got better. Lots of practice.'

'Da paints now. You probably already knew that.'

'I did not.' And why would he, when he'd been keeping everyone in his family at arm's length for so long? 'Listen, I owe you both an apology. I've been a blind fool, and I've treated you both badly.'

Finn nodded. Martin had obviously filled him in. 'Will I try to rustle up a healthy breakfast out of that rubbish you've got in your fridge?'

Frank smiled. 'That'd be grand.' He turned to Martin. 'Finn's going to help me get fitter.'

'Finn's the man for that,' said Martin.

'Aye. He's a good friend.' It was just the two of them now that Finn was working away in the kitchen and it felt awkward, but only because there was more unfinished business to be addressed. 'So are you.'

Martin's eyes were filling. Jeez, he was such a baby. But that was Martin. That was his brother.

'I was only ever trying to look out for you, FB.'

'I know, Marty. I just couldn't see it before last night. I shouldn't have cut you out. I should have seen Billy for what he was. Will you be all right?'

'Aye. Finn's putting me on a health kick too.' He tapped the side of his head. 'A mental health one.'

'Finn's the man.' They'd said it before and Frank had no doubt they'd be saying it many times in the years to come.

'Finn is the man,' said Martin, as if to confirm that prediction.

Over breakfast, they talked some more, reframing past events as they did. Then they got to the sticky subject of Martin and Bronagh.

'I got myself into an awful black hole after I heard about Billy, and Eve was the only one I could talk to. She understood,' said Martin.

'Probably because she was going through the same thing. That can help. But if all you do is keep it to yourselves, it becomes self-destructive. You should explain to Bronagh. She'll understand,' said Finn.

'Finn's right. If you love Bronagh, you need to share everything with her,' said Frank, making a personal note to take his own advice. 'Have you spoken to her?'

'A few messages but we've not really spoken since I left Belfast. I er, I'm a bit scared to, actually.' Martin's eyes were filling up again.

Frank wanted to comfort him with stories of kids, and dogs, and adventures. He wanted to make the nightmares go away for his wee brother, but they were men now and the world didn't work that way. There were some things Martin had to do on his own. 'Why don't you try her now?'

Martin looked at Finn. Finn nodded in approval. He gritted his teeth. 'Okay.'

Frank and Finn began to clear up the breakfast things. They could hear the muffled sounds of Martin talking in the dining room.

Finn checked the time. 'Six minutes. He must have got through anyways. You should come over and scatter Billy's ashes with us. It'll give us all some closure.'

'Maybe. I'm going to talk it through with Netta first. She's at work now but she wants to meet you.'

'Does Netta make you happy, Frank?'

It struck Frank that Finn had asked almost the exact same question he'd asked Benoit. He'd shaped it differently but what he'd meant was had Benoit managed to do the thing Frank had failed to do? And now Finn was asking, had Netta succeeded where Ellen had failed. 'Very much so.'

'And Fred there, is he a good companion?'

Fred was hoovering up the crumbs on the floor with his great long tongue. At the mention of his name his head shot up and he cocked it to one side, his dopey gaze fixed on Finn.

'He's the best,' said Frank.

'We talk about getting dogs, me and the lads. Ren's dog died last year. He's lonely without him.'

'They're your new gang, Ren and Rebel,' said Frank.

'I guess so. Except this one's a more equal partnership. Don't worry though. I still have time for the old gang.'

'When you see Rebel again, tell him I found it. He'll know what I mean.'

Martin came back into the room, looking a bit brighter. 'She's agreed to see me and talk next week after the kids go

back to school. She's taken them to Portrush to see her
family, so I've time to sort out a return. Ma and Da will let
me stay at theirs. I tried calling them but there's no answer
at home, or on Da's mobile.'

'Probably out shopping or something. Have you tried
Siobhan?' said Frank.

Martin pretended to shudder. 'Not sure I'm ready for
the Siobhan effect just yet.'

Frank tried her number. It went straight to voicemail.
'No answer. I haven't had a reply to the message I sent her
either. Probably nothing. We'll try again later. What do you
fellas want to do today?'

'It would be nice to go back to the old places, like when
we used to visit before,' said Martin.

Frank smiled. 'I was thinking the same thing. A lot of
them are gone now but there's one pub still standing, and
you already know the landlord.'

Frank let Martin and Finn go into the Hope and Anchor
first. It had had a couple of minor refurbs since they'd last
set foot in it, but it was still pretty much as it was the last
time they came.

Adrian was behind the bar. He saw them and his face
broke into a big, broad grin. 'Well look what the cat dragged
in. It's the Three Amigos. Older, wiser and twice as ugly.'
Netta had called them that too, except she hadn't laced it
with sarcasm. But he expected nothing else from Adrian, his
oldest and dearest friend. Although, now that he'd seen his
brother and cousin in a new light, Frank might have to think
about revising that description.

69

THE FULL INITIATION

Frank had messaged Netta to ask if she'd take care of Fred when she got home, as they were spending the afternoon at the Hope and Anchor. Shortly after, he sent her a picture of the three of them with Adrian, all looking more than a little merry. She took this to mean Martin and Frank's differences had been resolved.

She went into Frank's first to collect Fred and took him round to hers. Having sent the dogs out to the garden, she made a cup of tea and put her feet up. It had been a busy day, a few minutes quiet wouldn't hurt. She closed her eyes, all set to drift away, but a knock on the door put an immediate stop to it.

She opened it to a party of three. Her heart sank. She'd accidentally answered the knock of the God-Squad. Normally she did a sneaky look from behind the curtains to ascertain whether she needed to pretend she was out, but she'd been caught on the hop. When she noticed the absence of literature or briefcases about their persons, she relaxed slightly. Two of them were at least eighty, so they probably weren't sales people either.

'Am I speaking to Netta?' said the youngest, a woman who could have been anywhere between fifty and early sixties. She was rubbish at guessing peoples ages, especially when they looked as good as this woman. There was one crucial factor she hadn't missed though. The woman's accent was from Northern Ireland. What with that and the cabin-sized suitcases they had with them, a light bulb switched on in her head.

'You are,' she said.

'Hello. I'm Siobhan. Frank's sister.'

'Hello, Siobhan. And you must be Mr and Mrs O'Hare.' Netta's former corporate past resurfaced and she shook their hands. 'Frank and the others are out at the moment, but please come in.'

She showed them into the lounge. 'Let me take your coats. Would you like some tea or coffee?'

'Tea would be lovely,' said Mrs O'Hare. 'We've come straight from the airport. They don't know how to make a good cup.'

'No pressure then,' laughed Netta. Mrs O'Hare frowned. Oh dear. Perhaps wait a while before she told any more nervous jokes. 'Make yourselves at home. I'll put the kettle on.'

'I'll come and help you.' Siobhan followed her into the kitchen. 'Sorry to have just turned up on your doorstep like this. We thought they'd be in.'

'Not a problem. There are biscuits in that tin, if you want to put some on a plate. Unless you'd prefer something more substantial?'

'We ate at the airport. Biscuits will be great. Are those all your dogs?'

'The one with the blue collar is Frank's. The other two

are mine. I'll leave them in the garden until you're all settled. They can be a bit boisterous.'

'The blue collar, you said? I can see more than a passing resemblance.'

'I often think the same. Especially when Frank's just woken up.'

Siobhan gave her a look, very similar to the one Mrs O'Hare had given her a few moments ago. Oops. Possibly too much information. Then, hallelujah, she laughed. 'So where are they?'

'They're in a pub. An old favourite of Frank's, the Hope and Anchor.'

'Isn't that Adrian's pub?'

'Oh! You know Adrian?' Stupid question, since Adrian appeared to know a hell of a lot more about Frank's family than she did.

'Of course,' said Siobhan. 'Only through Frank though, with him being Frank's oldest friend. At least, he is now Billy's gone.'

'Billy?'

'Er, yes. Maybe I should call Frank to see how long they're going to be,' said Siobhan.

'It's okay, I'll call him. Why don't you take the drinks in?'

Netta called Frank. It certainly did sound like the whole family knew Adrian, but then that was highly likely, seeing as he was Frank's oldest friend, according to Siobhan. *At least, he is now Billy's gone.* That had to be Billy Mac, there couldn't be two Billys. But gone? Did that mean he'd left town, or the planet? The planet, presumably. Billy Mac must have died, and it was probably recent. She wondered if Frank knew.

When he picked the call up, the first thing she heard was the song in the background, 'My Perfect Cousin'. Next, came a bit of man giggling, some phone fumbling and finally, Frank himself: 'Well if it isn't the most beautiful woman in the world.'

It was corny and sweet, and probably came from a place of inebriation. Normally, she'd have found it more amusing and done some silly phone flirting, but she had urgent business. 'Frank, your parents and sister are here.'

'Shit. We're on our way.'

Netta had always thought of Frank as a fully grown, fully developed adult male, but standing in her lounge with his hands behind his back and looking very sheepish was a naughty boy who happened to be sixty-one years old. The other two were even worse. The man who had to be Cousin Finn was blinking furiously, and Martin was staring at the floor.

'And I suppose you're all very proud of yourselves with your afternoon drinking, getting sloshed,' said Mrs O'Hare, marching up and down in front of them like a sergeant-major in full dressing-down mode. Any minute now, she'd be calling them an 'orrible lot.

'Sorry Ma,' the three men-boys muttered.

'And as for you, Martin O'Hare. Running off like that and frightening the hell out of us. You left your wife with three fatherless children. Do you hear me, Martin? Not to mention the two, from your other women. I hope you're thoroughly ashamed of yourself.'

Martin mumbled something that sounded like, 'Yes Ma.'

'And let's not forget the business with that woman whose name shall not be spoken.'

'Ma, that was a misunderstanding,' said Frank.

'Quiet!' Mrs O'Hare was on a rant that wouldn't go

amiss in a pulpit and she was not about to be contradicted. She had reduced three fully grown men to quivering wrecks and sent the dogs fleeing for their lives into the breakfast room. Netta was in awe. Even her own mum wasn't this impressive.

'Whether it's a misunderstanding or not is something only Bronagh can decide. And I hope for your sake, Martin, she agrees with your brother.' She gave Frank a withering look that seemed to shrink him a tiny bit more. Then she returned her glare to Martin. 'You will be returning home with us on Sunday. But for now, your father will deal with you. Gerry.'

Mr O'Hare, who had hardly said a word since his arrival, stood up. 'Son, you and me need to have a talk.'

Martin looked like a man who'd just been given a death sentence. Frank handed his door keys over to him, and father and son went next door.

Mrs O'Hare rounded on Frank and Finn. 'And don't think I've finished with you two either. Gallivanting around Scotland. On a road trip, no less, when you were supposed to be bringing him home. You are in my bad books and will remain there for some time to come.'

Siobhan took her mother's arm. 'Come on now, Ma. Have a seat. They're very sorry, aren't you fellas?'

Frank and Finn stammered and muttered an affirmative.

'I'll make some more tea,' said Netta feeling like a bit-part actor in some long running family saga.

'Or coffee. Who wants coffee?' Frank had suddenly found his voice.

'Sorry about all of that,' he said when they were in the kitchen and out of earshot.

'Nonsense, I'm enjoying it.' Netta smirked. How could

she have ever thought things were getting boring with her and Frank?

He gave her an embarrassed grin. 'It's not funny.'

'Oh, but it is. Your mother's a formidable woman. She had you three squirming like worms on a stick. What do you think's going on next door?'

'Da will be giving him a talking to. Then they'll be working out what to do to get Martin back with his wife.'

'I wasn't sure, after…'

'Oh the battering days are long behind us now. Ma knows that. She just can't get out of the habit of asserting her authority now and then. It'll all have blown over soon.'

Finn came in with the empty biscuit plate. 'Siobhan's suggested more biscuits.' He puffed out his cheeks. 'I think we got off quite lightly with that one, what? Hello Netta. It seems strange having a proper introduction after I've just been yelled at for the last half hour in your living room but anyway, it's nice to meet you.'

So she was finally face to face with the one and only Cousin Finn. Netta had pictured a cross between Huckleberry Finn and John-boy Walton. Needless to say, he was nothing like either of them. He was more like the kind of personal trainer you signed up with because you couldn't think of anything nicer than being praised by him for managing a push-up without collapsing.

'Is it safe to go back in yet?' said Frank.

Finn eyes crinkled. He had quite the loveliest eyes, deep brown and kind. 'Only if you have very good biscuits.'

Netta reached for the biscuit tin. 'In that case, it's lucky for you pair that I recently stocked up on Marks and Spencer's finest.'

. . .

Netta and Siobhan were relaxing in the lounge, finishing off a bottle of wine. After a hastily codged together dinner, the others had gone over to Frank's. One of Frank's bedrooms was used as an office, so Netta had offered up one of hers. Siobhan had jumped in before anyone else.

'I meant to say earlier, I love your dress,' said Netta.

'Thanks. I designed it myself. I've a woman makes them up for me.'

'God, you're talented. Is that what you do for a living?'

Siobhan pulled a face. 'I wish. No, I work in HR. When I was a kid I wanted to work in fashion. Grand ideas that came to nothing. You know how it is.'

Netta nodded. 'I do. Life has a habit of messing things up.'

'Well, parents do anyway.'

'Oh I see. Do you want to talk about it?'

Siobhan shook her head. 'No, it's not worth the effort. But thanks for asking. And thanks for putting me up.'

'Are you sure you wouldn't have preferred to stay next door?' said Netta.

'Definitely not. I've had more than my fair share of that lot this week. It's nice to have a quiet hour with a sane person for a change.' Siobhan patted Maud who was sitting on her lap. 'I wouldn't mind a little dog like this. I've a touch of empty-nest syndrome. My kids have left home now, and I recently got rid of the biggest kid of all. My husband. He was a useless fecker. We get on all right, like, but he was such a drain on me. A dog would be much less work.'

Fecker? Netta liked that word. She tried it out: 'I don't get on with my ex. He's a manipulative fecker.'

'Like Ellen. It was a bad day when Frank met her. He has told you about Ellen, hasn't he? I'm not dropping him in it again?' Siobhan gave her a wicked smile. 'You're not too great at hiding surprise. You didn't know Frank and Adrian were ever that close. And I'm guessing you don't know about Billy either.'

'Put it this way, I only recently found out Adrian and Frank went that far back, and all I know about Billy Mac is that he once wrote some band reviews in a fanzine, and Adrian thinks he's a wanker.'

Siobhan laughed. 'Well Adrian would know. Fanzine, was it? Would that be *Can*, by any chance? That was their big claim to fame, the three of them. One very limited edition that only their mates bought.'

'The three of them?'

'Billy, Frank, or Frankie Boy as they used to call him. And Eve. Oh. You don't know about Eve either.'

Well that was one mystery solved. FB was Frankie Boy. And as there was only one name left to frame, she had a good idea who Eve was. 'No, but I'm guessing she went by the name of Ana Manic. And by the look on your face, I'm guessing there's a lot more to it.'

Siobhan sighed. 'What do you want to know?'

'Everything. I want the full initiation.'

'Well, aren't you the brave one? I hope you're prepared for a long night.'

70

THAT WAS A MOMENT

Having given his room up to the parents, Frank had spent the night in Robyn's room. Lying in bed and staring up at the walls, he noticed how oppressive they were. Rob had been going through her purple phase when it had last actually been her room. They were still purple. He heard the front door closing and went out onto the landing to investigate. As he suspected, Ma and Da were up. It must have been them.

He went down to the kitchen for his morning coffee and heard someone in his studio. He stuck his head around the door and saw that it was Da. 'Morning, son. Your ma's gone over to see Siobhan and your young lady.'

Frank smiled. Netta was a few years younger than him but young she was not. Still, it was all relative he supposed. 'D'you want a coffee, Da?'

'Go on then, while your ma's not here. She's got it into her head that caffeine's bad for me.'

Frank took the coffee into the studio. Da was standing in front of a painting he'd finished before the Easter break. He put the drinks on the little table he'd bought for him and

Netta to sit at. 'I've a gallery exhibition coming up in the autumn. That one's going in.'

Da patted his arm. 'It's good. The colours. The skyline, how do you manage to get it so straight?'

'I learned it from you. One of the first things you taught me was the importance of a steady hand.'

'Ah but that was house painting.'

'Same thing. Martin said you paint now.'

'I do, but not like this. Your ma keeps going on about me having lessons.'

'I could teach you,' said Frank.

'You're a bit too far away.'

'I'm going to be coming over more.'

'She'd like that.' Da sat down at the table. 'You've not done any decorating yourself for a while.'

'No. I've been helping Netta with hers though. We did a lot of work on it.'

'Aye, it looks well loved.' He sipped his coffee. He didn't need to say more, the implication was clear. Frank's house was unloved. Da was a man of few words, but every one of them counted.

'Da, how come you only had me do the decorating? How come you didn't do anything special with Martin?'

Da's brow furrowed. 'Because Martin had no interest in it, and he didn't need help in that way. He was always good with his hands. I did other things with him and Siobhan.'

'He doesn't think so.'

'Your brother has a short memory. He forgets the hours I spent helping him with his reading. Those books of yours, the Famous Five and the Hardy Boys. He was desperate to read them just because they were yours. They said he was a duffer at the school, but he just had trouble with words. Look how well he's done for himself.'

Ma came in through the French windows. 'Is that you drinking coffee, Gerry?'

'It's all right Ma, it's decaff. It's healthy coffee.' Frank hoped she wasn't as good at seeing through his lies as she used to be.

Ma looked put out. 'Oh. Well maybe you should drink that more often, Francis. You're looking very unhealthy. You could do with taking a leaf out of Finn's book.'

'It's all in hand, Ma, don't worry.'

'Right, so. Get your coat, Gerry. Netta's taking us to meet her parents.' She pointed a finger at Frank. 'You stay here, and don't let Martin out of your sight.'

Siobhan came round not long after they'd gone. She seemed a bit tetchy, but then didn't she always? Except perhaps yesterday when Ma was letting rip. Gloating was what she was then.

Finn was already up when she got there. Martin came down shortly after. He took one look at her and snorted. 'Come on now, Siobhan, crack your face why don't yer.'

'I'll tell you what I'll crack in a minute, your fucking skull,' she hissed.

Martin put his hands up in front of him. 'Whoa, what's up with you, Little Miss Sunshine? I thought you'd be over the moon. You tracked me down. We all got a bollocking, and you're the golden girl again.'

'Golden girl? Golden girl, is it? You have no idea, do you? Do any of you wankers know what I have to put up with? No, you don't. Because you're in hiding.' She pointed to Frank, and then to Finn. 'You're too busy lighting candles and telling people to be calm. And as for you.' She jabbed Martin in the chest. 'You're too preoccupied with letting Eve

Macintyre cry on your big gullible shoulder to notice your
marriage going down the pan. Who do you think persuaded
Bronagh to hear you out, huh? Who do you all think spends
hours listening to Ma wailing and gnashing her teeth over
youse lot and your oh so many misdemeanours? Shall I give
you a clue? It's me. Yep, little ould me, cleaning up after the
lot of yer like a good little woman. Well who's looking after
me, eh? Not youse feckers, that's for sure.'

Finn bravely opened his arms out to embrace her.
'Steady on there, Siobhan.'

Siobhan held out her hand to stop him coming any
closer. 'Don't Finn. I beg of you. Don't tell me to breathe
slowly. I know you mean well, but it's a little grating, you
know? I just need you all to step up to the plate. That's all.
Just behave like fucking adults.' She put her hand on her
forehead. 'I'm away back to Netta's. I get more sense out of
those dogs than youse three put together.'

Frank, Martin and Finn watched Siobhan storm back
through the garden and disappear into Netta's. Martin let
out a slow whistle. 'Fuck. That was a moment. D'you think
it's the menopause?'

Frank and Finn did a joint sharp intake of breath. 'You
can't be saying stuff like that. Not only is it patronising and
misogynistic, it's probably wildly inaccurate. Siobhan will be
post-menopausal by now,' said Finn.

'Finn's right. That was offensive,' said Frank.

'Was it?' said Martin, looking genuinely perplexed.

Frank rolled his eyes. 'Yes. Where have you been living,
in a cave?'

Martin shrugged. 'In that case, what was that all about?'

'I think she's just had enough.' Frank suddenly remembered, he'd forgotten to ask Da what the special thing was
that he did with Siobhan.

71

EYES AND EARS

Siobhan shut Netta's back door and turned the key. She had to get away before she let herself down and blubbed. She sank down onto the sofa. The little dog, Maud, jumped up on her lap and the bigger one, Betty, lay at her feet. She ran her hands along their backs and started to feel calmer.

It was Ma who'd set her off in a bad mood. Wasn't it always? All Siobhan had asked was if she was happier now that things were sorted. Ma had given her a filthy look and said: 'I'll be happy when he's back with Bronagh. We've had enough marital disasters in this family.'

It was the look that did it. The look that told Siobhan which marital disaster in particular Ma was referring to. Because yes, it always came back to her. Her brothers were useless shites in the marital area. Martin had his two horribly failed marriages and had very nearly screwed up his third. Frank and Ellen were a car crash from start to finish but somehow, her quiet little divorce was the one that always got Ma riled up. How was that? She'd given it her best shot, even though she'd known in the first year she'd made a dreadful mistake marrying Dermot. But she stuck it out.

They'd raised a happy family and done all the right things. When the divorce came through, she and Dermot went out for a meal together and wished each other well. Ma should be proud of her.

Thank God, Netta had taken them to meet her parents before Ma said any more. They'd planned it last night when Siobhan told her she needed to talk to her brothers about doing more. Unfortunately, she'd lost it before she had a chance to sit down and talk to them in a reasonable adult way, thanks to Martin. She'd ended up looking and sounding like a crazy woman. No doubt they'd be laughing their heads off at her. Knowing Martin, he'd be blaming it on the menopause. Ignorant fecker.

She buried her head in Maud's fur. It was a bit doggy but kind of nice. She should definitely get a dog. And she should apologise to Finn. He was a sweetheart. They didn't deserve him for a cousin.

She didn't realise Frank had come in until he was in the room. He sat next to her and put his arm around her. She couldn't remember the last time he'd done that. If ever. He kissed her head. He'd definitely never done that. 'I'm sorry. I've been a terrible brother and son.'

She sniffed. 'Yes you have.'

'I'm going to be coming over more often.'

'They're so old, you know? And Ma never lets up.' A big tear plopped onto Maud's back. 'She's always going on about me divorcing Dermot. I'm sure she blames me for Martin running off.'

'Sure, that's not fair.' Frank gave her another squeeze. It was oddly comforting.

'You're right, it isn't. Da needs you, Frank. We all do. You've been away too long.'

'I know. I'm listening. I'm so sorry. The others are too. They're just too scared of you to come over and say it.'

She wiped her eyes and tried out a laugh. 'They're such babies.'

'You can say that again. Listen, do you want to go out tonight? The boys are mad keen for a curry. Do our parents eat curry?'

'We do have curry in Belfast, you know. We are quite cosmopolitan these days. It has been known to pass their lips.'

Frank bumped his shoulder against hers. 'Ah but there's curry, and there's Birmingham curry.'

After the curry, which was actually very good, they went to Adrian's grotty pub. Ma was not too impressed and she told Adrian so, but her standards slipped surprisingly quickly after a couple of drinks. There was a DJ on. She had a little dance with Netta. She liked Netta. She was a good one for the craic. Best of all, she was easy to get on with. Siobhan could talk to her.

Halfway through the night, Frank sat down next to her. 'How's it going?' Her brother was happy at last. Adrian was right about Netta, she brought him out of himself. But there was more to it than that. It had to be something to do with Martin and Finn. She wasn't part of their little club so she didn't know what it was. Not yet anyway.

She looped her arm through his. 'Grand. You've got yourself a lovely woman there, Francis. Don't lose this one.'

'I'll try not to.' He fiddled with his beer mat. She sensed he was building himself up to something. 'Martin said you told him about Billy going with Eve when she was my girl-friend. I'm curious as to how you knew?'

'About the two of you, or about Billy and Eve?'

'Both, I guess. I thought we'd managed to keep it under the radar.'

'Come on, Frank, you must remember what it was like. Eyes and ears everywhere. I knew about you and Eve because you were seen. I knew about Billy and Eve because the gobshite loved to brag.'

'That figures. Do you know anything about that day the Balaclavas took Billy? I'm sure Billy wouldn't have informed. Unless he'd done it to impress Eve, what with her old man being a cop. But I can't see it somehow. And anyway, how would the Balaclavas have known if he had?'

'Like I said, Billy was always shooting his mouth off. He told everybody about those guns. He didn't need to inform, he just needed to tell enough people on the streets. What happened to Billy was nobody's fault but his own. Loose talk costs lives,' she said, remembering the slogan that was on every wall in those times. 'Except no lives were lost that day.'

Frank smiled. 'Thanks. I just needed to know.'

She patted him on the knee. 'No bother. I'm away to powder my nose. Do me a favour and talk to the parents.'

Siobhan fixed her lipstick in the ladies. She'd said enough to Frank to put his mind at rest. He didn't need to know Eve was meeting Billy that day to tell him she was having his baby.

She smacked her lips together and pressed a tissue between them. Under the radar, her arse. As if. Of course the Balaclavas knew about Frank and Eve. They'd put two and two together and decided it was him who'd grassed about the guns. That's why they had to know it was Billy with his big mouth. They'd done the right thing, her and Da. It hadn't been their finest hour but they'd had no choice. It was either Frank or Billy. Frank was theirs, and Billy Macintyre was a spiteful, greedy snake who poisoned everything he touched.

She'd tried to help Eve to get away from him by getting word to her dad through the network of whispers and secrets. Siobhan had taken a big risk herself with that one. Nobody wanted to be found out for passing information to the other side, no matter how insignificant. But some people just don't want to be helped, do they? Siobhan had heard about Eve's awful abortion, some sleazy so-called doctor across the border. That was probably Billy's doing. Eve's ould man would have made her have the baby in secret and put it up for adoption. Or he'd have taken her across the water to get the abortion done properly. A woman who knew a woman who knew Eve told Siobhan it had messed her insides up completely. No more babies. Poor cow. Frank didn't need to know about that either. Wasn't it enough that Billy had stolen the only two women he'd pinned his hopes on?

A wicked part of her would have liked to have seen Billy trying it on with Netta. She didn't know her well obviously, but Siobhan had the feeling Netta would be impervious to his so-called charms. From what Netta had said about her ex, she'd be able to spot a manipulative bastard miles off. Last night, she'd given her the full, uncensored version of Frank's history. At the end of it, Netta had been left in no doubt about the Eve and Ellen effect, and Siobhan was in no doubt that Frank had finally met the right woman.

She examined herself in the mirror, then went back in and waited to be served at the bar. Frank was talking to Da. Her dear old da. She remembered all the hours he'd spent making that first house of hers habitable. It was the thing he loved to do, his distraction. Frank had helped a bit with that house. Decorating was the gift Da had shared with him. Martin had the books. Da was always there helping him read, just so he could tell his big brother he knew the words. These days they'd say Martin was dyslexic, but schools were crueller places when they were kids.

But Da had saved the best for her. Eyes and ears. She was his, and he was hers. He'd shared with her the gift of knowledge, and together they'd kept the family safe.

'You're looking very well, Siobhan. Divorce suits you,' said Adrian.

She'd always liked Adrian. He wasn't exactly a looker, but he was funny, clever, and kind. Back in the day, those calls with him helped her get through the endless weeks of flip-flopping between worrying over Frank and hating her life with Dermot. She'd felt empty when they drew to a natural end. Many a time since, she'd been tempted to call him, just to chat. Just to feel a little less lonely. But she'd always talked herself out of it, not wanting to come over as too desperate. Still, he'd called her out of the blue. And he'd kept her number. That had to mean something. And anything was better than those fecking dating-site weirdos.

She gave him her best smile. 'Yes, it does.'

He smiled back. 'Can I get you a drink? Or would you prefer a dance?'

Adrian dropped Siobhan off outside Netta's. It was a beautiful morning and Siobhan was feeling something she hadn't felt for a long time. Attractive. She'd spent the night with a decent man who told her he'd had a secret crush on her for years. That was the kind of surprise she could handle.

She'd only got halfway up the path when the door opened. Martin stood in the doorway, a ridiculous grin on his face. 'Ooh, walk of shame.'

'Fuck off, Martin. Shove your double standards up your arse.' She pushed him out of the way and went straight upstairs to get changed.

There was a tap on the bedroom door just as she pulled on a clean top. 'Are you decent, Siobhan?' It was Ma.

Siobhan let out a heavy sigh. She might as well get it over with now. 'Come in.'

Ma stood in the doorway fiddling with her jumper. 'I just wanted to say, you go girl.' She raised her fist in the air like one of those athletes on the winner's podium. The geriatric version, obviously.

'Right! Thanks Mammy.'

'I'll leave you to pack.' She started to close the door, then she opened it again. 'You're a good girl, Siobhan. You're my rock. Well, you and your daddy.'

Siobhan waited until the door was fully closed before dropping down onto the bed in shock. 'Well fuck me.' Where the hell had that come from? Must be something in the water over here. Or maybe it was that Birmingham curry.

72

HE'S OUR EEJIT

Netta went upstairs to find Siobhan. The bedroom door was open. Siobhan was at the window, looking down onto the street where Frank, Finn, and Martin were gathered.

She tapped on the door. 'I was just coming up to tell you Finn was leaving, but I guess you can see that.'

Siobhan turned to look at her. 'Thanks, but I'll leave those three to wring out the last bit of man love before he heads off. It's been a long time coming. Can I ask you something? Do you think I was mad to spend the night with Adrian?'

'Not at all. He's lovely. Not the sort who'd take advantage of a woman,' said Netta. Adrian was quite the dark horse, now that she thought about it. 'I think he likes you.'

'Thanks. I needed to hear that. I'm not the sort who takes advantage of a man either, by the way. I like Adrian too, and it gets lonely sometimes.'

'I know.' Netta was going to add on both counts but she could see there was no need.

'Will we keep in touch?' said Siobhan.

'I'd like that.'

'And about that business with your man, Doogie. I wouldn't worry about it. Frank will tell you when he's ready. That might take some time though. He's a bit of an eejit.'

Netta laughed. 'Yes, but he's our eejit.' The wine had loosened her tongue the other night and she'd confided in Siobhan almost as much as Siobhan had confided in her. But it was true, there was nothing to be gained from pushing it with Frank. It really didn't matter.

'Too right,' said Siobhan. 'You'll take care of him, won't you? Don't feel sorry for him though, he'd hate that.'

'Of course. We take care of each other. No pity involved. That's not how we roll, as the young folks say.'

Siobhan opened her arms and gave Netta a hug. 'I knew I was going to like you, as soon as I saw you.'

'And I knew the same. As soon as I heard you calling Martin the Scarlet fucking Pimpernel.'

Siobhan's eyes narrowed for just a second. Then she tipped back her head and laughed out loud, and so did Netta. They were new friends. Maybe in time, they'd be more than that.

73

WE HAVE HALF A DAY

'I've done a once over in your cupboards, Frank. Not good.' Finn was standing outside his van, all ready to go.

Frank smiled. 'Is that you putting me on notice, Finn Meister?'

'It is. When I get back home, I'm going to send you a list of healthy foods to look out for. And we'll get your exercise plan going as well.'

Frank gave Finn a salute. It didn't sound much like fun but he knew he was going to be in good hands.

'You're in for it now, FB,' said Martin. 'Let us know when you're back home safely, cousin.'

Finn nodded. 'We're doing that road trip next year, for sure. Adrian's up for it, I talked him into it last night.'

'Adrian will agree to anything when he's drunk,' said Frank. 'I'll talk to him about it next time I see him.'

Finn gave them both a hug. 'I'll see youse both again soon.'

'He turned out good, didn't he,' said Martin as they watched Finn drive away.

'He turned out very good,' said Frank. 'And so did you. Will you let me know how you get on with Bronagh?'

'Will you answer my calls?'

'Absolutely.'

Siobhan came out of Netta's house and joined them.

'You just missed Finn,' said Frank.

She waved him away. 'I see plenty of Finn. Anyway, I thought you three would want a bit of special time to sign off your rekindled bromance. I just came out to let you know the taxi will be here in half an hour.'

Martin had a stupid grin on his face. 'Talking of romance. Have you heard from Adrian?'

'We've exchanged a couple of messages. Not that it's any of your business, Martin.'

'So it's more than a one-night stand then?' Martin just didn't know when to quit.

Frank was expecting Siobhan to slap him straight down but she just smiled: 'We shall see. Frank, Da's still over yours. Can you go and tell him?'

'Sure.'

'Thanks. Oh and Frank, Ma's being awful nice to me. Have you said something to her, by any chance?'

'Me? No.' Frank swung his gate open. He wasn't lying exactly. He hadn't spoken to Ma, but he might have had a quiet word with Da.

Da was in Frank's studio looking at the painting he'd liked so much yesterday. 'I can't get over the beauty of it.'

'Would you like it? I can bring it over next time I come.'

'It's for your exhibition, and it would probably cost more than I can pay.'

'I can paint another one for the exhibition, and I don't

want any money for it. You can pay me in kind. I'm thinking of doing some decorating.'

'Nice try, son, but I don't decorate now. I'm too old, and I don't need it anymore.'

'Consultancy basis only. I'll do the work, you can give the directions. Do we have a deal?'

Da smiled. 'We do.'

'The taxi's on its way. I'll get your bags.' Frank went up to his bedroom to get them. So that's what the decorating was all about. Da's coping mechanism. Suddenly it all made sense.

Frank and Netta waited on the street until the taxi disappeared around the corner. After all those years of avoiding his family, he hadn't wanted them to go.

Netta took his hand. 'We have half a day before everything's back to normal. Half a day of just you and me. How do you want to fill it?'

He pulled her hand to his lips and kissed it. 'Let's talk.'

'I think you should go to scatter Billy's ashes and make your peace with Eve,' said Netta. 'It helped me seeing Doogie again.'

Doogie. He'd told Netta everything except the bit about going to Doogie's place. He'd tell her soon enough, when he'd built his self-esteem up a bit more.

'I'll come with you if it helps,' she said. 'Not to the scattering though, that's something the three of you should do with Eve.'

'The Billy Mac Survivors Club.' Frank's mind drifted to Ellen. She wasn't a survivor, although he couldn't pin that one on Billy. He'd have to call Gavin to see how he was doing. It was time to have him in his life again.

'Will you go then?' said Netta.

'Yes. I will.' He would go. He would see Eve and tell her he was sorry for her loss. Then he'd spend time with his family. He might even bring his da back with him and together they'd do some decorating. Maybe they'd sit down in his studio and paint together. Just him and Da.

Netta stroked his cheek. 'We still have the rest of the day. What do you want to do now?'

Frank took her in his arms. For today, all he wanted to do was spend time with the woman he loved. Tomorrow, he would make plans. And he would most definitely buy a new phone.

∾

Be the first to know about Hazel's latest news and the general goings on in her life. You can follow her in all the usual places or join her **Readers' Club** and get regular monthly newsletters, a free novella and the occasional free story.

https://hazelwardauthor.com

A WORD FROM THE AUTHOR

Hello

I hope you enjoyed reading this story. If you did, would you mind leaving a review?

Your reviews are important. They help me to reach more readers and they help other readers to decide whether this book is for them.

You can leave a review at your local Amazon store .

To find out more about other stories written by me, read on…

READ NETTA'S COMPANION STORY, BEING DOOGIE CHAMBERS

If this book leaves you wanting to know more about the world of Netta Wilde and her friends, you can join Hazel's **Readers' Club** and get **Being Doogie Chambers,** a free book available exclusively to members of the club.

https://hazelwardauthor.com/readers-club/

READ MORE NETTA WILDE STORIES.

BEING NETTA WILDE

Two women. Two timelines. One heart-wrenching story.

A lonely woman. A single decision. A second chance at happiness.

★★★★★ 'One of my books of the year'

★★★★★ 'A riveting book that l didn't want to finish.'

★★★★★ 'A beautiful story about personal growth, love, loss and friendships.'

FINDING EDITH PINSENT

Two women. Two timelines. One heart-wrenching story.

★★★★★ 'Outstanding!! Wow. Just wow.'

★★★★★ 'A rollercoaster ride and feelgood heart-warming experience.'

★★★★★ 'Edie is so realistic, you will fall in love with her.'

SAVING GERALDINE CORCORAN

One shameful secret. One hidden letter. Two unlikely guardian angels.

★★★★★ 'A truly powerful story told brilliantly.'

★★★★★ 'Sadness, love, humour, surprise. You name it I felt it.'

★★★★★ 'Superbly written and well worth reading, but be prepared to cry and laugh and cry again!'

EDUCATING KELLY PAYNE

How to learn about love … the hard way.

★★★★★ 'The writing is phenomenal, the characters so real you can really see into their soul.'

★★★★★ 'I loved it! I'm wiping my eyes as I write.'

★★★★★ 'Kelly's journey is a cracker.'

MEETING ANNETTE GREY

Two strangers. One park bench. One life changing conversation.

★★★★★ 'Absolutely brilliant.'

★★★★★ 'Layered with deep emotions, intricate character development and a compelling storyline.'

LOVING NETTA WILDE

Look out for the final book in the Netta Wilde series, coming soon.

BEING DOOGIE CHAMBERS

A free novella, exclusive to members of Hazel Ward's Readers' Club.

Printed in Great Britain
by Amazon